THE NEMESIS ORIGIN

Dean Crawford

ISBN: 150851271X

ISBN-13: 978-1508512714

I

Mount Llullaillaco, Puna de Atacama
Argentina
1570

'Your time has come, Chaska.'

The interior of the tent was dark, filled with deep shadows that seemed to move with the buffeting winds that rumbled outside like demons crawling up the walls. Small candles flickered weakly in the bitterly cold air as Chaska huddled beneath thick blankets, her dark and wary eyes framed by jet black hair. She sat in one corner of the tent, behind her an older woman named Karu, a village elder, densely braided her hair with beads and decorative ribbons.

Chaska was revered as the most beautiful girl in the village by far, and it was that beauty that she now hated the most for she knew what awaited her outside. No family had accompanied her on her journey, for they were not blessed to visit this most sacred of places. Somewhere outside in the darkness she could hear the sound of chanting, the croaking tones of an old man who had probably been through this ritual a hundred times, his melodic singing rising and falling with the winds that howled across the lonely mountains.

Karu was about the same age as Chaska's grandmother, but her features held none of the familiarity of family or even friends. Every single person who had accompanied Chaska on the long journey was a stranger, likewise chosen, some said by the gods themselves, to travel into the upper realms where few dared to tread. That the journey was sacred was known to all among the empire, but there was a sad finality about this journey that enshrouded those who had accompanied Chaska. The apocalypse that had consumed their world, the invaders from the east with their guns and their diseases, had decimated Chaska's people through war and pestilence. Now, with almost all of their strongholds and cities fallen, this would be the last time the realm of the gods was visited by humans.

Karu gently parted the braids of her hair and cupped her chin in one hand, her voice soothing as she murmured softly in Quechuan.

'This is a great day, for you shall travel to meet Viracocha, the father of the gods. There, you will reside in paradise alongside Him, and speak to us of the future through the shamans.'

The tent rumbled as fresh gusts of icy wind swept past outside as though seeking her out. Chaska shivered and pulled the blankets tighter about her shoulders as Karu finished braiding her hair and stood. With a hunched gate, Karu shuffled across the tent to a drawstring bag and produced from within it a beaker that she handed to Chaska.

'Drink, for it will prepare you for your journey.'

Chaska looked down at the beaker to see within a dark liquid that reflected the candlelight like oil as it swirled. It smelled sweet and looked thick, and she recoiled from it instinctively as she had done many times before.

'Do not be afraid,' Karu urged. 'It will help you.'

Reluctantly, Chaska reached out and took the beaker of *chica* into her hands, and with a deep breath she held it to her lips and drank. The *chica* was cold, but it felt hot as it flooded into her stomach. She winced as she handed the beaker back, her head beginning to swirl.

'Good girl,' Karu said. 'Your mother would be proud.'

Karu put the beaker away and then turned to Chaska, a motherly expression on her features as she reached out with gnarled old hands.

'It is time; come.'

Chaska felt a deep twinge of fear as she reached out from beneath her blankets and Karu pulled her to her feet, the blankets falling away to reveal the finest dress that Chaska had ever worn. Tightly woven patterns of geometric shapes adorned the material, and woven into its fabric were fine threads of pure gold. On Chaska's fingers were rings likewise of pure gold, each one worth more than her father would earn in his entire life; in the flickering candles she glowed with tiny flames of light reflecting in the gold.

'You are beautiful,' Karu said with a broad smile, 'truly fit for Viracocha's side.'

Taking Chaska's much smaller hand, Karu led her to the tent entrance and reached out to push it aside. A gust of cold air rippled through the tent and Chaska shivered again as she was led outside, her shoes crunching on thick snow.

The mountains splashed across the horizon all around her, the sky aflame with burnished rivers of molten metal in the glow of the sun rising far behind the ranges. Banners of clouds ripped and torn by the vigorous winds tumbled across the sky, the snowcapped peaks below bathed in a rich orange glow. The cold wind whipped her hair into a frenzy of snaking black lines as she was turned by Karu and looked ahead to where a path wound its way to the very peak of the mountain.

Hundreds of royal aides turned to look at her, shivering as they lined the path with flaming torches that gusted and crackled on the wind. One by one they began to chant in time with an old man who waited for Chaska with one bony hand resting upon a staff at at his side.

'Go now,' Karu urged her softly. 'Your name means *very bright star*, Chaska, and that is what you shall become.'

Karu's hands guided her gently towards the old man, and as Chaska stepped forward she realized that she had lost her balance, and yet felt oddly calm. Her stomach churned with warmth despite the bitter cold, and her head swam as though she were extremely tired as the *chica* flowed through her bloodstream. She briefly remembered the same smell of *chica* from her past, her father drinking the beer outside their family home far away to the north. Grief pinched at Chaska's eyes as she thought of her parents and her brothers and sisters, so far away.

Your mother would be proud, Karu had said. Chaska's only comfort emerged as she realized that her family would probably already be awaiting her at Viracocha's side, for the fearsome *conquistadores* had been almost upon their village before she had been spirited away by the elders.

The old man, Qasa, beckoned her forward with a smile, his few remaining teeth like broken moss-covered gravestones guarding the entrance to an ancient cave. From other tents appeared five more girls, likewise dressed in elaborate clothes and with their hair braided, all young and all beautiful. They joined Chaska, their own chaperones helping the girls to link hands. The company made Chaska feel better as Qasa turned and began leaping and dancing and cackling as he made his way between the flaming torches and beckoned the girls to follow him.

The girls stumbled their way up the rocky path, icy cold snow seeping into their shoes and the bitter winds chilling their bodies. With a start, Chaska realized that the path was lined not just by royal servants but also by warriors, their flaming torches and the weapons of war in their hands. They chanted and hummed, their eyes seemingly fixed upon Chaska as she walked among the other girls toward the top of the mountain. At the peak, silhouetted against the blinding flare of the rising sun, she could just make out warriors standing in a ring around a single, smaller figure who stood alone in their midst.

Qasa reached the top of the mountain, the howling winds tugging at his threadbare clothes and wispy white hair. He seemed oblivious to the bitter chill as he thrust his staff towards the sky and his cries and chants reached new heights. The girls reached the peak, and as one they stood in a row facing the brilliant sunlight as the ring of warriors opened, the bravest and most noble remaining in the Empire gesturing for the girls to enter the ring.

Chaska looked inside and saw a lone girl.

Unlike Chaska and her companions, the girl awaiting them could not be called beautiful. Her eyes were too large, deep black discs that seem to reflect everything they saw as though the girl did not want to be a part of the world in which she lived. Her mouth was pinched, her lips thin and her skin sickly pale. The only thing that she shared in common with Chaska and the others was her densely braided black hair and her hugely elongated skull.

Chaska gripped the hands of her companions as she moved to stand in front of the strange child, and could feel likewise their tightening grip. The wind howled and swirled around them as Qasa danced and cackled, hopping and skipping from one foot to the next as he chanted and moved around them, thrusting his staff at the heavens above. Behind them, Chaska heard the warriors move to form a row, could hear the snapping and crackling of their torches and see the occasional spark whipped away by the bitter wind.

Chaska glanced nervously at her companions. All of them wore the same expression, a combination of melancholy, regret, and hope. Unlike the warriors, unlike the royal servants and Qasa, their skulls too were conical, extending far further back than was natural. Chaska recalled the years of pain in her youth, at odds with the immense pride of her family and the respectful gazes of all who crossed her path. Since she had been born she had been chosen for her beauty, and that beauty had been enhanced by the tribe when they had placed the wooden boards either side of her infant skull and forced it to grow into a conical shape that was unlike any of the other children in the village. She had spent most of her early years in pain, and only when those boards had been removed and the pressure eased on her weary skull had she begun to live what had passed for an ordinary life. Now, that distant pain was but a memory dulled by the *chica* that she had drunk.

Chaska knew that the girl who stood before them now had endured no deformation of her skull at the hands of the shamans. The girl before them had been born exactly as she was, and that was why she was so revered and likely raised in the palace of Machu Picchu: she was a child of the gods, quite literally.

Karu and the other servants joined them upon the mountain peak as Qasa cackled and howled, competing with the brisk gales assaulting the peak. With a sudden flourish of shouts and hollers at the endless vault of the heavens above, Qasa slammed his staff down onto the icy earth at their feet and then pointed at the warriors behind Chaska and her companions.

The warriors let out a deafening howl that sent a shiver of fear plunging through Chaska's body as they ran around the outside of the ring trailing sparks from their flaming torches. They encircled the girls and in the blinding light of the sun she saw one of the warriors move behind the strange girl in the centre, and in his hands was a strip of thickly knotted cord.

The warriors accelerated into a sprint as they roared their battle cries, the light of their torches surrounding the girls with a ring of fire and sparks. Qasa howled and turned on the spot as he beat the rocky ground with his feet, and then he raised his staff with one final screech, his eyes shut tight as he slammed it one more time onto the ground and pointed at the girl in the centre of the ring.

A warrior's club flicked with rapid movement and crashed down onto the strange girl's elongated skull. Chaska thought she heard a dull thump as she saw the girl's black eyes flare with surprise and then the light of life vanished from them. She crumpled beneath the blow to her knees and then toppled sideways onto the cold rocks, her wide dark eyes seeing no longer. Chaska glimpsed the warrior who had struck the girl reach down and whip the thickly knotted cord around her neck before twisting it tight.

Qasa raised his arms and staff to the bitterly cold skies in silence as

Chaska heard more dull thumps all around her. In her confused state it did not cross her mind what would happen next until it was too late.

A brief vision of her parents flickered through Chaska's mind and she gazed at the sun as though imploring for one last touch of her mother's hand, one last caring word from her father, and then with sudden brutality the sunlight vanished into darkness.

II

Machu Picchu
Peru
1911

'How much further?'

The dense heat of the jungle clung to Hiram Bingham's skin like a heavy blanket as he struggled up the rocky hillside. The foliage ahead was thick and rose up into a massive canopy that obscured the cloudy white sky above, only thin shafts of sunlight reaching the shadowy forest floor.

'As far as is required,' Hiram replied.

The high altitude air was thin and Hiram's lungs felt as though they had shrunk with every meandering step he had taken up the mountain. Already high in the Andes before they began the trek, and suffering from headaches and nausea brought on by the thin air, most of Hiram's team had fallen by the wayside thousands of feet below. Only a few hardy native trackers accompanied him, laden down beneath heavy burdens of supplies.

Hiram hacked with a machete at the dense foliage, the weapon heavier with every blow he made to clear a path toward a peak that he could just see through the dense canopy. He raised his hand to deploy the weapon once more but then hesitated as he saw a gigantic spider clinging to the vines, its banded legs bright orange against black and its massive pulsing abdomen glistening with moisture. Hiram change the angle of the blade and brought it down on another vine nearby as he made his way around the dangerous arachnid and clambered over a rocky boulder blocking his path.

Hiram was not following a map, for where he was headed no maps existed. His only guide were the legends and stories of the people he had met at the foot of the mountains; their recollections and fables an unreliable and often disheartening promise of unspeakable wealth and untold discoveries awaiting in this most remote region of the world. He had heard about a mysterious lost city in the jungles high in the Peruvian Andes for years, but no one in Cusco had believed his stories because it was already believed that the last capital of the Incas was the city of

Choquequirao.

'That way.'

Hiram's guide pointed between two massive tree trunks to where a shaft of bright sunlight beamed through the forest. Melchor Arteage was a peasant farmer recruited by Bingham in Mandor who claimed to know the location of the city, his native *Quechua* tongue translated by Sergeant Carrasco, the only member of Bingham's team to make it this far, and a small boy named Pablito who claimed to have climbed to the city once before. Having crossed the Urabamba River some two thousand feet below them, they had climbed for hours with little sign of the supposed citadel.

Hiram nodded and aimed towards the gap, his shirt drenched with sweat and the satchel slung over his shoulder weighty with the handful of stone trinkets he had discovered further down the hillside. Made of nothing more than the rock of the mountain upon which he climbed, to Hiram the trinkets could easily have been made of diamonds for their worth was equal in his mind.

Hiram scrambled over a damp boulder and slumped, breathless, as he turned and looked out over the densely forested gorge that plunged away beneath them through veils of ephemeral cloud. He reached into his satchel and pulled out a tiny carved figurine, one that likely depicted an ancient sun-god of Peruvian culture known as *Inti*. Hiram could not be sure if the figurine belonged to the Inca, but then he had never seen anything quite like it before from any culture of the Americas. It was this tiny figurine that had led him from the open plateau of Paracus to the soaring mountains of the Andes, all based upon the supposition of Melchor Arteage who insisted he had seen the image of the figurine once before.

Hiram leaned one elbow against the boulder and looked over his shoulder at the hillside to where the sunlight beamed between the two trees. For a moment he considered how much further up the hillside he had to climb, but then he realized something about the light. The lower edge of the shaft was dead straight, a perfectly horizontal line that did not appear in nature. Hiram squinted and shielded his eyes with one hand as he examined the line, and then he put the figurine back into his satchel and clambered further up the slope even as Melchor Arteage reached the boulder.

'I thought we take rest?' the guide complained, Carrasco translating.

Hiram did not reply as he scrambled up through the foliage and hacked away at the dense vines, forging a path toward the light. As he brought the machete crashing down upon the packed vines, the blade shuddered and he heard a ringing as it struck stone. Hiram slid the machete into its sheath and grasped at the vines with his bare hands to pull them away from the dark, moss covered surface of a rock wall.

Hiram stared at the wall before him, his chest heaving with the exertion and his eyes wide as he scanned the surface and saw the unmistakable signs of human engravings in the bare stone. The wall stood as high as his head and seemed to vanish to either side through the dense jungle. Built from stones that appeared to have no mortar between them, the rocks rested upon each other in perfectly dovetailed shapes as though purposely cut to fit.

Carrasco scrambled to Hiram's side and stared at the engraved stones.

'This is it,' he said. 'This is the place Arteage spoke of.'

Hiram searched along the wall as he followed the engravings. Images of shamans and sun gods, geometric patterns and spirals adorned the cut stone, and as Hiram made his way along he finally found what he was looking for. He gasped as he looked upon an image of the sun beaming down upon a figure that bore a wide angular head that was more conical than a human skull. The figure was dressed in ornate clothes that bore no relation to other engravings Hiram had seen across Peru by other cultures.

Hiram reached into his satchel and produced the figurine he had been holding just moments before and he held it up alongside the engraving. The bizarre proportions of the figurine matched the icon before him in the rocks.

'You see,' Carrasco said. 'This is the place.'

Hiram dropped the figurine into his satchel and reached up to the top of the wall as he dug his boot into a groove between the ancient stones and hoisted himself up. He rolled onto the surface above and came to his feet to see another wall of similar height above him. Hiram grabbed the nearest, thickest vine he could see and clambered up onto the top of the next wall, and then five more before he broke out of the forest canopy and realized he was standing on a massive plateau. Behind him, he realized that the series of walls were in fact terraces of perfectly joined stone, almost certainly for agricultural use like the stepped gardens he had seen years before in India and Thailand.

Hiram turned and took a single pace forwards and then dropped to his knees as he stared upon the sight of majestic grandeur that greeted him.

Atop the mountain ridgeline and veiled within trees and vines was a vast citadel that stretched as far as he could see, an immense city of terraced fields, stone temples and brickwork houses all forged from the solid stone of the mountain. Hiram turned and stared out across the immense mountain ranges of the Andes, ribbons of cloud drifting across the forested peaks as though he had ascended toward heaven itself.

Carrasco, a shorter and stockier man than Hiram, finally managed to scale the walls and breathlessly joined him on the terrace. His skin was sheened with sweat but his eyes were alive with delight as he surveyed the enormous city.

'We found it,' he gasped.

Hiram got to his feet and pushed the hat on his head back from his forehead as he surveyed the city and noted the large temple dominating the terraces ahead. Enshrouded in vines, creepers and trees, Hiram could nonetheless detect the angular lines of its walls, a building that could only possibly be the dwelling of the most powerful members of the civilization that had built this tremendous city.

'We must keep going,' Hiram said.

Pablito appeared and tugged at Hiram's shirt as he shook his head. Hiram frowned down at the child, who gabbled an excited statement and then turned and fled down the terraces and vanished back into the jungle.

Hiram made to move forward, but Carrasco's hand on his arm forestalled him.

'Wait,' Carrasco said. 'Pablito said that nobody has returned from this place, that it is haunted by the ancients who lived here. This is a sacred place, not to be intruded upon.'

Hiram pushed Carrasco away with a scowl of irritation. 'I know what is said, and most of what is said is nothing but hot air. Either you are with me or you remain with the cowards further down the hillside. What will it be, Carrasco?'

Carrasco's broad shoulders slumped as he glanced over his shoulder at the forest descending away from them into the plunging depths of the mountains. The Urabamba River flowed somewhere deep between the precipitous mountain slopes, veiled now by thick banks of cloud. Hiram knew that Carrasco would not want to go back down having come so far, and Carrasco reluctantly nodded.

Hiram made his way up the terraces, seeking paths where the vines had not crept in and where the growth of trees had been hindered by the stone walls and passages that wound between the countless buildings entombed within the jungle. Hiram had no doubt whatsoever that what he had found was at least a palace and perhaps the fabled last resting place of the Inca civilization, placed as it was upon the precipitous peak of the mountain and virtually invulnerable to any form of attack from below.

The temple ahead loomed above them, ranks of steps carved from solid stone and laced with thick vines and creepers leading to an entrance as black as night. Hiram climbed without fear, Carrasco following directly behind him as they reached the top of the steps and hesitated before the entrance. Hiram reached to his belt and unclipped a hefty flashlight that he tapped before aiming the beam into the gloom. He resisted the temptation to glance at Carrasco for support or advice, knowing that any sign of weakness might send his companion running back down the slope. Instead, he straightened his back, lifted his chin, and strode directly into the darkness.

The cloying heat of the jungle gave way to a cool, almost cold breath of stale air, as though the interior were haunted by the long-dead remains of its architects. The interior of the temple was clad with vines much as the exterior was, but these creepers were thinner and weaker, even the power and absolute patience of nature struggling to pierce the perfectly built walls. Hiram's flashlight beam picked out an altar of some kind that was engraved with various geometric designs associated with the Inca. Hiram noted evidence of scat all around, much of it desiccated, revealing that the temple had been open to the elements for perhaps centuries. As he approached the altar, he noted a larger engraving on the wall behind it. Clad in moss and draped in creepers, he could nonetheless see the unmistakable shape of a distorted human face staring out at him from the depths of prehistory.

Hiram slowed as he reached the altar, and as he looked down at it he realized that it was not an altar at all. A stone block, perfectly shaped and smoothed by countless hands, the block was capped with an ornate lid, a sarcophagus the likes of which Hiram had not seen since observing similar constructions excavated in Egypt. As he stared down at the top of the sarcophagus and aimed the flashlight beam at it, so the shape of the form within leapt into life as the engraved surface was illuminated.

Hiram knew without doubt what lay within the sarcophagus, fully recognised the distorted shape of the skull and those baleful wide eyes that he had first seen in the bizarre figurines he had collected as far away as Paracus, on Peru's Ica coastline. Believed by the local inhabitants to be an ancient depiction of gods, Bingham had taken a chance that they were more than just depictions.

'Here, help me with this.'

Carrasco moved to the far side of the sarcophagus as Hiram set the flashlight down nearby, the beam cutting through the musty air and illuminating them as he reached down and curled his fingers beneath the lid. They looked at each other and Hiram nodded once, twice and then a final third time. On the third nod both he and Carrasco heaved with all of their might against the weight of the sarcophagus lid.

In the gloomy darkness, the rumble of rock against rock echoed like the growl of some unspeakable beast as the lid shuddered across the top of the sarcophagus. Hiram dug his boots into the ground and pushed hard as he leaned his weight behind the lid, Carrasco, likewise pushing with all of his might, and they saw it slide clear, and with a deafening crash it dropped onto the stone steps and cracked in two. The crash echoed through the temple as though the building were protesting the violation of its secrets.

Hiram grabbed the flashlight and directed the beam into the interior of the sarcophagus, and he heard Carrasco mutter of prayer under his breath and make the sign of the cross as he stumbled away.

Inside the sarcophagus lay the bones of what looked like a child, huddled up in a foetal bundle and its desiccated skin drawn taut across the skull. The eyes were hollow pits and much of the remains had long since decayed to dust, but he could see strands of wiry black hair poking from the skull cap. Hiram leaned in and saw the tell-tale glint of gold woven into the fabric of the child's ancient clothes that glittered in the flashlight beam. But his gaze barely lingered on the gold, drawn instead to the bulbous and conical skull.

'Sweet mother of Mary,' Hiram finally whispered as he looked down at the contents. 'I found it.'

'We should leave this place immediately,' Carrasco said quickly from nearby the temple entrance. 'This place, it is not of this earth.'

Hiram stood up and directed the flashlight beam at Carrasco's face.

'You will speak nothing of this,' he snapped, 'and you will do exactly as I say. Bring the bearers up here but not into the temple. I will package these remains and you and your men will carry them back down the mountain.'

Carrasco shook his head, beads of sweat and worry glinting on his forehead.

'No, I cannot,' he blubbed. 'To move the remains would bring the bearer's soul great torment!'

Hiram reached down to his belt and drew his service revolver. The sound of the mechanism clicked loudly as he cocked the weapon and aimed it at Carrasco.

'Do you want your men to carry these remains down the mountain, or *yours*?'

Carrasco threw his hands up either side of his head, his features twisted with anxiety as he turned and hurried towards the temple exit.

Hiram watched Carrasco flee and then he turned back to the remains before him. He could barely contain the smile that spread across his features as he saw his fortune glitter like the gold before him in the flashlight beam. He had spent many years searching the jungles in the hope of making his name with a great discovery, and now that time had come. Nobody, anywhere in the world, would be in any way prepared for what he had found.

Hiram lowered his pistol and slid it back into the holster at his waist, then hurried towards the temple exit. He would need to carefully document the remains first and take photographs before ensuring that the contents of the sarcophagus were properly wrapped and sealed, for there was no way he could allow his bearers to see what they were carrying. Most would run for miles rather than…

Hiram stopped at the entrance to the temple as he saw Carrasco's body lying on the steps before him, eyes staring lifelessly up at the sky and his left temple a bloodied mess where it had been crushed by the blow of a weapon. Hiram's hand flashed to his pistol but it never made it to the weapon as a new sound reached his ear. The unmistakable click of a pistol hammer as it was drawn back. Hiram felt the tip of the weapon's cold barrel pressed into the side of his head.

'Do exactly as I say,' a voice said, 'and you will get to live the rest of your life in peace.'

III

Chicago Field Museum of Natural History
Chicago, Illinois
Present-day

'What's an Australopithecus?'

'Why did the Tyrannosaurus have such small arms?'

'If we evolved from monkeys, how come there are still monkeys alive?'

Dr Lucy Morgan stood in the central hall of the Field Museum and raised her hands to forestall the flood of questions rushing upon her from the excited group of children she was shepherding between the exhibits. She turned to face them, her long blonde hair glowing in the light that beamed through the museum's massive windows. She replied in a soft but commanding voice that gained the complete attention of her charges.

'Australopithecus is an extinct form of human that evolved in Africa several million years ago, not a monkey,' she explained. 'The Tyrannosaurus did not much use its arms for the purpose of hunting, mating, or eating, and so over time the arms devolved compared to the rest of its body. Finally, we did not evolve from monkeys but *alongside* the apes. Our species has changed over millions of years but so have the apes at the same time – the monkeys of today do not look like the monkeys of seven-million-years ago.'

One of the children, an inquisitive boy with spectacles and floppy brown hair, frowned as he looked at Lucy. 'How did the Tyrannosaurus clean its teeth, then?'

'It didn't,' Lucy explained. 'The first warning you would have got that a Tyrannosaurus was nearby would have been the stench of all the rancid meat rotting in its mouth.'

A ripple of delighted disgust chortled through the crowd of children as Lucy led them between large glass cabinets filled with the remains of human ancestors. During her career with the Field Museum, Lucy had excavated many of the remains herself, most usually out on the plains of Africa where so many ancient human ancestors had been discovered. Arranged as they were in the glass cabinets, it was easy to see the gradual changes that had evolved ancient human ancestors into modern

Homo sapiens. Through the glass, Lucy could see other visitors to the museum examining the remains, peering in and pointing at the various species on display. Grandparents and children, tourists, a tall man in a blue suit, people of all ages keen to learn about history.

'How do you know that these are not just really old monkeys?' asked another child, a young girl who was clasping one of the museum's brochures. 'They all look the same.'

Lucy smiled, having heard the same questions many times over during the tours she gave to schoolchildren when they visited the museum.

'There are many features that distinguish our ancient ancestors from us and from the apes along with whom we evolved. Probably the most obvious is the changes in leg and pelvis structure as our ancestors descended from the trees and began walking upright on the open plains. For me, the most compelling evidence is the position of our spines. Reach around to the back of your necks and press where you can feel your spine enters the skull. Can you all feel it?'

The children all reached around behind their necks and Lucy could see them all nodding and smiling as they probed the bones of their spines.

'Well, now look at the apes skeletons or those of our very oldest ancestors. Where do the spines enter the skull on them?'

The children peered at some of the fossils inside the glass cabinets and their sharp eyes quickly noticed the difference.

'The spine is going into the very back of their skulls,' said the child with the glasses.

'That's right,' Lucy said. 'Present-day apes and our own oldest ancestors still walked on all fours for the most part, and their spines entered the skull in a place that allowed them to look forwards while being on all fours. As we evolved to walk upright on the open plain on two legs, so the entry hole for our spines gradually moved until it is where is today, allowing us to look forwards naturally while walking on two legs. It is adaptions such as this that show how we evolved over many millions of years to become who we are today.'

The children were silent as they considered this new piece of information, and Lucy felt a glow of warmth inside as once again she saw how simple evidence could be presented to the children that made perfect sense of the complexities of evolution while allowing them to make their own judgements.

'I still don't get how somebody's bones knew how to move place in order to help us?' asked another young boy with curly brown hair.

'That's not how it works,' Lucy explained patiently. 'As we learned to live on the savannahs and it became helpful to be able to stand upright and see further, so those individuals who naturally had a slightly more upright gait would have been given an advantage living in that environment. That would have allowed them to hunt better, survive better, avoid predators better and find a mate easier, which would then have passed those advantageous traits on to their children. Those people who did not have such an upright gait would have found life a little bit harder and would have been less likely to mate, meaning they would have no children and would not have been able to pass on their traits. After long enough only the upright people would remain. That in essence is how evolution works, passing on the traits that work well to our children until only the things that work well remain.'

The children remained fascinated by the fossils around them and Lucy could see that they were accepting of her explanations. Their teacher, a friendly man named Clive, smiled in gratitude or possibly relief to see the children enraptured by the museum's exhibits.

'Feel free to walk wherever you want to,' Lucy said to Clive as she moved to stand alongside him and watch the children peering in at the remains inside the glass cabinets. 'I'll be in my office for most of the day.'

'Are you sure you don't want to look after thirty kids all day instead?' Clive suggested. 'You're clearly a natural at it.'

Lucy smiled. 'Being a natural doesn't mean it's something I want to do; that's why I became a scientist and not a teacher.'

'Can't blame me for trying.'

Lucy gave Clive a pat on the shoulder and took the opportunity to slip away from the fascinated children, and headed towards an access door that led to private offices kept out of sight from the general public. She strode up to the door and tapped in her personal security code into a panel beside the door, and the door clicked open and allowed her to pass through.

Lucy strode down the main corridor, glancing briefly left and right through glass windows into various laboratories where staff scientists were working on the museum's many projects. Recently excavated fossils were being cleaned, new species discovered in far-flung corners of the globe examined and recorded, ice cores retrieved from distant Arctic shores measured and examined for signs of climate change. Lucy passed them all by and then turned to her own office, opened the door and stepped inside. She closed the door behind her and strode across to a small desk that contained a computer and several files.

Lucy Morgan was not a senior scientist at the museum and so was not blessed with a large office, but she liked the view across the museum's lawns and the cosy feeling the small room gave her, which was warm even in Illinois' bitter winter months. Across one entire wall opposite the window, were ranks of tiny shelves upon which were stacked countless specimen jars containing bones, fossils and exotic species collected over centuries by explorers and suspended in alcohol to preserve them.

Lucy slumped down into her comfy office chair and stared out across the lawns at the bright blue sky outside, wishing she was in the field rather than cooped up in the museum. She was lost in her thoughts when a sharp knock rattled against the office door.

'Come in?'

The door opened and Lucy was surprised to see the man in the blue suit she had spotted in the main hall standing in the doorway looking at her. On impulse, she stood from her chair and the man smiled as he held out a card toward her.

'My apologies, doctor,' the man said, his voice heavily accented in what could have been Russian. 'I hope you do not mind me contacting you in this way?'

Lucy took the card and look down at it, reading quickly the name Vladimir Polkov and a title across the top of the card that read: Moscow Institute of Anthropological Studies.

'You never thought to try the phone?' Lucy quipped.

Vladimir smiled. 'I did, but my English is not so good and I thought it better to meet you in person. Having seen you teaching those children, I believe I have done the right thing.'

'How did you get in here?'

'I watched you input your code into the security door,' Vladimir shrugged. 'Again, I apologise.'

Lucy glanced again at the card briefly and then laid it down on her desk as she beckoned Vladimir into the office. Stocky and with thickly gelled black hair, something about Polkov seemed off to Lucy, as though he were a bad actor in a B-rated movie.

'What can I do for you, Mr Polkov?'

'Please, it is Vladimir, and I was wondering if you could help me with an investigation we are making?'

Lucy gestured to a spare chair in the corner of the office as she sat back down. 'Sure, shoot.'

'It is something of a delicate matter and I am not quite sure where to start.'

'Delicate?'

'It involves an excavation that occurred within the borders of a country which would not be happy with Russian investigators being present.'

Lucy raised an eyebrow but said nothing, letting the silence provoke the Russian into speaking further.

'My superiors have become interested in a discovery that was allegedly made in the deserts of Israel some years ago, the remains of a very ancient tomb in which bones were found and excavated. It is our understanding that those remains were then taken to America, but from there the trail has gone cold.'

This time it was the Russian who fell silent and allowed the silence to build.

'I'm not aware of any recent discoveries being made in Israel,' Lucy replied with a vague shrug. 'Not in anthropological terms, anyway.'

'But you are aware of discoveries, however?'

'Fresh archaeological digs are ongoing in Israel at all times,' Lucy agreed. 'We try to keep up with the flow but given the country's complex history there are far too many to document.'

Vladimir smiled with thin lips only, his eyes fixed upon Lucy's. 'My superiors have gone to great lengths to follow what happened in Israel, and have solid evidence that you were there and were present at the excavation site. They know and understand that you may not be able to speak of what you found, just as they are aware that you would love to do so given the nature of your discovery and that it was stolen from you.'

Lucy Morgan remained silent for a long time, her gaze likewise affixed to the Russian's but her mind was already travelling back several years to the dusty plains of the Negev desert. She had been sent there by the Field Museum in order to make archaeological excavations, but while present she had found herself on an entirely unconventional dig that she had kept secret from her employers. Guided by the expertise of native scientist and former mentor Doctor Hans Karowitz, and by her own instincts, she had eventually located an extraordinary tomb which she had successfully dated as being in excess of seven thousand years old.

Working alone in order to maintain absolute secrecy, she had been about to complete her excavation and have the remains flown out of the country when she had been betrayed by the very benefactors who had privately funded the dig. Imprisoned and isolated, it had only been the efforts of her mother and a roguish American former soldier and investigative journalist who had been willing to travel into Israel to rescue her that had kept her alive. Lucy Morgan knew that she had faced death and had absolutely no intention of having anything more to do with either Israel or anything that had been found within its borders.

'I was on holiday in Israel some years ago,' Lucy replied, giving the exact response that the Defense Intelligence Agency had instructed her to so many years ago. 'I did quite a lot of digging in the Negev area, but I can assure you I came back with nothing more than fossils of shells and some ancient pottery. I can show them to you, if you wish. They are absolutely fascinating examples of Neolithic and even Paleolithic origin.'

Vladimir leaned forward, his elbows resting on his knees and his hands clasped before him as the smile slipped away from his features.

'My superiors are willing to pay handsomely for any information that might help us locate the remains that were found in Israel.'

Lucy began to warm to her theme. 'They want to pay for my shells? That's great! Please, let me arrange them for you, and you can choose the ones you feel will please your superiors best. My personal favorites are the ammonites, some really good examples and almost pristine in the preservation of their features in the rock strata.'

Lucy stood up from her seat and reached across for a drawer that contained a collection of shells and assorted fossils. Opposite her, Vladimir stood up and one large hand pushed the drawer shut and pinned her hand in place.

'My superiors will only make the offer once,' he said. 'I do not wish this to become any more difficult than it needs to be.'

Lucy, her hand pinned beneath the Russian's, smiled sweetly as she erected a thin veil of confidence over her sudden fear.

'If that's your idea of a threat, then you just lost yourself a sale. I'll keep my shells. Now get out of my office and don't come back.'

Vladimir kept her hand pinned in place for a moment longer and then he turned and whirled from the office.

As soon as he closed the door behind him, Lucy exhaled heavily and slumped into her chair. It had been a long time since anybody had mentioned the things that had occurred in Israel and reminded her of the extraordinary, almost unbelievable discovery that she had made and been forced to abandon. To deny any knowledge of its existence pained her far more than the Russian would ever have known, especially as the Defense Intelligence Agency had forced her to sign nondisclosure agreements assuring that she would never share with anybody what she knew.

Lucy thought for a moment. She had not been alone in knowing of what had happened in Israel, and non-disclosure surely did not apply to individuals who already knew what she did. The Russian had threatened her, and what annoyed her most of all was that her work on the scant remnants of the remains she had been able to smuggle out of Israel without the agency's knowledge now concerned something far more important that archaeological curiosity.

Lucy turned to look at a mock human skeleton standing in one corner of her office, used for instructional purposes during lectures across the country. She looked down to one of the skeleton's hands, the index finger of which was somewhat longer than it should have been, the genuine bone perfectly disguised among fabricated replicas.

Lucy reached out and picked up the phone to dial a number she thought she would never actually ring.

IV

Englewood, Chicago

'It's ten dollars a slice and you either pay up now or you clear out.'

Reginald *Hood* Dyson rubbed his hands together against the cold of the night as he watched the addict's eyes flicker at the threat of his next fix being snatched away from him. Dyson's voice was soft, but the crisp night air carried the sound well enough that she could hear it from thirty yards away, delivered as it was with enough force to scare his next customer into parting with money before he had even tested the goods.

Nicola Lopez leaned against the corner of South Princeton and West 63rd , close by the "L" elevated rail line as she watched the deal go down amid crumbling tenement blocks and boarded up houses long since abandoned. Englewood was a neighborhood on the decline, blighted by crime and poverty. She had been following Dyson for two weeks, the former convict a dealer with connections to some of the major cartels operating out of South America. Dyson had spent more nights in Cook County Jail than Lopez had spent eating hot meals, a career criminal with enough muscle and reputation behind him to control an entire block on the city's south side.

Like most all dealers, Dyson operated in an area that looked every bit the drug dealer's paradise. From where Lopez stood she could see makeshift fires burning beneath the overpass where homeless people sought refuge from the bitter cold. It would be easy for an onlooker to think that all of them were simply low-life's living one day to the next in search of their next fix, but times had changed. Many of the people huddled over the meager flames had once lived in decent houses, commuted to decent jobs, raised decent children. Now in the turbulent wake of the economic crisis, all that they had left to their name were the clothes in which they stood and the memories to which they clung.

Lopez focused on Dyson and ignored the mumbling masses shuffling from one fire to the next. The dealer already had a package in his hand and was waving it demonstratively to his potential customers, a small group of whom had gathered around and appeared to be squabbling among themselves as to who would pay. It remained a marvel to Lopez that people in such dire straits had anything to pay for drugs with, but then again she knew that many of them fuelled their addiction with muggings, thefts and other criminal acts; the drug trade the source of some seventy percent of all crime in American cities.

Dyson handed the package over to a wiry, greasy-haired man with painfully thin features and a wild glint in his eye. Dyson was passed back in return greenbacks dirtied with age and use, much like the people handling them. Dyson pocketed the cash and offered his customers a mock salute, his smile bright in the flickering glow of the firelight and glinting with a gold tooth that Lopez knew he'd had fitted two years before, upon his release from jail; a celebration for the dropping of convictions due to lack of evidence and the interventions of a lawyer whose motivations were at best obscure.

Dyson swaggered off through the miserable masses as he made his way towards the 4x4 in which he had travelled from the west-side, and the vehicle that Lopez had followed him in. She pushed off the wall and circled back around the towering concrete pillars that supported the overpass above, the hiss and rattle of traffic rolling in and out of the city on the nearby I-94 an uncaring symphony to the misery.

As she walked past her car, she glimpsed her reflection in one of the windows, long dark hair and equally dark eyes against olive skin. Lopez was only a little over five feet tall, dressed in a tight-fitting leather jacket, jeans and boots and with her hair tied back in a ponytail. She walked out from behind the car toward the 4x4 and intercepted Dyson.

Dyson looked up as Lopez stepped into view and he slowed, one corner of his lips curling up in a gruesome smile as he came to a stop and shook his head. His dark eyes looked her up and down for a long moment before he finally spoke.

'Nicola Lopez,' he sneered. 'I thought that you would have learned to give up the last time you tried to send me down. Lack of evidence, if I recall?'

'Two years in Cook County being somebody's bitch, if I recall,' Lopez replied. 'Fancy heading back there?'

Dyson's grim smile vanished as his features hardened. 'I'm not going back to county, and you got nothin' on me. You looked around you, Lopez? This ain't no safe place for a lady.'

Lopez glanced at the cold metal of the overpass above them, the debris and rubbish gusting on the breeze.

'Perhaps you ought to leave then?'

Dyson burst out laughing and then in a flash a pistol appeared in his hand and he aimed directly at Lopez. 'No witnesses, no evidence but what they'll find left of you floating in Lake Michigan.'

Lopez raised a perfectly arched eyebrow and smiled as she tapped the breast of her jacket.

'Pinhole camera,' she said, 'wirelessly transmitting to a recording device in my office. Smile asshole, you're on camera threatening a bail officer with premeditated homicide.'

Dyson's snarl collapsed into a panicked grimace as he hurriedly stuffed the pistol back beneath his jacket and his white eyes sought a route of escape.

'You don't got power of arrest!' he insisted.

'Not until you pulled the piece on me,' Lopez agreed as with one hand she pulled a nightstick from inside her jacket. 'Now I got all the power I need. On your knees, hands behind your head!'

Dyson snarled again as he raised his hands behind his head, and Lopez took a pace toward him as she reached down for a pair of manacles attached to her belt.

The blow came from behind her, something hard and heavy slamming between her shoulders and knocking the breath from her lungs. She crashed onto the cold ground as the nightstick flew from her hand. The weight of a man landed on top of her and before she could react, somebody grabbed her wrists and yanked them into the small of her back. She heard a cackle of delight from just behind her right ear and a stench of foul breath as the man on top of her whispered.

'Bet your camera didn't see me. Been a while since I had myself on top of a pretty little thing like you.'

Lopez looked up and saw Dyson striding toward her as he pointed. 'Get that camera off her and shut it down!'

The man on top of her rolled her over and pinned her arms beneath her. Lopez recognised the scrawny face of the man to whom Dyson had sold the drugs, his wild eyes and stained teeth like a row of uneven tombstones between thin lips. The man unzipped her jacket and reached in, and Lopez saw his expression change from one of delight to one of lust as his hand moved over her breast and he gripped it tightly. His breathing accelerated and she saw him lick his lips as he looked down at her and then up at Dyson.

'Man, we could take her.'

Dyson looked down at Lopez and a cruel grin spread across his features, the gold tooth glinting in the faint light.

'The camera first,' he insisted. 'I know where her offices are 'cause my lawyer had to deal with her bail bondsman crap when he got me out of jail. We'll go pay a visit when we've finished with her and make sure there's no record of this.'

The scrawny man, his hand still grasping Lopez's breast, grinned in anticipation as he fumbled in search of the camera inside Lopez's jacket. He hunted for several long seconds before he frowned in confusion.

'There ain't no camera here,' he said. He pulled on something inside Lopez's jacket and a microphone appeared in his hand.

Dyson's gaze moved from Lopez toward her car, which was parked behind one of the massive concrete pillars. From where they were, a camera mounted on the dashboard would have had a clear view of both Lopez and Dyson and, if the lens had a high enough resolution, also be able to film the transaction he had just conducted.

'Clever girl,' Dyson said as he looked down at Lopez. 'That's the thing about you bail collectors: you're that little bit more cunning than the police. What say we turn that against you?'

Dyson reached down and pushed the scrawny man off Lopez as he drew his pistol again and held it to her chest, then with the other hand grabbed her collar and yanked her to her feet. Dyson shoved Lopez towards her car and jammed the pistol into the small of her back.

'Keep walking.'

Lopez stumbled forward as Dyson pushed her toward her car, changing his grip so the pistol was shoved under the small of her neck. They reached the car and Dyson pushed hard again so that her knees cracked against the vehicle's front fender. Dyson shoved his weight against Lopez and bent her over the hood of the vehicle, and with the pistol pressed to her neck he moved his head next to hers as one hand cupped her chin and lifted her head to look at the vehicle's windscreen. There, on the dashboard, the camera lens stared unblinkingly out at them.

'That camera is going to record everything that's going to happen to you now,' Dyson snarled. 'And then I'm going to go retrieve all that lovely footage and keep it, maybe watch it every now and again when I want to remind myself what it's like to take a *chiquita* like you from behind.'

Dyson pinned Lopez in place with his weight, the pistol still jammed against her neck as with his other hand he reached down and began trying to fumble with his jeans. She could hear the cackling of his accomplice and the sound of a belt being undone.

'The camera feed is live,' Lopez spat. 'Local law enforcement will be here within minutes.'

'Minutes is all I need, honey,' Dyson replied with a grim chuckle. 'That's what jail does to you. You reap what you sow, Lopez.'

Dyson shifted position as he reached down in an attempt to unzip his fly, and as his weight shifted off of Lopez's back she hooked one heel around Dyson's ankle as she pushed hard off the car's hood and jerked her head backward.

The back of Lopez's skull impacted Dyson's nose with a crack as she grabbed the pistol with her left hand and pushed it away from her neck. With a boot hooked around Dyson's ankle, the big man was instantly thrown off balance and Lopez immediately lifted one boot onto the bumper of the car and pushed hard to throw Dyson off.

Lopez whirled away from the car in one smooth motion and her right fist cracked across the scrawny man's sneering face even before he realized what had happened. A spray of grey and broken teeth flew from his mouth as he collapsed onto the ground.

Dyson let out a roar of anger and jumped up, one hand holding his jeans up as the other aimed the pistol at Lopez. She spun on her heel and flicked one boot up in a graceful high kick that smashed into Dyson's wrist before he could get a shot off, and then she lunged for the pistol.

Lopez managed to get a grip on Dyson's hand and she twisted savagely. Dyson let out a growl of pain his body doubled over as he fought to get hold of Lopez's face and twist her away. Lopez instantly bit down on Dyson's hand and heard him scream as he tried to yank his fingers away from her bite. She pulled Dyson up as he twisted away and threw him over her shoulder as she twisted the pistol hard in his grip.

Dyson slammed down onto the unforgiving asphalt as the pistol was ripped from his hand. Lopez stood and aimed the weapon down at Dyson, who stared up at her with features stricken with pain.

'Assault and attempted sexual assault,' Lopez growled with grim satisfaction as she stood over the cowering man. 'That should go down well on film alongside drug dealing and possession of an unlicensed weapon.'

Dyson said nothing but he looked to one side, somewhere behind Lopez, and she turned to see the scrawny man staggering to his feet and holding his bloody mouth, and behind him dozens of men all advancing toward her. Most were wrapped in multiple layers of clothing, their haggard faces bearded and their eyes hungry now for more than just food. Lopez's shirt had been yanked from the waist of her jeans and her collar ripped to expose bare, olive skin above her right breast, her hair shaken loose into long black veils that framed her face.

More sounds from behind and she turned to see other homeless men advancing around her car and cutting off any escape.

'Bail bondsman,' she snapped as she reached down and pulled an identity badge from her belt and held it high above her head. 'This is police business and there's a camera in the car with a live feed to the local station.'

The advancing ranks of men did not stop shuffling toward her, their eyes devoid of anything approaching emotion that she could recognise. Desperate men, with nothing to lose in this life and everything to gain. She realized belatedly that three square meals a day in jail or prison was infinitely preferable to their suffering outside in the elements of a Chicago winter.

'There ain't no cops watching!' Dyson yelled as he scrambled to his feet and backed away from Lopez. 'You can have her!'

'Back off, now!' Lopez yelled as she aimed her pistol into the sky and fired a single shot.

The gunshot caused many in the crowd to flinch, but others were now looking at her in a way that she knew would mean nothing would stop them. She glanced over her shoulder at Lake Michigan, the only possible means of escape a leap into the frigid black water as she began backing away and aimed the pistol at the shuffling hordes gathering before her.

She saw Dyson and his scrawny friend scramble away through the ranks of men as they sought their escape. She had fourteen rounds left in the Glock pistol, and she counted at least thirty men closing in on her from all sides. The closest of them reached out for her pistol, his features alive with a volatile mix of excitement and desperation.

Lopez aimed her pistol at his head and made to squeeze the trigger.

A deafening gunshot crashed out and was followed by four more as a sudden blaze of sirens and vehicles pulled beneath the underpass, bright headlight beams sweeping in to illuminate the shuffling vagrants.

The crowd whirled in surprise and scattered away from Lopez, running on unsteady legs back towards the salvation and anonymity of the fires and the shadows. Lopez lowered her pistol, suddenly aware of her heart pounding inside her chest as four black vehicles screeched to a halt in front of her. Lopez holstered her weapon as the door of one of the vehicles opened and a man stepped out.

He was tall, a black overcoat rippling in the cold wind, his bituminous skin dark. He walked with his hands in the pockets of the coat, apparently impervious to the chill, his features without emotion. He moved to within a couple of yards of her and watched her for a long moment before speaking in a voice so deep it sounded as though he were underwater.

'Nicola Lopez?'

'Who the hell are you?'

Lopez glanced at the vehicles and their distinctive plates and recognised them as government pool cars, something she had seen many times before in her career as a bail bondsman and occasional contractor for the Defense Intelligence Agency.

'I'm your savior,' the man replied.

'I had everything under control.'

'Of course,' the man said. 'Just like Dyson and his accomplice?'

'They got away.'

'Only as far as the highway,' the man replied. 'My people will pick them up. I take it they are worth quite a bit of money to you. I'd be happy to hand them back over, if you can spare me a moment of your time.'

Lopez surveyed the man for a moment longer.

'What did you say your name was?'

V

The interior of the vehicle was much as Lopez remembered government vehicles being: smart but spartan, with a smoked glass screen between the rear and front seats where two agents drove the vehicle back towards the city.

Lopez sat on a rearward facing seat with Aaron Devlin opposite. Upon closer inspection, she figured he looked a little old for a DIA field agent, somewhere in his late forties, his hair speckled with gray and his physique surrounded by a palpable aura of competence that verged on the threatening. His dark eyes watched her for what felt like an eternity as the car whispered along the asphalt.

'You want a photo?'

'I already have several. I've been studying them for some time.'

'I bet you have.'

If Aaron Devlin had ever possessed a sense of humor, Lopez wasn't sensing it.

'You've got quite an attitude, Ms Lopez,' Aaron said as he opened a file on his lap. 'You seem to be doing quite well for yourself running Warner and Lopez Incorporated.'

'It's Lopez Incorporated,' she corrected him. 'And yes, things are busy and time is money. What do you want?'

'It must be tough having to do all of this work on your own,' Aaron observed as though not hearing her last. 'And I suspect you're wondering where Doug Jarvis is?'

During the course of five investigations for the Defense Intelligence Agency, her superior officer had been Douglas Jarvis, a former Marine officer. An elderly man with a wealth of experience of intelligence gathering, Jarvis had been something of a mercurial boss who had been willing to take chances with the lives of those under his command in order to advance the needs and requirements of the United States government. There was no doubt in Lopez's mind that Jarvis was a patriot through and through, but it had been her decision to cease working for the DIA over a year previously due to the inherent and increasing risks to life and limb.

'I really hadn't thought about him,' she replied. Aaron did not reply as he continue to leaf through the file. 'Be sure to send on my warmest regards.'

Aaron looked up at that, as she had intended – her tone conveyed anything but the warmest regards.

'I have not met him,' Aaron informed her. 'I've been sent here by a different branch of the agency.'

'I don't work for the government anymore.'

'I'm not here to ask for your work, I'm here to ask merely for a little help in finding somebody. I understand from your record that doing so is something at which you excel.'

Lopez shrugged. 'If you can call digging crap out from under stones a skill.'

Aaron closed the file and folded his hands over it. 'I'm here to talk about Israel.'

'Beautiful country, never been there.'

'But you have a connection to somebody who has. His name is Ethan Warner.'

Lopez smiled tightly. 'Then why don't you go ask him?'

'We tried. Unfortunately, we have been unable to find him.'

'Shame, can I go now?'

'I think you know where he is.'

'I think you know nothing,' Lopez replied. 'I haven't seen Warner in almost a year.'

'So I see from the file we have on Warner and Lopez Incorporated.'

'*Lopez* Incorporated.'

'Of course,' Aaron smiled without warmth. 'Warner took off. I suppose that must have left you feeling rather jilted, to say the least?'

'What's your point, Devlin?'

'That you probably do not hold Mr Warner in high regard, and therefore it might be of some interest to you to have him found so that you can bring him to task for leaving you to work alone here in Chicago.'

'It was a mutual decision,' Lopez replied.

'That so?'

'He suggested he might want to leave, I agreed.'

Aaron raised an eyebrow. 'Is setting fire to somebody's motorcycle and punching them in the face what you consider an agreement?'

'It was an emotional moment,' Lopez shrugged. 'What's this

about?'

Aaron leaned forward in his seat as the street lights flashed by silently outside.

'I have a problem, Ms Lopez, and at this time the only person we know who may be able to help is beyond our reach. There have been some discoveries, recently, that bear similarity to excavations made in the Negev Desert in Israel some years ago, discoveries in which Ethan Warner was involved. I have it on record that both you and he signed nondisclosure agreements regarding these events, so I find it highly unlikely that you would truly have no idea at all where Ethan Warner has disappeared to.'

'I find it highly unlikely that you think I would give a f…' The sound of a truck's horn blared outside the vehicle as it rushed past in the opposite direction. '… where Ethan Warner has disappeared to.'

'He was your partner for several years.'

'He was a pain in my ass for several years. People move on. He outlived his usefulness.'

Aaron leaned back in his seat and shook his head. 'Was your relationship something more than business?'

A tiny smile curled from the corner of Lopez's sculptured lips.

'You're starting to outlive *your* usefulness, Devlin,' she replied. 'I don't know where Ethan Warner is and frankly I don't give a damn. For all I know he's disappeared up his own ass.'

Aaron sighed and looked out the window at the passing city.

'There is more to this than just the government needing to speak to Ethan Warner. There could be immensely important implications in what's happening, and right now we're trying to play catch up because there are others way ahead of us.'

'Others?'

'Need to know,' Aaron replied, 'and like you said, you don't work for the government anymore.'

'Then we're done here,' Lopez informed him. 'How about you be a good boy and drop me, Dyson, and his crony off at Cook County Jail?'

Aaron watched her for a moment longer, and his reply was as deep and rumbling as the road beneath them.

'So be it.'

*

It was close to midnight by the time Lopez finally got home.

True to his word, Aaron Devlin had ensured that both Dyson and his accomplice had been delivered to Cook County Jail, along with Lopez's car which she had found parked by the sidewalk after she had booked Dyson. She had also taken the precaution of downloading the video of both Dyson's drug deal and assault attempt directly at the jail, just in case any of Dyson's accomplices evolved any intelligence and attempted to break into her offices and snatch the evidence away before she could bring it to court.

Lopez pulled into her parking slot and killed the engine, then sat quietly for a moment and rubbed her eyes. She was working eighteen-hour–days, and could not really remember the last time she had taken a break to do anything other than wash, eat, or sleep. The sheer number of bail jumpers and the scale of Chicago meant that tracking down any one perp was like looking for a needle in a haystack, and as she had found out on numerous occasions, grabbing a needle sometimes hurt.

She got out of her car and walked towards the apartment block she had lived in for the past five years. Her apartment had been paid for by the proceeds of her very first investigation with Ethan Warner, which at least meant that her cost of living was appreciably lower than most people living in the city. That was just as well, because since working alone as a bail runner, her income had dropped dramatically: most all bail companies employed several agents to track down and apprehend bail jumpers. Doing it solo was widely considered to be something of a lost cause, the romantic notion of a bounty hunter shattered by the sheer difficulty and low financial reward of hunting down individuals alone. Without Ethan Warner to back her up, every successful mission was the result of a long hard slog that often lasted weeks.

Lopez walked wearily up the steps toward the apartment entrance and was surprised to find a woman sitting at the top of the steps. Young, with long blonde hair and green eyes, the woman had obviously been waiting for some time because she got to her feet the moment she laid eyes on Lopez.

'You must be Nicola?' the woman said.

'You must be psychic.'

The woman smiled and extended a hand. 'Sorry, my name is Dr Lucy Morgan. Ethan told me a lot about you. Is he about?'

'Sure he is,' Lopez replied as she shook the proffered hand, 'somewhere. If you find him, let me know; it seems everybody in the damned city's looking for him.'

'He's not here?'

'Hasn't been for a year or so,' Lopez replied. Despite being tired, she could tell that Morgan was not of the same ilk as Dyson or Devlin, and she remembered enough of the name to recall that she was some sort of scientist. 'You'd better come up.'

Lopez's apartment was larger than most and reasonably well decorated, her feminine eye for tasteful furniture marred only by her natural disregard for tidiness. Magazines were scattered across the leather couch, a couple of small beer bottles stood on a glass coffee table in the center of the lounge, and a fairly impressive stack of dirty dishes remained untouched on the kitchen counter.

'It's a nice place you've got here,' Lucy said politely as Lopez shut the door.

'It was until I moved in and forgot to tidy. Make yourself at home in any space you can find.'

Lucy perched on the couch and watched with some consternation as Lopez un-holstered her pistol and laid it on the kitchen counter, followed by a nightstick, two savage-looking blades and what might have been brass knuckles.

'Tools of the trade,' Lopez said with a faint smile as she saw Lucy's concerned expression.

'Ethan said that you were bounty hunters.'

'Law enforcement assistance,' Lopez replied as she tossed her leather jacket across a table and then slumped into a well-used armchair nearby. 'We're like street cleaners, sweeping up the trash and the dregs of society. Beer?'

'I'm good,' Lucy replied as Lopez pulled the cap from a bottle and took a deep swig.

'What do you want Ethan for?' Lopez asked. 'I thought that the case he worked with you finished some years ago?'

'In Washington, DC, so I recall,' Lucy replied with a nod. 'It's about where he met you, correct?'

Lopez replied simply by inclining her head in acquiescence.

'Ethan kept in touch the year following my return to Chicago,' Lucy explained. 'He saved my life in Israel and remained friends with my mother Rachel, so I got to hear about your work, from time to time.'

'Must have been fun,' Lopez replied.

'Ethan didn't say anything about the details. I got the impression he probably wasn't allowed to.'

'That's government contracting for you.'

'I think that what happened in Israel has happened again,' Lucy said simply.

Lopez set her beer bottle on the coffee table between them and looked at Lucy for a long time. Because of the nondisclosure agreements signed by herself, Ethan and anybody else involved in the case, they had shared little information on what had happened. Lopez had only met Ethan when he had arrived in Washington, DC in search of a crazed Baptist minister by the name of Kelvin Patterson, whom it was alleged had paid Lucy Morgan to go in search of the remains of angels buried in the deserts of Israel. What Lucy had found had not been the remains of angels at all but something far more earth-shattering: the seven thousand year old remains of a creature not of this earth.

What Patterson had been intending to do with the DNA of those remains had so appalled Lopez that she had not really allowed herself to think about it. She had seen the consequences of the pastor's actions in the deaths of many innocent people and had no wish to be involved in the case any further. In fact, virtually all of the cases that she and Ethan had worked for the DIA had involved a variety of paranormal or supernatural events, many of which had nearly cost them their lives.

'This is kind of Ethan's area of expertise,' Lopez explained. 'Have you contacted his family?'

Lucy nodded. 'I spoke to his sister, Natalie, and she said that they speak to him regularly by phone but that they have no idea where he is.'

'Why doesn't that surprise me?'

'Natalie promised that she would tell him that I was looking for him, but she admitted that contact with Ethan is sporadic and it could be weeks or even months before he speaks to her again. I don't know who else to turn to.'

For the first time Lopez recognised a hint of fear in Lucy's tone and instinctively her disinterest vanished as she leaned forward in her seat.

'How do you know that somebody has made a similar discovery as the one in Israel?'

'A man came to see me this morning,' Lucy explained. 'He insisted I share with him everything I knew about what was discovered in Israel. When I explained that I knew nothing, he threatened me.'

'Do you know his name or where he came from?'

'His name was Vladimir Polkov, and I think he was Russian or at the very least Eastern European.'

'And do you know anything about what was discovered in Israel?'

Lucy nodded. 'I know a great deal about it, because I've been studying it for the past five years.' She reached into her bag and produced a clear plastic cylinder. Inside the cylinder was a bone that looked a little like a finger bone but was much, much longer. 'I think they were looking for this.'

Lopez peered at the bone for a moment and saw the label stuck to the outside of the cylinder. Inscribed with the word 'Negev' and a date from five years previous, she did not need to ask what the bone was.

'Who else knows that you have that?' Lopez asked.

'Just Ethan, because it was he who gave me this bone. He liberated it from the remains that I excavated in Israel and handed it to me before my return to Chicago, and before he met you in DC. Ms Lopez, I don't know who is watching me but I think they know that I'm lying and I'm not sure what they're going to do next. I really need to find Ethan Warner – will you help me?'

VI

Office of the Director of National Intelligence
Tyson's Corner,
Virginia

'I want to speak to you plainly and in complete security. You are under no obligations and your presence here remains covert. No non-disclosure protocols are in operation, as I have asked you here on trust and reputation alone.'

Lieutenant General J. F. Nellis was a former United States Air Force officer who had recently been appointed DNI by the current president. Just one year into the role and he had already aged visibly, swamped by the sheer volume of information he was required to process as a matter of daily routine.

'That's the first time anybody has said that in an agency capacity. What gives?'

Former Defense Intelligence Agency operative Douglas Ian Jarvis sat opposite the DNI and tried not to look nervous. Almost as old as the director himself, Jarvis had spent some twenty years working for the DIA and been involved in some of the highest-level classified operations ever conducted by elements of the US Covert Operations Service. Most of them he would never be able to talk about with another human being, even those with whom he had served. Jarvis knew the rules and had obeyed them with patriotic fervour, more or less, his entire career. Which was why he was now feeling uncomfortable.

There had been no warning of the meeting. He had been woken at five in the morning by a polite knock at his bedroom door. Not the front door of his house – his *bedroom* door. Two agents, both armed, had disabled his alarm and accessed his house before waking him at gunpoint to inform him that he should not panic, that he was required for a meeting that must be conducted without observation of any kind.

Jarvis, unsurprisingly, had believed himself the victim of a terrorist abduction and had almost shot the two agents with the pistol he held under his pillow, but one of them had uttered two words that had both shocked him and belayed his trigger finger.

Majestic Twelve.

'You served the DIA for two decades, the last five years of which you operated a covert unit tasked with high-level, low-footprint investigations into unusual phenomena. By your own design, the outfit was conceived to be completely deniable, and capable of infiltrating government agency programs under the umbrella of its official investigative charter.'

Jarvis blinked. 'We stole data, exposed corruption and investigated paranormal events.'

Nellis smiled and took the hint. They could talk as he had requested and dispose of the formalities.

'At what level was your non-disclosure agreement ordered?'

'Cosmic,' Jarvis replied, 'Level Five. Orders came from the Pentagon, which department I do not know. All five of the investigations we conducted were *sealed terminal*, never to be released for public consumption.'

Nellis nodded as he looked down at folder before him. 'Tell me, how did you come into all of this?'

'Short story?'

'As concise as you can be.'

Jarvis began to feel a little more at ease, but he still picked his words with care as he spoke. He didn't know the DNI well enough to be sure of whether this was going to end with him being hung out to dry for revealing state secrets.

'The program I led was not designed by me but was inherited. It had its origins in something known as Project Blue Book, a series of systematic studies of the UFO phenomena conducted by the air force. It started with Project Sign, then Project Grudge, before becoming Blue Book. Designed to determine if UFOs represented a threat to national security and to analyse data gathered from sightings, it was scrapped in 1970.'

'And then resurrected later?'

'The CIA had numerous projects running through the seventies and eighties, like Project Stargate which investigated psychic phenomena and remote viewing, and units like MK-ULTRA which studied everything from hallucinatory drug-induced assassins to microwave mind-control and use of animals as weapons of war. All of these programs were eventually shut down, but a few years back I was approached by the DIA to start up a small unit that unified the disparate threads of previous CIA-led programs, and create a more covert study of such phenomena. Essentially, we were willing to investigate events that other agencies rejected as fantasy.'

Nellis leafed through a few pages of the folder. 'What was the catalyst for this sudden *volte-face* of the DIA?'

'An event that occurred in Israel,' Jarvis said, and then let his voice trail off.

Nellis looked at Jarvis for a moment. 'You can speak freely here, Doug.'

'No, sir, I cannot,' Jarvis replied. 'Lives have been taken as a result of the Pentagon's determination to preserve security over that operation.'

Nellis held Jarvis's gaze for a long moment. 'I can tell you, Mr Jarvis, that you never received orders from the Pentagon regarding these issues and operations.'

Jarvis stared long and hard at the DNI before he replied. 'Say that again?'

'You never received orders from the Pentagon regarding these issues and operations,' Nellis repeated. 'Your non-disclosure agreements, although legally and technically valid in a public setting, hold no weight in this office.'

'Who gave the orders?' Jarvis asked, stunned.

'I'll get to that,' Nellis replied. 'Israel?'

Jarvis sighed. He was an old man, now, and he realized that it wasn't like the Pentagon or anybody else could steal his young life away from him. If he was ever going to be able to come clean about the operations he had conducted, now was the time and Nellis was the man.

'I take it you are aware of the alleged events that took place in Roswell, New Mexico, in 1947?'

'The supposed crashed flying-saucer,' Nellis nodded.

'Nobody knows what happened that day, but what we can be sure of is that *something* happened and that it was highly important to the government of the time. The stories of the wreckage actually being a weather balloon weren't bought by anybody; it was a cover-up, all right, and within months of the event programs like Project Sign started up to investigate UFOs. The government spent millions trying to understand what happened, but its people just didn't have the skills to properly investigate such unusual events. After Project Blue Book was closed, the agencies involved adopted a *wait and watch* policy. They figured that if it happened once, then maybe something similar might happen again.'

Nellis blinked in surprise as he continued to study the file. 'Are we the only ones involved in this?'

'Not at all,' Jarvis replied. 'NASA recently heavily redacted a press-release that had been leaked to the media. Within it, from a NASA published study entitled *Archaeology, Anthropology and Interstellar Communications*, a paragraph was revealed that suggested they're preparing for contact from extra-terrestrial species. If what you're looking at there is the files the DIA publicly maintain on such events, it's on page eighteen.'

Nellis flipped to the relevant page and read aloud from it. *'These scholars are grappling with some of the enormous challenges that will face humanity if an information-rich signal emanating from another world is detected. By drawing on issues at the core of contemporary archaeology and anthropology, we can be much better prepared for contact with an extraterrestrial civilization, should that day ever come.'* Nellis looked up at Jarvis. 'Is this serious? You think that they're expecting an invasion?'

'Not exactly,' Jarvis smiled. 'NASA was likely using previous human invasions of other countries in history to compare to the arrival of an alien species here on Earth, but you can guess how the public reacted to such an official paper. After what happened in 1977 with the WOW Signal, I suspect the Pentagon wasn't too happy with NASA's more recent leak.'

'That *what* signal?' Nellis asked.

'The Wow Signal was picked up by the Big Ear Radio telescope of Ohio State University on August 15, 1977 as part of the SETI Project, the Search for Extra Terrestrial Intelligence. It bore all the hallmarks of an intelligent, non-terrestrial and non-solar system origin and lasted seventy-two seconds. Other, more recent signals have been detected from earth-like systems but are suppressed by the media.'

'It was an alien broadcast?' Nellis asked.

'By all the standards applied to such signals, yes,' Jarvis confirmed. 'It was intelligent, technological, and came from a star system other than our own.'

'It's been government policy for some time to suppress anything that might be considered controversial that NASA or other space agencies might discover.'

'Such as France,' Jarvis agreed, 'who have a full-time department called *Geipan* dedicated to the study of UFO sightings. The British recently operated a similar department but shut it down, or at least the public face of it. After what happened in Israel, the powers that be in Washington want all allied countries to cease further investigations into UFO activity to avoid generating unwanted public interest.'

Nellis reached the relevant page on Israel in the file before him. 'This material is heavily redacted; I can't figure out what it actually refers to.'

Jarvis took a deep breath, and let it all out.

'In the Negev Desert of Israel, a palaeontologist by the name of Dr Lucy Morgan excavated a seven thousand year old tomb, and inside it she found the skeletal remains of a bipedal, non-human figure.'

The room filled with a deep silence as Nellis absorbed the information. 'Go on.'

'Morgan vanished, along with the remains, and with a delicate political summit underway between Israel and Palestine, official US interference was impossible. Instead, I was tasked with organising a rescue and retrieval mission: liberate Lucy Morgan and tie her into a strict Non-Disclosure Agreement, and ensure that the remains she discovered were secured by the agency and spirited away.'

Nellis nodded, reading from the file and no-doubt filling in the redacted gaps as he went.

'The mission was a success and led to your further operations.'

'Four more,' Jarvis said, 'in New Mexico, Florida, Idaho and New York, and involving various rogue agency-operations that were brought to a close. All were successful, but the unit was wound-down after the final operation in New York City.'

'What happened?'

'A rogue CIA unit governed by MK-ULTRA, a supposedly defunct Agency program, hunted down my two lead operatives and forced them into hiding for over six months. After the situation was resolved, the two in question walked away from the DIA and vowed that they would never work for the government again. I haven't seen either of them since.'

Jarvis saw Nellis wince as he listened, and then he closed the file and looked at Jarvis.

'A situation has developed and I need your help.'

'I've been out of this game for almost two years,' Jarvis replied. 'My contacts have moved on, as has the technology. I don't know that I would be of any use in…'

Nellis raised his hand to forestall Jarvis, a smile touching his craggy features as he searched for the right words before he spoke.

'My role here is that of a cipher,' he said. 'I have the title of Director of National Intelligence, but that role has been engineered to deny me access to the Black Budget, to the Pentagon's Special Operations Department, to various sub-agencies operating across the globe and to any high-level clearances afforded the directors of those agencies. In short, Mr Jarvis, I'm sitting here as an administrator and nothing more, and I don't damned-well like it.'

Jarvis hesitated for a moment before he replied. 'Majestic Twelve.'

Nellis nodded and his voice dropped an octave as though he were afraid that somebody might be listening, even in an office in one of the most secure buildings on the planet.

'Is a rumoured cabal of former politicians, intelligence leaders, and military-industrial CEOs responsible for running the show we call humanity from behind the scenes. When you believed that you were receiving orders from the Pentagon, you were, in fact, operating on behalf of Majestic Twelve.'

Jarvis rubbed his temples with one hand. 'Why have you brought me here today?'

'I want you to re-start your unit under my command, and get to the bottom of what Majestic Twelve is attempting to achieve.'

'I doubt that will be possible, sir,' Jarvis replied. 'As I mentioned, both of my lead agents were compromised and later refused to work for the DIA any longer. Neither of them have any desire to perform more operations for us, and I don't even know where one of them is.'

Nellis nodded, clearly having memorised the names of the individuals concerned.

'Nicola Lopez runs the bail bondsmen company Warner & Lopez Inc out of Chicago. Ethan Warner, former United States Marine, is off the grid and has not been seen for almost a year.'

Jarvis nodded. 'You're not going to get Lopez out of Chicago, and if Ethan's decided to get off the radar then you won't find him.'

'I agree. We've already tried.'

'Why now?' Jarvis asked. 'What's this really all about?'

Nellis leaned back in his seat. 'I received direct orders two months ago, allegedly from the Pentagon, to maintain a watch on Dr Lucy Morgan as a person of interest to United States security. It's not every day I get direct orders regarding a single individual – that kind of attention is usually reserved for international terrorists and war criminals. Having personally researched her background, I could find absolutely no evidence of her being a threat to national security. I did some quiet digging, and none of my contacts at the Pentagon issued those orders.'

Jarvis raised an eyebrow. 'What did you do, sir?'

'I did as I was told,' Nellis grinned, 'and I waited to see what would happen. Sure enough, Lucy Morgan has been making some strange movements, working into the early hours in her apartment, buying chemicals and such like that are normally used for laboratory experiments. The CIA listed her as somebody perhaps intending to create bombs, but none of the chemicals she has bought can be used to create any explosive device that I know of and besides, she's a model citizen and respected scientist.'

'Not to mention a patriot,' Jarvis added. 'Lucy's no terrorist.'

'I had a few agents research her history, made connections with her presence in Israel some years ago, and with it numerous highly-redacted files. No clear trail, but enough to suspect that there was more to the ordered surveillance than met the eye. More digging linked Ethan Warner to Israel at the same time, and from there his link to you at the DIA.'

Jarvis masked his uncertainty with a smile. 'Stirling work, sir.'

'But I can do no more from here,' Nellis replied, 'and now Lucy Morgan has taken a vacation and vanished completely.'

Now, Jarvis leaned forward in his seat. 'How long?'

'Two days,' Nellis replied, 'right after she was observed speaking to one Nicola Lopez.'

Jarvis could not help the smile that creased from the corner of his lips as he pictured Lopez in his mind, her firecracker temper and sarcastic wit.

'They're up to something,' Jarvis said finally. 'Lopez might be helping her in some way.'

'More than that,' Nellis said. 'Morgan was approached by a Russian the day prior to her disappearance, a man by the name of Vladimir Polkov. He's the son of Yuri Polkov, a famed fossil smuggler and all-round enemy of the state. We didn't have the ability to obtain recordings, but if a fossil smuggler is interested in a fossil hunter's work, and Lucy Morgan has been conducting private studies of some kind…'

'… then she's found something new,' Jarvis completed the sentence. 'And you think that Majestic Twelve might be watching her, too.'

'I need you to get onto this, Doug, quietly,' Nellis implored him. 'Your former commanding officer, General Mitchell, recommended you in the highest terms to me as a reliable agent and patriot. Whatever's going on with Morgan and Lopez, I need to find out, and if it leads me to identifying the members of Majestic Twelve, then I can start doing my damned job properly and root out the corruption that has blighted the intelligence community for so long.'

Jarvis rubbed his jaw thoughtfully. 'What resources will I have?'

'Not much,' Nellis admitted. 'Two trusted agents as a security detail, what tech and data I can send you directly, a jet and a budget, of course. It goes without saying that this will be un-official operations; no paper trail, no direct contact after this meeting. You'll be supplied with a satellite phone and all necessary visas, if required. We need to move fast, Doug. What do you say? Do you think you can track Lucy Morgan down?'

'Definitely,' Jarvis replied. 'But Warner? I honestly don't know.'

VII

Pitlochrie, Cairngorns
Scotland

'Your target is a Caucasian male, approximately forty years of age, and with extensive military experience. He has a one-hour head start and is considered highly dangerous. Do not attempt to apprehend him on your own: locate, identify, and report in for reinforcements.'

There were forty infantry soldiers standing in the light drizzle that fell from low scudding clouds obscuring the peaks of the Cairngorns. A broad valley bordered the bitter waters of a river that flowed, it seemed, from a wilderness untouched by human hands, bleak and steep hillsides of black granite and windswept grass. All of the soldiers were dressed in British style disruptive pattern material khakis and heavy black boots, and they cradled SA-80 rifles in their gloved hands. Before the infantry stood their commanding officer, a major of the regiment who gestured to the barren hills around them.

'Your target has extensive survival experience and is known to be capable of enduring in even the harshest environments for weeks on end. He is able to fashion weapons from the barest minimum of resources and is a highly disciplined expert in camouflage and concealment. For his age, he is known to be in impressive physical condition and is possessed of a high degree of tenacity. He will not surrender even if found, and has a temperament that will likely result in him physically defending himself if cornered. You have forty-eight hours to find him.'

The major surveyed his men one last time and then saluted. 'Good luck, dismissed!'

The forty soldiers turned and jogged away in formation, leaving the asphalt road, and the sound of their thumping boots becoming dull and muted as they journeyed out across the sodden landscape with a pair of sergeants leading them.

The major watched as the small platoon followed the faint trail left by their quarry barely an hour before, and wondered if indeed they would be able to track him down. His regiment had spent much time training in the art of camouflage and concealment, as well as the complex skills required in tracking and trapping fugitives. The entire objective of the new training regime was designed specifically to give the British Army the ability to track down terrorists and other undesirables who may decide to hunker down in the most remote and inaccessible regions of the British Isles, a new and interesting tactic deployed by enemies of the state wishing to avoid detection.

For some time, the greatest fear of governments in the Western world had not been the massive terrorist organisations such as Al Qaeda and Islamic State, but rather the actions of so-called *lone wolf* terrorists, those that were impossible to track, invisible to detection by the sheer nature of their status. Living mostly off the grid, without cell phones or access to the Internet or bank accounts and driving licences, a true lone wolf could strike almost at will and disappear just as quickly, if they were possessed of the will and intelligence to plot and execute an effective terrorist attack. It was Major Jonathan Wilkinson's job to train British infantry to track down that lone terrorist and finish him off before he had the chance to strike.

A squall of bitter rain splattered against the major's combat fatigues and he pulled his beret down a little tighter about his head as he walked back towards the four-ton vehicle parked nearby. He reached the door and opened it to a billowing cloud of welcome warmth coming from the interior of the cab as he climbed inside and slammed the door shut. The driver, a regimental corporal, sat behind the wheel and waited patiently as the major picked up a folder he had left on the dashboard and opened it.

'From what I gather, this chap has never been found in any of the seventeen exercises he has run with us. Not bad for a damn Yankee, I'll give him that.'

The corporal nodded but said nothing as the major scanned down the pages of the file and tutted to himself. 'A former United States Marine, apparently. Well, we can't have Yanks running around making fools of our boys, eh?'

The corporal smiled and nodded, and the major rubbed his hands together as he peered through the rain splattered windscreen at the now very distant platoon of soldiers as they broke up into smaller groups, barely visible against the rough terrain.

'Rather them than me,' he said, more to himself than to the corporal next to him. 'Bloody freezing out there, and there's a depression coming in. I wouldn't be surprised if it snows tonight, bloody awful conditions to be out hunting for some damned confederate escapee.'

The corporal nodded once more and the major looked across at him. 'You're bloody quiet, considering you've landed the easy job of driving me around. I'd have thought you'd be been a bit more cheerful?'

The corporal turned to look at the officer, a pair of cold grey eyes fixing upon his as with one hand he drew a pistol from beneath his combat jacket and nudged it against the major's flank.

'Rather them than me,' he drawled in an American accent.

For a moment the major thought that he was in danger of losing his life as an image of newspaper headlines documenting the shooting of a senior army officer by an unknown lone wolf terrorist flashed through his mind. Then the corporal winked at him and the major's fear turned to anger.

'Bloody hell!' he blustered with indignation as he pointed out of the windscreen ahead of them. 'I've just dispatched forty men to find you, Warner, and you're sitting here in the cab of my bloody truck! What the hell have you done with my driver?'

'He's taking a nap in the back,' Ethan Warner replied with a casual smile as he indicated the back of the truck with a nod of his head.

'You're supposed to be evading and escaping my men!'

'I know, but it's *bloody awful* out there,' Ethan replied as he mimicked the major's accent.

'The British government is paying for you to educate my soldiers,' Major Wilkinson uttered in disgust, 'not sit here talking to me.'

'Your troops are being educated,' Ethan insisted. 'If they are stupid, they will follow the trail that I left leading out into the wilderness yesterday. It will be a very long walk with very little at the end of it. If they are smart, they'll notice the slightly newer trail that I left one hour ago that loops around the edge of those hills and comes right back here.'

Major Wilkinson looked at the row of low hills obscured in cloud and tutted again. 'This is not what I had in mind when I agreed to you training my men.'

'Good,' Ethan replied as he put his pistol away. 'Tracking people down is not a business of following them from A to B to C. You have to expect the unexpected, be prepared for anything, including outright deception. If your boys track me down in the next hour, they get the night off for doing a good job, and given that they are battle-hardened British infantry, I fully expect them to achieve that. If they don't, they'll have learned a valuable lesson: don't follow an old trail when a new one presents itself.'

'I'll let you present that explanation to the Ministry of Defense when they summon you to explain why you're not out there hiding in a bloody bush somewhere getting wet like my men.'

'Because I'm not stupid,' Ethan said with a cheerful smile. 'Now, in the interests of you not running after your troop and informing them of my deception, I'm afraid I'm forced to place your comfort into the hands of your competent NCOs and infantry.'

Major Wilkinson looked at Ethan with sudden consternation written large across his features.

'And what the bloody hell is that supposed to mean?'

*

Ethan liked the silence, especially after Major Wilkinson's prattling had been stiffled by a gag and Ethan had placed him in the back of the truck along with his hapless corporal. With both of them fully bound, they would either be spending a few very cold hours in the back of the truck until they could work themselves free or their faithful troops would return, having seen through Ethan's deception, and would be able to relieve them of their suffering.

Ethan pushed the back of the truck closed and then pulled his hood up against the icy rain tumbling from the clouds.

Time to disappear.

Ethan set off at a brisk walk in the opposite direction to which the infantry troops had disappeared, again a pre-planned diversion. Ethan, having plenty of experience of the brutality of Scottish winter weather, had no intention of spending two nights out in the wilderness when storms were blowing in from the north-west. While the troops were trying to figure out what had happened to him, he fully intended to be sitting at home with his feet up, and that home was over five miles away across the rolling hills, nestled deep in a valley high in the Cairngorns and far from a civilization he had long grown tired of.

Ethan moved quickly, using every feature of the ground beneath his boots to help conceal his passage. Where possible, he hopped from rock to rock, avoided leaving tracks in the damp soil and thick grass that would betray his passing. He changed direction frequently, and occasionally backtracked on purpose by fifty yards or so before setting off on a new course. He used river courses routinely, knowing that although dogs could detect the scent of his trail through the water downstream, by moving from rock to rock when those rocks were just below the surface of the water his scent would be washed away by the flow within minutes. Likewise, whenever joining a river, he first moved in the opposite direction intended before reversing his course, giving the impression that he was travelling downstream when in fact he was moving upstream.

At other times, he would seek to cover large areas of ground extremely quickly, striding forcefully up steep hills and running down the other side, in order to put the maximum amount of distance between himself and the British troops. Likewise, he would also follow popular tracks used by hikers and dog walkers in order to conceal his own path amid those of others. Within an hour, he was revelling in the silence four miles away from the lonely road where Major Wilkinson and his driver were, if they were lucky, being discovered by the troops.

The Scottish Highlands had been the remotest place that Ethan had been able to find work while still remaining out of sight of society at large. His past with the 15th Expeditionary Unit, Fourth Marines in Iraq and Afghanistan, and his extensive experience in both tracking lost souls and capturing bail runners in Illinois, had provided him with the necessary credentials to obtain employment as a survival instructor. Before coming to the British Isles, he had worked in Nevada and Arizona, often spending days or even weeks alone in the desert with small groups of highly trained former soldiers, dedicated survivalists, and even *preppers*, those who believed that the apocalypse was coming and sought to sharpen their survival skills before the supposedly imminent collapse of civilization. But remaining in the USA had still, from time to time, put him into contact with people he no longer wished to speak to, and therefore he decided that the best place for him was anywhere but America.

Ethan descended the side of a steep hill toward a lone cottage that sat perched on a narrow precipice overlooking a vast valley. The tumbling clouds above split briefly to allow bright sunbeams to sweep the valley floor and glitter on the creek that ran through the middle. Dense pine forests dressed the valley, and not for the first time Ethan paused and surveyed the extraordinary landscape.

Ethan had no television in the cottage, no Internet and no cell phone. Instead, he employed a small private accountanting firm in the nearby town of Inverness to maintain his bank account and take any mail or calls that he might receive. Once a week, Ethan would make the journey into the town to shop for food and to pick up any messages before disappearing again into the wilderness. Thus had his life been for the past six months and he had absolutely no intention of changing it.

Ethan had modified the cottage somewhat since acquiring it, insulating it against the bitter Scottish weather and improving its fuel-oil efficiency while stockpiling stores of water and tinned food. He discovered that beyond the reach of the rest of the world came a peace that he had not felt for many years, perhaps since his childhood, and that peace was far preferable to the rush and bustle of a major city, the crime, the expensive of living, and the hassle of enduring those around him. Ethan had always been something of a loner, and now instead of fighting that feeling, he was embracing it like never before and wishing he had done so decades ago.

Ethan strode to the front of the cottage and glanced briefly at the very top corner of the door, where he had placed a tiny pebble between the door and the jam, an indicator and a warning in case anybody had attempted to enter the property while he had been away. The pebble was still in place as he unlocked the door and walked in.

The cottage had only a small living room, an equally tiny kitchen, and a downstairs bathroom, the water for which was gravity fed from a tank in the attic. Two bedrooms upstairs, and an *en suite* in the main room completed the property and provided Ethan with everything that he needed and nothing that he didn't. Warm, compact and filled with a library of books stacked on every available shelf and in mountainous piles in corners of the rooms. Fiction, non-fiction, photography books, National Geographic magazines, New Scientist: everything and anything that fascinated Ethan.

Adorning the walls were small number of photographs, mostly of Ethan's parents and his sister Natalie. Only one other stood in one corner of the room, an image of Ethan standing with an attractive, olive-skinned woman with a bright smile and a mercenary glitter in her eyes. Ethan glanced at the picture of Nicola Lopez as he shrugged off his jacket and tossed it onto the nearest couch, then he made his way into the kitchen.

Living in the silence of the open wilderness had attuned Ethan's ear to any new sound with remarkable rapidity, and thus Ethan's hand froze in motion just before he switched the kettle on as a distant but unfamiliar noise reached out to him. Ethan stared into the middle distance and closed his eyes as he let his ears focus on the noise: a faint crunching and a vague hum that ebbed and flowed with each blustering of the wind outside. A vehicle, probably a mile away and upwind, the tires crunching against the crumbling gravel of the old track that led to the cottage. The wind was funnelled down the valley outside from the west, giving advance warning of any approaching vehicle.

Ethan turned and without hurrying he walked back into the living room and reached up to the old beams that lined the ceiling. There had been eight when Ethan arrived at the property, supporting the upstairs bedroom floor. The cottage itself was over two-hundred-years old and built the old way. Now, there were ten beams, two extra ones installed by Ethan himself to look as much as a part of the building as the rest but each hollowed out, hinged and containing a variety of weapons. Ethan reached inside and pulled down a .9mm pistol in its case along with two magazines, each with fifteen rounds. Within ten seconds, the pistol was out of its case, the magazine installed and Ethan was moving toward the rear of the house.

As he opened the back door and slipped outside, he could clearly hear the vehicle approaching the cottage. Nobody knew where he lived and nobody had any business coming out there.

VIII

Ethan crept around the side of the cottage as the vehicle pulled up outside, and he heard the engine switch off. He crouched against the cold stone wall and listened as the door opened, then shut with a clunk. Clean, crisp, a new vehicle - not one of the old farmers' Jeeps that rattled around the hillsides in search of lost sheep. Footsteps, not heavy, cautious and hesitant as they approached the front door. The sound of a knock, not generally the actions of an insane assassin bearing down upon him.

Ethan peeked around the corner of the cottage and saw a woman standing at his front door, her hood up but wisps of blonde hair twisted this way and that by the blustering wind. Jeans, hiking boots, a bag over her shoulder.

To his surprise, she seemed to notice she was being watched and turned to look straight at him. Ethan stepped out as he recognised the face and for a moment he didn't know what to say. Words finally reached him as though of their own accord.

'I wasn't ready for that.'

Lucy Morgan raised an eyebrow as she stared at Ethan and then at the gun in his hand.

'My God, do you people walk around with weapons all the time?'

Ethan tucked the pistol into the small of his back and managed an apologetic smile. 'You learn to be cautious,' he said by way of an explanation as he walked towards her. 'What on earth are you doing all the way out here, and how did you find me?'

'I had some help from a mutual friend,' Lucy Morgan replied. 'She told me to send you her *best regards*.'

An image of what passed for Nicola Lopez's *best regards* flashed briefly through Ethan's mind, an image of his burning motorcycle and aching jaw when he had left Chicago, and he could not help the wry smile that curled from one corner of his lips.

'I'll bet she did. But even Nicola didn't know I was out here.'

'Well, it only took her three days to track you down for me, so I guess she knows you better than you think.'

Ethan felt an odd sensation of melancholy sink through him as he realized that Lucy was probably right. Not many people had gotten as close to Ethan as Lopez had, and they had worked together for many years before circumstances came between them. Lopez had saved his life on more than one occasion and he had returned the favor more times than either of them cared to remember. But that was the past.

'You'd better come in,' Ethan said as he gestured for Lucy to follow him around to the rear of the cottage.

During the course of his investigations for the DIA, Ethan had come into contact with a number of civilians with whom he had kept in touch sporadically over the years. Lucy Morgan was one of those people. A brilliant palaeontologist and researcher, Lucy had made her name discovering the remains of some of mankind's oldest ancestors on the blistering plains of Africa's Rift Valley. Ethan's own natural interest in such things had meant that from time to time they corresponded, but since Ethan's change of career, he had not maintained contact and so now he found himself quite concerned as to why Lucy would have travelled halfway round the world to see him.

Ethan busied himself making coffee for them both and lighting the fire. Thick logs spit orange flame as warmth spilled from the hearth and filled the cottage with heat, light and a comforting scent of wood smoke.

'You've really managed to find a forgotten corner of the world out here,' Lucy said as Ethan handed her a chipped mug of steaming coffee.

'I found myself gripped by the need to be forgotten,' Ethan shrugged as he sat down opposite her in his favorite rocking chair, a big soft one in which he had spent many happy hours reading.

'Was life really that bad?'

'It wasn't bad, I just needed a change. Why are you here, Lucy?'

Ethan watched as Lucy Morgan reached down for the bag she had bought with her, and then lifted out a plastic cylinder which contained a bone. Ethan recognised the bone immediately as the one that he had liberated from the remains Lucy had excavated in Israel. With the DIA in control of the remains which had been spirited away to a top secret hiding place, the bone that Ethan had liberated had, for him, been the ideal gift for Lucy when she had been rescued from Israel.

'So, you studied it then,' Ethan said as he looked at the bone.

'I've spent every spare moment of the past few years studying it,' Lucy confirmed. 'I couldn't do it through the university or the museum without raising suspicions, and I've always believed that somebody has been watching me ever since what happened in Israel.'

'It's not impossible,' Ethan replied. 'The US government's black budget runs into tens of billions of dollars; small change for them to assign an agent or two to keep an eye on what you're doing.'

Lucy nodded as she stared down at the bone in the cylinder.

'I made sure that I did my research off hours at home, or in my lunch break or my days off, times when it would not raise suspicion and I could work without interruption.'

'And what have you found out?'

The discovery of a seven thousand year old tomb with alien remains inside had raised all kinds of questions in Ethan's mind, as it had done so many others. Solid, irrefutable evidence of the presence of an extra-terrestrial species not just on Earth but at the very dawn of human civilization raised all sorts of doubts and questions over the origin of human beliefs and religions worldwide.

'I started out by confirming the age of the specimen,' Lucy explained. 'Finding the remains in a seven millennia old tomb did not necessarily mean that the bones themselves were of the same age. They could have been interred later, perhaps even recently, so it was essential to match the remains to the tomb itself. I extracted material from within the interior of the bone that could not have been contaminated either by handling or other external influences, and radiocarbon dating confirmed that age of seven thousand years.'

Ethan rubbed his jaw as he looked at the specimen, his coffee forgotten as he considered the magnitude of what Lucy was revealing.

'You know why the DIA kept this find under wraps, don't you?'

'They think a public announcement of the find would cause chaos,' Lucy sighed. 'They think that the inevitable collapse of religion, especially in the Western world where it's already in rapid decline, would create a crisis of identity for the human race.'

'And you think differently,' Ethan guessed.

'I think that the revealing of this evidence, of its implications, would be the beginning of a new *enlightenment*. Those who simply believe in religions, regardless of evidence to the contrary, would be forced to face up to the fact that we are not special, not the product of a god. We are, in fact, likely *inferior* to many other species out there, especially those that have mastered the art of space travel. It could herald the beginning of a new age of reason and logic that has suffered so much in the face of rising religious extremism over the past few decades.'

Ethan shrugged uncertainly. 'That's a hell of a gamble to make with seven billion lives. Nobody really knows quite what would happen if this became public. Is that why you're here? Are you intending to do something about it?'

'No,' Lucy admitted. 'I'm here because I think other people are intending to either obtain these remains from me or from the US government.'

'What other people?'

'The Russians,' Lucy replied. 'I was approached in Chicago a few days ago by a representative, somebody claiming to be working for a collector in Russia. They wanted to know about the remains that were found in Israel and whether I had any access to them. I played dumb, naturally, but I don't think they bought it. I'm pretty sure I've been followed ever since.'

Ethan's eyes flicked to the cottage front door but Lucy waved him down.

'Not here,' Lucy assured him. 'Nicola helped me vanish from Illinois; she was really very clever. She employed a double, booked flights on my behalf so they could not be tracked to me, and then booked two further decoy flights under my name before sending me off. She told me what to do when I landed at Gatwick Airport near London, to take different trains, stay in hotels and halfway houses, pay cash only. I'm confident that nobody but Lopez knows I'm here.'

Ethan nodded. Lopez was every bit as much of an expert at vanishing as he was. Once, after a lengthy investigation in the forests of Idaho, they had been forced to go underground for more than six months, moving from city to city, wearing disguises and essentially vanishing from the system in order to evade rogue CIA agents intent on hunting them down.

'Fine,' he said eventually. 'Why would they have suddenly taken such an interest in things that happened years ago?'

'I can't be sure, but it may have something to do with what Pastor Kelvin Patterson was doing with the DNA that he managed to extract from the finds that I made in Israel.'

Kelvin Patterson, a Baptist minister on an apocalyptic mission for the supposed benefit of mankind in Washington, DC, had been convinced that the remains Lucy had found in Israel were not the remains of alien beings, but in fact those of angels. Intent on converting human beings into angels by injecting them with genetic material from the remains, specifically US Senators who could lobby on his behalf, he had murdered many innocent individuals.

'Have you managed to extract DNA from that bone?'

'I got a full profile, everything that Patterson was looking for. But unlike him, I spent the last three years analysing the strands, and it's what I found that I believe the Russians are hunting for and I'm pretty sure they're not alone.'

'Tell me.'

'I think you'd find it hard to comprehend, or even to believe.'

'You can let me be the judge of that,' Ethan insisted. 'You've come here for help, I'm assuming, and like your mother before you I can't help you unless you tell me everything.'

Lucy sighed, and as the fire crackled behind her she replied.

'The DNA contains…'

The fire spat a particularly loud crack just as the window to the cottage shattered and a spray of glass flew through the air. Ethan turned his head away at the same time as Lucy as a sudden deafening chatter of automatic gunfire hammered the wall of the cottage.

IX

'Get down!'

Ethan hurled himself across the living room and grabbed Lucy's collar. He pulled her onto the ground between the couches and shielded her body.

The gunfire sprayed around the room as it shattered the windows and spat choking clouds of plaster, wood, and dust through the air. Ethan pulled himself along the floor in a belly crawl as he reached behind him and pulled the pistol from out of his jeans, then rolled along to the window and watched the bullets hammering the ceilings and walls.

The deafening gunfire ceased abruptly and Ethan could hear the wind rumbling outside the window. He glanced at the damage to the interior of the cottage and noted that all of the bullets had gone high, spraying mostly across the ceiling and the beams rather than down towards where people would be walking or sitting.

In an instant he knew what was coming next. He scrambled to his feet and ran in a low crouch to Lucy's side where he could grab her..

'Move, now!' he whispered.

They ran out of the living room and into the tiny kitchen just as Ethan heard two metallic thumps come from behind him followed by a loud hissing sound. He turned to see a pair of smoke grenades roll across the lounge, one of them landing on the sofa. Ethan pushed the kitchen door closed and then pointed at the corner of the room.

'Stay there and stay down,' he said as he turned to the back door.

Lucy crouched into a tiny ball in the corner of the kitchen as Ethan opened the back door of the cottage and crept outside, careful to close the door behind him and turn the key in the lock. He pocketed the key and then hurried around to one side of the cottage.

Behind him, the hillside soared up towards low tumbling clouds that were darkening in the late afternoon light, low enough to conceal the peaks of the hills. The terrain was rough and it was at least a hundred yard climb to reach the cloud line and the safety of the fog, and he knew that they would not be able to make it without being spotted.

Ethan peered around the corner of the cottage and saw two men standing with automatic weapons pointed at the front of the cottage, both of them wearing masks and both of them apparently waiting for the smoke grenades to take effect.

Whoever they were and whatever they wanted, they did not want either Ethan or Lucy dead or they would not have bothered using smoke grenades – they would have tossed live ones inside. Ethan peered at the weapons they were holding and recognised instantly the ubiquitous shape of the AK-47. A tough, simple, and hardy weapon, it suffered from one fatal flaw; its huge inaccuracy. It was a widely known feature of the weapon that a man could stand fifty yards from a barn door, open fire on full automatic, and not have a single bullet hit the door due to the violent flexing of the rifle's barrel that sent rounds flying everywhere but at the target.

Ethan hurried back to the kitchen door and opened it. He reached out for Lucy's hand.

'I hope to hell you can run fast,' he said as he pulled to her feet and pointed up the hillside behind them.

'We'll be seen,' Lucy protested.

'That's what I'm hoping,' Ethan replied as he propelled Lucy up the hill. 'Let's go!'

Lucy, still grasping the bone cylinder in one hand, hit the hillside at a pace that surprised Ethan as he began sprinting in pursuit. He had quite forgotten that Lucy was probably ten years his junior, and likely not shy of running given her slim physique. Ethan pumped his arms and leaped with surprising agility for his age as he followed her up the hillside and away from the cottage.

Ethan risked a glance over his shoulder and saw smoke billowing out the windows from the interior of the cottage, the smoke inadvertently veiling their escape from the two men watching the front of the cottage. But the smoke only lasted as long as the wind was in a favorable direction, and moments later he heard a shout and saw one of the men pointed up at him.

'They're on to us,' he called to Lucy. 'Keep moving!'

Lucy did not look back as she kept running toward the top of the hills, their peaks lost in thick cloud. Ethan powered along behind her and risked another glance behind him to see the two masked gunmen already climbing the hill. Ethan turned and dropped to one knee, aimed down the hill and fired two shots, the rumbling wind snatching the sound of the gunfire away, feeble and mute compared to the destructive symphony of the AK-47s.

Their pursuers hurled themselves flat onto the ground of the hillside as the shots rang out, but Ethan had purposefully aimed high. He had no idea who the men were but Ethan was not in the business of killing in cold blood and he had every intention of catching both of their pursuers alive. Ethan turned again and ran hard, surprised to see Lucy already reaching the cloud line as she scrambled up the hillside.

A rattle of gunfire pursued Ethan up the hill and he flinched, but he kept moving. His lungs and throat felt rough from the exertion of climbing the hill, and his thighs felt numb as he struggled through the damp grass and over wet rocks as the clouds began to close around him.

The gunfire from behind ceased and Ethan took one last look back down the hillside to see the two men standing and watching him. In an instant they both raised their rifles, and with a start Ethan realized that this time they were aiming directly at him. He saw the two weapons' muzzle flash flare brightly and he hurled himself to one side as a series of deep thumps impacted the soft soil around him.

Ethan scrambled to his feet and sprinted as fast as his wearying lungs would allow up the hillside as he plunged into the fog and cried out breathlessly.

'Lucy?!'

He heard his name called out distantly from somewhere above and he kept moving, a little slower now as the gunfire behind him ceased and he began trying to conserve his energy.

'Keep calling until we see each other!'

Lucy, her own voice breathless, called several times over until he saw her figure emerge from the gloom ahead, her hands resting on her knees as she sucked in air. Ethan struggled his way to her side, his own breath sawing in his throat as he rested one hand on her shoulder and pulled her gently along with him.

'We have to keep moving,' he insisted. 'They've got vehicles and they're not going to give up easily.'

Lucy struggled alongside him and he could hear the concern in her voice. 'We can't survive out here without jackets and protection.'

'I know, we just have to keep moving a little longer.'

Ethan crested the ridge and despite his exhaustion, he began jogging gently down the opposite side and encouraged Lucy to follow him at the same speed. Lucy recovered more quickly from her exertions than he did and she followed him down the steep hillside toward the valley below. The damp and foggy air clogged their eyes and hair with globules of moisture that clung to their clothes and skin, a faint drizzle falling all around them and the dense fog deadening all sound.

Ethan moved as quickly as he dared on the slippery, dangerous hillside, conscious of the risk of breaking a leg or ankle. He reached the valley floor and emerged from the fog with Lucy close behind, and instantly he dropped to one knee and controlled his breathing as he tried to focus all of his attention on the muted sounds around them.

The rumbling wind that had alerted him to Lucy's vehicle was now likely concealing the approach of the gunmen's vehicle from the east, which was where he felt certain they would attempt to intercept him. There were a number of farmer's tracks that wound up the hillside and descended into this valley perhaps a mile to the east, tracks that the vehicle could easily negotiate.

'We should have taken the car,' Lucy said.

'We would never have gotten to it.'

'I can't believe they found me here,' Lucy shook her head. 'I was so careful.'

'We don't know that they're Russian, yet. They did have AK-47s, but so does just about every other criminal gang in the world. It's entirely possible they anticipated this move on your part, and instead been looking for me for some time.'

Lucy managed an unconvincing smile of gratitude. 'What do we do now?'

'We get caught,' Ethan replied. 'Follow me.'

Ethan ignored Lucy's quizzical look as he set off across the valley, hoping that he could reach the next hilltop and the cover of the fog before the gunmen's car could reach the valley and spot them. He walked hard, getting into his stride and hoping that Lucy would dig in behind him and keep moving. After a couple of minutes, he looked behind and saw her keeping pace, her head down and her breath puffing in dense clouds as she focused on nothing more than keeping up. Suitably impressed, Ethan began climbing the next hillside.

He was halfway up when he heard the sound of an engine and turned to see the gunmen's vehicle careening down a hillside less than a mile away behind them, the driver evidently struggling to maintain control on the rough terrain as he turned onto the valley floor and accelerated.

'Get into the fog cover as fast as you can!' Ethan shouted to Lucy.

Lucy climbed past him and kept moving as Ethan watched the Jeep approaching the foot of the mountain side on which he stood. It was probably a hundred yards below him, too far to use a pistol to take out the tires or even the engine. Such small weapons were simply not capable of that kind of accuracy. But with both men inside the vehicle, he realized he could delay them a little longer.

Ethan crouched down onto one knee, then rested his left elbow on the top of his left knee to support the weapon as he aimed carefully at the approaching vehicle. The wind was blustering from his right sufficiently that it would affect the travel of the bullet, and at a hundred yards there would be a small amount of drop to the bullet due to the effect of gravity. Ethan had thirteen rounds remaining and he knew damn well the first one would probably not be a hit, but that was not what he needed.

The Jeep closed in as Ethan arrested his breathing and squeezed the trigger.

Ethan fired five shots, each of them closely grouped in the hope that a couple of impacts would be enough to force the gunmen to fall back.

On the third shot, the Jeep swerved to the left and broke away from the climb as it sought to escape the salvo of gunfire. Instantly, Ethan stopped firing and capitalised on his success as he turned and continued running up the hill, determined to put as much distance between the Jeep, himself, and Lucy.

Ethan ran up into the cloud cover, the incessant mist and drizzle drenching him and chilling his skin as he caught up with Lucy where she was waiting for him on the ridgeline, her breath coming in ragged gasps.

'I can't do that too many more times,' she protested.

'Me, either,' Ethan replied, 'but we have to keep moving. Go, now!'

Ethan jogged down the hillside with Lucy close behind, but this time he could hear the Jeep in the distance, its engine struggling and whining, and he realized that the gunmen had abandoned the track and instead had charged the hill directly.

'They're coming right for us!' Lucy yelled as she realized what was happening.

'Get down!'

Ethan grabbed Lucy as he dashed towards a particularly large tuft of grass and a mound of shiny black rocks jutting from the bleak hillside. He threw himself down behind them and huddled with Lucy alongside him.

There was no way that they could outrun a vehicle, and Ethan knew that they had no chance of survival unless they stayed in the fog where they could not be seen. If you couldn't run away then you could only hope to *sneak* away.

The Jeep broke over the crest of the hill, its headlights on and casting dim beams through the foggy air as it began to descend toward the far side of the valley. It skidded to a halt and sat for a moment on the valley hillside, and then the two gunmen got out and began surveying the terrain around them.

'They know we're hiding,' Lucy whispered.

'But they don't know where,' Ethan replied. 'We've got to hope they're not any good at tracking and that they'll go past us in the fog and give us a chance to escape.'

Ethan peered around the edge of the boulder behind which they were hiding and saw the two men ease away from the cover of their vehicle as one of them knelt down and studied the grass around them. Almost immediately he looked up directly toward Ethan's hiding place.

'You were saying?' Lucy whispered urgently.

Ethan saw the two men jerk to their feet and aim their rifles at the boulder as they began marching across the open ground toward them. Faced with an impossible fight, Ethan knew that there was only one thing he could do. He leaped up and rested the pistol on the top of the boulder as the two gunmen exposed themselves and opened fire, several shots cracking out. The two gunmen threw themselves down onto the muddy wet grass.

'Go, now!'

'Go where?' Lucy shouted as she leaped to her feet.

Ethan was about to answer when a fresh voice rang out loud above the gunshots.

'Halt, stop where you are!'

Both Ethan and the two gunmen looked down the hill through the fog and saw figures running toward them, cradling their rifles and shouting commands as they advanced. The two gunmen whirled and opened fire on the advancing group of men as they began retreating back towards the Jeep.

In an instant, the shadowy figures dropped into prone positions and began returning fire up the hillside with a deafening clatter of SA-80 rifles as the British infantry advanced by sections and rapidly closed on the fleeing gunmen. Ethan got up from behind the boulder as he heard a vehicle's engine start up, and he saw the Jeep swing around and accelerate away back over the ridgeline and vanish from sight.

The British soldiers advanced on his position and he hurriedly slipped the pistol back into his jeans and showed his hands as empty as the troops rushed up to him and one of them grabbed his collar.

'That was far too easy, sunshine,' the infantry corporal said as he looked Ethan over. 'And Major Wilkinson has a bone to pick with you.'

Ethan glanced at where the Jeep had vanished over the ridgeline. 'Good, he might be able to help us.'

X

'You've got a lot of explaining to do.'

The cottage was filled once again with warmth and a rich orange glow from the crackling fire as Ethan sat down opposite Lucy Morgan.

'I know,' Lucy replied. 'Being shot at kind of broke my flow.'

After the unexpected appearance and gunfight with the two masked men, and Ethan's subsequent explanation to Major Wilkinson, the British officer had posted sentries all around Ethan's cottage and agreed to provide protection for twenty-four hours. Ethan had made rapid repairs to the shattered window to seal out the bitter cold, and Lucy had busied herself tidying up the debris from the bullet strikes before they had settled down to eat. It had been then that she had discovered that the files she had left inside the cottage had been stolen by the two gunmen, one of whom must have entered the building when Ethan and Lucy had fled up the hillside.

'Major Wilkinson is pulling some strings with the Ministry of Defense to see if we can identify who the gunmen were or where they came from,' Ethan said. 'I didn't manage to get any plates, but it's possible they may be able to pick up the vehicle travelling through local towns and start identifying them from there.'

'They must've followed me, despite everything,' Lucy said. 'You're living out here in the middle of nowhere and suddenly they turn up on your doorstep. Whether they predicted I would come here or not, I've dragged you into something and I had no idea it would become so dangerous.'

Ethan shrugged. 'I can't say that I'm happy about it, but it's not like it's the first time this has happened. You were telling me about something you found in the DNA from that bone of yours.'

Lucy leaned back in her chair, the firelight glowing on her features as she replied.

'The strands of DNA that I extracted from the bone show clear evidence of human strains alongside them. The remains that we found in Israel are not those of an entirely alien species but of some kind of hybrid.'

Ethan stared at Lucy for a few moments in the silence as he digested this new piece of information. He recalled that in Washington, DC, pastor Kelvin Patterson had attempted to meld human and alien DNA in an attempt to create angels to bring about the second coming. As insane as his plan had been, Patterson had had possession of alien bones and remains for some time, all of which had been pilfered from the scientists he had hired to find the remains in the first place. It was not entirely impossible that he had come to the same conclusion as Lucy, and thus had his plan for the Second Coming been born.

'How can you tell?'

'It's all to do with what we used to call junk DNA,' Lucy explained patiently. 'In the genetic sequence of DNA there were long strands that made no sense whatsoever and were simply termed *junk* because it was not believed they had any active processes ongoing. However, in recent years we've come to understand that even this supposedly junk DNA has a role to play. What's become clear from my study of this bone segment is that within the semi-active DNA are strands that have a purpose other than guiding cellular division.'

'Pretend I'm an idiot,' Ethan said. 'I like baby steps when it comes to science.'

'The DNA sequences are ordered in a particular way,' Lucy explained patiently. 'The way they are ordered does not correspond to any biological processes known to man. That does not mean, of course, that they have no biological process attached to them, but it does lead me to suspect that their purpose within the DNA is not so much as a biological marker as a message.'

'A message?' Ethan repeated as he raised his eyebrows in surprise. 'You think that there's a message in the DNA?'

Lucy nodded as she set her mug down.

'A number of scientists have postulated that the best way for alien species to have left messages or markers of their presence on earth would not be the classic idea of leaving a monument or rock carvings or similar because those messages would not endure for as long as a species that may be living on any given world. Their idea was that the best place to leave evidence of their passing would be in the genetic structure of the creatures that they encountered, because although those creatures may evolve over millions of years into species entirely distinct from those witnessed by passing aliens, the DNA would still hold the messages left behind. As long as life survived, so would the messages.'

Ethan stared into the flames of the fire for a moment. 'So you're saying that if ET wandered past Earth when the dinosaurs were walking around, and left a message in dino – DNA, then technically we should be able to find that message in the species alive on the earth today.'

'Technically, yes,' Lucy replied. 'The dinosaurs, or more specifically the raptors, survive now as many species of birds. If what you have outlined occurred, we would expect to find that genetic message surviving in the genes of birds.'

Ethan shook his head in wonder, quite surprised at how often advances in science revealed new ways in which the message of life could be passed across the universe.

'I'd never have thought of something like that.'

'Well, until Crick and Watson discovered DNA, nobody else had, either. The point is that this discovery goes far further than just potential messages in the genetic sequence of species. There is a theory known as panspermia.'

'I've heard of it,' Ethan replied. 'It's the idea that life is common in the universe, that complex organic molecules form naturally in deep space and are then carried to new born planets by comets, kick starting life all around the universe.'

'That's exactly right,' Lucy agreed, for the first time showing some sign of enthusiasm and delight in her work. 'Complex organic molecules have been discovered floating in gas clouds throughout our galaxy, some of those molecules just one step away from proteins and amino acids, the basis of all life on Earth. Panspermia is no longer just a hypothesis, it's a solid and valid scientific theory and provides the means for life to travel across the vast distances between stellar systems, and spread the basic chemicals of life wherever it can be found.'

'How does this tie in with the message in the bone DNA?'

'I'm not sure, yet,' Lucy admitted. 'But if the creature that we found in Israel was indeed a hybrid, then its genetic code must have been blended with that of a human. If you recall, although tall and with many features very different to ours, it was nonetheless bipedal and with a humanoid appearance. It's generally considered highly unlikely that humanoid figures would be a commonplace result of evolution around the galaxy. Certain features such as eyes, ears, grasping hands, and limbs are of course likely to develop, but the appearance of any intelligent alien species we would expect to be vastly different from our own. It is my conclusion that this hybrid creature was part human, and if the message encoded in its DNA is present, then there is every likelihood that same message is present in some humans today.'

Ethan raised an eyebrow as he considered this new idea.

'A bloodline,' he murmured as he thought back to his work in Israel. 'Kelvin Patterson was obsessed with the bloodline. He thought it was something to do with angels breeding with humans, like the Biblical legend of the Nephilim.'

'If there is any chance that an alien species did interbreed or otherwise genetically alter our ancestors, then the traces of their work should be present in the blood, or in the DNA, of certain peoples. It's my hypothesis that the clearest signal of any extra-terrestrial intervention in human development would be found in the oldest civilizations and the oldest remains that we can locate. I was in the process of researching various ancient civilizations and trying to determine which would be the most likely to harbor the evidence that we seek when Vladimir Polkov showed up.'

Ethan rubbed his jaw with one hand, a day's growth of stubble rasping beneath his fingers as he thought for a moment.

'That could be almost anywhere,' he replied finally. 'If I remember correctly what your mother told me, mankind evolved in Africa and expanded out in all directions, inhabiting the Middle East, Far East, the far north and Europe.'

'Well, that's one of the other interesting things I've been looking into.'

Lucy made to reach for her missing bag and then sighed as she remembered that it was no longer here.

'You've got a good memory,' Ethan guessed. 'I'm sure you could fill in the details.'

Lucy sat for a moment as she gathered her thoughts.

'I started looking into the research of people involved in something called pseudo-archaeology. It's essentially a fringe branch of science that until now hasn't really been science at all. Its proponents believe that the current model of human civilization's evolution is incorrect and that in fact we were able to develop complex societies many thousands of years before we originally thought.'

'You're talking about the kind of people that believe in Atlantis?'

'Not so much Atlantis,' Lucy replied. 'The thing with Plato's *Atlantis* is that the name is simply the one he gave to a rumored advanced city that existed somewhere in the Atlantic, beyond the Pillars of Hercules, which are what we now call the Rock of Gibraltar. If you take away the name and everything associated with it, then what you have is an eminent individual from an ancient civilization merely claiming to have heard of the existence of a much older civilization.'

'Okay, so how much evidence have you found?'

'Quite a bit,' Lucy replied. 'Mainstream archaeology does not involve itself in claims of ancient civilizations predating current history, and accepts only that our earliest civilizations evolved in what we refer to as the fertile crescent, areas of the Middle East, Iraq, Iran and so on that border the Persian Gulf. However, in recent years cities have been discovered deep in the jungles of India and other countries that clearly predate those civilizations, pushing back advanced human endeavor by thousands of years. The best known is Cabo de San Antonio, off the west coast of Cuba.'

'What's there?'

'A geological survey team discovered an entire sunken city beneath half a mile of water, filled with geometric megalithic structures like multiple pyramids arranged in rows that the scientists involved said they could not describe in terms of natural geological formations. They have beautiful sonar images of streets arranged around the pyramids. It's old enough to have existed during the last Ice Age, up to fifty thousand years ago. Ancient stories of the Maya and native Yucatecos people tell of an island state of advanced peoples that was swallowed by a flood. Samples collected from the site are of polished granite, not the limestone that forms the entire northwest Cuban peninsular. The closest natural granite is in the centre of Mexico.'

Ethan sat in silence for a moment. 'You think that such sunken cities are the origin of ancient flood myths?'

'The end of the Ice Age raised sea levels immensely as the glaciers that once covered the entire northern hemisphere receded,' Lucy explained. 'Any coastal cities built by advanced civilizations would have been easily swallowed by the oceans.'

'How many are there?'

'Dozens,' Lucy said. 'The Cambay Ruins off the coast of India were discovered in 2001, with artifacts such as bones, pottery and wall sections from the site dated at some nine thousand years old. The city of Yonaguni off the southern coast of Japan is at least five thousand years old and contains stepped walls and a massive pyramid about seventy feet below the surface of the sea. The walls of the city show evidence of men having working the stone, and the inhabitants are believed to have been the Jomon, the first culture to have developed pottery, who lived up to twelve thousand years ago.'

'And you are intending to go out there and search for something to support your theory,' Ethan surmised with a wry smile.

'That was the plan,' Lucy admitted. 'I'd managed to put aside some savings to fund the expedition because I knew that the museum would not support any such research. I was virtually ready to book flights when the Russians appeared.'

Ethan thought for a moment.

'The Defense Intelligence Agency confiscated the remains that you found in Israel, and could hardly have failed to examine them. What do you think the chances are that they will have discovered the same things that you have?'

Lucy inclined her head to one side as she thought for a moment. 'It depends. The DIA have never approached me and asked for any advice or even what I was researching that led me to find the remains. They have one piece of the puzzle, and it is possible even that they will find the message in the DNA, but what the hell they'll be able to do with it I don't know. The problem is that the message in itself is useless without a means of decoding or deciphering it.'

'You didn't say anything about deciphering,' Ethan pointed out.

'Ah,' Lucy said, suddenly excited as she returned to her theme. 'Now that's the really interesting bit. You see, the message in the DNA of the bones we found in Israel is only one half of the message. We have no idea what language or dialect might be used, although we would hope for mathematics or perhaps even binary code, something universal that all advanced species would presumably recognise. But that's not the reason I'm here.'

'It's not?'

'No,' Lucy replied, her face falling suddenly as though she had just recalled why she had journeyed across the globe to find him. 'Have you ever heard of Saethre–Chotzen syndrome, or Hydrocephalus?'

'Never,' Ethan admitted. 'What are they?'

'They're rare congenital disorders that cause the human skull to deform or fail to expand in the correct way as a child grows,' Lucy explained. 'Their origins lie in some kind of genetic mutation, and I've been working on the DNA from the bone to figure out if those mutations come from human genes modified in ancient history.'

Ethan raised an eyebrow. 'Seriously? You think that some modern illnesses may be connected to those remains we found in Israel?

'If a species altered our DNA in some way by breeding with humans, then it's entirely possible that in doing so they created a new line of illnesses.' Lucy pulled a photograph from her pocket and handed it to Ethan. 'This is Bethany O'Learey, from River Grove, Chicago. She is two-years-old and is suffering from the syndrome.'

Ethan looked at the image of a smiling, bright-eyed little girl with rosy cheeks and soft brown hair. Her entire skull was encased in some sort of metallic device.

'It's a brace that is holding her head together after cranial surgery,' Lucy explained, seeing Ethan's reaction. 'But the illness has other side effects, including heart issues, spinal fusing, and renal problems. She's dying, Ethan, and I've been watching it happen for the past year.'

Ethan looked up at Lucy as he put the pieces together for himself. 'You're looking for the cure.'

'I'm looking for the genetic material of any human being who might have been a hybrid with the alien species, that is fresh enough to extract DNA from and search for the gene that causes these illnesses,' Lucy said slowly. 'My guess is that someone, somewhere, once carried the origin of this and many other diseases. That person, whoever they were, would have been extremely important to those who followed them. Their remains would quite likely have been preserved extremely well, perhaps well enough to extract the DNA required to decipher the cure to this illness and perhaps save Bethany's life.'

Ethan considered the ancient cities to which Lucy had referred to.

'And you want to go and find the oldest possible site of an ancient civilization in the hopes of discovering the remains that you're looking for.'

'You're quite bright, really, when you try hard,' Lucy managed to smile.

For a moment Ethan was reminded of Lopez's snarky wit. He shook the memory off and glanced at the clock above the fireplace. It was already after eight, the Highlands outside black as night: perfect for moving unobserved.

'This cottage is compromised,' Ethan decided. 'There's not much point in me sitting here waiting for the next bunch of gun-wielding goons to turn up, and certainly no sense in you waiting around. Does Rachel have any idea where you are?'

'None,' Lucy admitted. 'After what happened in Israel, I decided to keep her on a need-to-know basis.'

'I know how that feels,' Ethan replied.

'She thinks I'm abroad on another dig, tucked safely away in Europe, which in some respects is true.'

Ethan rubbed his forehead and sighed heavily as he realized that he could hardly walk away from Lucy, now, when it was clear that she was intending to go straight for the oldest human civilization she could find. Although Ethan did not have an idea of who had attacked them, and could not even be entirely certain of why, what he was sure of was that they would continue to pursue Lucy. If they now had her most treasured files, then it did not take a rocket scientist to figure out that they would follow the same leads and would likely end up in the same places.

'They're going to follow you,' Ethan pointed out. 'Whether it's the Russians or somebody else, somebody wants to know what you know and they're not going to give up.'

Lucy's smile faded again.

'That means I'll need some kind of protection,' she replied, 'somebody who has experience of working in these kinds of conditions, somebody upon whom I can rely.'

'I'm not in this business anymore,' Ethan pointed out.

'I've *never* been in this business,' Lucy replied. 'I'm supposed to quietly dig up fossils and prepare them for museums, not run around the Scottish Highlands getting shot at. I can't do this on my own. You've spent the last year hiding away from everything – if getting away from the rest of the world is what you want, I can take you to places that people have not seen for thousands of years.'

'You've got a destination already?'

Lucy nodded and clearly did not need her files to inform him of her plans.

'The site in Israel where we found the remains is associated with ancient tribes that lived in the area during that period, and during the work I found numerous images depicted on rock faces, including engravings. I had photographs of them all, but they were in the bag we lost. However, it's not hard to show you.'

Lucy took a notepad from her jacket and a small pen, and quickly sketched an image. Ethan looked at the drawing, of lines emanating downward from a semi-circle.

'What is it?' he asked.

'An ancient petroglyph that portrays the sun,' Lucy explained. 'It's common throughout the ancient world in various similar forms, but this one stands out as exceptional because I have also found it at one of the supposedly impossible cities beneath the waves. The photograph was taken by divers examining the top of a pyramid, and the light from the shot by chance illuminated the engraving beneath a layer of sea moss.'

'Where was this pyramid?' Ethan asked.

Lucy smiled conspiratorially.

'You help me and you'll find out,' she said, 'if you want to.'

Ethan glanced at the crackling fire and the piles of books that had kept him company for so many months, and then he made his decision.

XI

London,
England

The apartment suite in which Yuri Polkov sat overlooked the broad green glittering waters of the Thames River, the Houses of Parliament and London Bridge visible to the right from the exclusive St Katharine's Docks. Two stories below, a private marina housed exotic yachts tucked away from prying eyes.

Yuri's old eyes scanned the cityscape before him, rooftops shining in the sunlight and reminding him of the glittering lights of the oilfields stretched across the Siberian wastes that had once been his home.

'The files you requested.'

Vladimir Polkov set a thick file of paperwork atop the polished mahogany desk behind which Yuri sat and then backed away respectfully. The old man continued to stare out across London before he seemed to break out of his reverie and looked down at the file.

'I requested the woman,' Yuri replied, his accent still heavily influenced by his upbringing, pride in his heritage preventing him from losing his Russian accent.

'She escaped,' Vladimir admitted. 'She had help from an American.'

Yuri continued to look down at the file as he replied. 'I have mountains of paperwork. I have libraries filled with thousands of books. I do not need files, for they are nothing without the person who collated them.'

'They have value,' Vladimir insisted. 'Do not dismiss them so easily.'

Yuri glared at his son and waved him away with an angry flourish of one veined hand. Vladimir turned without further protest and marched out of the office, closing the door quietly behind him.

Yuri looked down at the folder and reluctantly opened it to see within a dense stack of paperwork hurriedly filed by Dr Lucy Morgan. Yuri did not read the paperwork, instead placing his hand atop the files as though by doing so he could somehow communicate with their creator.

Yuri Polkov had followed the work of Dr Lucy Morgan for almost six years and found himself thoroughly fascinated by what she had achieved, despite the intervention of a crazed US pastor and the United States intelligence service. That they had, as far as his sources could reveal, confiscated one of the most amazing finds any scientist could ever hope to have made in their career and prevented her from even studying it, was a tragedy for which he had great sympathy. Lucy Morgan should by now have been a household name, not a low-grade researcher buried somewhere inside Chicago's Field Museum.

'You deserve this,' Yuri whispered to himself and in a moment of wistfulness hoped that Lucy Morgan could hear his words. 'You will not be forgotten.'

Yuri removed his hand from the folder and then began to read, all the while aware that his theft of her files was a crime. He had wanted the woman, not the work, for from her he could learn of the greatest secret ever concealed from mankind and reveal it to the world.

Yuri Polkov had been born the only son of a farmer who had scratched a meager existence from the unyielding permafrost of Siberia's bleak plains. His parents had struggled their entire lives to provide what they could for him and, to his eternal gratitude, that had included a solid education in a local school largely funded by the oil refineries that provided accommodation and education for the children of workers based out on the lonely ice fields. Yuri's parents had invested what they could to ensure that Yuri also benefited from this unique opportunity and he had learned to read at an early age.

As Yuri had grown older so his parents had grown weaker, their constant toiling in the fields and the bitter winters wearing them down until it had fallen to Yuri to support them as they had once supported him. But working alone, unable to afford to hire helping hands and witness to his parents terminal decline in health, a rage had been born in him that he had been unable to quell. Unable to provide for them via honest means, Yuri had been forced to turn to his wits and guile in order to improve their terrible circumstances.

In the event, it had not even really been crime that had saved them, not in the truest sense anyway. Yuri's early reading had fostered a fascination with fossils and dinosaurs, and that fascination had grown into personal study of geology, geography, palaeontology and other disciplines of science. Unable to afford a place at university, Yuri had whiled away countless cold nights reading any book he could get his hands on, and as his knowledge of palaeontology had grown so too had his awareness of the black market in fossils that thrived behind the scenes across the globe.

Yuri had originally intended to pursue an honest trade in fossils and the remains of species that he found in the Motherland, however the government of the time lay claim to anything found on Russian soil as being the property of the Politburo. To claim remains of any kind for oneself, or indeed to profit from them in any way, was punishable by the severest means. Nonetheless, as Yuri began to employ his knowledge of palaeontology in the pursuit of rare fossils, so the temptation to sell them for profit became too great to bear.

At the age of twenty three, while working in the permafrost of Siberia in early spring, Yuri made the discovery of a lifetime. There, suspended in ice before him around the edge of what had once been a Siberian tar pit, were the remains of a perfectly preserved juvenile mammoth. The freezing temperatures had preserved the animal to an astounding degree: the fur seemed as alive as the day the animal had died, the tusks in perfect condition, even the eye sockets not desiccated as with so many similar specimens. Yuri guessed that the animal must have died in a snowstorm and been frozen within hours of its demise before any predators or insects could gain access to the body. Over thousands of years more ice and snow piled over the remains, partly crushing them but otherwise preserving the body intact.

Yuri had immediately been faced with a dilemma. He was not a scientist or official with any significant connections, so he knew that if he reported the mammoth remains they would be whisked away to Moscow and established scientists would lay claim to the fame associated with the remains. Yuri Polkov of would merely be a small name attached to the find but would benefit from none of the excitement that would surround such a magnificent specimen. Yet, if he embarked upon the uncertain course of smuggling the remains out of Russia for sale in some other country, he ran the risk of arrest and imprisonment in one of Siberia's notorious jails.

In the end, Yuri had decided to excavate the remains himself; a task made easier by his access to large farm machinery belonging to his father. He had managed to excavate the mammoth and place it upon a trailer which he towed behind a tractor into one of the barns. He had then prepared a permanent container for the remains, which he had filled with densely packed snow before placing the mammoth in the container and packing it in with it more snow and ice before sealing the lid shut.

With the mammoth sealed inside the container and preserved by the ice, which was in no danger of melting due to the intensely low temperatures of a Siberian spring, Yuri had placed his parents into the care of friends as he prepared for what would become the longest journey of his life. With four trusted associates in whom he confided his astonishing find and with their shared intimate knowledge of the Siberian tundra, they had travelled out into the wilderness and spent two days photographing and documenting the remains before resealing the container and burying the mammoth once again in the ice. With the evidence of his find established, his four associates returned home while Yuri travelled south and escaped the Soviet Union via a container ship bound for Europe.

It had taken Yuri three months to establish a sale to a collector based in Montreal who had both the means and the funds to help Yuri smuggle the mammoth out of Russia. The deal was simple: Yuri would give up the remains of the mammoth for precisely half of its value on the black market, in return for the dealer ensuring that both he and his parents were spirited out of Russia and provided with the cash from the illegitimate deal with which to begin a new life in the United States.

Two months later Yuri and his parents had landed safely in Canada, while the remains of the mammoth had been successfully transported across the Bering Sea and into the collector's hands without the Russian government's knowledge. As far as Yuri was aware, they still did not know that a crime had taken place out on the lonely Siberian wastes.

The value of the illegal sale and the assistance of the Montreal collector's less savoury friends had provided Yuri and his family with a new home, documents and all of the legal paraphernalia required to begin their new life. In a time when it was still possible to move unnoticed and establish new lives, before computers, before the intensive surveillance of governments, Yuri had been able to provide for his parents until their deaths a few years later, their passing following a period of great happiness rather than the suffering they had endured for so many years previously.

Yuri success prompted him to continue on his path and over the next few years he had successfully smuggled numerous fossils from sites as diverse as Alberta, Montana, China and even Mongolia. Each sale that he achieved to private collectors swelled his bank accounts, and the contacts he made in the underworld laundered the money that passed through them. By the time Yuri was thirty five years old he was a millionaire with properties scattered across the United States, his fossil smuggling business carefully concealed behind the facade of a real estate company operating out of New York City.

Somewhere between his arrival in America and his retirement from the business of smuggling fossils, Yuri had become fascinated with the concept of out of place artifacts, a generic term given to objects that were found in archaeological digs that had no right to be there. The most famous example of such an artefact was the Antikithera Mechanism, an extraordinarily complex solar calendar that had been constructed by the Greeks two thousand years before. Remarkable in its complexity and accuracy, the device had once been believed to be constructed by aliens and handed to the Greeks as the catalyst for their sudden technological advancement.

Although that hypothesis had rapidly been dispelled by the hard work of archaeologists on the mechanism, the potential and possibility that extra-terrestrial intelligences had influenced the advancement of mankind had become an obsession for Yuri. He had spent years searching for evidence to support the hypothesis, and his efforts had not been without fruit. Virtually every single society and civilization in known history bore legends that had traditionally been interpreted as creation stories, or myths of dragons flying through the air or imagined gods created to explain the origin of mankind on the Earth. Yuri, like many others, had come to believe that these legends and myths had some basis in reality, their apparently supernatural flavour merely a consequence of witnesses' inability to construct a suitable explanation for the things that they had experienced.

Yuri looked down at the folder before him as he recalled so many examples of ancient gods that could in fact have been ordinary people witnessing extraordinary technology at a time in human history when such an experience would have been indistinguishable from magic. He felt certain that Dr Lucy Morgan did not share his beliefs, for he had attempted to contact her on numerous occasions regarding her work in Israel and had received no reply. Likewise, her work in other fields revealed no evidence of interest in out of place artifacts or indeed the alien intervention hypothesis.

Yuri opened the file and sifted through the papers, and instantly his eye was caught by a secondary file that contained images of a number of archaeological sites around the globe. What struck him immediately about the sites was their location, far from the places where people, even archaeologists, would normally spend time searching for evidence of ancient historical artifacts. Perhaps, he mused, Vladimir had been right after all.

Yuri reached out with one hand and pressed a communication button on his desk. Instantly a speaker came to life and his son's voice reached him from elsewhere in the house.

'Yes, papa?'

Yuri picked up a single sheet from the secondary folder and examined the image upon it as he spoke softly down the phone, an undersea wilderness dominated by huge stone structures and an unusual icon embedded beneath swaying sea moss.

'Prepare the jet,' he instructed his son. 'We leave this afternoon.'

'Where are we going, father?'

Yuri set the piece of paper down and looked out of the windows once more at the London skyline.

'Japan.'

XII

Yonaguni Island,
South China Sea

The Japan Airlines Boeing 777–200 descended through a layer of broken cloud with barely a hint of turbulence as Ethan peered out of his window at the vast island emerging from the North Pacific below them. Lucy Morgan sat next to him, buried in a series of books that she had bought with her in an attempt to replace some of the major details within the files that had been stolen from Ethan's cottage in the Scottish Highlands.

'Remind me again,' Ethan said as he watched the island passing by beneath the aircraft as it circled towards the airport. 'Why are we in Japan?'

Lucy did not look up from the books as she replied.

'Yonaguni Island is the location of one of the very oldest cities of ancient times, rumoured by some to be perhaps ten thousand years old.'

'I'd never heard of it until you mentioned it to me in Scotland,' Ethan admitted as he heard the Boeing's undercarriage whine down.

'That's to be expected,' Lucy replied, 'as the entire city is under the water. Yonaguni is a formation of rock situated just off the coast of the island, and is shallow enough for us to dive,' she explained. 'It was discovered quite some years ago and there has been a great deal of debate in the scientific literature over whether the formation is the result of natural processes or has been hand carved by man. The debate is the result of mainstream archaeology's insistence that there were no active complex civilizations ten thousand years ago, therefore how could there be any complex structures built at that time?'

'So we were still running around throwing spears at antelope when this city supposedly was built?'

'In a sense,' Lucy agreed. 'The dawn of civilization seven thousand years ago was preceded by a long period where mankind essentially grasped the concept of agriculture and in many cases were no longer living the life of the hunter gatherer. However, dwellings were made of things like daub, straw, mud bricks and other natural building materials: there were no major construction efforts or anything approaching what we would call cities.'

'So farming communities then,' Ethan surmised.

'Very basic ones,' Lucy nodded. 'The big mystery of course is how rapidly mankind went from such simple dwellings and pursuits to the sudden emergence of major cities and complex technologies. It's different when you're talking about something like the Egyptian pyramids, for which the tombs of the very builders themselves have been found. They were built in a time where the Egyptian Empire was already powerful and had sufficient manpower and resources to create such incredible constructions. But go back another couple of thousand years and there is simply no way that human beings had either the numbers or the coordination to achieve such remarkable structures, and yet there they are.'

'And you think if we dive on this place, this Yonaguni, we might find something that leads you toward a tomb of some kind or some remains?'

The Boeing trembled as it settled into the wind currents and lined up for landing, and Lucy glanced out of the window at the mountainous island as it passed by.

'This country, Japan, is from where we inherited the legends of dragons. The original Japanese manuscripts that contain mention of dragons, however, do not describe flying reptiles with wings and pointy tails and big teeth. Translated directly, they describe objects that fly noisily through the air and often emit or trail fire as they pass by. Many modern scholars interpret this description as an observation of things like ball lightning, comets striking our atmosphere and other natural phenomena, but a closer inspection of the manuscript reveals that these supposed comets often changed direction or came to a complete halt in the air. Some even landed amid flames. Obviously, that's not what comets do.'

'So you're figuring that what these ancient Japanese witnesses were describing was in fact flying craft of some kind,' Ethan said.

The Boeing settled onto the runway with a thump and the engines wound up as they went into reverse thrust as massive air brakes extended. Lucy spoke up a little above the noise of the engines as she replied.

'You have to have an open mind to say the least,' she admitted. 'We have to remember that these people were trying to describe something that was either beyond their scope of understanding or for which they did not have adequate words to accurately interpret what they saw. If you turn the problem on its head and ask yourself whether it's likely that they were indeed seeing massive flying reptiles breathing fire..?' Ethan smiled and tilted his head in acquiescence. 'Exactly, it's actually *less* likely that they were witnessing some sort of unknown flying creature than some kind of flying vehicle, mainly because we know that flying vehicles are at least possible – we're in one right now.'

'They're only possible *now*,' Ethan countered, 'because we have the technology to build one. I imagine that the early Samurai would have been left speechless by a role of Sellotape, let alone a flying vehicle.'

'It's not the only evidence we have of unusual events occurring in ancient Japan,' Lucy said as the Boeing taxied off the runway toward the terminals. 'There is an extraordinarily well documented event from 1812 concerning the appearance of a large sphere that was washed up on a beach off Harashagahama, called the *Utsuro-Bune* incident. Witnessed by many people, and recorded far afield without any deviation from the facts in the oldest recorded documents, from the sphere appeared a woman with red hair who carried a box of some kind. The woman is described as not being a native of Japan but being recognisably human and speaking a language that none of the witnesses understood. She refused to let anyone near the box, which was said to be fairly small and covered in colored lights that flickered and flashed as though by magic. The sphere in which she travelled was covered in unusual symbols.'

'I don't suppose there's any physical evidence of this woman, the flashing device she was carrying or the sphere that she arrived in?'

'No,' Lucy admitted. 'The woman returned to her sphere and the sea. The story endures on the strength of multiple witnesses on the record and the consistency with which the event was described. Even some of the harshest sceptics are willing to concede that clearly something, or somebody, did indeed wash up on that beach. Who or what it was remains unknown.'

The Boeing's engines whined down as it parked in front of the terminals. Ethan remained sitting as virtually every other passenger on the aircraft got up and began fumbling to get at their luggage from overhead lockers, and wondered not for the first time why they even bothered. Nobody was going anywhere until the doors were open.

'It's a thin line of enquiry,' Ethan decided. 'A couple of legends and the site of what might or might not be an ancient city buried under the waves.'

'Right now neither present much to go on,' Lucy admitted, 'except for the sun icon. There are numerous sites around the world that could harbour what we're looking for, but this one ranks as the oldest. If there's nothing here, or we determine that the site is in fact a result of natural formations, then we simply move to the next and work our way forwards in time, so to speak.'

Ethan looked up. 'How many sites have you got to visit?'

'All in all, about thirty eight.'

Ethan's face dropped. Lucy smiled as she patted him on the shoulder. 'Actually, it's just six that I can be sure are worth our time.'

'And how are we going to get out to this remarkable formation of yours?' Ethan asked as he got out of his seat and began filing with Lucy toward the exits.

'I have some friends who have dived the site repeatedly over the past few years,' Lucy explained as they walked. 'They're archaeologists who also have an interest in the potential of out of place artifacts and evidence of civilizations older than the commonly accepted dates. I took your advice and emailed them via a new account I created in a false name in an attempt to cover our tracks.'

'Good,' Ethan said as he stepped off the plane and onto the concourse and was able to walk normally. 'Like I said, the Russians may anticipate this move but anything we can do to slow them down will be a bonus. How many times have you dived in open water?'

'Enough times not have a problem,' Lucy replied. 'My friends are waiting for us, so let's get a move on.'

Ethan threw Lucy a mock salute and followed her towards the customs and arrival terminal.

*

'They've landed.'

The interior of the vehicle was outfitted with plush, cream leather that contrasted sharply with the glossy black interior and the panels of deeply polished mahogany. The windows were tinted, concealing the occupants from the outside world.

Yuri Polkov shut off the communicator in the armrest of his chair through which the driver had informed him that both Lucy Morgan and her mysterious American escort had landed at the airport not more than ten miles from where Yuri's vehicle now drove towards an exclusive hotel. Yuri's private Learjet had shadowed the JAL flight from London and now Yuri had sped past Lucy Morgan through customs, his private flight status affording him swifter passage.

'I don't understand what they are doing out here,' Vladimir admitted as he searched through Lucy's files and struggled to make a connection. 'I thought that they would return to Israel, the place where they found the original remains?'

'As did I,' Yuri replied, 'that's why I told you that papers and files are no substitute for the mind behind them. Lucy knows things that we do not, has an understanding that we do not, and for now we are forced to pursue her.'

'The only thing I've been able to find that makes any sense is this,' Vladimir said as he handed his father a glossy photograph. 'She's been collecting images of this place for months.'

Yuri took the photograph and studied it. It appeared to be a sonar image, or perhaps one taken by satellite, that showed the south-east corner of Yonaguni Island. There, just off the coast, a distinctive series of geometric shapes emerged from the sea floor. Although Yuri was fully aware of the power of nature to carve extraordinary forms through volcanic and other processes, the sheer complexity of the site that he was looking at defied any natural explanation.

A central, temple like area was elevated high above the seafloor on a diamond-shaped plateau that was surrounded by pathways, steps, angular altars and other perfectly aligned features that screamed human architecture.

Vladimir handed him another sheet of paper that contain scribbled notes in Lucy's hand, marking the depth of the remains and including charts that showed the original coastline prior to the last Ice Age.

'According to these charts,' Vladimir said, 'the last time this site would have been above water and habitable was around three thousand years ago.'

'The end of the Ice Age caused the melting of the massive ice caps,' Yuri agreed. 'Sea levels rose dramatically over a period of just centuries and swamped many coastal plains and cities. Some believe that this deluge was the origin of the flood myth from the Bible, as so many different peoples could have witnessed it and the event was dramatic enough to have remained in human memory and later been recorded.'

Vladimir shook his head as he leafed through the files.

'The site has been dived over and over again,' he said as he examined Lucy's records. 'Nobody has found anything except shards of pottery and wood, much of which has been dated as in excess of ten thousand years old, but according to this could easily have been washed up at the site from elsewhere. Scientists dispute that the site can be gauged from the result of the debris found around it.'

Yuri handed back the sonar image of the monument as he glanced out of the window of the limousine towards the island's south-east coast.

'We will need diving equipment,' Yuri informed his son, 'and a means to travel to the site without being seen easily by either Lucy Morgan or this man who is accompanying her. Do we know anything about him?'

'As a matter of fact we do,' Vladimir said as he handed his father another image. 'It turns out that this is the same guy who showed up in Israel when Lucy was there. His name is Ethan Warner, a former journalist and United States Marine. He has a history of working for the US government as well as in various war zones and danger spots around the world. He could prove a problem for us.'

Yuri looked down at the picture of Warner, probably taken some time in the last five years. Wavy light brown hair framed cold grey eyes and a wide jaw, and Yuri could tell from the image taken of Warner crossing a road in Chicago that he was in good physical condition. Once a soldier…

'Inform our men that Lucy Morgan is the priority,' Yuri decided. 'If this Ethan Warner decides he wants to get in the way, then they are to deal with him as the situation dictates.'

Vladimir nodded enthusiastically as he picked up the phone from beside him on the seat and began dialling.

'Don't worry, papa,' he said. 'I will deal with Ethan Warner personally.'

XIII

'We've been out here many times before, there won't be any problems.'

Michael Spader was an American archaeologist who had travelled to Japan after marrying his wife, Ishira, when she decided to return to her homeland to continue her own research into ancient feudal Japan. A native of Ohio, as far as Ethan could make out Michael seemed to be the kind of free spirit who just went along with everybody else, and had an easy-going nature that provided Ethan with some kind of reassurance that he and his wife knew what they were doing.

Michael was at the wheelhouse of the small boat *Jest* as it crashed through the waves along the island's south shore. Ishira was busily unpacking and preparing the diving equipment alongside Lucy, who had suddenly developed a very business-like attitude towards the expedition. Ethan shrugged off the jetlag weighing down upon him with an effort as he stepped towards the bow of the boat where Michael was guiding it through the brisk seas.

'How deep are the remains?' Ethan asked, shouting to be heard above the engine and the crashing water.

'In places it's not much more than ten feet,' Michael explained. 'In others, more like fifty but it's all accessible. I'd imagine a maximum dive time of thirty minutes plus decompression.'

Ethan looked up at the bright blue sky, filled with light, cumulus clouds flaring bright white in the sunlight. The ocean was brisk, but in shallow waters *Jest* would easily be able to anchor. He looked up at the steep cliffs lining the nearby shore, seeking weak spots or points of ambush from which the boat would be easily visible on the ocean.

'You look like you're staking the joint out,' Michael observed.

'Habit of a lifetime.'

Ethan glanced across to the rucksack he had bought with him, somewhat reassured by the knowledge that a 9 mm pistol was safely tucked inside. There had been no way he could have dared to attempt to slip a weapon through customs either when leaving the USA or arriving in Japan: even though he technically had the knowledge and ability to do so, the chance of him being flagged up and thus exposed was too great to take. Instead, he had elected to contact a former buddy from the Marines who was still on active service and based in Okinawa, and through him he had been able to obtain the weapon despite Lucy's concern.

'I didn't expect you to be carrying,' Michael said to him.

'I didn't expect you to know.'

Michael grinned. 'I didn't, but I do now.'

Ethan dropped his voice an octave so that Ishira would not overhear him. 'Lucy is being followed, and the people following her are not afraid of guns. I thought it best to be cautious.'

'And you were going to tell us about this *when*?' Michael demanded, the smile gone from his face.

'Now,' Ethan replied without rancour. 'You're not in any danger, and we're far enough out here that we'll see any trouble coming long before it reaches us.'

'That's not particularly reassuring. We heard about what happened to Lucy in Israel, that she was abducted and held by terrorists or similar. Are they the same ones following her now?'

'No,' Ethan replied. 'These guys are a different bunch and we don't know exactly who they are.'

'Smashing,' Michael uttered. 'First sign of trouble and we're out of here, no questions asked.'

'Agreed,' Ethan replied. 'Just wanted to let you know.'

'Obliged, I'm sure.'

Ethan walked over to the diving gear and began busying himself preparing his own kit. Due to the relatively shallow nature of the dive they would be using a standard nitrogen and oxygen mix, with only a slight excess of oxygen to minimise the chances of nitrogen bubbles forming in the blood if they were forced to ascend too quickly. Ethan wanted the ability to get out of the water fast if anything went wrong, and despite the fact that they had departed the United Kingdom in great secrecy and left a complex trail behind them he had long ago learned to always err on the side of caution.

'The kit's ready,' Lucy reported as she made a final check on the oxygen gauges.

'Five minutes!' Michael called from the wheelhouse, and Ethan heard the engine note whine down slightly as the boat approached the dive site and pulled in towards the coastline.

'The currents are strong here,' Ishira informed them, 'and the water contains a high volume of plankton and algae that can bring visibility down to less than five metres at times. Maintain close visual contact with each other and make sure you start your ascent with at least five minutes extra time available, because you'll be fighting the currents to stay in position and will burn through your supply far quicker than during your descent.'

Both Ethan and Lucy nodded in agreement as they began pulling on their wetsuits, and Ishira hefted their oxygen tanks onto their backs and helped clip them into place.

The boat's engine died down as Michael manoeuvred *Jest* into place directly overhead the flooded city, and moments later the clatter of a stainless steel chain rattled out across the rolling waves as he threw the anchor overboard. The anchor chain clattered through its stays and then slowed and pulled taut as the boat swung around into the current. Michael visually gauged the water passing the bow and then called out to them.

'About four knots from the south-west,' he reported. 'It will be a little less down there but even so, I'd recommend using tethers just in case.'

Ethan shook his head. 'If either one of us is pulled clear by the currents we'll surface and let off a flare. It's better for the boat to come after us than to be hindered by tethers when we need to move freely across the site.'

Michael shrugged but did not argue, although it was clear he felt that the waters were too choppy and the currents too strong to free dive the site.

'Are you sure about that?' Lucy asked him as they pulled on their flippers, *Jest* rocking and plunging on the swells.

'We'll start on the north-east corner of the site and then let the current move us down across it,' Ethan informed her. 'It's sensible to let the current do the swimming for us. Once we're done, we'll ascend and have plenty of energy to maintain position.'

Lucy nodded her agreement. 'Okay, but it's a fairly big site so depending on the visibility we may have to split in order to see everything.'

'And what exactly is it that we're looking for? That icon in the photograph?'

'Yes,' Lucy replied. 'Just keep an open mind and think about what you've learned so far. If there's anything down there that could give us some pointers as to where we need to go, then pick it up or photograph it.'

Ethan pulled his oxygen mask on as he turned to sit on the edge of the boat with his back facing the water, Lucy moving alongside him. They checked each other's oxygen supply and with a thumbs-up to each other Ethan held his mask in place as he went backwards over the edge of the boat. He only just heard Michael's last comment before he plunged into the cold water.

'Did I forget to mention the hammerhead sharks?'

The water flooded around Ethan's body, and despite the highly effective thermal wetsuit he could feel the cold water on his hands and face. Ethan quickly orientated himself as he saw Lucy plunge into the water beside him amid a shimmering galaxy of bubbles, one hand over her mask as she reached back and tightened it in place and then gave him another thumbs-up.

Ethan looked around and saw that the water was presenting fairly good visibility, tinged with blue rather than the dull green that signalled a high organic content and reduced visibility. He looked down and was surprised to see that some ten feet beneath him was a perfectly flat surface of rock that extended away into the distance, marred only by clumps of mosses. It appeared to be made of sandstone, and almost instantly he spotted a perfect right angled corner to it just a few yards away.

For some reason he had expected to have to descend further to find the remarkable temple of which Lucy had spoken, but he could see already that it was nearby. He allowed his own natural weight to draw him down toward the surface of the monument as Lucy descended and moved to one side to hover over the edge.

Ethan swam to join her and looked down to see the side of the monument drop away onto a series of terraces, each of them cut at perfect right angles. Ethan had heard of numerous examples of natural phenomena creating such sharp right angles and angular features, most famously the Giant's Causeway in Ireland. But here there was a difference: the monument itself stood alone and rose above the vast plain of the seabed. There was no evidence of erosion or loose rock that would have been evident had the effect of currents or similar been responsible for shaping the monument over geological timescales.

Ethan surveyed the overall shape of the monument. Despite the obvious geometric nature of the various structures that jutted from its surface, when Ethan swam away from the monument and looked at it as a whole it seemed clear to him that it was a natural formation that had later been modified by human hands. There seemed to be no plausible reason for human beings to have built such a large blocky construction, with no immediate obvious point of entry to any kind of interior. However, if they had instead been presented with a large feature such as the monument on a shoreline with an existing geometric shape that could be altered and upon which could be erected buildings, then it seemed likely that it would be used for as long as it was available to them.

Ethan looked across the surface of the monument and then considered the closeness of the shore of the island. His eye was drawn to the underside of the boat's hull nearby, the water shimmering through the surface in bright beams. He looked again at the terraces on the right of the monument and suddenly he realized what he was looking at.

Ethan tapped Lucy shoulder and gestured to the boat before pointing at the terraces below them on the right of the monument. The terraces had always confused scientists who advocated the man-made nature of the site because the steps were too large for natural human movement and so had no apparent reason for being constructed or carved. But the monument had also been covered up by rapidly rising sea levels, and the terraces rose up in the direction of the nearby shore.

With a series of hand signals, Ethan indicated the lowest of the terraces near the front of the monument and pointed at the boat. Then he indicated the water around them, and raised his level hands in front of him up towards his head and over it and then pointed at the next level of terraces and the boat once more.

Lucy frowned for a moment and then her eyes widened as she realized what he was suggesting. The monument was not something built by human hands but modified as sea levels rose around it. The monument had been used as a dock, fresh terraces cut further and further away from the front of the monument as sea levels gradually rose in the wake of the Ice Age.

Suddenly, the so-called temples and altars made sense. They were not constructions in themselves, but features that had been carved smooth in order to build upon them: loading bays, steps, perhaps even a market where the so-called *temple* now stood. The altar may even have been a primitive sundial calendar, charting the passing of seasons for fishermen who might have lived and worked at this place. Only when the water became too deep and the level of the terraces reached the top of the monument was it finally overcome by the waves.

Lucy nodded, a look of delight in her eyes as she patted Ethan shoulder, clearly agreeing with his hypothesis of what the monument had actually been. Typically, in ancient civilizations, the presence of a natural harbour or a well-constructed dock had led to the establishment of major ports, from which major cities had then grown. The monument could easily represent all that remained of one of the oldest Japanese societies ever to have existed.

Ethan turned and saw that the monument extended some sixty yards long by perhaps forty wide and was at least eighteen yards deep. The terraces descended down on one side, while the temple beneath him extended down onto the surface of the main monument itself. Lucy produced in her hand a laminated map that she orientated to show the shape of the monument beneath him. Ethan could quickly identify the temple and the terraces, and also the shape of the angular altar to which Lucy pointed emphatically. Ethan nodded and turned to follow her as she began descending to where the altar should be.

The altar, a diamond-shaped feature extending up from the flat surface of the rest of the monument and located in front of the main temple, was covered in clumps of sea moss and clams. Sometimes referred to as the "*turtle*", its perfectly ordered shape struck Ethan as far too geometric to possibly have been carved by anything but human hands. He swam behind Lucy as she came to a stop at the front of the altar and began pulling chunks of moss away from the surface.

Ethan noted a movement in the distance to his right and turned to see the ghostly form of a hammerhead shark drift like a marine phantom through the endless abyss. It seemed to watch him for a long moment with one cruel black eye on the tip of its massive head, and then its tail flicked and it accelerated out into the gloom once more.

Ethan turned back to Lucy and watched her clean the surface of the rocks and then begin to examine them closely. Ethan peered in from over her shoulder and quickly saw what she was looking at.

The rock had been engraved deeply with a single disc from which extended a series of lines radiating out from the bottom of the disc as though depicting a sun shining down toward the ground. There were no lines pointing upward. Ethan nodded, recognising the image as one that Lucy had shown him as being present in Israel. She had said that there was no known link between the Egyptians and ancient Japanese Jomon who had lived on Yonaguni Island.

Ethan prepared the camera and then began photographing the engraving, both with the altar itself in view and also close-up on the detail of the icon. Lucy noted the position and orientation of the engraving on the altar and then pushed away and ascended above the monument as she sought more locations to investigate.

Ethan turned and saw another hammerhead shark emerge from the gloom behind them, circling slowly and swinging its great head from side to side. Its massive flanks were criss-crossed with scars from countless fights with other predators, and it easily outsized every shark he had seen up to that point.

Ethan ascended, tapped Lucy shoulder and indicated the shark, and as he did so he saw the three shapes approaching them swiftly from the south, metallic black blocks with the unmistakable shape of men behind them. The underwater jet-skis rushed in and Ethan could see each of the men holding a projectile, metallic harpoons with wicked glistening tips.

XIV

Ethan grabbed Lucy's shoulder and pointed at the onrushing jet-skis before he pushed her upwards towards the shadowy hull of the *Jest* above them. He saw the panicked look on Lucy's face as she realized that they were being pursued, but she obeyed instantly and headed towards the boat as Ethan turned to confront the machines.

Each was powered by two small motors that left a stream of bubbles behind the vehicles, and they were fronted with a Perspex bow-shield behind which the men huddled as they spread out. Ethan knew at a glance that he had no chance of defeating the three without first taking control of one of the jet-skis, and he glanced briefly at Lucy and judged the distance between her, their boat and the onrushing machines. Confident that she could reach the boat before the machines reached her, Ethan swam immediately for the shallow water atop the monument. Just a few fathoms deep, the shallow water would take the advantage away from the machines and give it to Ethan as they would not be able to climb and dive faster than he could and would be limited in their ability to attack all at once.

Ethan kicked for the temple, keeping an eye open to his left as the machines rushed in. One of the men aimed a wicked harpoon and fired, the projectile rocketing toward Ethan and leaving a thin swirling stream of bubbles behind it. Ethan rolled and turned head-on towards the projectile to minimise his profile and the harpoon flashed by scant inches from his right shoulder, close enough that he felt the turbulence of its passing ripple against his wetsuit.

Ethan reached the top of the temple and turned to see the three jet-skis fan out, one to each side of him as the centre machine rushed headlong toward him. The man in control of it aimed his harpoon and Ethan knew immediately that he would wait until the last minute to be sure of a certain hit before he fired. Ethan reached down to his belt and unclipped his oxygen tank as he faced toward the onrushing jet-ski, waiting for the operator to fire the weapon at him. The machine loomed larger and larger, and he could hear the whirring of the propellers inside the motor and could see the eyes of the man operating it behind the shield.

The harpoon fired in a cloud of bubbles and Ethan immediately dropped to his knees and crouched down as he slid the oxygen tank from his back. The harpoon rushed over his head as Ethan surged to his feet and swung the oxygen tank like a battering ram at the machine. The pilot tried desperately to turn aside but was far too slow to react as Ethan swung the oxygen tank over and down behind the shield to crash into the pilot's head with a dull thump that smashed his forehead against the control column.

The jet-ski slammed into the surface of the temple, then twisted sideways in a cloud of dislodged sand as Ethan pulled his oxygen tank back on and strapped it in place as he swam towards the careering machine. The pilot was hanging limp in his seat, his arms floating out to either side of his body as blood spilled from his forehead and stained the water with scarlet clouds.

Ethan grabbed the pilot and yanked him from the seat as he jumped onto the jet-ski and twisted the throttle grip. The machine surged away from the surface of the temple as the motors engaged and Ethan flew out over the deep blue abyss and dove downward as he searched for the other two vehicles.

He saw them immediately as they rushed in toward him, both of their operators moving in for the kill. Ethan kept diving as he made an effort to draw them away from *Jest*, one eye on his depth gauge. As he dove away he spotted the silvery glint of an expended harpoon lying on one of the narrow shelves of the monument. Ethan turned his jet-ski and descended alongside the shelf, ancient carved stone flashing by as he reached out with one hand and grabbed the harpoon before turning away from the monument and descending further. He glanced over his shoulder and saw the remaining two jet-skis still pursuing him, both of them aiming harpoons at him but too far out of range to shoot.

He twisted the controls of the jet-ski and it turned sharply to head back towards the two pursuing vehicles. Ethan tucked down behind the bow shield to prevent them from firing their harpoons at him but he knew as soon as he had passed they would probably fire over their shoulders in an attempt to injure him. But Ethan had no intention of letting them go by without further evening the odds.

The two vehicles spread apart, aiming to pass either side of him so that one or other of his assailants could take a perfect shot. Ethan waited until the last moment before he turned his machine to the right, gambling that the man on his left was likely right-handed and would thus be forced to take a more complicated shot over his left forearm where the protective screen would get in his way. Ethan aimed towards the remaining vehicle and banked his own machine hard over so that its hull protected him from being shot at close range.

As the jet-ski passed by Ethan stuck his hand out with the harpoon pointing in the same direction as he was travelling and shoved it directly down into the vehicle's starboard turbine as he snatched his hand away. He heard a muted clattering sound as he saw the harpoon fired from the other vehicle flash by just behind and above him. Ethan grabbed his controls and turned to pursue the expended harpoon and he glanced over his shoulder to see the damaged jet-ski veering away in a tight turn as its pilot fought for control, the harpoon lodged in its turbine blades.

Above them against the shimmering surface of the ocean, Ethan glimpsed the shape of a hammerhead shark as it coasted into the cloud of blood swirling near the surface, two more joining it as they closed in on the unconscious pilot's body.

Ethan dove after the descending harpoon and managed to snatch it in his hand as he turned back towards the remaining undamaged jet-ski. From the corner of his eye he saw *Jest's* anchor being pulled up and he knew that Lucy must now be safely aboard. The remaining jet-ski turned towards him once more, the pilot's harpoon again reloaded as he accelerated towards Ethan at maximum velocity.

Ethan glanced at the damaged jet-ski and saw that the pilot had shut down the blocked turbine and was now turning back towards the fight. Ethan looked at the boat above and decided to take his chance. The onrushing vehicle loomed in his vision and Ethan knew that the pilot was seeking merely to maintain his attention so that his companion could close in for the kill.

Ethan held onto the controls as lightly as he could and waited. The onrushing machine loomed up and he saw the pilot's eyes widen in shock as he realized that Ethan was not going to break off. The pilot yanked his controls to one side but Ethan simply turned to match his attacker's course, and at the last moment Ethan pushed up and away from the jet-ski and let go of the controls. Freed of his body weight and with the passing water now dragging Ethan away, the jet-ski continued on its course for a split second before it smashed into the other machine with a cracking sound of crumpling plastic and metal as the two vehicles collided at near maximum velocity.

The pilot doubled over as the two machines spun and smashed together, the bow of Ethan's jet-ski plunging into the pilot's side and smashing him from his seat. The pilot's oxygen mouthpiece and mask were ripped from his face by the force of the impact and he tumbled helplessly in the abyss, a spiralling trail of glistening bubbles behind him.

Ethan looked up and saw the sharks now tearing in a frenzy at the injured pilot's body, a rapidly expanding crimson cloud reducing visibility at the surface. Ethan kicked off as hard as he could toward the murky shape of *Jest's* hull. He reached down once again and unclipped his oxygen tank as he looked down and to his right and saw the damaged jet-ski struggling to climb towards him, its weight and that of its driver too much for the single engine. Ethan shrugged off his oxygen tank, took a last deep breath from its contents, then pulled the mouthpiece out and shoved the oxygen tank in the direction of the pursuing machine.

Freed of the extra weight Ethan began ascending rapidly towards the surface of the nearby boat, and he looked down to see the damage jet-ski swerve to avoid the tumbling oxygen tank, slowed further by the obstacle in its path before it vanished as Ethan ascended through the gruesome cloud of blood tainting the water.

To his right he saw the hammerheads thrashing around the corpse of the diver, now a shredded mess of rubber, blood and bone, the sharks entirely consumed by their feeding frenzy. Ethan looked up and saw *Jest* looming above him and moments later he burst onto the surface and kicked away for the boat.

'Ethan!'

He heard Lucy cry out as he swam towards the boat and heard its engine growling as it moved toward him. Ishira was at the controls as Michael reached out with one hand toward Ethan. Ethan swam as close to the boat as he dared in the crashing waves and reached out to grab Michael's hand as with the other he grasped the side of the boat and began hauling himself aboard.

Lucy helped as Ethan rolled onto the deck and pulled off his mask.

'Get us out of here,' Ethan grasped as he fought to remove his flippers.

'It's not just divers,' Michael said as he pointed out across the ocean.

Ethan looked to his right and saw a speedboat rushing toward them, the sleek hull crashing through the waves.

'Who the hell are these people?'

'How about we have this chat later and concentrate on staying alive?!' Michael suggested as he turned and grabbed a rifle from its case and handed it to Ethan.

'Incoming!' Ishira yelled.

Ethan saw the speedboat rushing toward their port hull at full throttle, two men with rifles hanging over the hull and aiming in his direction.

'Get down!'

Ethan hurled himself flat onto the deck, his fingers instinctively finding the rifle's safety catch and trigger in unison with the same fluidity he had once possessed as a Marine fighting in Afghanistan's Tora Bora caves. The weapon came up into his shoulder even as he saw the first burst of muzzle flash from their attackers' weapons as they sprayed a lethal hail of automatic fire across the boat's deck. Ethan, enveloped in a bubble of adrenalin fuelled silence, ignored the bullets that zipped and tore into the deck around him as he breathed slowly and took aim. A Marine instructor's words drifted unbidden through his mind.

All the automatic fire in the world is useless against one well-placed round. Shoot slow son, and you'll shoot sure.

The shooter raked the deck as the speedboat turned away at the last moment amid crashing surf and shining metal. Ethan's breathing stopped for a single second as he squeezed the trigger once.

The round hit the shooter low in his belly as the speedboat raced past and bounced on the churning waves. Ethan saw the man's mouth gape open in shock as he folded over at the waist, his legs crumpling beneath him as he collapsed onto the speedboat's deck.

Ethan looked over the barrel of the rifle and saw at least three other men in the rear of the speedboat. He stood up and rushed to the bridge, keeping one eye on the speedboat as it circled out for another pass. The adrenaline was pumping through his veins now like a freight train powering through the night as he leapt up the steps two at a time and pointed at their attackers.

'Turn the boat around,' he ordered Ishira. 'Head straight for them.'

'We can't fight them!'

'We sure as hell can't outrun them,' Ethan snapped back. He glanced out of the bridge windows to see the speedboat racing toward them again. 'Take them down the left side!' Ethan shouted as he jumped back down to the deck.

Ethan ran low to the stern of the boat, sliding onto his belly and aiming across the port stern. A crackle of gunfire snapped across the wind as Ethan slowed his breathing. The speedboat soared past, two men firing their weapons from the hip with aimless abandon in the hopes of catching a lucky hit. A salvo of bullets splintered *Jest's* hull close to Ethan's shoulder and showered him with debris.

As the boat thundered by Ethan aimed at one of the shooters, taking advantage of the low aspect movement now that the speedboat was moving almost directly away from him. Despite the pitching of the boats across the waves, the target was easier to track. Ethan held his breath and fired two rounds, double-tapping the trigger as he aimed for the man's torso.

The first round missed, hitting the deck low and to the man's left, but the second round hit him straight through the neck, a fine mist of blood spraying into the wind as the man was hurled backwards to sprawl on the deck in a tangle of limbs and spilled blood.

Ethan rolled over and shouted to Michael above the wind.

'Turn her around!'

Michael responded without argument this time, the boat wheeling around on the churning surface of the ocean as she chugged her way back toward their attackers.

Lucy struggled across the heaving deck and hurled herself down alongside Ethan.

'We can't keep this up forever,' she said. 'Sooner or later one of us is going to get hit!'

'They're coming back!' Michael shouted as the speedboat suddenly turned hard into them and rushed head-on once again.

Ethan glanced at the towering cliffs nearby and then at the surface of the ocean ahead. The waves were crashing across rock features just below the surface, and to his amazement he realized that the Yonaguni formation was large enough to breach the surface, that it was not entirely submerged.

'Run away from them! Bring them down the port side!' Ethan shouted.

'I thought you told me not to run away?!' Michael yelled back.

'Do it, and let them see you do it!'

Ethan shifted his position slightly and aimed his rifle aft as he heard the speedboat's powerful engines growling and the familiar rattle of gunfire as the men aboard opened up once again. The shots went wide and high, the speedboat too far away for accurate shooting and its motion through the waves spoiling their aim.

Michael threw the throttles wide open as he aimed for the rocks jutting from the ocean surface as Ethan fired two or three shots in the general direction of the speedboat and then tossed the rifle down and ran to the wheel house.

'Don't turn until I tell you!' Ethan shouted above the wind.

'We'll hit the rocks, and they're closing on us!'

'Stay on course!' Ethan roared as he looked back and saw the speedboat rushing toward them. 'Come right, five degrees!'

Michael responded immediately, drawing the speedboat in toward *Jest's* port hull, the speedboat pilot aiming for a close pass as he accelerated toward them. Ethan looked over his shoulder and saw the rocks looming large before them.

'We'll breach our hull!' Michael shouted.

'Stay on course!'

The speedboat thundered toward them, the gunmen aboard struggling to shoot their automatic rifles as the boat thumped and bounced on the waves. Ethan saw the reefs ahead, white water smashing into the ancient rocks, and then he saw the gunmen take aim as the speedboat roared alongside them.

'Now!' Ethan yelled as he reached past Michael and hauled the throttle closed.

The boat heaved in the waves as the thrust from its engine vanished and it heeled violently to starboard as Michael spun the wheel and ducked down as a rattle of gunfire crackled out above the roar of the speedboat's engines.

The speedboat thundered by and hurled a wall of spray up against

Jest as the gunshots flew wildly past the decks, barely a single round impacting the boat. Ethan watched as the sleek vessel raced past them and then smashed into the reefs with a crash of shattered fibreglass and rending metal.

The hull shattered with a grinding metallic roar that Ethan could hear even above the labouring engines. The crew were hurled into the waves as the pilot's face smashed into the windscreen with a dull thump and a puff of windswept blood. The speedboat's hull stripped away as it careered over the rocks and its engines were ripped from their mounts. Ethan saw a thick cloud of black smoke billow from both of the speedboat's engines as limp bodies toppled over the taff-rail into the ocean in a tangle of flailing limbs. The speedboat tumbled off the far side of the reef and began turning in lazy circles on the surface of the water, spitting flames that began to burn their way along the hull until it slowly began to sink beneath the waves.

'That'll do,' Ethan smiled grimly as he lowered the rifle and stood up.

In the churning water, Ethan saw more hammerheads circling the bloodied stain where the speedboat had sunk.

Ishira began guiding the boat to shore as Lucy, clearly shaken by the encounter, moved to Ethan's side.

'Who are they? What do they want with us?'

'I don't know,' Ethan admitted. 'You get what you needed?'

Lucy nodded. 'That icon we found engraved in the rocks proves that we're on the right tracks, but this monument is simply a natural rock foundation that people later modified and built upon. Any artifacts that may have been nearby would almost certainly have decayed or been washed away.'

Ethan rubbed his temples. 'Well I hope you have a good Plan B, because there's no way we can stay here. They're on to us now and we need to disappear as fast as we can.'

'I'm all in favour of that,' Michael muttered from the wheelhouse.

'I'll book a flight as soon as we get to our hotel,' Lucy said.

'We're not going to the hotel,' Ethan insisted. 'If they found us out out here they'll probably be waiting for us at the hotel. Where is it that you need to go next?'

Lucy sat down and pulled a laminated map from her kit that she opened out on the deck at her feet.

'I don't know for sure,' she admitted, 'but all we can do is try another site of a similar age. The icon on Yonaguni's altar was facing east, but the altar itself was facing south-west, and the direction of sacred altars and images was important to ancient cultures.' Lucy took a pen and sketched a line roughly heading south west from Yonaguni and out across the Malay. 'The oldest known ruins that I can be sure rival Yonaguni in age are to be found here.' She pointed at a spot on the map to their south west. 'The icon at Yonaguni points out over the Pacific Ocean to nowhere, but the altar points toward this site.'

'Mahendraparvata, Cambodia,' Ethan read from the map. 'What's there?'

'An ancient city, much older than the more famous Angkor Wat. It was only found a few years ago and I'm pretty certain that if we found that sun icon here, we'll find it there. If we don't, then the trail's already gone cold.'

Ethan surveyed the coastline for a few moments before he made a decision.

'Okay, this is what we're going to do. We need to find a way to get to Indonesia, and from there I can find us a passage to Cambodia that won't involve passports.'

'How on earth are you going to do that?'

'I do have friends too, y'know.'

XV

Defense Intelligence Agency,
DIAC Building,
Washington DC

Agent Aaron Devlin strode toward an elevator bank on the third floor of the defense intelligence agency DIAC building. Ever since the events of 9/11 security had been tight, with all elevators guarded at all times and repeated security checkpoints ensuring that not only could nobody get into the building without proper authorisation, but that it was also impossible to move *through* the building without obtaining the necessary clearances.

Nowhere, however, was security tighter than on the fifth floor.

New protocols initiated the previous year, and policies implemented by Congress and by the president himself had resulted in crushing blows against security for many of the most powerful agencies, including the CIA, NSA and DIA. Human rights lawyers had attempted to strip them of their powers, to peel back layers of security due to supposed breaches of human rights during surveillance and other data gathering programs. Powerful members of the agencies, concerned about the potential for loss of data and gathering ability, had ensured that an old branch of the intelligence services had been resurrected, and access to this new branch was both highly classified and restricted. Although the intelligence agencies of the United States government were overseen by an Intelligence Director, the role itself created in the wake of the war on terror, there remained segments of the intelligence community that it was felt operated best autonomously. The cabal, little known outside of the community itself, was now located on the DIA building's fifth floor. Aaron knew its members only by their code names, for each individual member of the group was both unknown to both those outside the group and to those within the group as well. The cabal's name was enough to provoke whispers among those who dared speak it.

Majestic Twelve.

Aaron reached the elevators and presented his pass code and identity key to the two armed guards manning their posts outside the elevator. A third form of identification was also required, but this involved no high-technology whatsoever. Despite intense research and huge investment in all manner of identity technology such as iris recognition, DNA scanning and complex facial recognition software, when it came down to high-level security requirements there was one thing above all others the ensured that nobody got inside the building who shouldn't: *human recognition*.

A screen beside the elevators flickered into life, the screen itself split into four, and on each of those four screens was a member of the intelligence services who knew Aaron personally. Many were former military officers, some of whom had served alongside Aaron. Before each of those individuals was a button, and they were required to either admit or deny access to the elevators by simply ensuring that Aaron was who he said he was. Each of them cleared Aaron for access, each of them at their desks either in the DIA headquarters itself or elsewhere in the intelligence community. All of them had been pre-warned that Aaron would be present at the elevators at a set time, a further security process that prevented a *lookalike* from gaining access.

The doors opened and Aaron stepped inside before the guards outside selected the floor he had been granted access to. The doors closed and the elevator began to climb to the fifth floor. Aaron subconsciously straightened his tie despite having done it many times already that morning, and he ran through his head what had happened so far and what he was required to report. Aaron had visited this floor only twice in the last three months, and on both occasions it had been as the bearer of bad news.

The elevator slowed and the doors opened to reveal a single corridor before him. At the far end were two double doors, and outside those doors were two armed guards already aiming their weapons at him. If the doors had opened and anybody but Aaron Devlin had been standing inside, they were under orders to open fire. Aaron waited for them to identify him visually and lower their weapons before he stepped out of the elevator and walked towards them. The two guards stepped forward, one maintaining his rifle at port arms while the other produced a scanner. Aaron halted before them and allowed the guard to wipe the scanner over him, seeking any evidence of explosives, bugging devices or any other treasonable baggage that might give them reason to prevent him from entering the double doors.

The scanner came up clean and Aaron walked forward as the other guard lowered his weapon and turned to the door's security panel. He accessed a code that neither Aaron or the other guard knew and the locks on the doors clicked. The guards stood back as the door opened automatically with a gentle hiss, and Aaron walked through.

The door hissed shut behind him and clicked as the locks sealed. Aaron walked across a narrow gap to where a second door, this one open, awaited him. He walked through the door and it too closed automatically behind him. His footfalls immediately sounded odd, muted and dull as though underwater, the hallmark of what was known as an anechoic chamber. Separated from the outside world by six inches of steel, followed by a six inch gap on all sides except for a supporting pillar beneath, and then six inches of steel outside that, the chamber insured that no electromagnetic energy could pass either in or out. Instead, all that led into the room was a fibre-optic cable that carried signals from twelve separate locations on a secure band.

Aaron moved to the centre of the room, in which was a large rectangular transparent container that looked remarkably like a coffin. Within were the skeletal remains of a humanoid form, one that Aaron had studied many times in the past few years. Normally interred in a secret warehouse deep in the New Mexico desert, the remains had been transported to the DIAC during the current crisis.

Other than the container the chamber contained no furniture, but for an array of speakers around the walls. Thus was the secrecy of Majestic Twelve maintained, along with the anonymity of its members and those who worked for them. Its greatest power was that not even its members knew who worked for them, nor those workers who they actually answered to. Voices were distorted, faces never seen, and the guards outside the room had no idea what they were actually guarding, only that nobody got in without the correct clearances.

'Gentleman,' Aaron announced his presence.

'Proceed.'

The voice was heavily digitised, completely unidentifiable. Aaron figured that it was possible at some extreme level for the fibre-optic audio feed to be hacked by some lone wolf computer genius and for somebody on the outside to listen in. However, all they would have to show for their efforts were a series of heavily digitised voices that any critic would immediately suggest had been created by the hacker themselves, the recording a fake.

'The operation is proceeding as planned,' Aaron said, knowing that his voice too would be masked by many layers of digital distortion. 'We have tracked our main target to an island in the South China Sea, and are attempting to obtain more information as we speak.'

'Do you have any idea of the item's location?'

'No, at this time we do not.'

The item, as it was collectively referred to amongst the members of Majestic Twelve, represented the furthering of a project that had been in motion for at least half a century. Aaron didn't know what the item was, and his gut told him that neither did the members of Majestic Twelve or indeed the target they were pursuing. The difficulty with maintaining such incredible security was ensuring each component of the team had enough information to conduct an effective investigation. At this time, Aaron knew only of events that had occurred in Israel some years before, and of the people involved in those events – the rest was withheld from him.

'And yet the target is in Japan?' said another distorted voice, its tone slightly different, enabling Aaron to differentiate between speakers.

'They are clearly following a trail,' Aaron replied. 'At this time we do not know what clues they are using to do so, but we do know that they have obtained help. The target is travelling in the company of Ethan Warner, a former United States Marine who was also involved in the original investigation in Israel.'

'We know of Warner,' said a third voice. *'His presence complicates matters. There are others who would like to obtain the item who are aware that Warner has been involved in government investigations in the past. Warner represents a clear target that they can follow.'*

'He also represents somebody who can do the work for us,' Aaron pointed out. 'I've read his file and he has extensive experience in this field. I maintain that our best course of action is to allow Warner to act on our behalf, allowing us to stay in the shadows, and then move in as soon as he obtains the item.'

'And risk him hiding it?' asked another voice. *'Ethan Warner no longer works for the government and may be driven by motivations other than patriotism.'*

'His past work with the Defense Intelligence Agency would suggest otherwise,' Aaron said carefully. 'However, he has an understandable mistrust of government as a result of some unfortunate incidences toward the end of his career. It is claimed in a number of official reports that he and his former partner business partner, Nicola Lopez, were targeted by the CIA for six months.'

'What happened in the past is irrelevant,' said a new voice. *'The present is all that matters. Warner represents an obstacle to our obtaining of the item. The wisest course of action is to intervene at the earliest possible opportunity and ensure that whatever happens, Ethan Warner does not beat us to it.'*

Aaron nodded, and then remembered that none of the men could see his movements.

'I have somebody on the inside, who will keep me informed,' he promised. 'But if the unthinkable should happen? If either Warner or Lucy Morgan should obtain what we seek, what should my orders be?'

A long silence pervaded the room, and Aaron wondered whether the methods required to maintain secrecy around Majestic Twelve were preventing them from forming a clear leadership. Then again, in this day and age of absolute responsibility, perhaps preventing a clear leadership also prevented any one individual from taking any blame for errors.

'Your orders are clear,' came the final reply from a voice just distinct enough for Aaron to be sure that he had never actually heard it speak before. *'The obtaining of the item is far more important than any other part of this operation. If its secrets were revealed to the public at large, we have no idea what the consequences could be. Such turmoil on a global scale would be unprecedented and our ability to contain it unknown. Lucy's work must continue to be suppressed at every level. Whatever it takes.'*

Aaron knew that he would hear no more from the men and that the implied action required was clear.

'Understood,' he replied. 'We know that they are in Japan. We'll bring them in before the week is out.'

Aaron heard a faint blip from the speakers as the connections were cut off. He looked down to his side at the remains in the container and suppressed a shiver of revulsion. Seven feet tall, and with a fused chest plate and massive cranium, the creature was both something human and something from another world, a horrifying chimera. That it was seven thousand years old made Aaron even more uncomfortable. Whatever it was, and whatever had happened, it was too important to be left in the hands of a former Marine and a low-level civilian scientist.

Aaron turned and walked to the door of the room. A pressure pad beneath his feet detected his presence and the door opened once again. Aaron strode out to the double doors and they also opened. He was scanned once more for recording devices by the two guards before he was finally allowed to walk back towards the elevator doors.

Aaron travelled back down to the third floor and was making his way towards his office when an agent hurried towards him with a panicked look on his face.

'We've lost them,' he reported.

'Tell me that's a joke,' Aaron snapped.

'We have two men dead,' the agent replied. 'The others were unable to keep track of Warner and Morgan after they made landfall. Whatever they found at the Yonaguni Monument they took with them.'

'Do you have any idea where they might be headed?'

'We have everybody working on it.'

Which, roughly translated, meant that nobody knew where they had gone. Aaron followed the agent back towards his office, pursued by the uncomfortable feeling that he was going to be forced to make unpleasant choices in the next few days to avoid having to be the bearer of bad news once again to Majestic Twelve.

XVI

Purot Tabing Dagat,
Philippines

'Are you sure you know what you're doing?'

The town of Purot was nestled against mountainous and forested hillsides that overlooked a perfect blue ocean that sparkled in the sunlight as Ethan stepped off a battered fishing trawler and onto a rickety jetty.

'Trust me, we're better off moving this way from now on,' Ethan replied to Lucy. 'If we can't be tracked, we can't be attacked.'

Ethan had spent two years working in the Philippines and Indonesia with his former fiancee, Joanna Defoe. Much of their work had involved exposing corruption in local governments, whereby major corporations were obtaining legal rights to land owned by fishermen in the wake of natural disasters such as tsunami. The government took control of the damaged land under the pretence of health and safety, but instead of returning the land to villagers instead allowed corporations to build new resorts and hotels in return for cash, the fishermen forced to move on and their livelihoods taken away from them. Once independent and proud villagers now laboured for miserable salaries as porters and servants in those massive hotels, their rights to ownership of the land revoked by the government.

As a result of his work, Ethan had made many friends among the ordinary people of the Philippines and it had taken only a phone call or two to arrange discrete passage for himself and Lucy aboard a small freighter bound from Japan to Sumatra. The local fishermen of the Philippines had been more than happy to pick him up as the freighter moved through the Sulu Sea, although Lucy had been most disconcerted about the nature of their transfer. Her hair was still wet from where she had hurled herself over the freighter's side with Ethan in hot pursuit, the captain turning a discreet blind eye to the exit.

'I'm not used all this creeping around,' she complained, 'or travelling this light.'

'That's probably why you got caught in Israel,' Ethan pointed out.

They both carried a single rucksack that contained their essential papers and passports, along with changes of clothes and what they could fit inside before they had hurried away from Japan. A waterproof cover protected the contents from their unscheduled dips in the ocean.

Ethan turned and paid the fishermen for their passage despite the old man's insistence that he take no money. Ethan was not an expert in local dialects, but he took the old man's shoulder firmly in his hand and squeezed it gently to convey the importance of the journey and the great assistance the fisherman had provided them with. The old man ceased his arguing and took Ethan's money with a toothy smile and a flurry of well wishes.

'Now what the hell do we do?' Lucy asked. 'Couldn't we have just taken the freighter all the way to Cambodia?'

Ethan set off along the jetty as he replied. 'We could have, if the freighter had been going to Cambodia. This is as close as we could get and frankly it's exactly where I want to be.'

'Do you have friends here?' Lucy asked as they walked into the small town and searched open fronted buildings that they passed.

'Kind of.'

'What's that supposed to mean?'

'Well, they were friends, and now they're sort of acquaintances.'

'*Sort of* acquaintances?' Lucy echoed uncomfortably. 'So what you mean is you know some people who don't like you?'

Ethan's jaw split in a wry grin. 'Now you're getting to know me.'

Ethan changed direction and began heading towards one of the open fronted buildings, outside which stood some thatch-weaved tables and chairs. There were few tourists at such a remote location, but Ethan wasn't looking particularly for tourists. He had already seen a man sitting outside, a fedora over his face as he reclined in a chair. He was wearing denim shorts over tanned legs, hiking boots and a loose white shirt unbuttoned to reveal a densely forested chest. On a table before him was a steaming cup of coffee, an unusual drink considering the heat and humidity.

Ethan came to stand in front of the man as Lucy moved alongside him.

'Let me guess, another heavy night at the bar?' Ethan asked.

The head turned slightly as the man heard the sound of Ethan's voice, and then one big hand moved lazily to lift the hat off his face as he squinted up at the new arrival. It looked as though the man had noticed something unpleasant tasting in his mouth as he screwed his face up and then replaced the hat.

'Piss off, Warner,' the man replied in a rough English accent.

Ethan grinned as he sat down in a seat opposite the man and gestured for Lucy to do likewise.

'That's no way to greet an old friend.'

'That's right,' the man replied from behind his hat.

'This is Lucy Morgan,' Ethan said as he gestured to Lucy.

The man still didn't remove the hat as he replied. 'Pleasure to meet you.'

'And this is?' Lucy asked.

'This,' Ethan introduced the man, 'is the finest bush pilot you'll ever meet. He goes by the name of Arnie Hackett.'

Arnie wearily lifted the battered fedora from his face and shook his head as he squinted at Ethan in the bright morning sunlight. 'You're a shameless scumbag, Warner. Every compliment that falls from your lips is tainted with the scent of treachery.'

'You're British,' Lucy observed.

'And I see you share Warner's keen detective skills,' Arnie replied with a raised eyebrow that appeared to cause his headache to increase in intensity. He let the hat drop back over his face and leaned back in his chair once more. 'If you'll excuse me, I have a great deal of sleeping to do.'

'I need to hire you for some work,' Ethan said.

'I'd rather sever my own testicles with a blunt coconut.'

'I can arrange that.'

Arnie removed the hat from his face once more with an irritated flourish and pointed at Warner. 'The last time I did any work for you I almost became a piece of bullet art. Trouble follows you around, sunshine.' Arnie glanced at Lucy. 'You'd do well to stay away from this guy.'

'I'd like to,' Lucy admitted, 'but we have a mutual interest that unfortunately means we're tied at the hip.'

'You have my condolences.'

'It's important, Arnie,' Ethan insisted. 'You'll be well paid.'

'I'd rather be poor, drunk and alive.'

'It's just a flight,' Ethan said.

Arnie chuckled and shook his head beneath his hat. 'It's never *just* a flight.'

'We need a ride to Cambodia, no questions asked.'

'There won't be any questions asked because there won't be any flight.'

'Arnie, Lucy is in trouble and we need your help.'

Arnie sighed mightily beneath his hat and finally tossed it irritably onto the table top before him. 'It's going to be one of those days. First a hefty bar bill, then a hangover and then you.'

'Third time lucky,' Ethan grinned.

Arnie leaned briskly forward on the table as he jabbed a finger at Ethan's face. 'You walked out of here with that damned fiancee of yours and left me with a ten thousand dollar bill for repairs to my last aircraft. What you paid me barely covered the cost.'

'You knew the risks,' Ethan said as he waved his hand dismissively through the air between them. 'Don't try and tell me you think you've been conned.'

'I had to forge new registrations in three different countries because of what you did,' Arnie snapped back. 'Those were major corporations you took on, and after you skipped the country they started focusing on everyone else who assisted you. I'm not just lucky to still be flying, I'm lucky to still be alive.'

'We just need to get out of here without being traced,' Lucy explained. 'I came here to do some archaeological digs and suddenly I find myself being shot at. The sooner we leave, the less chance there will be of somebody catching on to us.'

'Why don't I find that reassuring?'

'I promise you Arnie,' Ethan said, 'it's just a flight we need. If we take a charter of any other kind the paperwork will lead straight to us. This way, we are out of sight and out of mind.'

'Just how I'd like you to be,' Arnie mumbled as he looked at Lucy. 'It will be double the normal cost, by the hour not by the flight.'

'Standard plus fifty percent.'

'Do you want to fly or not?' Arnie peered at him.

'I'll pay,' Lucy insisted. 'I won't be able to draw the funds out without drawing attention to you, so I would have to find another way of paying you.'

'Don't give him any ideas,' Ethan warned her. 'You don't know where he's been.'

'I won't even be walking towards my aircraft without payment upfront, in full,' Arnie insisted.

'I've got a thousand bucks on me now,' Lucy said.

'You have?' Ethan asked

'You have?' Arnie echoed as he peered at the rucksack slung across her shoulder. 'Good, that will get you halfway across the ocean. I can drop you out there and you can swim the rest of the way.'

'How about you show us your aircraft before we start paying you money?' Ethan suggested. 'That last wreck you dragged us about in was on the verge of falling apart.'

'It was in perfect flying condition until you got on board,' Arnie protested as he grabbed his hat and dragged himself wearily to his feet. 'Bullet holes and aeroplanes don't generally go together.'

Ethan got up as Arnie turned away and dumped the fedora back onto his head. Lucy stood and joined him as they followed the pilot away from the bar toward a dusty path that led down between dense ranks of palm trees.

'He's got a hangover,' Lucy pointed out, 'and he looks like he hasn't washed in a week. You sure you want him to be flying us anywhere?'

'If you want to travel incognito then people like Arnie are your only bet,' Ethan advised. 'Besides, he's from the old school of flying, does everything by the seat of his pants. If we run into trouble it's a pilot like Arnie who'll be able to get us out of it.'

The path wound down from the town towards a large bay of deep azure water that sparkled in the sunlight, ringed by an immaculate crescent of white sand. Ranks of fishing boats, their sails stowed and their cargoes being unloaded, crowded the ramshackle jetties that lined one half of the beach. Ethan followed Arnie down onto the beach and past the jetties to where a large twin-engine aircraft floated on the water, moored to a low jetty.

Ethan was not an expert on aircraft but he could recognise some of the more classically shaped airframes and the one before him now was a fugitive from the golden age of aviation. The Consolidated PBY Catalina was painted white and looked like a giant dove as it sat on the immaculate blue surface of the bay. A veteran of World War II, the amphibious Catalina had a long hull with an equally wide wingspan atop it, two large piston engines set into the high wing either side of an angular glass cockpit with multiple windows. On her rear fuselage, two bulbous Perspex viewing bubbles that had once held cannons glinted in the sunlight, and a large side door was open with a ramp that extended down onto the jetty. Capable of landing both on the water and on land, the Catalina had been renowned during the war for its reliability, durability and extremely long range.

'Well, you can't have been doing too badly to have upgraded so well,' Ethan called to Arnie as he surveyed the Catalina.

'Are you kidding?' Arnie protested. 'I had this thing dragged from the jungles where it crashed about forty years ago and spent most of the rest of my money bring her up to flying condition, or what at least passes for flying condition in this corner of the world.'

As they approached the aircraft, a young Asian woman stepped out of the interior and into the bright sunlight. Wearing boots, shorts and a loose fitting shirt, her eyes were concealed behind aggressive black sunglasses and her long black hair tied in a ponytail behind her head. Arnie gestured towards the woman as they walked down onto the jetty.

'My wife, Yin Lee,' he introduced her. 'Yin is my co-pilot, or captain if I'm drunk enough.'

Yin directed a curt nod at Ethan and Lucy as she cleaned her hands on a rag, evidently having been busy fixing something inside the aircraft. Now that they were standing closer to the Catalina it became clear to Ethan that despite the white paint flaring in the sunlight the aircraft was very much a work in progress. Oil streaks stained the wings and many of the panels that had once been mangled in whatever crash had originally damaged the aircraft looked as though they had been beaten back into shape on Arnie's forehead.

'Are you sure this thing can make it all the way to Cambodia?'

'Are you sure you can pay me to *get* you all the way to Cambodia?' Arnie shot back.

'We'll get you the money,' Ethan promised, 'one way or the other. I suspect you'll need it to finish your repairs and turn this wreck into a proper aircraft. When can we leave?'

Arnie looked at Ethan and Lucy for a long moment, evidently weighing up the pros and cons of risking his quiet life for some extra cash. As if on cue, Lucy opened her bag and pulled out a thick wad of American dollars. Displaying a hitherto unsuspected mercenary streak, she grinned at Arnie with a glint in her eye.

'Should be enough for a decent paint job,' she suggested mildly.

Arnie winced, at himself rather than Ethan and Lucy, as he took the wad of cash and turned to call over his shoulder.

'Lock the repairs down and check the tanks,' he said to Yin. 'Let's get her ready for flight.'

XVII

'Repeat it to me, slowly.'

Yuri Polkov rested his chin on wiry hands that were interlocked before him as he looked up at the two men. Both of them were standing with their hands clasped before them, bulky muscles stretching the fabric of their cheap suits. Both were square headed, broad jawed former soldiers and if they'd had a brain cell between them they would not have known how to use it.

'They slipped away from us,' said the first man, Sergie, his head pulled down upon a thick neck as though he feared Yuri might throw something at it. 'We did not dare follow them too closely. We can't find them anywhere.'

Yuri looked away from the two men and out across the broad open water to where the islands of the Philippines crouched low against the horizon. The yacht upon which he sat was one of several owned by his company and berthed in Singapore, and had been diverted to the South China Sea as soon as Yuri's jet had lifted off from O'Hare International in the United States. He had fervently hoped to have laid his hands upon Lucy Morgan and have brought her to the yacht by now, but instead he found himself baffled as to how easily Morgan had escaped.

'She could not have known we had followed her here,' Yuri pointed out to the two men standing before him. 'And yet you managed to expose yourself and scare them away in the space of a single morning?'

The second man, Abram, shook his head. 'They were already on their toes. They dove a site off the coast of Yonaguni but came under attack from gunmen. They fled, then boarded a freighter headed south, so we took passage on another vessel sailing the same route. But when we docked, they were nowhere to be seen. Either they got off before they left, or they got off before they docked again. I don't know if something spooked them or not, but the guy who was with her looked sharp, like he might be ex-military.'

'They were covering their tracks,' Sergei added. 'One of them might have contacts in the area.'

Yuri clenched his interwoven fingers in frustration. 'Are you sure you saw them board this freighter?'

'One hundred per cent,' Abram nodded. 'The vessel is still docked less than twenty miles from us. There are a lot of small fishing vessels out here. If Morgan or her companion knew local people, they could have left the freighter and found passage ashore. Smugglers use the technique regularly.'

Yuri leaned back in his seat folded his hands in his lap as he looked at the thugs before him. Hired by his son Vladimir, who lacked his father's sense of decorum, both of the men were idiots for hire. If the man with Lucy Morgan was in any way familiar with either military life or the criminal underworld, he would have spotted Sergie and Abram for what they were from a hundred yards away. That could have been enough for him to take flight, especially if he was aware of the sensitive nature of what Lucy possessed.

'Dismissed,' Yuri uttered and waved the two men away.

Yuri listened to the sound of the water slapping against the yacht's hull as he thought hard. He was not the only person pursuing what Lucy possessed, of that much he could be sure, and now he wondered who else might have entered the game at such a crucial juncture. The value of Lucy's knowledge and of what she might find was almost incalculable, not something that could be measured in millions or even billions of dollars. It represented a paradigm shift in human nature, a turning point that would go down in history to be remembered for millennia, and Yuri Polkov was determined to be the man whose name would be associated with that turning point.

'Vladimir!'

Yuri's son strode out onto the deck from the yacht's interior and moved to sit opposite his father. 'Yes, papa?'

'I want you to dismiss all of your thugs. Send them back to the *Gulag* or wherever they came from.'

'But these men are loyal father, and will do…'

'They are buffoons!' Yuri snapped, barely able to contain his fury.

Vladimir ground his teeth in his jaw, and Yuri wondered what his son had promised those idiots of his in return for their work. Money? Drugs? More?

'We must seek to locate Lucy Morgan once more, and this time we will face them ourselves.'

'They're as slippery as eels,' Vladimir replied with visible distaste. 'They will see us coming and flee long before…'

'Ah, my son,' Yuri murmured, 'so often do you judge. Your distaste for Doctor Morgan is born of the fact that you were unable to persuade her to talk in Chicago, that your supposed charms had no effect on her. Your solution is anger and the threat of violence, yet that response is the very reason they flee us.'

'We should have grabbed her when we had the chance and made her talk!' Vladimir slammed his fist down on the table.

Yuri merely smiled and shook his head. 'No, my son. We should have taken her to dinner and shared her fascination and her enthusiasm, encouraged her to share her secrets by choice, not by force. Then, and only then, would we have disposed of her.'

Vladimir smiled tightly. 'It would help, papa, if I knew what we were looking for?'

Yuri sat back and exhaled softly as he glanced out over the oceans.

'We seek the answer to a question about human history that nobody has been able to explain,' he said. 'The ancient ancestors of modern humans had existed in a hunter-gatherer state for hundreds of thousands of years. But suddenly mankind began building cities, forming agriculture and advanced technologies, and that growth blossomed simultaneously in widely separated geographical areas, from the Indus Valley to the Levant to the Americas.'

Vladimir leaned back in his seat, clearly disinterested but humoring his father's obsession.

'Surely that's just natural growth after the end of the Ice Ages?'

'There had been some developments, simple dwellings, domestication of animals and rudimentary agriculture. But then the people of the Indus valley began the construction of major cities around five thousand years ago. At the same time the Sumerians began to build cities in Mesopotamia, between the Euphrates and Tigris Rivers. There is no record of gradual development or progression because the cities sprang up almost instantaneously. Both civilizations supposedly independently invented the wheel and a script called cuneiform. The Indus valley script, known as Dravidian, hasn't been fully deciphered even today.'

'How big were these cities?' Vladimir dutifully asked.

'They were home to up to forty thousand people,' Yuri replied. 'They had domestic bathrooms, flushing toilets and drains built using burnt and glazed bricks. They had public basins with two layers of bricks with gypsum mortar and sealed by a layer of bitumen. The Mesopotamians built docks, seaworthy vessels for trade and developed extensive irrigation comparable to modern agriculture. The Egyptians rose at about the same time. Egypt's first King, Menes, ruled some five thousand years ago in its capital Memphis, but the kingdom was ancient even then and had already developed its hieroglyphic script, again apparently out of nowhere.'

'And you don't think that this could have happened naturally?' Vladimir asked.

'It's possible,' Yuri conceded, 'but it should have taken longer than it did, and it seems that the ancients suddenly acquired knowledge sufficiently advanced to still be used today.'

The Babylonians, Yuri explained, were descended from the Sumerians, and their mathematics was written using a sexagesimal numeral system: one which has as its base the number sixty. From this derived the modern day usage of sixty seconds in a minute, sixty minutes in an hour and three hundred and sixty degrees in a circle.

'So what's the issue here?' Vladimir asked. 'If this is all well known, why are we chasing Doctor Morgan half way around the globe?'

'Because Lucy is on the trail of something far, far bigger,' Yuri explained. 'She may be on her way to finding fresh remains that contain not just proof of extra-terrestrial influence on both human development and even evolution, but that they left us a message in those remains.'

Vladimir stared at his father silently for a few moments. 'A message?'

'A message,' Yuri repeated, 'one that has long been rumoured through the religions of mankind, the divine word of gods. But we are now talking about real historical events that match the supposed myths of a thousand religions. We are familiar only with the religious histories that survive to this day, but they have existed in many differing forms for millennia. Oral tradition was the only way for ancient civilizations to record their past until scripts suddenly appeared simultaneously around the world: the Neolithic script, Indus script, Sumerian and Bronze Age phonetics all appear around six thousand years ago. In all of their creation myths, these early civilizations almost identically describe gods who came down from the skies and passed to them great knowledge.'

Vladimir himself had read of the legends of the Sumerians, Egyptians, Amerindians, and Japanese, describing such visitors as traveling in fiery chariots, flaming dragons or giant glowing birds that descended noisily from the sky. Encouraged by his father, he had been required to digest vast volumes of material that to him was being spouted by pseudo-scientists and fringe fanatics.

'That's crazy,' Vladimir said. 'Surely our ancestors would have recorded such things in greater detail?'

'What makes you think that they didn't?' Yuri asked. 'The fingerprints of such events are found in almost every religious text on Earth.'

'Where?' Vladimir uttered, baffled.

'Ezekiel speaks of such events in the Bible,' Yuri said. '"*And I looked, and, behold, a whirlwind came out of the north, a great cloud, and a fire infolding itself, and a brightness was about it, and out of the midst thereof as the color of amber, out of the midst of the fire. Also out of the midst thereof came the likeness of four living creatures, and this was their appearance: they had the likeness of a man.*"'

'I don't suppose that a passage in the Bible is going to alter the future of humanity, papa,' Vladimir smiled. 'We all know that it's not a historical document.'

'True, but real historical documents and evidence?' Yuri challenged. 'NASA launched its Voyager space probes in the seventies with solid gold discs aboard, bearing greetings in fifty-five different languages. One of those was ancient Sumerian. Why would they include a script that is several thousand years old and no longer used by humanity?'

Vladimir rubbed his temples in a sign of weariness and Yuri fought to control the outrage surging through his veins. His son thought him a fool. Yet Yuri's journey was the purest that he had ever conceived. For once, for the first time since his youth, Yuri was seeking a noble path, one that would secure his legacy for millennia to come. He would be ever remembered as the truth, the light, he who had heralded the new *enlightenment*.

'Our purpose is the eradication of blind faith,' Yuri said finally. 'The exposure of the remains that Lucy Morgan discovered in Israel or similar artifacts will finally bring about an awakening among the *so-called* faithful. How many thousands of years have human beings murdered each other, oppressed each other, hounded and tortured and exiled each other on the basis of nothing more than blind *faith*?'

Yuri spat the word as though it tasted foul. Vladimir raised an eyebrow.

'You can lead a horse to water…' he replied.

'Pah!' Yuri snorted. 'Faith is nothing. The very word describes an inability to trust one's own beliefs, that faith is required. Around the world, Islamic militants murder school children for wanting to go to school, mutilate female genitalia, punish women for being raped and burn the flags of other nations in the name of faith. The Catholic Church opposes contraception and abortion, spreading lies and disinformation to do so, hoards a fortune worth hundreds of billions of dollars while lamenting poverty, and has routinely avoided prosecuting members of the church who have abused children in their care. What part of all that is the light or the truth? Religion, in all of its guises, is the darkness my son, it is the evil that it claims to stand against. Lucy's work, properly exposed to the world, will crush religion in an instant.'

'Or strengthen it,' Vladimir murmured in reply. 'What do you want me to do next?'

'Have a little faith,' Yuri replied with a cold smile. 'Lucy Morgan first got into all of this while searching for alien remains in Israel, as you know. Israel is part of the Levant, the cradle of civilization. Twelve thousand years ago the Levant was a very different place, a lush and fertile land, and the Sumerian legends describe the origins of their civilization there through unusual means.'

'Like the Bible?' Vladimir asked.

'Sumerian legends tell of a god named Enki,' Yuri explained. 'Enki rose out of the Persian Gulf in what is described as a diving suit, and is depicted as an amphibious being. Many legends in the region also state unequivocally that Enki came from under the sea. Enki is the culture bearer for the Sumerian civilization, who is said to have brought them the arts of writing, agriculture and tool making.'

'And you think that perhaps Lucy, having seen the first set of remains she found taken away from above the United States government, is now hot on the trail of something else?'

'Yes,' Yuri replied, 'but more than that I think she was able to study the remains before the government took them away. I think that she discovered a link, a trail that may lead her to something more. The United States government presumably does not have that link or has not yet discovered it. Given Lucy Morgan's tenacity and expertise in her field it would not surprise me if she had got the jump on the government.'

Vladimir frowned. 'Then what do we have that makes this all worthwhile? Lucy Morgan may be following a *wild-goose-chase*, as I think the Americans call it?'

Yuri leaned down beneath his seat and lifted out what looked to Vladimir like a stone libation bowl, dirtied with age. Yuri set the bowl between them on the table.

'This, my son, is the Fuenta Magna. It was found in 1958 near Lake Titicaca in Bolivia. As you can see it features beautifully engraved anthropomorphic characters and zoological motifs characteristic of the local culture.'

'It's lovely,' Vladimir uttered without interest. 'Make your point, papa.'

'It is often referred to as the Rosetta Stone of the Americas, and is one of the most controversial artifacts in South America as it raises questions about whether there may have been a connection between the Sumerians and the ancient inhabitants of the Andes, located thousands of miles away. The reason for that are the inscriptions, here on the edge.'

Vladimir peered at the writing running around the rim of the bowl's interior. 'It looks a bit like hieroglyphics.'

'They're better than that,' Yuri replied, 'they're in two different scripts. One is the ancient language of Pukhara, a forerunner of the Tiahuanaco civilization native to Bolivia and Peru. The other is proto-Sumerian, a culture that rose in the fertile crescent thousands of miles away.'

Vladimir looked up at his father. 'Could the Sumerians have sailed across the oceans and met the Pukhara?'

'Their civilizations had only just managed to begin the rudimentary basics of agriculture, Vlad',' Yuri explained. 'Sailing around the globe wasn't just unlikely, but truly impossible.'

Vladimir shook his head. 'I still don't understand, papa. What if we do find these remains and we do understand the message that is within them? Why is it so important?'

Yuri sighed heavily as he realized the extent of his son's incapacity to understand the importance of what he was pursuing.

'Because it underlines more than just human evolution – it reveals the fact that our development as a species has been guided. *We had help*,' he explained. 'Because it brings to an end more than just religious conflict, the centuries and millennia of which have cost millions of lives for absolutely nothing. Because it could reveal not just that humanity's development has been guided at some point in our past by intelligences not of this Earth, but that life at large in the universe is, in fact, guided. That we are not merely the product of natural processes, but that the spread of life in the universe may have been deliberately engineered, perhaps even by species that have long since passed into extinction. We are not pursuing just remains in a dusty desert, my son, we are pursuing the final chapter in our understanding of how we came to be here. We are seeking the actual origin of life in our universe, the true nature of *God*.'

Vladimir stared at his father as the depth of their quest began to finally sink in. The younger man glanced up at the skies as though searching the heavens, and as he did so Yuri too looked skyward at the light cumulus clouds drifting through the endless blue.

It was then that he saw the tiny speck of an aircraft climbing away from the nearby islands, and heard the sound of the engines as they passed overhead. He shielded his eyes with one hand and easily identified the shape of the aircraft, its distinctive fuselage and wide straight wings bright white as they reflected the sunlight flaring off the clouds beneath them.

The Catalina was heading south west, right out over the ocean. Although there were isolated islands in that direction the aircraft was still climbing, already through five thousand feet. That put its likely destination is at least a hundred nautical miles away and probably more as it sought the colder high altitude air to cruise more efficiently.

Yuri lowered his hand as he watched the aircraft disappear above the cumulus clouds and spoke without looking at his son.

'Contact our IT experts and have them access local flight plans filed from the islands. Find out if there are any Catalina recorded as being due to depart the islands today.'

Vladimir craned his head back toward the faint noise of the passing aircraft.

'You think they're aboard?'

'If I were looking to leave the area in a hurry and did not want to be traced, I would charter a private aircraft and make sure the pilot had not filed a flight plan. If we don't find one...'

Vladimir nodded as he got out of his seat and hurried away.

XVIII

Cambodia

Ethan awoke to a nudge on his shoulder. He opened his eyes as the sound of the rumbling engines and rattling interior of the Catalina invaded the blissful oblivion of sleep, the cabin half in shadow but intersected by brilliant halos of gold and orange light blazing through the port windows. Yin, Arnie's co-pilot, satisfied herself that he was awake before she moved away across the interior of the Catalina's fuselage and shook Lucy Morgan's shoulder.

Ethan sat up on the cramped seat where he had managed to grab a few hours' sleep, his joints aching and his legs numb from the vibrations coming from the Catalina's twin engines. He stood up and moved to one of the bulbous viewing panels near the rear of the fuselage and crouched down to look out. Blankets of tattered stratus cloud glowed orange as they passed by several thousand feet below them, and through the gaps he could see a coastline even further below, the waves flecked with white rollers.

'Where are we?' Lucy asked as she sat up in a seat with a blanket wrapped over her shoulders.

'Crossing the Cambodian coast,' Ethan replied, 'assuming Arnie knows where the hell he's going.'

The flight had been a long one, and despite the Catalina's impressive range Arnie had been required to land at an airstrip he knew deep in the mountain wilderness of Java. Despite his reservations Ethan had been forced to allow Arnie to choose his own course, mainly because they were required to avoid any major airports to prevent their passage being recorded. Arnie's contacts, of whom Ethan guessed the less he knew the better, included a couple of airstrip operators who also had access to the *Avgas* which fuelled the Catalina's aged piston engines. Landing on a makeshift airstrip atop a mountain ridge almost entirely enshrouded in cloud had been an experience that neither Ethan nor Lucy would forget in a long time, but to Arnie and Yin it had all seemed like business as usual. Not for the first time, Ethan wondered what Arnie got up to with his aircraft when tourism season was off.

Ethan made his way to the cockpit and clambered into the co-pilot seat alongside Arnie, who was scrutinising a map and checking off their position via his instruments. A modern screen in the centre of the cockpit held a GPS display and Ethan could immediately orientate himself to their position.

'How much farther until we land?' he asked.

Without looking up, Arnie pointed at the GPS display which showed a large inland lake far from Cambodia's coast.

'That is Tonle Sap Lake, south of Angor Wat. It's the closest location I can take you to without attracting too much attention. The lake is massive so we'll land well south of the temples where all the tourists are. From there, you're on your own.'

'How much further north of the lake is this place that Lucy is looking for?'

'According to this map, it's a recently excavated temple site about twenty five miles north of Angkor Wat. There's not much in the way of public transport out there and you're pretty much on the edge of the mountains and jungles. Rather you than me.'

Ethan spotted Arnie's smug grin but he chose not to respond. He took one last look at the astonishing vista outside the cockpit windows, the broken cloud far below reaching the base of distant mountains that soared into the powder blue sky, their rugged peaks bathed in the dawn sunlight, and then he made his way back into the interior of the Catalina to see Lucy sipping from a mug of hot coffee.

Yin passed Ethan one of the mugs as she made her way forward, and he sat back down in his seat and gestured with a nod of his head towards the cockpit.

'Arnie reckons that we'll land within an hour on the lake to the south of Angor Wat. After that we've got to make our own way north.'

'That's fine,' Lucy replied. 'Believe me, out there nobody is going to find us unless we want them to.'

'And just where is it that we are going?'

Lucy pulled out a map from her bag and unfolded it until it showed a particular area of mountainous and jungle terrain in the north of Cambodia.

'Mahendraparvata is an ancient city of the Khmer Empire in Cambodia,' she explained as she moved to sit next to him. 'The location of the city has been known for years, but most of it remained concealed by forest until it was uncovered by a recent archaeological expedition. Apparently they had the use of advanced airborne laser scanning technology.'

'What's there that is so important to us?'

Lucy pulled out a photograph and showed it to Ethan. He instantly recognised the sun icon from the underwater temple at Yonaguni, a semi-circle of radiating lines of various lengths extending downward from the sun. But this one was located on a carved stone that looked as though it were atop a structure of some kind, the tops of the forest canopy visible surrounding the monument.

'And this was taken at Mahendraparvata,' he surmised.

'Just two years ago,' Lucy confirmed. 'The name Mahendraparvata means '*Mountain of the Great Indra'*. It is derived from Sanskrit words and is a reference to the sacred hill top site commonly known as 'Phnom Kulen' today where Jayavarman II was consecrated as the first king of the Khmer Empire in the year 802. The name is attested in inscriptions on the Angkor-area Ak Yum temple.'

'802 AD?' Ethan echoed. 'That's a lot more recent than the Yonaguni site engraving.'

'Much, but the inscription on the Yonaguni monument is the closest physically to this one, and I cannot believe that such a close location is not somehow connected, especially as the Yonaguni altar faces toward Mahendraparvata. My guess is that whoever carved the inscriptions at Yonaguni passed on the tradition to those who lived at Mahendraparvata, or they at least in some way inherited the religion or beliefs behind the inscription.'

'So, what are we going there for if we already have an image of the icon?'

'That's the interesting bit.'

'I had a feeling that you were going to say that.'

Lucy pulled out the image of the icon from the Yonaguni monument and held it alongside the one from Mahendraparvata. 'Notice anything?'

Ethan stared at the two images but he could see nothing particularly different about them.

'They look the same to me.'

'The lines, radiating outward from the sun,' Lucy encouraged.

As though sunlight had suddenly burst from the image, Ethan

spotted it.

'They're slightly different lengths,' he realized. The radiating lines varied from one icon to the next. 'But that could be an error on the part if the person who carved them.'

Lucy shook her head.

'These people built temples as big as modern buildings with no mortar, constructed from nothing but perfectly carved rocks. They built the temples at Angor Wat, complexes as big as modern towns, with ornate carvings from thousands of tonnes of rock. They knew how to carve an icon without screwing it up.'

'So what does it mean?'

Lucy smiled as she looked at the two images. 'It means that there could be a message inside the differences *between* the two images. It means that if we can decipher that message, we can follow the directions it gives us. These icons are trying to tell us something.'

Arnie walked down from the cockpit and jabbed a thumb over his shoulder.

'Yin's taking us in toward Angkor Wat. Your destination is about twenty-eight miles north of Siem Reap, below Phnom Kulen mountain in Siem Reap Province. You'll have a hell of a time getting there as there's nothing to follow but goat tracks; the area is filled with bogs and reed beds, and to cap it all, the entire zone is a landmine hazard from back in the heady days of the war here.'

If Arnie had thought that he might dissuade Lucy from going any further, he was about to be very disappointed.

'I know,' Lucy replied. 'An archaeological expedition to find Mahendraparvata was co-led by the University of Sydney and London's Archaeology and Development Foundation. The team uncovered dozens of temples out there and even figured out a reason why the civilization collapsed. I've studied their work extensively.'

Arnie nodded, turned and marched back toward the cockpit. 'Good to hear. 'We'll be landing in fifteen minutes.'

'He's not much interested in digging,' Ethan said to Lucy. 'What happened to the city? Why did it vanish?'

'Deforestation,' Lucy explained. 'Quite the warning shot across modern civilization's bows once again. Virtually every single ancient society collapsed because its population exceeded the ability of the land around it to support them. The city of Mahendraparvata declined as water management issues and a growing population starved the area of resources.'

'Bleak,' Ethan agreed. 'I still don't understand why we actually have to travel to this place.'

'Because the photograph I have here doesn't show any context,' Lucy explained. 'If we're going to decipher what this message is, then we need to know how they relate to each other. Sun worship was a common religion among ancient societies for obvious reasons. I'm hoping that if we can obtain some kind of orientation information from the site at Mahendraparvata, then it might tell us something about what the messages mean.'

'I don't know if we'll be able to get Arnie to stick around,' Ethan admitted as he glanced towards the cockpit.

'We'll have the advantage by then,' Lucy pointed out. 'Nobody knows that we're here, right?'

Ethan heard the engine note change and the Catalina began descending toward the ethereal layer of clouds below. He got up and made his way forward to the cockpit to see both Arnie and Yin engrossed in their navigation duties. The Catalina descended into the cloud, both pilots silently monitoring their instruments as the aircraft flew in zero visibility through the glowing orange and gold mist. Ethan and Lucy both got into seats just behind the cockpit door and strapped in as the aircraft bounced and gyrated in the turbulence billowing up from the land below.

It was almost ten minutes before the aircraft emerged from the cloud base and Ethan got his first glimpse of the Cambodian wilderness. A patchwork of rice fields, the ankle-deep water reflecting the warm broken sunlight in silvery patches, stretched before them between thickets of dense jungle draped in veils of mist. Ahead, vast mountain ranges vanished up into the clouds, and before them was a wide strip of water burnished by the sunrise as though some careless giant had laid an enormous copper sword across the plains.

'It's beautiful,' Lucy murmured, momentarily stunned by the scenery before them.

Arnie pointed to the water and gave Yin a thumbs up, his wife nodding as she guided the Catalina toward the water. Ever descending, the Catalina passed over the rice fields and Ethan could see women toiling far below, men guiding oxen through the fields, white specks against the green that stopped moving and probably were looking up at the aircraft as it passed overhead.

'There is no radar coverage out this far,' Arnie announced to Ethan. 'And none at all out over the ocean. Nobody could have tracked us here. We'll land at a remote spot on the lake and let you both out.'

Ethan nodded and reached across to pat his friend on the shoulder. 'I appreciate you doing this for us, Arnie.'

Arnie responded with a vague scowl but said nothing as he returned his attention to the instruments. Ethan and Lucy watched in silence as the Catalina flew out over the lake, just five hundred feet above the surface of the water as Yin expertly orientated the aircraft to face into the wind, while at the same time picking a landing spot far to the lake's western shore.

Ethan watched as Arnie wound the flaps down and drew the throttles back, the Catalina descending ever closer to the water and slowing until Yin finally flared the nose and the Catalina shuddered as its hull touched down on the water. The entire aircraft vibrated as it thundered along the surface of the lake and then gradually began to slow.

Yin guided the Catalina close to the shore as Arnie leaned one arm back across his seat and looked over his shoulder at them.

'No boat aboard, I'm afraid,' he reported with a smile that suggested anything but disappointment. 'And no jetties long enough for us to moor. You'll be taking a dip.'

Ethan pretended not to notice Lucy's angry glare as he made his way to the Catalina's side hatch and opened the latches before sliding the door back. Green water stared up at him, and he ensured that the waterproof bag inside his rucksack was sealed before he threw it over his shoulders and, without further hesitation, jumped into the deep green water.

Ethan kicked out for the shoreline as he heard Lucy jump from the aircraft and splash into the water behind him. It took less than a minute for him to find his feet on the floor of the lake and wade his way out to the shoreline, Lucy just a few yards behind and still wearing a scowl on her face.

She crawled from the water and stood up, drenched, with her hair hanging limp from its ponytail as she dragged clumps of reeds from her clothes. Behind her, Ethan heard the Catalina's engines clattering once again; the aircraft turned to face out across the lake and a faint spray of seawater hit Ethan in the face. Moments later, the engines rattled and spat before the propellers stopped turning and a deep silence descended upon the lake.

Arnie poked his head through the cockpit's top-hatch and called to them. 'Twenty-four hours. You don't show, we don't stay, go it?'

Before Ethan could reply, Arnie ducked back inside the cockpit and slammed the hatch shut.

'Well, that's that then,' Ethan said. 'Where to now?'

Lucy, her face now permanently set in an angry grimace, stormed past Ethan as she climbed towards a road that encircled the lake.

'North,' she snapped without elaborating. 'We get to the town at Siem Reap by the river, and we'll figure out the rest from there.'

Ethan suppressed a smile as he climbed after her toward the road.

XIX

Mahendraparvata, Cambodia

Ethan had ridden some fairly untrustworthy vehicles in his time, but the rickety and unstable motorcycle on which he now squatted pretty much ranked as the worst.

It had taken them two hours to trek around the outside of the lake's western edge before they had encountered a small village and a local farmer who was willing to take them in his truck to Angkor Wat. A further bumpy hour later, and with Lucy in no better mood, they had arrived close to the massive temples. Ethan had seen images of the complex a thousand times before, but even so he was overwhelmed by the sheer size of the ancient city complex. The presence of so much architecture seemed to soften Lucy's mood a little, although they had no time to stay and investigate the ruins.

The journey further north, upon the ancient motorcycles that Ethan had managed to hire from a local vendor in Angkor Wat, had taken a further three hours after a rest for lunch, and now the sun was descending to the west and the battered old engines clattered beneath them as they reached the slopes of Mount Kulen. The road was little more than a rutted clearing of dust and stones, and the motorcycle's suspension had frozen rigid many long decades before. Ethan led the way with Lucy grimly hanging on behind on a second motorcycle and apparently following the blue cloud of haze puffing from the exhaust of Ethan's machine.

It took another hour of riding over the rough road, cracked and pot-holed from monsoon rains, to reach what the locals called the *River of A Thousand Lingas*. A popular tourist destination that was silent at this time in the afternoon, its waterfalls crashed nearby and Ethan could see a massive 16th-century reclining gold Buddha carved out of solid rock at Preah Ang Thom.

They rode on along the ever-narrowing tracks, volcanic rocks and muddy courses, carefully crossing decrepit wooden bridges, and carving a path through jungle streams that whispered and sparkled in the sunlight beaming down through the canopy above.

At a clearing along the edge of what appeared to be a series of damp, clogged bogs downstream from the crashing waterfalls, Ethan and Lucy were forced to abandon the motorcycles. The tracks petered out into a narrow pass alternately rocky or filled with deep, slick mud from where the seasonal rains had thundered down the mountainsides. High reeds concealed large tracts of shallow water that led up to the edge of the mountain, itself enshrouded in jungle and broken cloud. The heat was intense, dense like a blanket against their skin, and the humidity high enough that sweat did not evaporate. Despite stocking up with water, Ethan recognised the dangers of dehydration in this harsh environment as he made his way between ever thickening banks of foliage with Lucy laboring a short distance behind.

Above them, the once blue sky had become overcast with sullen clouds and across the hillsides Ethan could hear the dull rumble of thunder as though giants were marching in pursuit of them as they entered the jungles.

'We're running out of daylight,' Ethan observed as he looked at his watch and hesitated on the hillside. 'Another couple of hours and we'll have to make camp.'

'We'll make camp at Mahendraparvata,' Lucy replied. 'The previous expedition cleared the area, remember? I don't fancy camping out in the middle of the jungle, especially if it's going to rain. I've spent enough time getting wet on this little expedition, so far.'

Lucy stomped past Ethan and plunged into the foliage. For a moment, Ethan was reminded of his time with Nicola Lopez in Idaho, where they had plunged through forests that were cold rather than hot, in pursuit of something not quite human. He shook the thought from his mind as he turned and followed Lucy, keeping a sharp lookout for snakes, spiders, and other unsavory creepy-crawlies that made the jungle their home.

During his time with the Marines, Ethan had spent months training in the jungles of the Philippines and had developed a healthy respect for the sheer volume of wildlife that called the tropical forests home. Virtually everything that lived there could harm humans in one way or another, from snakes large enough to eat a grown man to scorpions with venom nasty enough to result in the loss of limbs, and spiders the size of dinner plates with fangs an inch long. Once he had actually seen a millipede as long as his arm scuttling through the undergrowth of the jungle, and the sight had sent a shiver down his spine as he had imagined one of those awful creatures plunging into his sleeping bag.

Lucy forged on, either unaware or unafraid of the jungle's insectoid offerings as she marched in search of the legendary city. Ethan maintained pace with her as they hacked, slashed, and clambered their way through the dense undergrowth, Lucy holding a GPS locator in one hand to keep them on track amid the dense jungle. It was her concentration on the locator that made her almost walk into the huge stone statue that abruptly confronted them.

Ethan looked up in awe at the sight of an immense, larger-than-life-size stone elephant that seemed to loom out of the forest before them. Lucy checked their position and nodded in satisfaction.

'We're getting close,' she said. 'Mount Kulen and Phnom Kulen isn't far away now.'

Ethan glanced about at the jungle and began to pick out stone structures hidden amid the dense foliage, isolated pagodas, monasteries, and secluded shrines.

'Mahendraparvata means the *Mountain of Indra, King of the Gods*,' Lucy informed him as they climbed. 'They worshipped this place as where the most superior of all divine beings resided.'

'I thought that was supposed to be Buddha?' Ethan asked, more than aware of his ignorance in such things.

'Most of these temples were dedicated to Shiva, the supreme protector of the empire. Others were erected to worship Vishnu, an icon of universal order and harmony. Shiva had three eyes that represented the sun, the moon, and fire, carried a trident in his hand, and was borne upon an ox.'

'Sounds like a mixture of Satan, Neptune, and the Hydra,' Ethan observed.

'All the world's religions have a common origin in much older civilizations,' Lucy acknowledged. 'Want to know who first fed thousands of people with nothing more than what he held in his hands? It was Buddha, thousands of years before Christianity was conceived. Vishnu was part of a triune religion with Shiva and Krishna, just like the Father, Son, and Holy Ghost. Krishna was born on December 25th of a virgin in a stable, an evil king tried to kill him when he was an infant, he preached to the people and predicted he would die to attone for their sins, was killed and resurrected, and all of it long before Christianity.'

'Don't shout that in the street in the Bible Belt,' Ethan advised.

'It's the legends that pass down,' Lucy replied, apparently not hearing Ethan's last or not caring, 'their names and locations changed to fit new times and new beliefs. Vishnu also carried a chakra, club, and a ball representing the earth, and rode a *garuda* that was half a man and half an eagle, hardly Christian lore. The Khmers worshipped some pretty weird gods, but what if their representations of those gods was merely their way of explaining something for which they had no Earthly example or point of reference?'

Ethan could think of no sensible answer as he continued to follow Lucy up the hillside through the deep jungle. As they climbed they began to pass isolated, vine-covered towers, massive moss-covered statues of elephants and lions, and sprawling lingas or stone carvings lying at the bottom of the jungle streams. Ethan's unpracticed eye could detect ornate inscriptions on porticoes and stelae, variously standing or lying amid the undergrowth, but Lucy forged on past them with barely a second glance.

He realized, belatedly, that she was following a nearby small stream that flowed down the mountain into the distant Siem Reap River, and from there along canals to the massive barays and smaller ponds built to store water for the colossal city at Angkor Wat. Mount Kule, he guessed, was home to the quarries that provided the stone that built the immense complex and other temple cities, and the source of the water upon which the city's population had depended.

'The city was the birthplace of the Khmer Empire,' Lucy said as she climbed. 'It doesn't get much more important than that. If there's a place where our mysterious logo might carry a message of importance to us, this will be it.'

Ethan gazed at gigantic stone lions at Srah Damrei and a massive moss-covered elephant at Damrei Krap. There were the brick temples of O'Thma, Prasat Neak Ta, and Prasat Chrei, surrounded by long grass and grown over with shrubs. The sun was sinking low towards the mountain tops when Lucy finally broke out of the forest into an open clearing. Ethan stumbled out of the forest behind her and looked up, and he instantly froze as his jaw dropped and he surveyed the astonishing sight before him.

The lone tangerine-colored temple tower of Prasat O'Paong emerged from the jungle as though in defiance of nature itself, tufts of long grass sprouting between its stones. Carvings of Shiva, Vishnu, and a row of *rishis*, or wise men, adorned immense lichen-covered stones at its base, half concealed by the vines and creepers snaking down the temple's walls.

'This is it,' Lucy said as she produced her map and studied it closely. 'The temple itself is a little further along the plateau.'

Ethan followed Lucy past the elaborate construction and back into deep jungle. 'I thought you said this place had been excavated?'

'I did, but it was only discovered recently and its extent is unknown. It could cover literally hundreds of square acres and we haven't even begun to examine what it contains.'

Lucy followed her map intensely until she arrived at what looked like the foot of a giant pyramid. Ethan looked up to see a gigantic three-tiered temple, the entire construction smothered in twisted vines as though green water had poured in torrents down its slopes and been frozen in time.

'This is Prasat Rong Chen,' Lucy said as she pocketed her map and looked at the temple before them. 'We have to climb to the summit; the engraving is up there. There is a pedestal that once held the linga where a Brahman priest performed the rite that made Jayavarman II absolute monarch.'

Ethan peered up to where the tip of the temple towered above the canopy. 'Ladies first,' he grinned.

Lucy reached up and began climbing, moving from vine to vine as she scaled the side of the pyramid with Ethan close behind. In the intense heat and deep humidity, even climbing the moderately-sloped sides of the pyramid required immense effort, and they were both sweating heavily when they reached the top. Ethan clambered alongside Lucy onto a narrow plateau covered in thick moss and grass sprouting from between cracks in the stonework. Ahead, in the center of the plateau, was a stone pedestal that looked not dissimilar to the one they had seen atop the Yonaguni Monument, thousands of miles away in the South China Sea.

Lucy hurried across to the pedestal, which was also entombed in mosses and lichen. She began hunting around the edges of it, peeling off small bits of moss until she found what she was looking for. Ethan watched as she uncovered an engraved image of the sun with its radiating beams of light, once again pointing down toward the earth.

Lucy pulled a compass from her satchel and set it atop the pedestal before she stepped back and used her cell phone to take a picture.

Lucy flipped a finger across the screen of her cell phone and selected the picture she had just taken. Then, she used one of the phone's *apps* to place the image alongside the one taken at Yonaguni Island. She turned the phone in her hand and held it out to Ethan.

'They're both engraved with lines pointing in the same direction.'

Ethan observed the images carefully and shook his head. 'Not quite. The engraving at Yonaguni is facing slightly more to the south.'

Lucy nodded, her face enraptured with excitement as she waved the phone up and down. 'That's my point, don't you get it? If Mahandrapavarta's icon is to the south and is pointing slightly north, and the icon at Yonaguni is *vice-versa…?*'

Ethan pictured a mental image of the separate locations of where they were standing now in Cambodia and the site of the monument at Yonaguni. Placed on a map of the Earth, he quickly caught on to what Lucy was getting out.

'They might be referencing a single location.'

'Not *might be*,' Lucy emphasized. 'Look at the longest line on each image of the sun beams.'

She held the phone out to him once more and Ethan observed that in both cases the longest line from each image of the sun was in a slightly different location.

'They're markers,' Ethan acknowledged. 'They're not pointing to each other, they're both pointing to *something else*.'

Lucy whirled and set her phone down on the pedestal as she pulled from her satchel a map of the world and unfolded it alongside the images. Using a compass, she measured the angle at which the longest line of the engraving on the pedestal was pointed, and then plotted a line from the position of the Cambodian temple on the map toward the east across the Pacific. Then, she drew a second line, this time from the location of the Yonaguni temple toward the east.

Lucy stood up and looked at the lines she had drawn on the map. Ethan moved to stand alongside her and his eyes travelled across the lines to where they intersected at a spot on the opposite side of the Pacific Ocean.

'Peru,' he said. 'How on earth would a civilization so old know anything about locations on the far side of the Pacific Ocean?'

'Exactly,' Lucy replied. 'More to the point, how would they know about this particular location?'

'What's special about it?' Ethan asked.

'It's a place called Nazca,' Lucy replied. 'It's the site of the famous Nazca Lines, enormous hieroglyphs in the desert that are only visible from the air. The civilization that created them is immensely ancient and had no access to aircraft. They could not see their own work in the desert, so why did they create it?'

Ethan shook his head. 'I have no idea.' He looked up at the darkening sky above. 'We need to get out of here while we still can.'

'You're damned right,' Lucy said as she packed her materials away into her satchel. 'We've got a flight to catch, if we're going to figure out what's over there.'

'It's going to be tough to get to Peru from here and not be observed or tracked.'

'We're not going to Peru.'

Ethan shot her confused look as she began descending the side of the pyramid, but he obediently followed her down toward the darkening jungle below. They reached the forest floor and Ethan jumped down alongside Lucy and was about to ask what she meant when he heard the click of multiple rifles, the distinctive sound of AK-47s as from the jungle around them emerged a group of men.

'That's far enough,' one of them said as he aimed at Ethan.

XX

Ethan turned slowly and raised his hands as he looked at the nearest man aiming an AK-47 at him. He was clearly a native, his English broken and heavily accented. The teeth in his mouth were stained and gapped as he gestured to Lucy with the barrel of the rifle.

'Get her down from there,' he ordered.

Lucy jumped down from the pyramid. 'You have no right to prevent us from climbing it,' she protested.

'I've got all the right I need,' the man replied as he tapped his rifle's barrel. 'Leave this place now, or you'll become a permanent part of it.'

The men had closed in around them and Ethan counted twelve, eight of them armed with the ubiquitous rifles, the other four apparently onlookers but carrying various weapons such as clubs or machetes. One of them carried a shuttered lantern that he opened to illuminate the gloomy forest in a dull yellow glow. The man set the lantern down beside the foot of the temple. Ethan knew they were far too distant from any local habitation to have merely stumbled across the temple, Ethan, or Lucy. He could only assume that they been hired to protect the temple.

'Who are you working for?' Ethan asked.

'We are working for nobody. We are simply protecting the heritage of our country from grave robbers.'

'We are not grave robbers!' Lucy snapped.

Ethan looked at the clothes the man was wearing, cheap slacks and a loose shirt that had seen better days. His hair was unkempt, his feet shoved into tattered sandals. He was holding the rifle in the grip of one hand without the shoulder strap in place and it wavered here and there, undirected and sloppy. A villager elder, Ethan surmised, probably quite poor and certainly not a soldier of any kind. And yet the weapon was perfectly clean, professionally maintained or perhaps even brand new.

'Whoever paid you put those words in your mouth,' Ethan replied to him. 'They provided you with the weapons. Whatever they promised you, they won't deliver.'

'We are working for nobody. We are simply protecting the heritage of our country from grave robbers,' the man repeated in a monotone voice.

Ethan glanced briefly at the other men in the crowd. They were all dressed in a similar manner to the elder and also holding their weapons at odd angles and with an insufficient grip to prevent the kickback that would drive the barrels upward into the air should they choose to fire. Ethan took a pace towards their leader and lowered his hands slightly as he puts a reasonable expression on his face.

'Whatever they paid you, I'll double,' Ethan promised.

The village elder's expression altered as he began to consider his options. Ethan moved a little closer. 'We're not grave robbers, we merely came here to study the engravings on the walls of the temple. You can even join us, if you wish to ensure that we do not take anything from the temple with us.'

The old man regarded Ethan for a long moment, his eyes drifting up and down as he assessed the man before him, and then as Ethan had hoped he looked over his shoulder for support from his colleagues. As soon as his head was turned Ethan lunged forwards and grabbed the rifle stock with his left hand as he slammed his right forearm across the elder's chest.

The rifle easily was snatched away from the older man's weak grip, and Ethan turned the AK-47 and pressed it against the man's chest. The entire movement had taken no more than two seconds and none of the men around them had either had time to fire or indeed showed any intent of doing so.

Ethan looked to the elder, whose face had crumbled in panic as he raised his hands either side of his head and began gabbling in his native tongue, beging for his life. Ethan grabbed his collar to silence him and then looked at the watching villagers, none of whom could shoot without risking hitting the old man.

'Who hired you?' Ethan demanded.

'Foreigner,' the old man replied hurriedly. 'Lots of money. They said to come out here and stop you both.'

'Us?' Lucy demanded. 'Specifically us?'

'Yes, you, the American man and woman.'

Ethan and Lucy exchanged a surprise glance. 'How the hell would they know we were coming here?'

'Did you get a name?' Ethan demanded of the elder.

The man shook his head. 'No, no name, but she was American woman, very friendly.'

'A woman?' Ethan asked in surprise.

He turned to look at Lucy, who in response appeared nonplussed until suddenly a realization dawned on her features. 'When I was in Chicago, I couldn't find you so I went to...'

Before Ethan could apply a familiar voice spoke from somewhere behind him in the tree line.

'Me.'

Ethan and Lucy turned as from out of the jungle strode a woman with a black ponytail, khaki shorts and hiking boots. Her dark eyes flashed exotically, a pistol held lightly in one hand down by her thigh. She looked like a cross between Michelle Rodriguez and Lara Croft.

'Nicola,' Ethan uttered in surprise.

Lopez gestured to the old man with a nod of her head. 'Let him go and give him back his rifle before he has a heart attack.'

There was a determined tone in her voice that Ethan had often heard, one that had not really ever been directed at him but at the bail-jumpers they had often arrested on the streets of Chicago. Ethan turned the rifle over in his hands as he released the elder, and shoved the weapon into his chest.

'My apologies, Tak,' Lopez said to the old man. 'I hope your payment was sufficient?'

'Yes, yes,' Tak replied enthusiastically as he backed away from Ethan.

'I should have known,' Ethan said as he turned to face his former partner. 'Either you followed us or you suddenly decided on a weekend break in Cambodia.'

'Who'd have thought it?' Lopez replied with a slight shrug.

'You followed me,' Lucy said as though betrayed. 'You've been following us the whole time?'

Lopez shot Lucy a pitying look. 'And you're surprised? You've been wandering around with one of the world's most controversial fossils in your pocket for years. Do you have any idea how much money it's worth?'

'You always did have a mercenary streak in you,' Ethan observed. 'What's your plan? Take the remains and sell them to the highest bidder?'

'Best bet,' Lopez replied. 'None of the governments involved in this want Lucy's discovery to be public knowledge because of the panic they fear it will spread. That means no country can lay claim to the remains without exposing them, which also means that they can be put up for sale on the black market without fear of arrest for smuggling.'

'And there was I thinking you were the honorable one of the pair,' Lucy uttered in disgust.

'Thanks very much,' Ethan replied, somewhat dismayed.

'Business is down,' Lopez said by way of an explanation. 'A girl's got to do what a girl's got to do, especially after this asshole decided to leave me carrying the can while he went off wandering around the world to find himself.'

'I took a sabbatical,' Ethan replied.

'You took off!' Lopez shot back as she jabbed her pistol in Ethan's direction. 'You left me to get by on my own! Do you have any idea how many hours I have to work just to make ends meet?!'

'Can we do this another time, please?' Lucy intervened as she moved between them.

Lopez nodded. 'That's fine. I'll just take the measurements you made and be on my way, thanks.'

'Over my dead body,' Lucy snarled.

'Don't tempt me.'

Ethan shook his head. 'You're no cold-blooded killer, Lopez. What's this really all about?'

'You don't get to ask,' Lopez shot back at him. 'By your own choice it's none of your business, now.'

Lopez took a single place and jabbed the pistol into Lucy's ribs. 'Your measurements, or I'll ventilate you right here and right now.'

Not used to having a pistol stuck in her side, Lucy hesitated no longer as her anger vanished and she reached into her satchel and produced a rubbing of the carving she had made and the measurements she had made alongside it. Lopez snatched it from her and tucked it into the pocket of her shorts.

'Nice doing business with you all,' Lopez flashed a bright smile as she backed away.

Ethan watched her go, certain that he would be able to track her and find out where she went. Lucy had said that they would not be going to Peru, and now he desperately wanted to know what she meant and whether Lopez would be heading in the wrong direction. He made no effort to stop her, and she was almost at the tree line when a hand reached out and grabbed Lopez from behind and rammed a pistol up under her ribs.

'I'll take that.'

Ethan's eyes widened in amazement as from the darkening tree line half a dozen camouflaged troops emerged, their weapons trained on Ethan and the villagers behind them. They spread out quickly, taking up firing positions, M-16 rifles held firmly in professional grips. Ethan heard the villagers behind him exchange a flurry of nervous whispers.

'This is supposed to be one of the remotest sites on the planet,' Lucy gasped in dismay. 'Where the hell are all these people coming from?'

Ethan said nothing as the armed soldier reached down to Lopez's shorts and slid his hand inside the pocket to retrieve the notes that Lopez had stolen. The soldier's hand lingered for a few seconds longer than it needed to in her shorts as he spoke softly in her ear.

'Nice doing business with you,' he smiled.

Lopez scowled at him but said nothing as the soldier pocketed the paperwork and backed away from her. Ethan watched in silence, his hands still in the air as the troops surveyed the natives before them.

'My apologies,' the leader of the small platoon said in an American accent. 'But my orders are to ensure that nobody leaves this place alive.'

Ethan glanced sideways at Tak, the old man understanding every word the American soldiers said and like Ethan knowing that these were no ordinary soldiers but most likely CIA paramilitary troops or some other covert unit. He saw a look of fresh resolve appear on the old man's face and his wiry old finger curl across the trigger of the AK-47 he still held in his hands.

'And who'd you take orders from?' Ethan asked the soldier.

'You'll never need to know.'

Ethan jerked sideways and lifted a boot to bring it crashing down on the lantern glowing beside the temple. His boot smashed through the glass and instantly the jungle plunged into near darkness.

In the dim illumination from the darkening sky above, Ethan saw the American soldier lift his rifle to aim at them, and in an instant Tak let out an enraged cry and opened fire. The bright muzzle flash of the AK-

47 illuminated the jungle clearing with jagged flashes of light as its clattering fire rattled out.

Ethan hurled himself at Lucy and threw them both down onto the jungle floor as the rest of the villagers likewise opened fire on the American soldiers, who leaped for cover and returned fire. Ethan saw Lopez break away from her captor and sprint into the darkened jungle

Tak got off half a dozen rounds before he was struck by two American bullets high in the chest and hurled onto his back. The villagers kept firing, their disorganized and chaotic attack sending bullets flying both toward the American soldiers and high into the jungle canopy. Ethan grabbed Lucy's hand as he got to his feet and dashed into cover behind the temple.

'Let's get out of here!' he hissed.

Lucy followed him as fast as she dared through the dense jungle, and turned south around the back of the temple and plunged down the hillside. The crackling gunfire ceased and Ethan heard American voices yelling in the darkness behind him. The villagers would have been completely outclassed by the American troops and had either been annihilated or were fleeing into the jungle, but Ethan felt certain the Americans would not pursue them, and instead return their attention to him and Lucy.

'The shooting stopped,' Lucy whispered as they ran.

'Only temporarily,' Ethan insisted. 'Keep moving!'

XXI

Ethan hurtled down the hillside with Lucy hot on his heels, and behind them he could hear the Americans plunging through the undergrowth in pursuit. He recalled that they were wearing jungle gear and were laden down with water, webbing, and weapons. Ethan and Lucy were encumbered only by their light rucksacks, but the soldiers' fitness would likely even the odds.

Ethan began to slow slightly as they descended the mountain side, knowing that even the slightest injury would render them unable to escape. Lucy closed in behind him as they ran, aiming for the open tracks used by the motorcyclists and tourists to reach the waterfalls below. Both of their mopeds were parked down there, and although Ethan was certain that such battered old vehicles would not have been stolen, he could not be sure that the headlights worked.

A shot cracked out behind him and he flinched instinctively as the round smacked into a tree to his right.

'Get in front of me,' Ethan insisted as he moved to the right and allowed Lucy to pass him.

Another shot impacted close beside Ethan's head and sprayed him with wood chips as he ducked down and followed Lucy through the darkness. Moments later, she found the path that they had followed up the hillside, a slightly clearer passage through the forest toward the waterfalls below. Lucy picked up the pace as she regained her confidence on the narrow trail, and Ethan likewise accelerated as they raced through the darkness.

'Why the hell are Americans shooting at us?'

'I don't know and stop talking, they can hear us!'

Ethan heard the crashing of the waterfall as they approached it, a useful feature that would help disguise the sound of their movement. He quickly began considering his options, wondering whether it might be better to hunker down in the jungle and hope the American soldiers would pass them by rather than continuing their headlong flight down the hillside. The solution came as another shot cracked out and narrowly passed between Lucy and Ethan in the darkness. Two highly accurate shots in an otherwise pitch black forest could mean only one thing: the platoon sharpshooter was using night-vision to pick them out as they ran.

Ethan began dodging left and right on the path in an attempt to spoil the sharpshooter's aim, but two more shots cracked out and hit the path almost at his feet. He heard Lucy cry out as though she had been hit as she stumbled, but she picked herself up and kept moving.

A voice bellowed out from the jungle behind them.

'Another step and we'll shoot to kill!'

'Keep moving!' Ethan growled ahead to Lucy, knowing that the soldiers were intent on killing them anyway.

The path plunged away down the hillside a short distance ahead and circled the elephant pool, the water just visible plunging into its limpid depths. Lucy ran down to the edge of the pool and circled it with Ethan close behind. They were almost at the edge of the tree line when a fresh shot cracked out and hit the path directly in front of them. Lucy skittered to a halt and Ethan almost collided with her as he turned and saw the shape of the sharpshooter silhouetted against the dimly illuminated sky at the top of the falls, his weapon aimed down at them.

Ethan spotted a bright red light appear on his chest, quivering slightly with the sharpshooter's heartbeat as he kept the weapon aimed directly at Ethan's body.

'That's as far as you go!' the sharpshooter called over the crashing sound of the waterfall.

Ethan desperately tried to think of a way out of the situation, but he knew that if he so much as flinched the soldier would shoot him dead. He could just about hear the sounds of the rest of the American platoon advancing behind the sharpshooter, and he realized that there was nowhere to go.

The remaining soldiers broke from the tree line and appeared alongside the sharpshooter above them. They had been reduced from eight men to six, evidently some of the villagers' bullets having found their mark, but that now meant the soldiers' blood would be up and there would be no quarter given to either Ethan or Lucy. In the middle of dense jungle and at night, there would be no witnesses to whatever was about to happen.

The leader of the American platoon directed a mock salute at Ethan as he nodded to the sharpshooter.

'Take them down.'

Ethan prepare to leap to one side in a desperate attempt to protect his own life when suddenly the sniper cried out and his weapon snapped up in the air and fired high, his face illuminated in a bright green light, a narrow beam streaking from the nearby forest to hit the soldier's face and blind him through his night vision goggles.

Ethan turned and without hesitation grabbed Lucy and sprinted for the tree line behind them. A crescendo of shots hammered the elephant pool as the remainder of the soldiers attempted to hit them without the benefit of night-vision. The bullets smacked into the path behind them and Ethan heard ricochets hit the trees nearby, and with a gasp of relief they plunged into the tree line and the dense cover of the undergrowth.

'Keep moving,' Ethan whispered harshly. 'We've got to make it to the motorcycles.'

To his right Ethan heard another figure crashing through the undergrowth, and they burst out onto the path directly behind him.

'You're welcome,' Lopez whispered as she ran behind him.

'Who the hell are they?' Ethan demanded as they ran.

'No idea. They must've followed you here.'

'Nobody knew we were coming,' Lucy snapped back from somewhere ahead. 'They just as likely followed *you*!'

'We'll deal with it later,' Ethan cut them both off. 'Nice work with the laser pen,' he added as they descended towards the main access road to the mountain.

Lucy reached the road first, Ethan behind as he spotted the motorcycles they had abandoned. He rushed over to them as Lopez broke from the tree line behind and hurried across.

'They haven't been tampered with,' Ethan said as he examined the engines.

'There would have been a lot of motorcycles here when they arrived during daylight,' Lopez guessed.

Lucy clambered onto a motorbike and made to use the kick start. Ethan grabbed her ankle to prevent her from starting the engine.

'No, push off and use the motorcycle as a pushbike. We need to get away as quietly as possible or they'll be onto us. They must have their own transport to have reached us so fast.'

Lucy nodded and pushed away toward the path that descended down the hillside, the moped accelerating slowly away. Ethan climbed aboard his own and then looked at Lopez.

'Get on.'

Lopez didn't hesitate to jump on the pillion seat, and Ethan pushed away as hard as he could with his feet. The scooter reluctantly began to move even as he heard voices shouting from behind them as the troops closed in on their position. The scooter gradually gathered speed and began to roll down the hillside, only the faint crunch of the tires on gravel giving their position away.

'Well, I didn't see us doing this so soon,' Lopez said to Ethan in a soft whisper.

'Don't get overexcited,' Ethan replied. 'If you hadn't pulled that stunt with the laser pen, I would have left you on this mountain.'

Ethan could sense the smile on Lopez's face in her tone as she replied.

'You and I both know you would never have done that.'

Ethan did not reply as he followed Lucy's moped down the hillside. They were gathering speed and the breeze was a welcome relief from the overwhelming humidity and heat. Through gaps in the forest below them he could see the flickering lights of Siem Reap in the distance, close enough that they would be able to hide among the crowds, if they could get off the hillside unobserved.

Then, above the crunching of their tires on the dusty road, Ethan heard a new sound growing in intensity. He turned his head as he tried to make out what it was, and quickly he was able to distinguish the rhythmic *thump-thump-thump* of rotor blades beating the air.

'Helicopter!' he yelled ahead to Lucy. 'They're sending one in! Use your engine now!'

Ethan clicked the moped into second gear with the clutch held closed, reached down to turn the ignition key on, and then dumped the clutch. The little motorbike growled into life as the back tire briefly locked up on the dusty path and then bit once more. Ahead, he heard a cough and a splutter from Lucy's machine, and then it whined into life, a cloud of blue smoke billowing from its exhaust.

Ethan twisted the throttle wide open and the little motorbike surged away. Flocks of birds vaulted in panic from the trees in thick clouds of wings that streaked across the dark sky above, and Ethan saw Lucy's bike quiver as its engine caught and she accelerated away.

'Watch out for the trees!'

Lucy swerved her motorbike further out toward the edge of the track, the plunging hillside vanishing to their right into a dense canopy of trees.

Lopez shouted out to Ethan above the wailing noise of the engine. 'They're coming in from the right!'

Ethan nodded as he glanced out over the jungle and saw the helicopter sweeping in, a black silhouette against the clouds. The thundering rotors vibrated through the motorcycle beneath him as a brilliant halo of light suddenly exploded into life and illuminated the dusty track as though it were daylight.

The track weaved between the dense jungle, switching back on itself every few hundred yards as it descended the mountain's precipitous sides. Ethan kicked the motorbike up a gear, swept it through a long right-hand bend that followed the epic curve of the mountainside as they plunged beneath a canopy of trees, then braked hard and switched back in pursuit of Lucy. Warm droplets of water showered down upon them as the heavens opened above, and Lopez's grip on Ethan's waist tightened as the bike leaned out almost to the edge of the drop. Ethan leaned into the turn as the rear wheel skipped and spun on the damp track. He twisted the handlebars to the right, counter-steering against the rear wheel's grip, and let it spin freely as he broadsided around the rest of the turn. He then opened the throttle wide, the bike coming upright as the track straightened out toward the next switchback, descending toward the lowlands of Siem Reap.

Within moments, Ethan's shirt was drenched with water, his hair and eyes thick and heavy with moisture as the rainfall began hammering the road ahead. He could already see Lucy slowing down, her motorcycle slipping and sliding, the dust having turned into slick mud as she tried to maintain control in the blinding light and heavy rain.

A deafening crack burst the air around them as the helicopter opened fire, and in an instant he saw a spray of woodchips burst from the foliage as a tree plunged out of the forest ahead, thick branches rushing down toward the track. Lucy swerved to avoid the falling tree and her motorcycle twisted sideways as it fought for grip.

'Get down!'

Ethan swerved out and they plunged beneath the falling tree, damp leaves and fronds slapping across them as the bike raced beneath the plunging trunk and out the other side. The motorbike weaved and kicked, and Ethan struggled to keep it upright as they shot out into clear air.

Ethan closed the throttle to give the bike a chance to steady itself and yelled over his shoulder to Lopez.

'Use the pen again!'

Lopez reached into her pocket and retrieved the laser pen as a fresh salvo of shots hammered the track through the rain. The torrential downpour was forcing the pilot of the helicopter to fly at an awkward angle along the mountainside to fight the brisk winds and keep the track beneath him in sight, the cockpit almost facing the motorcycles as armed men fired from an open hatch on the helicopter's port fuselage.

Lopez activated the pen and aimed it at the cockpit, and suddenly the helicopter jerked violently to the right and veered away from the hillside as the pilot was blinded by the laser beam.

The troops aboard the helicopter fired again at the motorcycles, and Ethan heard the front tire squeal as something struck it and it buckled under the blow. The tires lost their grip as all balance was ripped from Ethan's hands and they toppled toward the dusty surface of the track racing past beneath them.

'Jump!'

Lopez hurled herself clear of the saddle, her arms out before her as she crashed down. Ethan hurled himself off and the breath was smashed from his lungs as he rolled across the muddy earth with his arms wrapped around his head. The motorbike bounced past him on its side, the metal engine scraping with a high-pitched squeal across the rugged terrain.

Ethan rolled to a stop and peered through eyes filled with damp grit. The helicopter had swung out across the valley, its rotors thundering as its pilot gave himself a chance to recover his eyesight from Lopez's laser pen. It was almost invisible through the blustering wind and rain, the cloud base above lowering with every passing minute.

Ethan heard the sound of an approaching engine and saw Lucy's scooter ride back up the hillside to join them.

'What happened?!' she yelled.

Ethan glanced at his motorbike's ruined front wheel. 'Lucky hit; they took out the wheel!'

Ethan knew that there was no way that they could all ride on Lucy's motorbike. He got to his feet as Lopez brushed herself down.

'We should make for the treeline down there,' Lopez pointed to a lower track than the one they were on.

Ethan was about to agree with her when he heard the sound of the helicopter's engine begin to rise again as it swung back toward them. He peered down the steep hillside and then along the track, where it doubled back on itself and descended below them. An idea sprang into his mind.

'Lopez, get on Lucy's bike and ride down there as fast as you can! When you get there, lay the bike down and make as though you're just getting up!'

'What the hell for?'

'Just do it!'

Lopez did not hesitate a moment longer. She jumped on the back of Lucy's motorbike and they rode away.

Ethan grabbed the damaged bike and hauled it upright. The front tire was lost, ragged rubber hanging on to the rim. He dragged it back into the treeline through the pouring rain as he heard the helicopter thundering back toward them, the searchlight emerging from the gloomy sky. He pulled the bike back and clambered onto the seat, then kicked down on the starter. The engine rattled wearily into life beneath him as fat drops of warm rain splattered onto his head from the dense canopy above.

He saw the helicopter swing out of the falling veils of rain and pull in alongside the cliff face, and then begin to descend as its searchlight picked out where Lucy and Lopez were on the track below. Blinded by Lopez's laser pen and out of sight through the clouds, the pilot had lost track of exactly where he had last seen the two motorcycles. The wind and rain gusted into Ethan's face as the helicopter's rotor blades thundered through the sky and he saw the shape of two soldiers in the back aiming their weapons down at the track below. The helicopter was within twenty yards of the cliff face and struggling to stay in position against the winds as it descended out of sight below the cliff edge.

Ethan twisted the throttle and the motorbike hurtled out of the treeline toward the edge of the track, the front wheel rattling on its rims across the rain splattered ground. He saw the top of the helicopter's rotors and the two soldiers leaning out of the side and aiming down at Lopez and Lucy, and then he hurled himself out of the saddle as the plunging abyss yawned open before him.

Ethan landed hard and grasped for a handhold as the motorbike flew off the edge of the cliff. Its engine noise faded instantly as it revolved lazily toward the helicopter below, and one of the gunners spotted its motion at the last instant.

Ethan grabbed hold of a dense clump of foliage and looked over his shoulder to see the man open his mouth to bellow a warning to the pilot, just before the motorcycle smashed into the helicopter's spinning rotors and they flew apart in a lethal cloud of blades and debris.

Ethan covered his head with his free hand and pulled his legs up protectively as shrapnel hammered the cliff face. The helicopter's engines shrieked as the vehicle banked away out of control and spun a complete revolution before it smashed down into the trees further down the hillside and the engines split open and ignited their fuel.

The helicopter exploded in a brilliant fireball that blossomed like a brief sunrise against the darkened forest below before it was swallowed by black smoke and the flames were quenched by the torrential downpour. Ethan managed to maintain his grip on the foliage as he dragged himself back up onto the track, and then turned and looked down below.

Lucy and Lopez huddled together on the track beside the remaining scooter, and he wasted no time in jogging down the track and doubling back to where they were. He saw Lopez look up at him and give him a thumbs-up as she called out in the rain.

'Nice to see you haven't forgotten how to show a girl a good time.'

Ethan helped Lucy to her feet. The scientist, dazed and shivering, looked up at him. 'Remind me why I asked you to join me out here?'

Ethan wrapped one arm around her and squinted up into the rain.

'We'd better keep moving. Those soldiers won't have missed that explosion.'

Together, Ethan, Lucy and Lopez turned and began the long walk toward the distant lights of Siem Reap.

XXII

Bangkok, Thailand

Aaron Devlin ducked his head to look out of the Bombadier Challenger 300's oval windows as the aircraft taxied in towards the airport terminals, and fought off waves of exhaustion that washed over him. All was blackness outside, twinkling lights marking the terminals and taxiways and the city beyond. Behind distant mountains, the first pale tint of dawn was touching the horizon, and despite sleeping for much of the journey Aaron felt lethargic as he heard the engines whine down and he unbuckled himself from his seat.

A cabin attendant unlocked the aircraft's boarding doors, and the door folded down to present a series of steps. Aaron had not even got out of his seat when two men boarded the aircraft and walked towards him.

'Well?' Aaron demanded.

Both men were dressed in combat fatigues and bore the insignia of the CIA's paramilitary Specialist Tactics Squadron. The senior of the two, Lieutenant Greg Veer, a shaven-headed veteran of the US military, handed Aaron a slim folder of transparent plastic within which was contained a map.

Aaron took the map and looked at it. Two lines were drawn from two separate locations, one in the South China Sea and the other in Cambodia. They intersected at a location on South America's western coast.

'Lucy Morgan?'

'The target evaded capture,' Lieutenant Veer replied.

'What of the man with her, Ethan Warner?'

'Also in the wind, and there was somebody else there too. A woman whom we have not yet identified.'

Aaron looked at the map, evidently recovered from Lucy Morgan by the STS team. The soldiers had intercepted Morgan in Cambodia, north of Angkor Wat, and that explained the line drawn from that location towards South America. The other line, drawn from Yonaguni Island, was clearly related to the work done in Cambodia. The problem was that Aaron had no idea what the lines represented: it could be some kind of directions, but he had no intention of flying halfway across the globe without being sure that there was something waiting for him at his destination.

'You had eight men, you were chasing two unarmed civilians, and yet they evaded capture and are still at large?'

'Like I said, they had help,' Veer growled. 'The third unidentified woman was armed, not to mention the fact that she had allied herself to large number of armed villagers. We lost two men during the firefight, with a third injured.'

'And then you lost a helicopter and the three crew aboard,' Aaron noted as he recalled the report he had read on the flight out.

'We did not witness the loss of the helicopter,' Veer snapped, clearly irritated at Aaron's accusation. 'But yes, the individuals escaped and we have no idea where they have gone. Judging by the map, it would appear that South America is the next target.'

Aaron glanced at the map for a moment and then tossed it onto the seat he had occupied for the past twelve hours.

'We cannot be sure of that. What were they doing when you found them?'

'They had climbed up some kind of temple in the jungle,' Veer replied without interest. 'We don't know what they were doing up there, but we do know that the unidentified woman intercepted them and took the map. I then took the map from her, but it may be that Lucy Morgan had further information on her person that we did not recover.'

'A temple,' Aaron murmured thoughtfully. 'Send the team back out to the temple and scour every inch of it. I want to know what Lucy Morgan knows, then we can figure out what she intends to do next.'

'What about South America?' Veer asked. 'If they are headed there, then they have a good head start. I recommend we prepare a team to be on standby in case they show up somewhere out there.'

Aaron nodded. 'Do it.'

The two soldiers turned away and marched from the jet as Aaron turned and picked up another folder, one that he had been reading on the long journey across the Pacific. He opened the file and flicked to a series of photographs taken several years ago by the DIA. One of them was of a Latino woman, long dark hair and exotic eyes staring out with a barely concealed contempt for the camera.

'Nicola Lopez,' Aaron murmured. 'What are you up to?'

Aaron reached for his cell phone and held it in his hand for a moment as he turned the pages of the file and observed a series of images taken at Yonaguni airport. Shot through a long-range lens, the images showed an elderly man exiting a private jet and boarding a glossy black limousine before being whisked away toward the airport exits. The details identified the man as Yuri Polkov, a Russian black-market dealer who had made his money stealing antiquities and fossils for sale on the black market to collectors and, in some cases, less scrupulous museums.

Aaron knew that Polkov was considered to be a violent criminal. He had built an impressive fortune through acquiring and selling stolen artifacts, and then had that fortune laundered through various legitimate businesses located around the globe, many of them involved in the legitimate trade of fossils and rare antiquities. The Russian was known to the FBI, but nobody had ever made any attempt to arrest him simply because his crimes were committed in countries that had no direct relationship with the United States. The US government knew that the antiquities Polkov acquired were not his by right, and that fact alone effectively made him a modern day grave robber, but with many of the items he and others acquired ending up in American museums, nobody had felt it worthwhile pursuing such a powerful man.

Now, Aaron had that reason. He dialled a number and waited for the line to connect, determined to get ahead of Lucy Morgan and secure the artifacts she sought before she ever laid eyes on them.

*

Cairo,
Egypt

'It's not my fault!'

Arnie was enshrouded in a deep cloud of irritability as he sat at the controls of the Catalina, his wife alongside him as the aircraft descended toward the vast, deep blue waters of the Mediterranean. The engines clattered outside as the aircraft bobbed up and down on the rapidly warming thermals rising up from the ocean below.

'They have resources,' Ethan replied, 'and they can track flight plans. As soon as they figure out where we've gone they'll be on to us.'

'And if we hadn't filed a flight plan we would have been shot down by the Egyptian Air Force, not to mention the military of various other countries we've had to fly over,' Arnie snapped back. 'I don't give a damn if you're being followed or not, my main concern is not being arrested or getting into an argument with a heat-seeking missile!'

Ethan scowled as the Catalina bounced violently on a gust of wind and he thumped his head on the cockpit ceiling. He turned and walked out of the cockpit, down into the Catalina's fuselage, grabbing handholds wherever he could to steady himself, and saw Lucy packing her gear while studying the images she had taken in Cambodia.

'Okay, you want to tell me why the hell we're heading for Cairo?'

'Because I think I may know the answer to what these images mean,' Lucy replied as she fastened her rucksack and threw it onto her shoulders.

'They're directions,' Ethan replied. 'I thought we had that sorted?'

'They are,' she agreed, 'but they're also...'

Lucy hesitated and looked to one side. On the other side of the aircraft, her boots propped up on the seat in front of her and her hands behind her head, sat Lopez. She regarded them with interest.

'Don't mind me,' she purred.

'I don't like her tagging along for the ride,' Lucy said to Ethan with obvious distaste.

'We wouldn't have got out of Cambodia without Lopez,' Ethan replied. 'We owed her at least a ride out of the country.'

Lucy looked back and forth between them. 'Does trouble always follow you two around like this?'

'Pretty much,' Ethan and Lopez replied in perfect chorus.

'Those soldiers, they were American,' Lucy reminded him. 'That means that the people who have been shooting at us are not Russians.'

'That means that the people shooting at us are not *just* Russians,' Lopez corrected her. 'It seems that whatever you're pursuing is on the shopping list of a lot of dangerous dudes.'

'That doesn't surprise me, but the fact that we don't even know if it exists makes me wonder why on earth so many people are in on the chase.'

Ethan and Lopez exchanged a glance before he finally spoke. 'The remains that you found in Israel all those years ago were confiscated by the Defense Intelligence Agency, who have probably been studying them ever since. Lopez and I know that there are small units within the government's intelligence agencies that operate autonomously, and who may well be able to send paramilitary troops after us in an attempt to confiscate whatever information we are carrying at any one time. They are unaccountable before Congress, as they were operating in Cambodia without the knowledge of that country's government.'

'So we're not just being chased by Russians, but by our own country.'

'Pretty much,' Lopez agreed.

Ethan heard the Catalina's flaps wind down, the aircraft experiencing increased turbulence as it descended towards the shallow seas off the coast of Egypt. Ethan knew full well that as soon as they landed and passed through customs at Cairo International Airport they would be flagged by the DIA, and anybody else who had an interest in them would know exactly where they were.

'Arnie isn't going to like it,' Ethan said, 'but we're getting off before customs.'

'Just like that?' Lucy raised an eyebrow. 'Egypt borders Israel, so they're pretty good on ensuring that people don't get into the country through anything but the proper channels.'

'Believe me,' Ethan replied, 'I know the territory.'

Ethan made his way to the side of the aircraft and looked out of the bulbous viewing port to see the broad blue Mediterranean drifting by beneath them. Arnie was bringing the aircraft in over the water, the distant hustle and bustle of Cairo just visible shimmering with a metallic glitter in the haze far to the south.

Ethan figured that the Catalina probably landed at somewhere around seventy knots. At this distance from Cairo, they would be well inside air traffic control radar range, but not yet close enough for Arnie to be talking to approach. In addition, radar was an unusual beast and not as absolute in its performance as many people believed. Heat inversions frequently caused aircraft traces to disappear before reappearing moments later, and Ethan knew that as long as Arnie was maintaining radio contact with local air traffic and he disappeared from their radars, they would not alert the rescue services to a possible downed aircraft provided the aircraft reappeared on their scopes before too long and radio contact was maintained.

'Get ready to get wet again,' Ethan said to Lucy.

Lucy looked out of the window in exasperation. 'You're not serious?'

Ethan hurried up to the cockpit where Arnie and his wife were preparing the aircraft for landing. 'You can drop us off here at Lake Bardawil, we'll find our own way into the city.'

Arnie looked over his shoulder at Ethan as though he'd gone insane. 'Er, we haven't landed yet.'

'Yeah, about that. Do you think you could just drop down for a bit and touch down as slowly as possible? We'll be gone before you know it.'

'You're going to jump?'

'Get her under twenty knots once we're down,' Ethan instructed. 'As soon as we're all off, power up and take off again. You'll only be off their scopes from maybe a minute or so.'

Arnie stared at Ethan incredulously and then looked at his wife.

'You said you couldn't wait to be rid of him,' Yin pointed out.

Ethan grinned. 'Now's your chance. Your transponder is set to altitude,' he said as he observed the cockpit instruments, 'but this far out and in the early morning, chances are they won't spot the descent if it's quick.'

'This is the last time, Warner,' Arnie grumbled. 'If I ever see your sorry ass aboard my plane ever again, I'll shoot you myself!'

'Always a pleasure,' Ethan replied. 'Twenty knots, remember?'

Arnie scowled and turned to concentrate on his instruments. Ethan hurried back down through the aircraft and gestured with a thumb over his shoulder towards the cockpit. 'The Catalina has a hatch on the cockpit canopy that we can climb out of. We can't use the main hatch in case the fuselage floods, so we'll have to jump.'

'I take it you know that there are great white sharks in the Mediterranean,' Lucy pointed out.

'Arnie's going to take us in close to the shore. We'll easily be able to swim to the beach and shouldn't be exposed for too long.'

'That's not the kind of reassurance I was hoping for!' Lucy shot back. 'How about: maybe this is a really bad idea and we'll just land on a runway like normal people?'

Ethan smiled as he glanced at Lopez. 'Sorry, we're not normal people.'

The Catalina was descending and Ethan could see the ocean rushing up towards them, a thin beach just a few hundred yards away across the water. Ahead, Ethan could see a spit of land that jutted out a fair way into the water and encircled Lake Bardawil.

'Come on, let's go.'

Ethan led the way to the cockpit and saw Arnie and Yin gently lowering the Catalina towards the water. Ethan reached up and popped the catches on the canopy hatch before pushing it up and over. A rush of warm air touched with sea salt and the unmistakable scent of the African coast wafted into the cockpit just as the aircraft thumped down onto the water. Ethan held on carefully as Arnie guided the aircraft in a straight line and the friction of the water bought its airspeed down.

'Welcome to Africa and thank you for flying Air Arnie,' Arnie called over his shoulder. 'Now get out before I throw you out myself!'

Ethan pulled himself up and out of the hatch, the roar of the two piston engines deafening as he manoeuvred himself carefully to one side of the fuselage and then jumped into the water now flowing sedately past the hull. The Catalina passed him by, her wake bobbing Ethan up and down on the water as he saw Lucy jump into the waves, closely followed by Lopez.

The Catalina continued on its way for several seconds, and then Ethan saw Arnie poke his head out of the hatch and with one hand direct an obscene gesture in Ethan's direction before the hatch slammed shut. Moments later, the Catalina's engines roared as she thundered away across the waves and took to the air once more.

The clattering engines died away into the distance as the Catalina turned towards the city and Ethan was left in silence on the bobbing waves. Lucy and Lopez swam to join him, Lucy looked increasingly distraught.

'If I'd known this was how you did business, I would never have come to you for help,' she uttered.

'You're welcome,' Ethan replied. 'We're now in your hands. Wherever it was you intended to go, you have the lead.'

Lucy rolled her eyes and kicked off towards the narrow spit of land encircling the bay.

XXIII

The Museum of Egyptian Antiquities, Tahrir Square, Cairo

The museum was located on Meret Basha on the eastern banks of the Nile, just north of Tahrir Square, a handsome building fronted with fountains and stone sphinxes, bustling with tourists. Ethan led the way, his features concealed behind sunglasses and a cheap tourist hat that he had found being hawked by an Egyptian vendor in one of Cairo's busy streets. The sun was beating down on the busy square as they made their way through the bustling crowds.

It had taken them almost three hours to reach the museum from the lake, hitching a lift into the city and booking into a cheap hotel in order to shower and change into hastily purchased clothes. Nobody took any notice of them, the hoteliers assuming them to be American tourists, and made no remark on their damp hair or creased and dirty clothing.

As they reached the museum entrance, Ethan hung back and allowed Lucy to lead the way inside. She walked with confidence through the vast halls filled with Egyptian mummies, the ancient remains of Rameses II, and the elaborate gold head mask of Tutankhamen attracting crowds of tourists, their cameras flashing as they photographed the famous relics.

Ethan watched Lucy walk up to a member of the museum staff and speak to him quietly. The man appeared surprised to have been approached at all, but then he seemed to recognise Lucy and moments later he was beckoning her to follow him. Ethan and Lopez again hung back as they followed Lucy and the staff member toward a series of locked doors near the back of the main hall.

'You have any idea what she's up to?' Lopez asked him.

'None whatsoever.'

'What's your stake in this?'

'She came to me,' Ethan replied. 'I don't have a stake. You?'

Lopez did not reply as they reached the doors and were led through into a laboratory of sorts, where sealed Perspex boxes contained antiquities that were being cleaned and prepared for display by museum staff. Lucy's new friend led them between the staff workers toward a series of offices at the back of the laboratory, and he called out.

'Dr El-Wari?'

From within one of the offices stepped an Egyptian man wearing spectacles and with receding black hair, his dark skin stark against his crisp white shirt. He took one look at Lucy and then spread his arms wide.

'Dr Morgan,' he exclaimed as he stepped forward and swept her up into an embrace. 'I thought we had seen the last of you in Egypt a long time ago, more was the pity.'

Lucy returned the embrace warmly, and then turned to gesture to Ethan and Lopez as she introduced them. El-Wari greeted them with vigorous handshakes and beckoned them into his office as he shut the door behind them.

'Dr El-Wari is one of Egypt's foremost experts on hieroglyphics and ancient Egyptian iconography,' Lucy said by way of an explanation. 'He may be able to help us.'

'Help you with what?' El-Wari asked.

Lucy produced from her rucksack photographs of the icons they had taken in Japan and Cambodia and laid them on the doctor's table.

'These images were taken by us in Cambodia and Japan,' Lucy explained. 'The sites where the icons were found were dated as being 800 A.D. and anything up to 3000 BCE. I wanted to ask if you'd seen anything similar in your work here in Egypt?'

El-Wari nodded. 'Many times. This is the hieroglyph for the sun god *Aten* and is found on many tombs and obelisks around Egypt. But I've never heard of it being found on any other monuments on the planet, and this version of it is slightly different. The length of the beams projecting from the sun are always the same length in Aten's hieroglyphic, but these are represented at variable lengths.'

El-Wari moved across his office to a large poster that had been laminated and stuck to the wall. Upon it were dense ranks of hieroglyphs, each with a translation beneath them in both Greek and Latin that Ethan guessed had been taken from the famous Rosetta Stone, a granodiorite stele inscribed with a decree issued at Memphis, Egypt in 196 BCE on behalf of King Ptolemy V. The decree appeared in three scripts: Ancient Egyptian hieroglyphs, the Demotic script, and Ancient Greek, and had provided linguists with a means to finally decode the mysterious

Egyptian hieroglyphs. The doctor tapped one of the icons, a round disc with sun beams extending from beneath it in exactly the same manner as the icons that Lucy had found in Japan in Cambodia.

Lucy nodded. 'Okay, can you think of the largest or most prominent hieroglyph of this kind in Egypt that you have found so far? Do you know where it is located?'

'I know precisely where it *was* located. The great Temple of the Aten was constructed in the city of el-Amarna, Egypt, and was the main temple for the worship of the god Aten during the reign of Akhenaten around 1353-1336 BCE.'

'You mean it doesn't exist anymore?' Lucy asked, somewhat deflated.

'The reign of Akhenaten, the father of the more famous Tutankhamen, was a unique period in ancient Egyptian history that created an entirely new religion by establishing a religious cult dedicated to the sun-disk Aten. Akhenaten shut down traditional worship of other deities like Amun-Ra and brought in a new era, though short-lived, of monotheism where the Aten was worshipped as a sun god, and Akhenaten and his wife, Nefertiti, represented the divinely royal couple that connected the people with their god. He built a new capital at Amarna along the east bank of the Nile River, setting up workshops, palaces, suburbs and temples. The Great Temple of the Aten was located just north of the Central City and, as the largest temple dedicated to the Aten, was where Akhenaten fully established the cult and worship of the sun-disk.'

'Can we visit the temple? Has enough of it remained to study?'

'The temple was destroyed by later pharaohs who considered the worship of the sun alone to be something of a heresy,' El-Wari explained. 'In addition, the temple did not have any icons engraved upon it. Instead, it was open roofed allowing worshippers to pray directly to the sun in the sky above, as opposed to previous religions within ancient Egypt that worshipped images of deities in temples and such like.'

'So a pharaoh comes along and suddenly begins worshipping the sun,' Ethan said, 'after thousands of years of the people worshipping other gods. Why would he do that?'

'Nobody knows,' El-Wari admitted. 'But there is much about Akhenaten that we do not know, and that stands out as different from other pharaohs both before and after. What few busts we have of him depict an unusual looking man with a long, slender face and what appears to be an extended cranium, as though he was deformed in some way.'

'Do we have any iconography from the temple at all?' Lucy asked.

'There is an engraving on the wall of one of the tombs in Amarna that depicts the shape of the temple. I think that the tomb belongs to somebody called Meryre, and the depiction of the temple includes a very large image of the sun disc of Aten. In fact, I think that…'

El-Wari hurried across to one of his shelves and searched through it for several moments before he produced a thick book that he dragged across to the desk and opened. He flipped through several pages before he found what he was looking for, a large depiction of ancient hieroglyphs that appeared to show a temple.

'Yes, here, look. The depiction of the temple, and the icon of Aten does not present equal lines but instead resembles the iconography you've showed me from Cambodia and Japan.'

Lucy seemed almost to begin hopping about from foot to foot as she grasped the doctor's arm. 'Do you know the orientation of this tomb when it was found?'

'East to west,' El-Wari replied, 'which would have meant that the sunbeams of the Aten cartouche would have pointed east.'

Lucy hurriedly pulled out a map that she had bought in Cairo, on which she had already redrawn the lines that extended from Japan and Cambodia to intersect on the coast of South America. Within moments, she had plotted a line east from Cairo, carefully transposing the angle of the longest beam from the temple icon to match the orientation of her map.

Ethan stepped closer, and to his amazement he saw the line extend and pass directly through the point where those from Japan and Cambodia bisected.

'It's a match,' Ethan realized. 'They're pointing to the same place as the other lines.'

'This isn't possible,' El-Wari protested. 'It's a coincidence. These civilizations would have had no contact with each other and would not have shared any kind of iconography.'

'That's not what the evidence is telling us,' Lucy replied. 'The civilizations were all connected by one thing, something that could traverse the great distances between them and was important enough to the people respectively that they recorded its presence in their religious icons over thousands of years. And all of it points to one place. Peru.'

'And what does that mean?' Lopez asked. 'What's so special about Peru?'

'You said that Akhenaten was deformed in some way?' Lucy pressed El-Wari.

'He was possessed of an unusual appearance,' El-Wari confirmed, 'and had a considerably extended cranium, perhaps as a result of deliberate deformation as a child.'

'Perhaps,' Lucy murmured. 'But then, perhaps not. This may be the very link that we've been searching for. I can't believe that I didn't make the connection earlier.'

'There is *no* connection,' El-Wari insisted. 'These cultures never made contact with each other.'

'Yet both Egyptian and Inca cultures mysteriously possess the same identical body of ancient art, architecture, symbolism, mythology and religion,' Lucy countered. 'Isn't it true that Victorian scholars, faced with this enigma, concluded that both cultures must have been children of a Golden Age parent civilization? Today, the parallels between the two cultures are not only being ignored by American and Western scholars, they're being suppressed.'

'Pah!' El-Wari scoffed. 'That's not science, it's pseudo-archaeology. Nobody believes that sort of thing.'

Lucy shot the doctor a harsh look and then stormed across to his book shelves. She scanned for several moments and then selected two thick tomes that she brought back to the table and opened side-by-side. Ethan saw a series of images that Lucy identified as she flipped through the books.

'Both the Incas and the Egyptians mummified their dead and interred them with crossed arms, gold funerary masks and gifts for the afterlife,' Lucy pointed out as she identified images in the books portraying identical appearances of the two cultures' artifacts. 'Both cultures built megalithic structures with incredibly precise stonework and masonry joined with metal clasps, trapezoidal entrances, and obelisks with hieroglyphic writing etched into the stonework. Both worshipped the solar icon of the sun, *Aten* for the Egyptians and *Inti* for the Inca. Both used animal symbolism on funerary masks as a representation of the third or *mind's* eye, both used the *ankh* and *staff* symbol for their gods, a symbolism found in many ancient cultures separated by thousands of miles and yet a correlation ignored by mainstream science. Anthropoidal coffins, reed boat construction, *tryptich* three-door temples denoting the same religious practices… the list is endless, doctor. It's staring us in the face!'

Ethan saw Dr El-Wari hesitate, trying to absorb a new line of thought that perhaps he had refused to consider before. 'These people could not have met,' he insisted. 'Their cultures are separated by not just thousands of miles, but by thousands of *years*!'

'No,' Lucy shot back. 'The city of Caral in Peru was built some five thousand years ago. Pyramid-shaped public buildings were being built at Caral at the same time that the *Saqqara* pyramid, the oldest in Egypt, was going up. Caral's pyramids were already being revamped when Egypt's Great Pyramid of Khufu was under construction.' Lucy was virtually radiating sunlight herself as she pointed at the icon of the Egyptian sun god Aten. 'We've been looking at this all the wrong way. We've been assuming that this image, this icon hieroglyph, depicts the *sun.*'

'It does,' El-Wari insisted. 'That's what it's famous for.'

'I think that's what it's *become* famous for,' Lucy replied. 'But I think it has more than one meaning, because we have all seen this icon before in a different way.'

'I don't understand,' El-Wari admitted.

'That makes two of us,' Ethan pointed out.

'Three,' Lopez added.

'If we put aside the assumption that none of these civilizations knew each other,' Lucy persisted, 'and we start looking at this hieroglyph as not that of a god being worshipped but of information being recorded, then we find that it also appears within the culture of a society that lived in South America for thousands of years. It was used by them to record information, a means to maintain records among a people that had no written dialect of their own.'

'In South America?' El-Wari echoed as he thought for a moment and then his jaw dropped as he stared at Lucy. 'You don't think that this is a message?'

'I don't think it's a message at all,' Lucy replied. 'I *know* that it's a message.'

'But it can't be,' El-Wari protested. 'If this is true, it throws into doubt virtually everything we know about the development of our civilizations!'

'And that's why so many people are pursuing it.'

'Do you want to fill in the ignorant among us?' Lopez demanded.

Lucy turned to face them.

'This is not a picture of the sun beaming light down upon the earth,' she said. 'This is a message written in a Peruvian language that is appearing all around the world at different archaeological sites. It is the image of something called a Quipu.'

'And what the hell is one of those?' Lopez demanded.

'It is the physical language of the Inca people of South America,' Dr El-Wari explained. 'Quipu are a series of knots tied into strings that are themselves attached to a circular ring that was often worn as a necklace. It was recently discovered that these devices, which had once been thought to contain only numerical information, are in fact able to record dialect.'

'I thought that the Inca were a relatively recent people,' Ethan said. 'Weren't they wiped out by the *conquistadors* a few hundred years ago?'

'That's right,' Lucy agreed, 'but archaeologists in Peru have found a 'quipu' on the site of Caral, indicating that the device was in use thousands of years earlier than previously believed. Previously, the oldest known quipus dated from about A.D. 650. They knew that the newly discovered Caral quipus corresponded to the very ancient period of Caral because it was found in a public building. It was an offering placed on a stairway when they decided to bury the building and put down a floor to build another structure on top.'

Ethan frowned as he connected the train of Lucy's thought with their own quest.

'So the quipu might be an ancient connection between cultures, and might also be the most recently used method of communication between them?'

'Precisely,' Lucy agreed. 'The Inca represent the most recent civilization that has a connection to this iconography. That means they may also be home to the most recent remains of individuals who carry what we're looking for. If Akhenaten might have had some connection to the remains we found in Israel, then perhaps the ancient Inca do, too; there may be remains of people there much fresher than those of ancient Egyptian pharaohs. The Inca were experts in the practice of mummification.'

'So, we go to Peru now?' Lopez asked.

Lucy shook her head and looked at Dr El-Wari. 'Many of Peru's ancient antiquities now reside in museums across the globe. They were scattered after the *conquistadors* conquered the Inca civilization in search of gold and other valuables that they plundered. Somewhere, we need to find a particular quipu, one is associated with the iconography we are seeing at all of these ancient sites.'

Dr El-Wari spoke softly.

'The largest collection of ancient Peruvian artifacts associated with the Inca civilization is not held in South America.'

'Where is it?' Ethan asked.

'In Germany,' El-Wari replied. 'At the Staatliche Museen zu Berlin.'

Lucy turned to Ethan. 'If there is a quipu that matches these icons, it may tell us everything we need to know to narrow down the location of the remains. We need to go to Germany, right now.'

XXIV

'The flight plan was filed from Cambodia to Cairo.'

Yuri Polkov looked at the paperwork that his son Vladimir handed to him as their private Learjet soared through billowing banks of cloud illuminated a deep gold and orange by the rising sun. The file showed the registration number of a privately owned aircraft, a PBY Catalina, that was based in the Philippines.

'What have we been able to figure out from what happened in Cambodia?'

Vladimir sat in the seat opposite his father and glanced idly out of the window at the brilliant sunrise. The glow cast his face half into shadow, and for a moment Yuri was struck by the way the light contrasted Vladimir in much the same way as his personality did. He was his father's son, and the darkness consumed them both far more easily than did the light.

'They were looking for something deep in the jungles north of Angkor Wat,' Vladimir replied. 'I managed to get some men up there but they didn't find much, at least nothing that we can make sense of.'

'Show me,' Yuri demanded.

Vladimir shrugged and tossed half a dozen small photographs onto the table top between them. 'As near as we can make out, their interest was in an engraving at the top of a pyramid. Some sort of capstone.'

Yuri placed the photographs into a line before him on the table and scrutinized them carefully. The pictures were poorly taken, shot by imbeciles on their cell phones with crude flashes to illuminate the gloomy jungle. It was only by chance that one of the shots had been taken at an awkward angle that cast into sharp relief the engraving on the side of the capstone.

Yuri peered closely at the icon and nodded to himself with a hum of satisfaction.

'What do you see?' Vladimir asked.

Yuri reached into a folder beside him and from it produced an image taken by a diver at the Yonaguni monument in Japan. He positioned the images beside each other and turned them to face Vladimir. 'What do you see?' He challenged.

Vladimir glanced at the photos without interest. 'Nothing but engraved rocks.'

'Engraved rocks two thousand miles apart, created by civilizations that lived at different times and yet producing the precisely the same icon. Don't you think that this image meant something to these people?'

'These people painted faces on rocks and worshipped them,' Vladimir replied with a disinterested smile.

Yuri shook his head and leaned back in his seat as he examined the images. 'This icon, that of the disc of the sun with radiating beams of light emanating from it, has been a feature of ancient civilizations across the globe for thousands of years. That in itself is not surprising, considering that most ancient civilizations worshipped the sun and the life that it brings to our planet, and that worship forms the basis of every major religion to this day. Every religion owes its creation to our ancient ancestor's worship of the sun.'

'Fascinating,' Vladimir murmured. 'But it doesn't bring them any closer to us. We still don't know where Lucy Morgan and Ethan Warner have gone.'

'No,' Yuri agreed, 'but these particular images give me a very good idea of where they might be *thinking* of going.'

Vladimir peered at his father, his interest suddenly peaked. 'What do you mean?'

'These icons,' Yuri gestured to the photographs. 'I might expect them to appear in widely separated civilizations from different eras of human development. What I would not expect is for them to be utterly identical in every feature, including the precise length of each of the beams of light radiating from them.'

Vladimir looked again at the images and noted that each of the beams was indeed the same length in each of the images, as though they had been carved by the same artist drawing from the same template.

'Coincidence?'

'I do not deal in coincidence, my son,' Yuri rumbled as he tapped the image of the icon from Cambodia. 'These icons actually mean something. They contain a message, something to be followed and understood.'

Vladimir shrugged again but said nothing. Yuri felt a desperate tug of melancholy for his son's lack of understanding, his inability to comprehend the magnitude of what it was they were actually doing and the knowledge that they sought.

'Every single ancient civilization worshipped the sun because it brought light and life to our planet. They understood that without the sun, there would be no life.'

'It doesn't take inherent genius to figure that out, father,' Vladimir replied.

'No, but it does require a respectable degree of intelligence to understand what that means for the present-day worship of gods of so many names by so many nations.'

'They don't worship suns, they worship deities.'

'And how did those deities come to be worshipped in the first place?' Yuri challenged. 'The world's holy books would have it that their words were transcribed from the voice of those very gods themselves, but they are so full of errors and inconsistencies that we know it cannot be true. Think about the words used to describe the gods themselves: that they are *the light of the world*, that they *come upon clouds*. Think about the legends and stories associated with them. The birth stories of the messiahs of so many religious icons match the dates and times of winter and summer solstices, the resurrection legends matching the dates of the coming of spring. Successive religions changed the names of the icons being worshipped in order to eradicate the memory of proceeding religions, condemning them as heresy. How do you think it is that the legend of Christ's resurrection comes at Easter, which was originally the ancient festival *Eostara* and had nothing to do with resurrections at all but with the coming of spring? Or that his birth is celebrated at Christmas, which was originally a celebration of the end of the winter where the sun was at its lowest point for three days before being miraculously resurrected three days later as it rose earlier day by day in the eastern sky?'

Vladimir shrugged. 'It's all fascinating, I agree, but it doesn't solve this problem.'

Yuri shoulders sagged. 'It does if you know where to look.'

Yuri took out a map of the Earth upon which he had transcribed two lines intersecting from Japan and Cambodia, matching the relevant lines from the engravings at the relevant sites. The lines met on the coast of South America, deep in Peru.

'When the images of the icons at these two monuments are aligned with each other according to their orientation upon the monuments themselves, the longest of each of the sun beams points directly to this location in Peru. While I'm sure that this is significant, I am not sure that it's the entire story.'

Vladimir leaned forward on the table and peered at the two lines. 'If the lines point to Peru, than what is Morgan doing in Cairo?'

'Precisely my question,' Yuri agreed, for once delighted that his son was following the same train of thought. 'If the lines themselves were the only story, then they would have proceeded directly to Peru. It would seem certain that the Catalina transported them out of Cambodia and brought them to Egypt. But I notice on the flight plan that the only occupants of the aircraft recorded on the plan were the pilot and co-pilot, and that the customs report shows them as indeed being the only occupants aboard the aircraft when it landed and was inspected by officials in Cairo.'

Vladimir looked down at the flight plan, attached to which was a photograph of the Catalina.

'It's a seaplane,' he noted. 'It's possible they may have been able to get out of the aircraft prior to it landing in Cairo.'

'Yes,' Yuri agreed. 'But why? Why would they get out in Cairo? What could possibly be here that could connect everything that has happened so far?'

'Do you think there's another icon in Egypt that might be of use to them?'

'Possibly,' Yuri agreed, 'and I don't doubt that we would find one if we looked hard enough. I also don't doubt that it would simply point in the same direction as the previous two, further confirming the importance of Peru to the search but adding nothing to our knowledge base. Lucy Morgan is smart enough to know where to go next, and she must have had some kind of breakthrough in order to be in Cairo at all.'

'I can send people in,' Vladimir said. 'We could have them within hours.'

'We don't need to have them,' Yuri assured him. 'What we need to do is ensure that Lucy Morgan finds what she is looking for.'

'You want to *help* her?' Vladimir asked, aghast.

'We need to follow them,' Yuri assured his son. 'Let them do the work for us.'

'That's not enough,' Vladimir replied. 'You know what happened to them in Cambodia. We found bullet marks all around that temple; fresh bullet marks. They were under fire, and further down the mountain side there were reports of gunfire and the crashing of a helicopter. We went down there and all we found was mangled metal. Every single body had been recovered from the site, and the helicopter itself had no registration or flight plan.'

Yuri nodded slowly. 'We knew we would not be alone in the search, and we knew that our rivals would be willing to use any means possible to obtain what Lucy Morgan possesses.'

'And that means they will clearly kill,' Vladimir insisted, his dark eyes burning into his father's. 'This is one crusade too far, father.'

'This is the most important crusade of all,' Yuri retaliated, and then he gestured out of the window of the Learjet at the brilliant sunrise blazing across the horizon. 'Did you know that the original Crusades, led by the Catholic Church, were not about regaining the Holy Lands for God at all? Their purpose was from where we get the expression "the riches of the East". Under religious rule, learning was forbidden and so Europe collapsed into a remedial state of understanding, exactly what the churches wanted: a populace too stupid to understand the world around them. That's why we call it now the Dark Ages. But in the Middle East, Islam allowed and even encouraged learning. They had astronomers and scientists that made fools of the people of Europe and their bigoted faith leaders, and so did the Vatican become jealous of their success. They instigated the Crusades and let millions of peasants spill their blood to swell the coffers of the Catholic Church.'

'I don't imagine the Pope will elaborate on that,' Vladimir pointed out.

'Much as they don't reveal why they enforce celibacy on their priests and Cardinals,' Yuri said. 'It's not about emulating Jesus. It was brought into force long before Rome fell, so that members of the church who died had no families to inherit their wealth, which instead went to the church. That greed, too, swelled the wealth of the Vatican over many centuries, until it has become the bloated monster that it is today, having gorged for so long on the wealth of others.'

'I'm not arguing with you, papa,' Vladimir said, 'but none of this will ever reach the ears of the people. Nobody will stand up and say such things, no matter how true they might be.'

'Which is why it is so important that we press on with this,' Yuri urged. 'We are the light, my son, and it is against the forces of darkness that we rally; the evil and the cruelty of religion. I would travel to the ends of the earth and wilfully surrender every last rouble that I possess, and have possessed in my entire life, for the chance to hold this discovery in my hands and say that I did the right thing. The *right thing*.' Yuri looked his son in the eye. 'This discovery, Lucy's discovery, *our* discovery, will bring an end to religious myth and conflict for all time, and bring us a fortune beyond avarice. It will be ours to bring unto the world, not Lucy Morgan's. America's enforced respect for religions that deserve nothing but contempt will pressure them to maintain a veil of secrecy over everything that Lucy does. We cannot allow that to happen, to deny mankind his second enlightenment.' Yuri sighed, and a cold grin curled from his lips. 'Nor should we deny ourselves the right to earn a handsome fee for displaying such wondrous remains and sharing their contents with the world.'

Vladimir stared into his father's eyes for a long moment and then he nodded slowly.

'I understand,' he said softly. 'What would you have me do?'

'Place your men at Cairo airport and have them maintain a permanent watch on the Catalina. I want to be absolutely sure that if Lucy Morgan and Ethan Warner attempt to escape Cairo, they do not do so aboard that aircraft. Start searching for them, but if you make contact do not approach or attempt to apprehend them. We will be far better served by following them to their destination and allowing Lucy Morgan to complete her work on our behalf. As soon as you locate them, find out where they're going, and this time we'll make sure we're ahead of them.'

The Learjet banked over and the seatbelt lights illuminated above their heads as the aircraft prepared to land. As the Learjet's graceful wing blocked the sunlight, Yuri saw his son's face consumed once more by deep shadows.

XXV

Ethnological Museum of Berlin,
Dahlem, Germany

'This is it.'

The museum was a blocky, modern construction that loomed out of the darkness as Ethan, Lucy, and Lopez strolled along the damp sidewalk towards it. The road beside them was filled with commuter traffic, rivers of headlights illuminating the drizzle falling from the dark and sullen sky above. The warm glow of the museum's interior ahead seemed unusually inviting as they hurried toward it.

'It's one of several of Berlin's national museums, and reputed to hold the largest collection of quipu anywhere on earth,' Lucy said eagerly as they began climbing the steps towards the entrance.

The museum was located in the Dahlem neighborhood of the borough of Steglitz-Zehlendorf, and shared a building with the Museum fur Asiatiche Kunst and the Museum Europaischer Kulturen. Ethan had never visited Berlin before, and was feeling somewhat disorientated by their rapid transit from country to country.

Lucy Morgan had, with Dr El-Wari's help, been able to secure their passage out of Egypt to Berlin via a chartered flight, their passage smoothed by Dr El-Wari's credentials. Once again, Ethan had been reluctant to use normal passenger aircraft, but with Arnie and the Catalina having flown out of Cairo barely an hour after landing and refuelling, there was no other way to get to Berlin in a reasonable amount of time.

'How will we know which one we're looking for?' Ethan asked as they stepped inside the museum. 'We don't want to be hanging about here too long.'

'We'll have to sort through them,' Lucy admitted as she led the way. Numerous tourists were milling through the collections, so Lucy kept her voice low she replied. 'One way or the other, we have to find the quipu before the Russians close in on us again. They're not stupid, and if they're following what we're doing now, they might attempt to decipher the clues themselves and get ahead of us. I don't really want an armed party waiting for us on the other side of the Atlantic.'

'You may not have to worry about that, if we're arrested here in Berlin,' Lopez pointed out. 'I'm guessing that most of these exhibits are alarmed, and I can see already that most of them are also behind locked glass cabinets.'

The museum was filled with an exotic array of artifacts gathered by German explorers over centuries from around the world. Full-size replicas of Amerindian shelters stood alongside rows of glass cabinets containing figurines and carvings from a dizzying array of cultures and civilizations stretching back through to prehistory. Ethan glanced this way and that at the elaborate displays as he followed Lucy towards a separate room that contained South American artifacts.

'We not going to be able to just pop one of these cabinets,' he observed as he saw the heavy duty locks guarding each of them, much like a jewellery shop. 'What's your plan?'

'I've been working on that,' Lucy replied mysteriously as she led the way into the South American exhibit.

The exhibit was slightly darker than many of the others, the lighting softer as though to enhance the sense of mystery around the iconic civilizations that had long been lost to the Spanish invasions and time itself. Images of great Maya, Inca, and Aztec strongholds dominated the walls, while cabinets stood in rows between the great images and were filled with countless artifacts; everything from shawls and sandals to solid gold carvings and masks with grotesque expressions that reflected the light in moving shadows as though alive.

Along each wall were a series of lower glass-fronted cabinets that contained exhibits at waist height, and among them were multiple rows of quipu. Lucy Morgan fished out the pictures of the engravings from both Cambodia and Japan and held them in one hand as she began methodically moving from left to right down the cabinets.

'This could take a real long time,' Lopez whispered to Ethan. 'We've got to assume that whoever is following us knows that we landed in Berlin.'

'We had no choice but to take a scheduled flight,' Ethan replied. 'The Catalina would never have got us here quickly enough and besides, I think Arnie would have suffered a coronary if we'd asked him to fly us to Berlin.'

'Do you think the Russians know what we're looking for here?'

Ethan shook his head as he watched Lucy making her way down the row of display cabinets, one finger gently drifting across the surface of the glass.

'Hell, even I don't know what we're really looking for here. I would have thought that a photograph would have sufficed, but Lucy couldn't find one online, and she says that these quipu are too detailed to decipher by imagery alone.'

Lucy let out a small grasp of excitement and one hand flew to her lips as she looked over her shoulder at Ethan and beckoned him to join her. Lopez followed with a disinterested look on her face as Ethan wandered across to Lucy's side and looked down. She pointed excitedly at one of the quipu before her, and Ethan raised an eyebrow in surprise as she laid the photograph down on the glass either side of the artifact.

'It's a perfect match,' Lucy whispered, her eyes shining with delight. 'This is the one.'

'Fabulous,' Lopez murmured wearily. 'Why don't we we just take a photograph of it and make our way out of here?'

'That won't be good enough,' Lucy insisted. 'That's not the way quipu work. The Inca did not have a means of writing down language in the sense that we do, so instead they used quipu to record numerical information by using differing lengths of cord and differing numbers of knots in each of those cords.'

'And you need the original piece to count the cords in each of the lines,' Ethan said as he looked down at the quipu.

'Exactly,' Lucy agreed. 'A quipu is made of cotton or camelid wool string in a two-dimensional array. The primary cord supports up to a hundred pendents. The pendents can bear subsidiary cords, which themselves can have subsidiaries, and so on, up to six levels in some instances. There may also be a set of top cords, attached so as to lie most naturally on the opposite side from the pendants. The pendents, subsidiaries, and top cords each carry a sequence of knots, which record information.'

'And you can read them?' Lopez asked.

'Kind of,' Lucy replied less certainly. 'In a canonical numerical quipu, each pendent or subsidiary displays a number: a positive integer, expressed in decimal notation. A "One" is represented by a figure-eight knot, figures two-to-nine by the corresponding long knot, and tens appear one level higher. Ten is represented by a single overhand knot on that level, twenty by a cluster of two overhand knots and…'

'Yeah, we get the picture,' Lopez cut her off. 'Let's just get the damned thing and you can count in your head okay?'

'If we leave it here, then the Russians will simply record the same information,' Lucy said to Ethan. 'There are plenty of experts in South America they can hire who are capable of reading quipu and deciphering what the message within it means. We'll be no better off than if we just sat here waiting to be caught.'

'How do we get that out of there without smashing the cabinet to pieces?' Ethan asked as he began looking for a fire extinguisher or something to hit it with.

'We *ask*, nicely,' Lucy replied.

She turned and strode across to one of the curators, and Ethan watched as they conversed for several moments before the curator finally nodded and hurried off. Lucy strolled casually back to Ethan's side, a knowing smile on her face.

'This is how work is done in the academic world,' she said. 'We cooperate.'

'He's going to let you handle that thing?' Lopez asked.

'We won't be able to touch it, but he's going to take it out of the cabinet to an examination room where we can study it more closely.'

'Can you figure out what it says?' Ethan asked.

'If you're asking me whether I can read a quipu, then yes I can read it. It is whether it will tell me what we need to know that is important, and how long it will take me to do so. Reading these things is a bit of a fine art.'

The curator returned and opened the glass cabinet, retrieving the quipu and then leading them to a small observation room set off to one side of the main museum. He laid the quipu carefully down on the table before Lucy.

'I can only give you about five minutes,' the curator told her in heavily accented English. 'The museum will be closing after that.'

'Five minutes should be fine,' Lucy replied. 'I'll take good care of it.'

The curator nodded and left the room as Ethan and Lopez moved to stand either side of her. 'You can read it that fast?' Lopez asked.

'Not a chance,' Lucy admitted. 'But now I can photograph each individual pendent and measure them. That will be enough detail to decipher it while we travel to South America.'

'We'd better keep watch,' Ethan said as he turned to Lopez.

'I'll be right behind you,' Lucy promised.

Ethan walked out of the room and turned back towards the Amerindian antiquities exhibit with Lopez by his side.

'I really don't know why we're doing this,' Lopez said. 'What on earth is worth chasing in all of this? Some bunch of bones in Peru?'

'You weren't there in Israel,' Ethan replied as they walked toward the glass cabinets. 'You didn't see what those remains looked like. If there are more of them, if they can be used to prove not just the existence of extra-terrestrials but their intervention in ancient civilizations and human evolution, imagine what will happen in the wake of such news becoming public. The Defense Intelligence Agency was quite happy to take those remains from Lucy and bury them away from view, and then force us to sign nondisclosure agreements in order that the news never got out – why would they do that? Why would they keep something so important so secret?'

'Panic,' Lopez replied without hesitation. 'They're afraid that every single religious headcase on the planet will go off their rockers and start blowing up churches, mosques, and synagogues wherever they find them, depending on whose side they're on. They'll scream that their god is the right one and that every other god is false, no matter what evidence is presented to the contrary.'

'I don't know,' Ethan murmured in reply.

'Are you kidding?' Lopez asked. 'Islam goes into meltdown if anybody even *thinks* about just drawing a picture of Mohammad, let alone blaspheming about him. They still hang people in Iran for not believing in Allah or being gay. Christians swear they're under attack in the USA despite being in a huge majority. Israel bombs the hell out of Palestine virtually every day, and Palestinians respond in kind just because they differ on who owns what land. You really think they'll take it sitting down that all of their faiths are based on nothing, that humanity might have been tampered with by an alien species, that their supposed gods might in fact have been little green men?'

'I don't think you give people enough credit,' Ethan replied, 'or rather perhaps governments don't. I think people would take it pretty well; they've virtually been expecting it for decades, now. Every day NASA and other agencies are finding earth-like planets orbiting stars light years from us. Everybody is pretty much waiting for science to find evidence of life on other planets or even signals from them. I think there is something else behind the secrecy, something else they want to protect.'

'I can't imagine what,' Lopez replied, 'just like you can't imagine why the Russians or the Americans are after it to. If they want to keep everything secret, surely they would be working together rather than against each other?'

Ethan stopped walking as he considered what Lopez and said.

'That's a very good point. Why *are* they working against each other?'

'Maybe Russia's invasion of Ukraine and the annexing of Crimea soured the water a bit between us?'

'Maybe,' Ethan murmured. 'But when it comes to something of this importance, politics doesn't always get in the way. Both countries would have equal motivation to maintain secrecy if it's global panic they worried about. Unless...'

'Unless neither of the people that are chasing us are American and Russian military personnel,' Lopez completed the sentence. 'Which would mean their motivations would be purely financial.'

'Those troops in Cambodia were a paramilitary unit, and that means they're likely not working for the military or the government directly but for departments of the government which work autonomously,' Ethan recalled. 'They're operating outside of congressional oversight.'

'Defense Intelligence Agency,' Lopez almost spat her reply with distaste. 'It could be Jarvis. He could be on to us already.'

Doug Jarvis, Ethan's former platoon commander in the Marines and long-time servant of the intelligence community, had retired over a year previously in the wake of Ethan and Lopez's long flight from the CIA and their final investigation together in New York City. The chances were that Jarvis would know enough to have picked up Ethan's trail, but it seemed unlikely that the DIA would have gone to him. Jarvis was an old man, now, and surely not willing to return to the field.

Ethan was about to reply when he looked up and saw the curator talking to two men, both of them in sharp suits and with muscular physiques barely contained by their jackets. The curator nodded and turned to point at the cabinets containing the quipu.

'I think it's time to leave,' Ethan said.

The two suited men looked in the direction of the glass cabinets and then both of them looked directly at Ethan and Lopez. Even from the distance between them, Ethan could detect the look of surprise and recognition on both the men's faces.

XXVI

Ethan burst back into the examination room with Lopez close behind him. 'We're leaving now!'

Lucy stood up from her chair as she snapped off more images of the quipu. 'I need another couple of minutes.'

'You need to leave now or we won't be going anywhere!' Lopez snapped as she strode across to the desk and yanked off her jacket.

Lopez wrapped the jacket around her right arm and without hesitation she drove the point of her elbow straight down into the glass case. The glass shattered and she reached in and grabbed the quipu from within the case and stuffed it into her pocket as Lucy stared aghast at her.

'Let's move!'

Ethan led the way out of the room to see the two suited men already marching toward them. He turned the other way and spotted an access corridor at the rear of the gallery, then made a run for it with Lucy and Lopez following close behind. Ethan crashed through the access door and into a corridor that led between rows of laboratories where staff scientists were cleaning and preparing exhibits for display. They looked up from behind transparent eye-shields at the intruders as they dashed past, Ethan leading the way out of the laboratories and into a service corridor.

He turned right to where signs in German directed him toward loading bays at the rear of the building.

'We can't escape the building,' Lopez whispered harshly as she followed him. 'There must be more of them outside.'

'We'll deal with them when we get there,' Ethan replied. 'Right now we just need to disappear.'

The corridor opened out onto a loading bay and warehouse, a set of sliding doors partially open to the cold night outside where two uniformed warehouseman were unloading a truck full of boxes. Ethan did not head for the open door but instead turned towards a series of racks where other similar boxes were stacked, Lucy and Lopez following him as he ducked down behind the boxes and waited.

The two suited men burst into the warehouse and immediately saw the open door. They hurried toward it and one of them called out angrily to the two warehousemen.

'Did you see three people come through here?'

The two warehouseman stared blankly back at the suited intruders but said nothing. Just as Ethan had expected, the two warehouseman understood nothing of English. More importantly, he recognized the accent of the leader of the two suited men: the same voice he had heard in the jungle in Cambodia.

'Stay here,' Ethan whispered to Lucy.

Ethan stepped out of cover with Lopez alongside him and they began walking toward the two American men, using their bodies to shield them from the view of the two warehousemen beyond. They were within just a few yards when the two men sensed they were being approached and turned to face Ethan and Lopez.

'Looking for us?' Ethan asked conversationally.

'As a matter of fact, no,' the American said. 'We're interested in the other woman.'

Ethan and Lopez exchanged a confused glance as Lopez shrugged. 'I didn't see any other woman.'

The American twisted his face into a gruesome smile as he began pacing toward Ethan. 'Give her up or this is going to get nasty.'

The American reached beneath his jacket and produced a pistol, his accomplice doing the same.

'Looks like it already has,' Lopez observed.

Ethan judged the distance between himself and the two American agents and he knew he could not make it before they were able to draw a bead and fire on him. He looked past them to where the two warehouseman and the truck driver had taken one look at the two guns and immediately turned and fled out of sight. He glanced left and right for any object that he could use to even the odds against the two agents, but he could see nothing and the two Americans knew that he was cornered.

'Give her up, now,' the American agent repeated, 'or you will both vanish forever. Two American losers on foreign soil when they shouldn't be there and with nobody looking for them.'

'You talking about us or you?' Ethan asked with a grim smile.

The American lost patience and raised the pistol to point at Ethan. 'We're done talking. Where is Lucy Morgan?'

Ethan was about to reply but another voice called out from their right. 'I'm here.'

The two American agents turned to their left just as Lucy Morgan burst from the racking with a hefty fire extinguisher in her hands. She aimed the extinguisher and a dense blast of thick foam hit the two American agents square in the face.

Ethan rushed forward and drove the knuckles of his right hand deep into the nearest American's throat to incapacitate him, then grabbed the pistol's barrel with one hand and cupped the agent's knuckles with the other before twisting hard and pulling the arm over his shoulder.

The blinded American groaned as he was thrown over Ethan's shoulder to slam down onto the concrete floor, the pistol simultaneously twisting from his grasp as Ethan turned the weapon in his grip and aimed it down at the American.

He had just enough time to see Lopez's right boot thud into the other agent's belly, as with one smooth motion she followed through with the other leg and drove her left knee up into the man's face as he bowed over at the waist. The agent sank to his knees as his consciousness slipped away, and Lopez grabbed his pistol from his hand.

Ethan looked up at Lucy Morgan, who tossed the fire extinguisher to one side with a metallic clang. 'Now what?'

Ethan and Lopez exchanged a glance, and then Ethan gestured with his head towards the open warehouse door. 'Let's go.'

Ethan hurried out of the warehouse and peeked left and right before making his way to the cab of the truck. The driver and two warehouseman had fled the vehicle and left its door open and the keys in the ignition. Furthermore, the driver had left his high visibility jacket in his seat. Ethan grabbed the jacket and threw it over his shoulders as he turned to Lopez and Lucy.

'Get in the back; maybe we can sneak out of here.'

Lopez and Lucy jumped into the narrow interior of the delivery vehicle, and Ethan shut the rear doors before hurrying back round to the front and climbing into the cab. He started the engine and yanked the door shut before aiming directly for the exits, neither of which contained anything more blocking his way than a simple barrier striped bright red and white, and a guard post. Being a museum, he figured there was little chance that the guard at the post was armed or would cast anything more than a cursory glance in Ethan's direction as he let the vehicle out.

Ethan drove down towards the guard post and saw inside a man in a smart uniform looking in his direction. Ethan had no idea of what security protocols might be in place at the museum, but he hoped that having already let the delivery vehicle in, the guard would have no problem in lifting the barrier and letting it out again. Ethan raised his right hand in a cautious wave and waited to see what would happen.

The guard looked at him for several long seconds from within his post just as a series of alarms began blaring out from the museum behind them. The guard leaped from his seat, then he drew a pistol from a holster at his waist and aimed it at the truck.

'Incoming!' Ethan yelled into the back.

Ethan slammed the throttle pedal down and ducked to one side to shield himself behind the dashboard as he heard the guard yell something and two sharp cracks of gunfire split the night air. The windscreen of the vehicle shattered as the bullets passed through above where Ethan had sprawled himself across the seats.

Ethan heard the truck's fenders smash through the feeble barrier, and he jerked upright and yanked the wheel hard to the right. The truck skidded sideways on the damp asphalt and then shuddered as its tires bounced before finally finding some grip and the vehicle accelerated away from the museum.

Ethan glanced in his mirrors and immediately spotted two large black SUVs accelerate out into the traffic flow from just behind him, and begin weaving and passing other vehicles in an attempt to catch the delivery truck.

'We've got company!' he yelled back at Lopez in the rear of the vehicle. 'Two SUVs, fifty yards behind!'

Lopez reacted instantly as she gripped the pistol she had taken from the American agent, and positioned herself near the rear doors of the truck, ready to hurl them open and return fire if it was needed. Lucy scrambled over a pile of undelivered boxes and poked her head through a small hatch into the cab.

'Where the hell do we go now?'

'I'm working on that,' Ethan shot back.

The road ahead was filled with red brake lights that glowed in the darkness as Berlin's rush-hour traffic began building up. Ethan could see no way past the traffic on the main road, and he knew that as soon as the truck was brought to a halt the men in the SUVs would be upon them.

Ethan jerked the wheel to the right and the delivery truck mounted the sidewalk with a series of deep thuds as he fought for control and began racing alongside parked vehicles as he approached a series of traffic lights marking a major intersection. The truck's headlights illuminated the startled faces of pedestrians who threw themselves clear of the onrushing vehicle. Ethan backed off the throttle to give them a chance to get out of the way before he raced past. He glanced in his mirrors and saw both of the SUVs mount the sidewalk in pursuit.

Ethan plunged onto the intersection and turned hard right away from the river, thinking quickly as he guided the truck down a two–lane highway. The traffic was dense but the wider road allowed him to take a line between the two rows of traffic, vehicles honking and voices hollering as they were forced to move aside from the larger truck as it accelerated between them. The river was to his rear, which meant that the airport was somewhere out to his right to the south-east.

He checked his mirrors again and saw both SUVs likewise forcing their way through the centre line of traffic. Both were modern vehicles, and although Ethan could not tell their age by the numberplates they carried, he was pretty damn sure that they would have all of the modern safety features of expensive vehicles of their type.

Ethan accelerated until the throttle was flat to the floor, but still the SUVs were closing in on him, their bright headlights flaring and reflecting off the mirrors and into his face. Ethan kept one eye on the road ahead as the truck reached sixty kilometres per hour, the leading SUV barely ten yards behind him. The road ahead was about to open up into three lanes, the traffic breaking up and giving the SUVs the room they would need to pass and block Ethan's path.

'Hold on tight!'

Ethan waited two seconds and then he dropped the truck out of gear and yanked up on the handbrake.

The truck's tires instantly locked up on the damp asphalt but there was no flare of red from the brake lights behind him and thus no warning for the pursuing SUVs. He fought to keep the wheel straight, the truck pinned between two lines of traffic and the SUVs behind him left with nowhere to go. The delivery truck shuddered under a massive impact and a crash of splintered glass and tortured metal as the first SUV smashed into the back of the truck. A second crash signalled the impact of the second SUV into the rear of the first.

Ethan disengaged the handbrake and slammed the truck back into gear as he stomped on the gas and accelerated away. He peered into his mirrors and saw the first SUV with its headlights now dark and figures just visible floundering behind the safety impact bags that had inflated upon impact from the dashboards, blocking their view.

'Two vehicles down,' Ethan chortled with glee into the truck behind him. 'We're in the clear!'

Ethan hurled the truck into a right turn to join the *autobahn* that would head south-east towards Schonefeld airport. The truck's headlights swung around to point down the new road and immediately a clatter of gunfire sprayed out in savage bursts of light and hit the truck's engine grill head-on. Ethan flinched and ducked to one side as he hit the brakes, even as the engine note of the truck altered, struck by rounds, and then one of its tires was blown out. The truck squealed as the tire deflated and the metal rim hit the road and bit deep into the wet asphalt. The vehicle swerved into a broadside and Ethan grabbed hold of the dashboard as it tipped and slammed over onto its side, the metal cage of the truck screeching along the asphalt before it hit the sidewalk and came crashing to a halt.

XXVII

Ethan hauled himself out of his seat as he struggled to orientate himself, sparkling chunks of glass spilling from his hair. The truck had spun a hundred and eighty degrees after crashing onto its side, the cabin now facing back the way they had come. Ethan took immediate advantage of the cover provided by the rest of the vehicle, and with one boot he kicked out what remained of the windscreen and clambered from the vehicle.

He slumped onto his knees and tried to clear his head. He looked up and saw that the traffic was being diverted around the scene by a series of bollards, as though workmen were busy digging in the road. But there were no workmen and now the crashed truck looked as though it was already cordoned off by police. Armed police.

The sound of running boots crunching on broken glass reached his ears. Ethan tucked himself in against the vehicle's front fender, the smell of leaking oil acrid in the air as the damaged engine spilled its contents onto the asphalt. He heard the back of the truck being opened and the shouts of men commanding Lopez and Lucy to come out with their hands behind their heads. Russian accents, angry and determined.

Ethan knew that Lopez would probably have concealed her pistol somewhere on her person, but the voices sounded far too efficient to neglect to search for the weapon. He could not tell how many there were, only that he was seriously outnumbered.

Ethan gripped his pistol tighter and prepared to take on the first man that appeared at the front of the truck to check the cab. He knew he would only have seconds to disarm and take them hostage in the hopes that he could trade Lopez and Lucy for one of their own.

In the distance he could hear sirens, and he hoped that the law enforcement they were trying to evade might now come to their rescue. If he could only hold them off just a few more seconds...

'Ethan Warner!' The name was shouted out like an accusation. 'We have them. Come out now with your hands in sight!'

The sirens were still too far away, no doubt held up by the same traffic that had hindered their own escape. Ethan could hear nothing but the click of a pistol being cocked.

'I'll kill the Latino first,' the voice growled.

Ethan cursed as he got to his feet with his hands in the air, the pistol held in plain sight as he got his first look at their attackers.

'Step forward and put the gun down on the ground, now!'

Ethan placed his pistol on the ground and took a step forward as three gunmen surrounded him. Lopez and Lucy were held between two men, and a sixth man was sitting in a vehicle nearby waiting for his colleagues to make their getaway.

The apparent leader of the group, a man with slick black hair and sly eyes whom Ethan assumed must be Vladimir Polkov, gestured to Ethan.

'Hand over the quipu.'

'I don't have it,' Ethan replied.

'One of you does, and it's going to end up in my hands in the next two seconds or we'll be rummaging through your dead bodies for it.'

Ethan forced himself not to look at Lopez as he recalled her putting the quipu in her pocket. Instead, his mind was spinning as he tried to understand how it was that so many people had ended up pursuing them. The men at the museum were clearly American agents, and yet now they were being confronted by Russian mercenaries. He was attempting to put the two together when there was a sudden screech of rubber on asphalt and headlights swept across them all as three new SUVs pulled in, glossy black vehicles on private plates. The doors to the vehicles swung open as one, the occupants spilling out but remaining hidden behind the doors as they aimed pistols at the Russians and a sharp American voice yelled out.

'Weapons on the ground!'

The Russians stared about themselves in amazement as they were suddenly out–gunned and outnumbered. Ethan and Lopez likewise exchanged a stunned glance.

'We're going nowhere without the quipu!' Vladimir yelled back as he grabbed Lucy Morgan as a human shield and pressed his pistol tight against her neck.

There was a moment of silence before the American replied. 'Then we have ourselves a problem. You don't hand her over, you're going nowhere.'

The sirens became louder as they closed in on the scene of carnage, and this time Ethan thought he could heard the distant, rhythmic *thump thump thump* of helicopter blades surging through the night air.

'You don't hand over that quipu, nobody is going anywhere!'

Vladimir bellowed defiantly back.

Ethan was about to speak when Lucy Morgan called out. 'Take the damned quipu and fight over it amongst yourselves!'

Ethan this time glanced at Lopez, and she pulled the quipu from her pocket and held it up in the air.

'Is this what you're looking for?'

The Russian yanked Lucy Morgan around, the pistol still pressed to her neck as his eyes locked onto the valuable artefact. 'Hand it over now or I'll ventilate her!'

'Give up on the theatricals, *Ivan*,' Lopez mocked. 'You want the quipu, you let her go. You go back to your vehicle with me and we go for a little drive so the Americans don't open fire and shred you and your goons, and I'll hand it over before you take off.'

Vladimir peered at her suspiciously and at the massed ranks of Americans aiming their weapons at him. Then he shuffled over to Lopez's side before hurriedly switching Lucy for Lopez and pressing the pistol against her neck.

'You try anything, it'll be the last thing that you do,' Ethan heard him hiss to Lopez.

Ethan watched in silence, the Americans also making no move to intervene as the Russians began retreating towards their vehicle, Vladimir using Lopez as a human shield once again as he backed up against the side of the vehicle and climbed carefully into the rear passenger seat. He hesitated there for a moment as his men got on board, and then he pulled Lopez into the vehicle with him and shouted a command.

'Go!'

The vehicle turned and accelerated away with a squeal of tires to vanish into the traffic flow seething past the crashed truck. Ethan turned and picked up his discarded pistol as he grabbed Lucy and pulled her out of sight behind the wreckage of the delivery truck.

'What the hell are you doing?' Lucy demanded.

'We don't know who they are,' Ethan replied as he peered around the edge of the damaged truck at the amassed vehicles.

'Mr Warner,' another American voice called, 'it's time to hand yourself over to the authorities before this gets out of hand.'

'I'm not going anywhere until you tell me who you are!' Ethan yelled back.

'We're running out of time,' called the voice again. 'If we don't leave immediately we will all be under arrest, and I don't believe that the DIA would want to have to dig you out of trouble overseas once again!'

Ethan frowned in surprise and cautiously stepped out, the pistol still held firmly in his grip as from around the side of the truck walked an old man in a sharp suit, the dark blue fabric seeming almost black in the German night. The man walked with his hands in his pockets as casually as though he were taking an evening stroll, and he offered Ethan a laconic smile as though he had seen the destruction that surrounded Ethan all before: which he had, many times.

'Jarvis,' Ethan gasped, 'I don't believe it.'

'Ethan,' Jarvis acknowledged him as he looked at the scene around them of crashed vehicles, bullet holes and traffic chaos. 'Nice to see you're still handy at working under the radar, keeping yourself to yourself, so to speak.'

'What the hell are you doing here?'

'Shall we leave?' Jarvis asked casually. 'I'd hate to have to deal with the paperwork required to clear up the mess you've made here, and I can explain everything on the way.'

XXVIII

'Where's Lopez?'

Ethan was sat next to Lucy in the back of one of the SUVs that was being driven by a government agent. Opposite them sat Doug Jarvis, his hands folded calmly in his lap and an appraising look on his face.

'We're following the Russian vehicle now but maintaining a safe distance,' Jarvis assured him. 'I suspect that they'll want to avoid any further confrontations with us and will not harm Lopez once they have what they want. I take it that she has the quipu?'

'She stole it,' Lucy Morgan confirmed with a barely concealed disgust. 'That artifact belongs in a museum.'

'She had your best interests at heart, and what she did to defuse the situation was incredibly brave,' Jarvis replied. 'I'm sure the quipu will be recovered in due course.'

Ethan shook his head in disbelief, barely able to comprehend how in the space of a few days he had gone from being so far away from the Defence Intelligence Agency and the unfathomable workings of Doug Jarvis's command, to sitting in a government vehicle with him as though the intervening years simply had not occurred.

'Why are you in Berlin?' Ethan demanded. 'How the hell did you even know we were searching for that quipu?'

Jarvis kept the serene smile on his face and offered Ethan a shrug. 'It's my business to know what's going on, Ethan. You of all people should know that.'

'You're retired,' Ethan reminded him. 'Dammit, you're old enough to remember the Civil War, you shouldn't be running around in the cold like this.'

Jarvis chuckled with what appeared to be genuine humor, although he could never be quite sure whether anything about Jarvis was as it appeared.

'I didn't choose to be here,' Jarvis admitted. 'And I'm not working for the DIA.'

'Who are you working for?'

Again, the smile and the shrug. 'Let's just say that those who occupy the heady heights of the intelligence community have been trying to unravel the corruption that has plagued many of the departments and agencies over the last twenty years or more. When they got to your business in Israel from a few years ago, they realized that they simply didn't have enough information to act upon so they called me to fill in the gaps. I have to say, it's been quite invigorating after a couple of years in retirement.'

Ethan leaned back in the seat and rubbed his hands down his face. 'What's your hand in the game?'

'Honestly Ethan, I don't have any. My job is to figure out, on behalf of those heady powers, what the hell is going on now. Those responsible for overseeing the activities of the intelligence community have figured out that they are not being told everything they should be, and they have a real compulsion to get to the bottom of what's happening here. My job is to help them do that. My first port of call was Lucy Morgan, and I followed her to you. As ever, it was then simply a matter of following the trail of destruction that you left behind.'

Ethan felt as though he had gone into a time warp and emerged two years previously. 'I never cause a trail of destruction – it's everybody else who keeps shooting at me.'

'Keeps happening, though, doesn't it,' Jarvis observed with a wry smile.

'Do you know why I'm here?' Lucy Morgan asked.

'Yes, I do,' Jarvis acknowledged with a nod as the smile slid away from his face. 'A truly noble cause in which I will assist with all the power that I can draw upon. I'm not here to hinder your mission, Lucy. My job is to try to ensure that you succeed, because with your success will come mine.'

'So you *do* have a bet in the game,' Ethan observed.

'I like to maintain a reputation of doing a thorough job,' Jarvis explained.

The SUV slowed and pulled over to the side of the road, and through the tinted windows Ethan could just about make out Lopez standing waiting for them. Jarvis leaned over and opened the door, and Lopez climbed in and slammed the door shut. Her gaze swept the interior of the SUV and settled upon Jarvis.

'You,' she uttered.

'Me,' Jarvis smiled back.

Lopez turned to look Ethan. 'May I borrow your gun?'

'He's here to help,' Ethan replied.

'He's here to help *himself*. Please, let me put him out of his misery and me out of mine.'

'A pleasure to see you again as always, Nicola,' Jarvis said to her. 'Believe me, I was quite happy spending my days gardening, not dodging bullets chasing you and Ethan halfway across the globe on yet another merry chase.'

'Obviously not happy *enough*, or you wouldn't be here. What is it this time? Another promotion?'

'I'm here to get you out of Berlin,' Jarvis replied. 'I have a jet waiting at the airport and it can take you anywhere you need to go.'

'Excellent,' Lopez replied with a smile. 'We'll get aboard and you can stay here, agreed?'

'Why did they let you go?' Lucy asked.

'They knew they'd never get out of the country if they didn't,' Lopez replied. 'The authorities would be alerted by Jarvis and his people, and they'd be in a cell within an hour of showing up at the airport.'

'Precisely,' Jarvis agreed. 'Volkov and his people want to maintain a low profile. Hard to do when they're chasing Ethan, here.'

Ethan turned to Lucy. 'Did you manage to learn enough from the quipu to figure out where we need to go?'

Lucy shook her head. 'It was too complex, too much information for me to absorb in one go. It would have needed an expert to decipher in that amount of time. We're not going to get ahead of the Russian,s now; they'll have the time to decipher the quipu and figure out where it is we need to go next.'

Lopez leaned back in a seat with a content smile on her face. 'Oh ye of little faith, you don't think that I would have done everything possible to ensure that they ended up without a good trail to follow?'

'What do you mean?'

Lopez shrugged innocently. 'I may have taken the time, while Ethan here was doing his Driving Miss Daisy bit around Berlin, to alter one or two of the knots on the quipu.'

Lucy Morgan grasped in horror. 'You tampered with an ancient and priceless artifact?!'

'No different from me messing with Jarvis's tie,' Lopez observed.

'You think I'm priceless?' Jarvis asked with a raised eyebrow.

'I think you're ancient.'

'So that means that when they decipher the quipu it may lead them in the wrong direction,' Ethan asked Lucy.

'The location of knots in a quipu dictate values much like numbers,' Lucy agreed. 'If they've been altered, then the information will be incorrect. But they still have the quipu and I didn't have enough time to photograph all of the pendents.'

'Then you'll be glad that we have images of it,' Jarvis said. 'You'd be amazed at how far the DIA got in their investigation into the remains found in Israel. Although we were forced to confiscate those remains from your expedition, Lucy, there has been a ceaseless study of those remains ongoing over the years. Connections have been made, mysteries solved.'

'Do you know where we need to go?' Lucy asked keenly.

'Right now, all that matters is getting out of Berlin,' Jarvis replied. 'The authorities will be onto our trail fairly quickly, so the sooner we can take off the better, and with so many other people tracking you our diplomatic flight status will be essential in keeping them at bay.'

'And *who* exactly is it that keeps following us?' Ethan asked. 'There were Americans at the museum, Russians waiting for us outside, and you presumably coming toward us from the airport. It's like half of the planet is after this quipu and what it could tell us.'

'The Russian interest in the quipu comes from a man named Yuri Polkov, a Russian black-market dealer in fossils who made his fortune back in the 1970s and 1980s dealing in a combination of rare fossils smuggled out of countries like China and Mongolia, and equally rare gemstones. Yuri pulled out of the black market game once he made his money, laundering most of it into properties around the globe. He has a portfolio worth a quarter of a billion and free capital worth about half of that.'

'It was a Russian who came to see me at Chicago's Field Museum,' Lucy replied, 'but he was not an old man. He was young, the same man who had a gun to my throat back there.'

'Vladimir Polkov,' Jarvis identified him, 'the prodigal son. He seems to have inherited his sense of criminal enterprise from his father, but unlike daddy, he has not curbed his excesses. The FBI has a file on him an inch thick but they haven't managed to make anything stick and

Vladimir avoids the USA as much as he can.'

'And the Americans at the museum?' Ethan persisted. 'Who were they? Lopez and I figured they might be STS.'

'That's the big mystery,' Jarvis admitted. 'It's certain that they are part of the US government but they're working under the jurisdiction of an agency that we have not yet identified, part of the shield of secrecy that is preventing the Intelligence Director from getting to the bottom of this. Whoever they are working for, they're not answering to Congress or even the White House, and we only have a name so far: Majestic Twelve.'

'A rogue command,' Ethan murmured. 'We encountered one of those out in Idaho a few years ago and it nearly cost us our lives.'

'And what about the SUVs that chased us down after we got out of the museum?' Lopez demanded.

Jarvis grinned tightly. 'They were my men, and would have got you out of here if you'd given them the chance to update you. As it is, they are nursing various cuts and bruises, and the damaged vehicles are being towed away by the German authorities.'

'Oops,' Ethan murmured without regret. 'Perhaps you should send your men in to say hello first, rather than following us in unmarked vehicles. This cloak and dagger crap got us down the last time around, Doug. How about you cut it out and tell us where we're going so we can get this all over and done with?'

Jarvis inclined his head and the smile reappeared. 'Fair enough. We're flying to Peru.'

'That's what the quipu said?' Lucy demanded.

Doug Jarvis produced a folder, which he opened to reveal an image of the quipu that they had attempted to decipher in the museum.

'How on earth did you know about that?!' Lucy gasped in amazement.

'The DIA made connections with the engravings found at the site of the Israeli excavation and the iconography of certain ancient cultures over a year ago, Lucy,' Jarvis explained. 'But such unusual relationships flew in the face of accepted history and so few staff were assigned to continue the work. One of them put in some serious hours and finally realized what the icons represented – ancient knowledge of another culture, much older than the Incas, thousands of miles away in South

America who used quipu to store information. The link allowed us to investigate further, and although we did not have all of the information you did, regarding Cambodia and Yonaguni, we were able to study hundreds of quipu preserved around the world, and located this one in Berlin.'

Ethan sat back in his seat and rubbed his eyes.

'You could have saved us a lot of time if you'd just approached us earlier,' he said.

'I would have done,' Jarvis replied, 'but since you both kept sneaking around, it was hard to track you down. Anyway, despite its many flaws the CIA is remarkably adept at obtaining information when required. Unfortunately, if the mysterious faction within our government is using CIA assets to further its aims then this very operation, conducted six months ago, may have alerted them to the DIA's work. Two agents were sent to photograph the quipu, and it was later deciphered by a South American specialist at Princeton University.'

'What did it say?' Lucy asked, her eyes bright with intrigue and excitement.

'Enough to interest the DIA and spark this new investigation,' Jarvis replied. 'The quipu is directing us toward a place called Nazca. Whatever is waiting there had better be worth it, because I'm damned sure we won't be the only people on site.'

'It will be worth it,' Lucy promised. 'The icons at Yonaguni and Mahandrapavarta also pointed to Nazca in the physical sense, and the curator of the museum told me who discovered that quipu. His name was Hiram Bingham, III.'

'A former member of the US Senate,' Jarvis recalled from memory. 'He had a stake in all of this?'

'Hiram discovered the lost citadel of Machu Picchu in 1911,' Lucy explained. 'It's estimated that Hiram excavated and transported out of Peru thousands of artifacts from the citadel, including mummies. Right after his discovery, he had a life-long involvement with the US government and became Lieutenant Governor of Connecticut and later a Republican Senator. It makes me wonder just what he might have excavated from the citadel to have brought him to the attention of the government in the first place, and perhaps what he might also have missed during his work in Peru.'

'Peru is mountainous, the terrain difficult,' Ethan pointed out. 'We'll need access, vehicles, a means to move freely. This jet won't cut it out there.'

Jarvis waved Ethan's concerns aside with a swipe of his hand.

'I've contacted the perfect person for the job.'

XXIX

Jorge Chavez International Airport
Callao, Peru

'You're absolutely sure?'

Aaron Devlin listened to the voice on the other end of the line before he acknowledged the details and set the phone down into its cradle in the corner his seat.

The Bombadier jet was parked on the servicing apron of Chile's largest international airport, and the voice on the other end of the line had been an agent in Washington, DC who had picked up a link between Lucy Morgan's work in Cambodia and the DIA's investigation into the remains excavated from Israel.

Warner and Morgan had been identified and pursued in Berlin, but once again had slipped away from Lieutenant Veer and another agent sent to apprehend them. A rapid egress from the scene, and an assessment of their activities, had enabled the agents to ascertain that Morgan had been studying an Inca artifact known as a quipu, and Aaron's contacts had quickly identified the precise quipu in question and sent him everything that had been learned from it during previous studies.

The DIA had deciphered the quipu approximately six months prior to Aaron's arrival in Peru, but had been unaware of its links to the archaeological sites in Cambodia and Yonaguni. Thus, the measurements and data contained within the quipu had presented no useful information and had been disregarded. Now, the information had been thrown into sharp relief by the revelatory imagery from the other sites, and its contents had stunned even Aaron.

The quipu detailed a particular location on a plateau deep in the deserts of Peru with astonishing precision, comparable to a modern Global Positioning System fix. Aaron's assistants had been required to ascertain where the quipu had first been found, because the coordinates were based on the quipu's original location. Many of the ancient Inca's artifacts had been destroyed by the *conquistadores* including quipu, which had been considered by the Christian invaders as *unGodly* with typically bigoted arrogance. However, hundreds had survived and in

2014 a set of twenty-five had been unearthed in an archaeological complex called Incahuasi, south of Lima. Six hundred years old, the quipu were perfectly preserved, and one of them stood out as exceptional, for it matched perfectly the icons found at the seven thousand year old burial site in Israel.

Orientating the data deciphered from the quipu with its location, Aaron's team had been able to get a fix on the location the quipu described: the Nazca Plateau. Aaron picked up an image of an aircraft seen landing at the airport the day before, an antiquated old seaplane that had in the space of a few days completed half a circumnavigation of the globe from Egypt to Peru.

'A Consolidated Catalina is not an aircraft designed to fly such distances,' he murmured to himself as he used the Internet to study the aircraft type.

Built during World War II for the United States Navy, Army, and Air Force as a long-range, amphibious reconnaissance and antisubmarine aircraft, the Catalina was renowned for its long-range and endurance. However, it was never really designed for all-weather operations, better suited to work in warm temperatures and low to medium altitudes. What interested Aaron was that the Catalina had last been seen on radar flying high into the Peruvian Andes on what had been filed on its flight plan as a sightseeing trip.

Aaron was no aviator, but he was fully aware of the dangers of flying in mountainous terrain. High elevations created various types of winds that could pull an aircraft from the sky and cause it to plummet into the ground. Most aviators avoided such conditions, rather than choosing to fly directly into them.

To his annoyance, Lieutenant Veer had lost track of Lucy Morgan somewhere between Cambodia and Cairo, where the Catalina had landed, but then picked them up again in Berlin after they had somewhat foolishly booked seats on a commercial flight. He considered it something of a triumph that he had decided to maintain a watch on the Catalina. Although he was certain now that they had not been aboard when the aircraft had departed Cairo, it was also obvious that Yuri Polkov was following the same aircraft, his private Learjet also identified at an airport near Berlin and now being tracked across the Atlantic, heading for South America.

Aaron examined a photograph taken in Berlin after an incident at the museum and on the autobahn nearby. Clearly, Yuri Polkov's men had pursued Lucy Morgan just as Aaron had, but they had been in possession of better information. Morgan's disappearance from the city with Warner in tow meant that fresh help had arrived to assist them, help with sufficient influence and power to spirit them out of Germany and away to South America. With so many parties now involved, it was difficult to track allegiances or fathom motivations.

Meanwhile, the Catalina continued its journey across Europe and over the North Atlantic. Aaron had resisted the temptation to have the aircraft's owners apprehended and questioned. Though he could not be sure, his instincts told him that the aircraft pilot was involved somehow and may well lead him to Lucy Morgan by a more roundabout means.

'What are they looking for in Peru?' he asked out loud.

The voice that replied came from speakers mounted in the aircraft, wirelessly linked to American spy satellites equipped to transfer secure communications outside of normal channels.

'Given their previous research, it would seem likely that they are pursuing further evidence located in or around the sites of ancient civilizations. What we cannot confirm is where they will go next. We can reroute spy satellites to monitor the area but their orbits are not sufficient to maintain a constant watch, and the aircraft you identified could easily depart the area and be missed.'

Aaron nodded. The Catalina's amphibious nature allowed it to land in places that would not be accessible to other aircraft. Flying in mountainous terrain beyond the reach of local radar, the aircraft could be lost in a moment and impossible to locate in such a vast and uninhabited country.

'We've got to get ahead of the game,' Aaron insisted. 'Apprehending Yuri Polkov and removing him from play could put us ahead of Morgan.'

'Polkov is a dealer, a mercenary seeking profit. He likely knows nothing that would benefit us, and his possession of the quipu does not threaten our position, for we already know of its contents and the locations it describes. Our purpose and priority is to confiscate everything that Lucy Morgan or Yuri Polkov find and ensure that they are unable to share any of their discoveries with the wider world.'

Aaron nodded as he picked up a picture that had been taken four days before Vladimir Polkov had approached Lucy Morgan. The agency had been following Polkov and his entourage around Chicago, Illinois. As his enquiries had concerned Lucy Morgan, his presence then flagged the CIA's interest, the agency having placed a permanent watch on Lucy ever since the events in Israel. Aaron had been on Morgan's tail almost immediately, but it was only recently that he had been able to assess much of the surveillance data that had been gathered on her movements during the period preceding the Polkovs' appearance in Chicago.

The photograph was a split image of Chicago's Lake Shore Hospital: one of Lucy Morgan walking inside, and a young girl who was being treated at the hospital for an unknown genetic disorder. Aaron stared at the image for a long moment before he spoke.

'What is Lucy Morgan's end game here?' Aaron asked out loud. 'Why do you think she intends to deliberately go against the conditions of her nondisclosure agreement with the DIA?'

The voice of Majestic Twelve's Number Three replied.

'The reasons why are irrelevant. All that matters is that she is attempting to expose national secrets and she must be stopped from doing so. This task above all others is the focus of your mission.'

Aaron nodded but his eyes were still affixed to the image of the young girl in the hospital.

'We have people working to ensure that Morgan cannot share what she knows.'

Aaron looked at another image, this time of Rachel Morgan, Lucy's mother.

'Whatever it takes,' Number Five insisted. *'If Lucy Morgan cannot be cajoled, or finds a way to conceal anything that she has discovered, then Rachel Morgan will become the focus of our campaign. Find a way to make it clear to Lucy Morgan that there is nothing we will not do to ensure her silence.'*

Aaron let his gaze drift back to the image of hospitalised child.

'Yes, sir,' he murmured in reply.

*

Nazca Plateau,

Peru

The Catalina's piston engines growled outside the cockpit as Ethan sat in the mildly vibrating seat and watched the mountainous terrain drifting past far below.

'I've been spending far too much time in airplanes, he said.

'You've been spending far too much time in *my* damned airplane,' Arnie growled in response.

'You took the government's coin and flew the damned thing here to help us,' Ethan replied, enjoying the pilot's discontent. 'I suspect that Jarvis paid you handsomely, so it's *our* airplane, for the time being.'

'If I'd known Jarvis was working with you, I'd have told him to take his money and smoke it.'

'But then you'd have missed all the fun.'

Arnie scowled but did not reply, watching the passing mountains instead.

Ethan felt somewhat relieved to now be at a higher altitude after spending such a long time aboard the Catalina as it weaved in between vast mountain ranges and plains, plunging through banks of dense cloud with nothing to guide them but Arnie's skill as a pilot. He and his wife, Yin, had guided the aircraft across terrain far from any radio navigation beacons using nothing more than a map, compass, and a stopwatch attached to the cockpit controls before them.

Jarvis had hired Arnie in Cairo, already aware of the need to make it to South America, and had arranged all the necessary paperwork for Arnie to be awaiting them at Peru's Jorge Chavez International Airport, this time operating as a sightseeing venture and archaeological expedition overhead the Nazca plateau. Jarvis's jet had remained behind at the airport, in Ethan's opinion a conspicuous advert to the Russians of their presence in Peru.

Jarvis and a faithful escort of two armed agents sat nearby inside the Catalina, Lopez and Lucy next to each other on the seat opposite Ethan. Lucy was peering through the Catalina's bulbous viewing port for her first glimpse of the famous Nazca Plateau. In one hand she held a replica of the quipu they had lost to Vladimir Polkov, and it was as though she, too, were counting down the distance to their destination.

'What's so special about this place?' Ethan asked as the Catalina began a gentle left turn, the barren mountains drifting by beneath its wing below fluffy cumulus clouds that trailed shadows across the desert.

'This is the site of the largest petroglyphs ever created by human beings,' Lucy explained delightedly, with the enthusiasm only a scientist could hold for aged scrawlings in the desert. 'There are countless gigantic figures, animals, and lines drawn in the deserts here, including lines that ran dead straight for mile after mile and line up with astronomical bodies. The creation is generally attributed to the Inca, but they were actually created by an even earlier proto-civilization as much as three thousand years ago.'

'What are the lines for?' Lopez asked.

'Again, nobody knows for sure. Some researchers believe they are astronomical markers, others that they are runways for extra terrestrial beings, others still religious pathways marched by their creators at certain times of the year to worship the seasons and the sunrises at various Equinox. If I am right, and they bear any resemblance to this quipu, then there may be more to them than that. They may indicate the presence of something far more important, something important enough to the Inca to completely transform hundreds of square miles of desert floor into a series of images that could only be seen from the air.'

'If they can only be seen from the air, then why did they bother making them?' Jarvis asked.

'That's the big mystery,' Lucy said. 'You don't make things that you can't see, unless you're building them for *somebody else* to see. I think we can all agree that there were no flying machines five hundred years ago in South America that were built by human beings.'

Ethan was about to ask another question when Lucy gasped and pressed her hands to the glass of the observation bubble as the Catalina banked again, and this time Ethan could see from where he was sitting the vast plateau opening up beneath them, and slicing across it endless perfectly straight lines vanishing towards the milky white horizon.

To his amazement, the lines seemed unperturbed by the fact that they often crossed rugged crests and valleys, their perspective still perfectly straight when viewed out of the Catalina's windows. Some of the lines had been widened to resemble what Ethan could only describe to himself in his mind as runways, perfectly long and straight as though somebody had started to build an airstrip on the plateau and then abandoned the project before laying the asphalt.

Between the endless lines and often branching off of them, where numerous pictographs: images of animals, birds, a giant spider, and even a monkey with a tightly coiled tail. Ethan peered out of the window at the amassed images and then looked across at Lucy.

'So, what are we looking for?'

'Anything that resembles this quipu,' Lucy replied as she laid the quipu out on the seat beside her.

Ethan looked to the quipu, resembling as ever a circular sun with beams of light emanating down around it. There were too many knots to maintain a mental image of them, so he merely stuck to looking at the length of the lines themselves and then turned and looked out of the window. Lopez and Jarvis watched below as the Catalina began gently circling the plateau in a wide arc. The occasional cumulus cloud drifted past and blocked the view, its shadow dragged below it along the scorching desert as though made reluctant by the incessant heat.

They circled for almost an hour, attempting to pick out lines and images that matched the quipu without success. Ethan glimpsed a massive image of a human being on the desert floor far below as he pushed away from the window, having heard Arnie calling from the cockpit. He walked up to the cockpit door as the grizzled old pilot looked over his shoulder.

'We're getting low on fuel,' he pointed out as he tapped one of the gauges amid the myriad controls of the cockpit. 'The air's thin at this altitude, so we're not getting the best fuel economy out of the engines. Short story – we're going to have to land soon.'

'I'll tell the troops,' Ethan promised. 'How far away from here will we have to land?'

'Aerodromo Maria Reiche, just south of the lines here, and somewhere I can get *Avgas* in decent quantities,' Arnie replied as he scrutinised a map.

'We're getting close,' Ethan said. 'Sooner or later we're going to be forced onto foot, again, and you'll be in the clear, don't worry.'

'It's not us we're worried about,' Arnie replied. 'Your friend there, the scientist. Jarvis said that she's on some sort of medical mission, right?'

'She's searching for a cure for somebody, on a hell of a long shot.'

'Well, it's not going to get any easier with those Russians chasing you around the globe. Your friend Jarvis has pulled some strings all right, but we're sitting ducks now. Best we can do is keep you in the air. The Russians aren't going to have any influence on the authorities, here, unless they start throwing money around, but if the US government is in on this, too, it's only a matter of time before they ground us. Whatever you need to figure out, you need to do it soon and get away from us so that you can't be tracked.'

Ethan nodded and patted his friend on the back. He walked down into the fuselage once more and approached Lucy.

'Time's almost up. Arnie's going to have to land within the hour.'

Lucy shook her head and ran a hand through her hair as she sought desperately for some sign on the desert far below.

'There's nothing there that fits,' she said. 'The quipu just doesn't match anything that we can see and it could take us hours of searching photographs of this site before we finally find what we're looking for.'

Ethan peered out of the window at the various images on the desert floor and then looked at the quipu once more. Despite the vividness of the images, there were far more straight lines than there were curves on the desert floor. He looked down at the quipu and then on an impulse he reached down and undid the neck of the quipu, then laid it back on the seat. The circular shape extended into a straight horizontal line, the beams of light from the sun now looking more like vines draped over the edge of a cliff, pointing straight down.

'Most of the lines in that desert are straight,' Ethan said. 'Do you see anything now?'

Lucy peered at the quipu for a long moment, then shifted her gaze out of the window as she sought something to compare it with. 'Nothing leaps out, but some of these lines run for immense distances. Even if we could get up to thirty thousand feet, we probably wouldn't be able to see the entire plateau.'

Ethan looked at the plateau below and his eyes caught on a vivid image of a hummingbird, drawn entirely from straight lines that hooked back on themselves to form the outline and the shape of its wings and tail. The elegant, long tip of its beak extended out in front of it and pointed away to the north east.

Ethan glanced at the quipu once more and then pointed at the bird. 'What about that one?'

Lucy looked down at the bird, its image prominently displayed upon a large plateau to the north of the desert where the other images were arrayed. She looked down at the seat where the quipu was laid and suddenly a correlation leapt into life before her. Ethan watched as she reached down and rearranged the various pendents of the quipu to match the orientation and shape of the hummingbird on the rocks far below, and to his amazement the different lengths of the quipu lines matched the size of the wings and tail of the bird.

'It's perfect,' Lopez muttered in disbelief.

'All but for one feature,' Ethan pointed out. 'The quipu image doesn't have a beak.'

'Yes, it does,' Lucy replied in awe as she reached down and took the longest pendent of the quipu and hooked it back from its current position at the rear of the bird so that it crossed the body of the hummingbird and ended as the beak, a perfect representation of the geoglyph in the desert far below them.

'I need a compass,' Lucy said hurriedly.

'There's one in the cockpit,' Ethan informed her, and without hesitation Lucy dashed past and hurried up to the cockpit, Ethan in pursuit.

'It's the hummingbird,' she said excitedly to Arnie. 'I need to know which direction it points.'

Arnie glanced out of the window to his left and saw the hummingbird motif on the desert floor far below. He took the controls from Yin and guided the Catalina through a wide turn as he set up to fly directly overhead the image in the direction of the beak.

'Stand by,' he said as the Catalina slowly lined up with the tail and beak of the bird.

Ethan watched as the Catalina descended below scattered cumulus cloud and the image of the huge hummingbird loomed into view on the desert below, the aircraft pointing directly in the same direction as the hummingbird's beak.

'Zero-three-zero degrees,' Arnie informed Lucy as he glanced at the Catalina's magnetic compass among the instruments before him on the control panel.

Lucy sat down in the cockpit's jump-seat and with a map, ruler, and pencil she marked the position of the hummingbird on the map and then drew a line heading away on a magnetic heading of zero-three-zero. The line traced across the wilderness and plunged deep into the Andes mountains, but Lucy shook her head.

'What's wrong?' Ethan asked.

'It doesn't point anywhere,' Lucy explained in confusion. 'There's nothing up there in that part of the mountains.'

Ethan peered past her out of the cockpit windows as Arnie banked the Catalina over the hummingbird's massive form below them. Beside it was a line that looked like a wide runway, narrow near the hummingbird and widening as it extended away at an angle very close to that of the hummingbird's beak.

'What about that line? Could that have anything to do with it?' he asked Lucy.

Lucy looked out of the window but she seemed none the wiser as the Catalina turned. It was Arnie's voice that reached them from the front of the cockpit.

'I'm not one for your crackpot theories, but there is something known as *magnetic declination*. It's the difference between true North, and the position of the magnetic North Pole. Your Inca friends of centuries ago probably would have had no knowledge of the magnetic North Pole, only the position of true North via the stars. Our compass points towards the magnetic North Pole, and the magnetic declination in this part of the world is negative six degrees west, which would match that line alongside the hummingbird's beak. Why not adjust your line on the map and see where it points then?'

Lucy stared wide-eyed at the pilot, her jaw dropping. 'Arnie, you're a genius.'

'I keep saying it,' Arnie agreed with a shrug.

Lucy redrew the line and Ethan could see her shiver with excitement as she jabbed the pencil at a point on the map.

'The quipu's knots state that it would take six days travel in the indicated direction to reach the destination it pointed to. Do you know what this line reaches at about six days travel in the indicated direction?'

Ethan leaned over to see the map and instantly recognise the name she had scribbled beside a cross deep in the Andes mountains.

'Machu Picchu,' Ethan said, 'the last citadel of the Inca Empire.'

'And the site that Hiram Bingham III found and excavated over a hundred years ago. We have to go there, right now,' Lucy said to Arnie.

Arnie through a mock salute over his shoulder as the Catalina levelled out on course toward the north-east.

XXX

Laguna de Huaypo, Chinchero
Peru

The Catalina touched down onto the sparkling waters of the lake, the aircraft trembling as it thundered across the waves and then began to slow. Less than a mile across at its widest point, the lake was surrounded by rolling hills and ramshackle sheds on its southern shore. Ethan could see evidence of basic housing and two or three parked vehicles nearby, and children rushing out toward the aircraft as it taxied in toward the shore.

Arnie swung the Catalina around to bring it alongside a rickety-looking jetty that poked out into the water.

'At least we're not going to get wet, this time,' Lucy observed as they unstrapped from their seats.

Arnie shut down the engines and clambered from the cockpit as Ethan and his companions assembled near the exit doors. Outside, Ethan could hear children's feet hammering down the jetty and could see through the windows two elderly-looking Peruvian men move alongside the aircraft and look up at it in wonder as Arnie opened the doors. A waft of clear mountain air breezed into the Catalina's hot interior as Arnie climbed from the aircraft onto the jetty with a rope. He loosely tied it around one of several posts nearby before hurrying up to the front of the aircraft, where Yin had climbed up to one of the cockpit hatches and hurled a second rope out to secure the aircraft's bow.

The children jabbered excitedly in a torrent of Spanish, Ethan completely at a loss as to what they were saying. Lopez stepped from the interior of the aircraft, a bright smile touching her features as she listened to the children and looked at Ethan.

'They're speaking a mixture of Spanish and *Quechua*, the dialect of the Inca,' Lopez explained as she listened to the children. Then her face seemed confused and she frowned as she listened to the children's voices and then looked at Lucy. 'They say it has been a long time since they have seen an aircraft land on the water. Normally, aircraft come out of the water and fly away into the sky.'

Lucy nodded as she looked at the lake.

'The Laguna de Huaypo is a place where unidentified flying objects are often seen,' she explained. 'To the extent that the locals barely take any notice of them anymore. However, a major event in 1983 was witnessed by a large number of local people. Supposedly, a UFO took off out of the water and flew low over the village at high-speed, causing many of the people to be knocked over as it accelerated by. A young boy was knocked over onto his belly and some sort of exhaust hit him as the aircraft passed overhead.'

'Was he okay?' Ethan asked.

'Yes, after receiving hundreds of stitches. The exhaust apparently lifted the skin off of his back and he had to be taken to a local hospital in Cusco where he made a full recovery. Surgeons at the time said they had never seen an injury like it, but there was no permanent damage.'

As she spoke, one of the elderly men who had walked down onto the jetty apparently understood her explanation and began jabbering in their local dialect to Lopez.

'They see many lights in the sky here,' Lopez translated. 'The lights never directly interfere with the people, and in fact seem to try and stay out of their way, as though they hide deep beneath the water of the lakes high in the mountains where even native folk cannot go. There are the remains of cities built so high in these mountains that the air is too thin for women to give birth, and even mules and other pack animals can only bear light loads, and yet those cities and buildings are built with stones that weigh hundreds of tonnes.' The old man looked at Lucy as he spoke and Lopez translated. 'How could these people have done this, when even we cannot work so hard at such high altitude?'

'You need to move,' Arnie said to Jarvis. 'The paperwork at the airport won't be hard for your Russian friends to follow, and they'll spot my registration pretty damned quick. If they're in South America already, they'll make a beeline for us.'

'I appreciate what you've done here, Arnie,' Ethan said. 'Chances are we're ahead of the Russians and the Americans, at least for now.'

Arnie grinned tightly. 'I did it for Lucy, and on the agreement that you would never show up anywhere near me again.'

'Benevolent as ever,' Ethan said as he extended a hand.

'Get out of my sight,' Arnie replied as he shook it, a twinkle in his eye.

'How far away are we from this supposed ancient city?' Lopez asked Lucy.

'About twenty-five miles, but most of it is uphill, as the city resides high in the Andes,' Lucy replied. 'It's a tough journey, to say the least.'

'Then we'd best get moving,' Ethan replied as he looked up at the sky. 'We've only got a few hours of daylight left.'

Ethan saw Jarvis conceal a wince as he imagined the distances they were going to have to cover without any kind of help. He glanced at the vehicles parked near the side of the road.

'Do you think you could get the locals to help us out here?' Jarvis asked Lopez. 'Maybe give us a ride to the mountain?'

Lopez spoke in Spanish to the two elderly men who were standing with their hands behind their backs and watching as Arnie and his wife worked on the Catalina to prepare her for flight. The two men looked at each other and nodded, each of them showing a toothless smile, and wrinkles that seemed as old and as deep as the gorges on the flanks of the mountains around them.

'Looks like we got ourselves a ride,' Lopez smiled brightly. 'Ladies first,' she gestured to Ethan.

Ethan turned to her with a wry smile. 'Remind me why it was we stopped working together?'

'You couldn't take the competition.'

Ethan shook his head as he walked towards the two battered sedans, both of which were painted dark blue, the coat just visible beneath a thick layer of dust that coated both vehicles.

'The Russians aren't the only people likely to be on our case,' Jarvis pointed out as he joined Ethan.

'Can't you call in support of some kind, give us the protection we need until this is all over?'

'My position here, now, is as unofficial as yours,' Jarvis admitted. 'The Intelligence Director cannot sanction operations out here in Peru without the agreement of Congress and lengthy negotiations with the Peruvian government. Technically, if I wasn't retired I wouldn't even be allowed to be here. We're on our own whether we like it or not.'

'Now you know how we felt on all those operations that you sent us on,' Ethan smiled grimly. 'Not so much fun being a deniable asset yourself, is it?'

Jarvis did not reply as they reached the vehicles, one of the old men hurrying ahead and jumping gamely into the driver's seat.

*

'We've got them.'

Aaron Devlin looked quickly at the paperwork handed to him by Lieutenant Veer, who had hurried aboard the Bombadier. Flight plans and passenger manifests detailed the Catalina's passage into Peru, where it had landed for both fuel and customs duties before continuing on using an Instrument Flight Rules flight plan. The destination was marked as Maria Reiche Neuman Airport.

'Cusco,' Aaron said as he examined the flight plan. 'What's there?'

'It's an ancient Inca city, long since rebuilt. There are considerable Inca remains in and around the city, so it's possible that is their final destination.'

'I'd believe that if it were not for the amphibious nature of this Catalina they've hired,' Aaron replied. 'Are there any major bodies of water between the point of departure near Lima and their landing at Cusco, and have they been registered as having arrived, yet?'

'Local air traffic has not recorded them as having landed yet,' Veer replied. 'There are several bodies of water on the flight path, most of them at fairly high altitude, but there is one in particular low enough and large enough that the aircraft could both land and depart, provided the local air temperatures were not too high.'

'Is it within the vicinity of any known Inca remains, any cities or archaeological sites of note?'

'It's within twenty or so miles of Machu Picchu,' Veer said.

Aaron did not need to be told what Machu Picchu was, its appearance iconic and photographed possibly more than even the Great Pyramids of Giza in Egypt. He thoughtfully rubbed his chin. Cusco was indeed an ancient Inca city, but a heavy rebuilding program and a dense modern population almost certainly ruled out the chance of any undiscovered tombs or similar archaeological sites being missed over the centuries. But Machu Picchu sat atop a mountain ridge high in the Andes and was surrounded by other archaeological sites of similar note, any one of which might yet be home to undiscovered remains Exactly the kind of thing that Lucy Morgan was looking for.

'Dispatch four men to the airport to await the Catalina's arrival. I want the aircraft searched this time. If they're not aboard, then we shall be forced to intercept them at Machu Picchu. Prepare your team for deployment and contact US Southern Command– we'll need a suitable aircraft for transport.'

'Understood. And the site in the Andes?'

Aaron thought for a moment. 'Tourists will have no access to the site at night, and the mountain roads are far too dangerous to traverse in darkness. Warner and his people will want free movement, so they will attempt to access the area before dawn and be gone before the first tourists arrive after sunrise.'

'That will require a tactical insertion of our team,' Lieutenant Veer informed him. 'There's no way we'll be able to reach the site and ascend the mountain ahead of Morgan.'

'Arrange it,' Aaron agreed. 'You and your men will deploy *en route* and set up a perimeter around the citadel. It's imperative that Lucy Morgan is allowed to find the remains that she seeks, after which we will liberate them from her and depart the area as if we were never there.'

The agent nodded, turned and hurried from the jet as Aaron retook his seat and tossed the flight plan down onto a table next to him. It was time to bring this entire episode to a close.

XXXI

Machu Picchu,
Andes, Peru

Ethan squinted up into the star-filled sky above as he stopped for breath on the endlessly winding trail high above a plunging gorge that descended towards the Urabamba River far below. The mountains loomed large above him in the darkness, their peaks enshrouded in dense forests and ribbons of cloud that glowed a faint blue beneath the light of a crescent moon.

The temperature was falling as they climbed. The track narrow and treacherous as it circled this way and that around the mountainside. Approaching the mountain's tip from the south rather than from the east, where the main service road wound its way up to the citadel, the old Inca Trail was less well-trodden and thus less likely to be blocked by the Russians should they have arrived first. From his vantage point, Ethan could see the main road zig-zagging back and forth up the mountain's eastern flank.

Lucy labored past him, her head down and arms swinging as she marched relentlessly up the track. Lopez kept pace with her easily, perhaps somewhat more at home here in South America. Ethan knew that she had grown up in the Vedeer Mountains of Guanajuato in Mexico, long before her family had attempted to find a better life in the United States. Lopez had been the only member to remain after her family returned to Mexico, and had ultimately ended up working for DC's Metropolitan Police Department. Behind Lopez, Jarvis and his two escorts trudged wearily in pursuit.

'This is why modern society doesn't build cities on top of damned mountains,' Jarvis gasped as he passed by.

Ethan squatted down quietly and watched the track behind them for a few moments in an attempt to determine whether they were being followed. As the sound of the team's footsteps faded away, he revelled in the deep silence of the mountains, reminded briefly of his foggy highland refuge in Scotland, half a world away. Nobody appeared behind them, and he turned his head to look out across the plunging gorge to the main road. He could see no evidence of headlights or detect any movement of pedestrians ascending the mountain. The citadel was closed to tourists during the night, and most began the journey down the mountainside long before sunset. Ethan knew that the earliest risers gained access to the highest peaks at dawn, and armed guards protected the site during daylight. If they didn't want to be caught up in a fire-fight with Peruvian officials, their work had to be complete before sunrise.

The car journey to the mountain on Peru's dusty and often untreated roads had taken two hours, and then there had been a long trek out and round to the south of the mountain to avoid the tourist trails.

'Checking our tail?'

Ethan saw Lucy squat down alongside him in the darkness.

'It's good practice, even alone up here,' he replied, and then looked again at the mountains. 'This place does seem remote enough for your alien interventionists to appear, in the sense that virtually every sighting of UFOs seems to occur in lonely places rather than city centers.'

'If they interacted with us thousands of years ago, maybe it was because we weren't so well connected as we are now,' Lucy speculated.

'How will you know if you've found the remains you're looking for?' Ethan asked. 'Won't they all look the same?'

'Do you remember what Dr El-Wari said about the Pharaoh Akhenaten? That his skull was deformed, a rare feature known today as Scaphocephaly?'

'Yes,' Ethan replied. 'You think that the same deformation will be present here?'

'There is a place about four hours' drive from here on the Paracas Peninsula,' Lucy replied. 'Stone tools have been found in the area, and cursory analysis has established dates as old as eight thousand years. But the big discovery there was of dozens of skulls, all of them massively deformed. The thing is, the phenomenon of skull deformation is not unique to the Paracas area. The Egyptians performed it, as did people on the island of Vanuatu in Melanesia, Malta in the Mediterranean, and the Olmec of Mexico among others. Most of these skulls are elongated as the result of artificial binding, whereas a number of the Paracas skulls show specific characteristics that would seem to indicate that they were in fact born that way.'

'How could you tell?'

'They had *non-human* features,' Lucy replied, and Ethan thought that he saw her shiver in the darkness. 'One is the presence of two small holes in the back of the skull, perpendicular to the cranial suture present in the parietal plate of the skull. Every normal human skull is composed of three major bone plates; the frontal plate and the two parietal plates which lie behind this, intersecting the frontal plate and making a *"T"* shape. The Paracus skulls have only two plates, an unknown feature of modern man, and some investigators believe that the two holes are fixing points for tendons and ligaments necessary to hold up the person's elongated head, just as similar holes appear in human jaws as fixing points for muscles and tendons.'

'Could it be a genetic disorder?' Ethan asked. 'Something inherited?'

'Perhaps,' Lucy conceded, 'but the big issue with the Paracus skulls is that ritualistic deformation could only alter the shape of the skull, not the skull volume. But several skulls excavated from a site called Cerro Colorado, adjacent to the main graveyard in Paracas, had a cranial volume more than double that of a normal human.' Lucy shivered again. 'In one case, a deformed foetus was found inside the mummy of its dead mother, its skull heavily elongated. Ethan, they were born this way. Something happened to these people thousands of years ago, something terrible.'

Ethan got to his feet. 'Let's not dwell on it too long. We've got a job to do here for Beth. We can swap horror stories later.'

Ethan jogged with Lucy around the corner of the trail, turning right to see the mountain open up before him, and high upon its peak the vast citadel of Machu Picchu. The immense mountain soared out of the gorge to rise high into the sky, the angular and geometrically-aligned city upon its peak a dark and brooding presence, a shadow against the great darkness of the heavens.

Lopez and the others had stopped just ahead of them and were likewise admiring the spectacular view.

'Keep moving,' Ethan insisted. 'If Vladimir and his goons get up there before we do, they'll hold the high ground and we'll never get into the city.'

As if on cue, a light down on the hillside caught his eye and he turned to see several vehicles climbing the mountain side, their headlight beams sweeping left and right as they negotiated the hazardous switchbacks.

'That's got to be him,' Lopez said.

'He'll have brought friends,' Ethan agreed. 'Our only bet is to get up there first and get this done before he arrives.'

Lucy did not hesitate and immediately began marching with even greater determination towards the ruined city. Jarvis followed wearily as Ethan hurried alongside the old man.

'Maybe you should sit this one out,' he suggested.

'I didn't come all this way to just sit on the side of the mountain and watch you get shot at,' Jarvis pointed out as he labored forward.

'No,' Lopez agreed, 'you normally do that from Washington.'

'Will you cut it out?' Ethan said to her.

Lopez shrugged and kept moving as Ethan turned to Jarvis. 'There's nothing to be gained by coming up here. Either we're going to pull this off or we're not, and I don't think that you being there is going to make much difference.'

'Thanks for the vote of confidence.'

'You know I don't mean it like that,' Ethan said. 'We were unable to bring our guns with us from Berlin, so we're unarmed. We have little chance of success against Vladimir's men, and I have no idea how long it's going to take Lucy to figure out where these remains are buried.'

'You need all the hands you can get, then,' Jarvis said with a finality that brooked no argument. 'I'm not sitting on my ass and letting you take all the flak.'

Ethan relented and walked faster as he left Jarvis behind and came up alongside Lopez. 'Any bright ideas?'

'Quit, and get out alive.'

'There's a little girl in Chicago relying on us to pull this off.'

'I know that now,' Lopez shot back, having learned of Bethany's plight on the flight from Berlin. 'But what use are we going to be to her if we're dead? There's no way we can defeat Vladimir in an open fight, we're not even armed.'

'We've gotten out of situations as tight as this before,' Ethan replied. 'We're going to have to improvise.'

'Excellent,' Lopez said. 'Improvise away then, captain.'

Ethan winced at Lopez's sarcasm and was about to reply when a faint droning noise rolled across the mountains. Ethan instinctively turned one ear to the noise and slowed as he looked over his shoulder and up into the blackened sky above them. Ribbons of cloud obscured the heavens and a sprinkling of stars that twinkled as he spotted the source of the engine noise. He could just make out a set of red and green navigation lights as they appeared from behind a bank of cloud. It took Ethan a few moments of observation to identify that the aircraft was climbing and turning as it did so, probably something that had lifted off out of Cusco's international airport.

'It's just an airplane,' Lopez said, 'nothing to do with us.'

Ethan squinted at the aircraft. The airport was probably forty miles away from the mountain, and any aircraft taking off on the airport's zero-eight runway would have turned long before it and reached Machu Picchu. Ethan recalled that most airports had a standard departure procedure which was followed rigidly by all aircraft, especially in mountainous countries such as Peru, to avoid unwanted collisions with the terrain.

'Then what's it doing all the way out here at night?' he asked.

The aircraft was almost directly overhead now and passing above banks of rippled cloud. Its high altitude meant that it was glinting as it reflected the light from a sun that had yet to breach the distant horizon, the dawn a pale streak of light between the mountains. Ethan kept his gaze fixed upon it and moments later he identified tiny specks spilling from the aircraft as though its baggage were being deliberately ejected in flight, bathed in the sun's distant glow.

Ethan needed only a moment more to be sure that it wasn't baggage that was spilling from the aircraft.

'It's a HALO deployment,' Ethan said as he identified freefalling parachutists rocketing towards the clouds above. 'High Altitude Low Opening deployment, we used it in the Marines in Iraq.'

'You think they're American?' Jarvis asked as he looked up at the aircraft departing to the north.

'I don't know, but even if they are they may not be on our side. We need to move fast!'

Ethan picked up the pace and joined Lucy and Lopez as they climbed the last few hundred yards toward the city. 'This could be the distraction we were hoping for,' he said to Lopez.

'You think? Now we have two armed groups opposing us, instead of one. How is that going to help?'

Ethan looked at Lucy. 'Whatever happens, you just keep your head down and do what you do. As soon as you find what you're looking for, you get the hell out of here no matter what happens and you get back to Cusco, understood?'

Lucy nodded, and Ethan looked over his shoulder again and craned his neck back to see the specks plummeting through the clouds and emerging beneath them, faintly illuminated by the glow of the moon. The parachutists were leaving their chutes closed until the last possible instant, an extremely dangerous but highly effective tactic, if performed correctly. He realized that it was doubtful that the parachutists were anything other than expert soldiers, almost certainly American and almost certainly members of the Specialist Tactics Squadron they had narrowly avoided death at the hands of in Cambodia.

'When the shooting starts, it's going to be chaos,' Ethan said. 'Let's make sure it's not us being shot at.'

'What's that supposed to mean?'

'Just follow my lead,' Ethan said to Lopez as they reached the walls of the city.

He looked up above him one more time, and this time he saw parachutes billow open like black petals against the darkening sky, could hear the cracks as they filled abruptly with air and slowed the jumpers to prepare them for landing. Even in the low light, he could spot the rifles in their grasp; Bergens dangling beneath them on cords.

Twelve men, highly trained and heavily armed.

'Let's go, move!'

One by one, Ethan and the team scaled the city's outer wall and dashed inside.

XXXII

Ethan dashed in pursuit of Lucy as she ran into the darkness towards the vast blackened silhouette of Machu Picchu. The aircraft was already departing to the north, and Ethan realized with certainty that it would not be returning. The men who had been dispatched from the aircraft would not be returning home without their mission being accomplished, and had been deployed without the permission of the Peruvian government.

'This way!'

Lucy's whisper was harsh in the darkness. Ethan ran hard behind her, trying to see ahead in the near pitch-black. The city was enshrouded in darkness, but the sky was beginning to glow with the first faint light of dawn, and Ethan could see both the city's larger temples silhouetted against the dawn and a large wedge-shaped mountain soaring even higher than Machu Picchu to the north.

Lopez ran alongside him, and behind was Jarvis and his two escorts, the old man jogging along as best he could. To the right, a series of bright headlight beams swept by the visitor center that was nestled at the base of the old city, the sound of car engines growling as the drivers pulled in and the sound of car doors slamming in the darkness.

'Hurry it up, keep moving!' Ethan whispered.

The city was divided into terraces that Ethan presumed were once used to grow crops to feed the city's inhabitants, the terraces descending away toward the sheer faces of the mountainside that plunged toward deep gorges far below. To either side of the great plaza, around which the city was centered, were ranks of buildings and temples, each with names like the Royal Palace and Tombs on the left of the plaza, the Sacred Rock at the far end of the plaza, and the Artisan's Wall on the right, behind which were ranks of houses that ended abruptly in the sheer face of the mountain's eastern flank.

Ethan hauled himself up off a final terrace and into the main plaza, Lopez alongside him as the two escorts behind hauled Jarvis up the ridge and onto the lawned plaza. Voices shouted out, Russian accents sharp against the night air, and a series of flickering flashlight beams sweeping this way and that as the Russians began ascending the terraces from below.

Ethan looked up at the almost invisible figures descending on parachutes, black against blackness and barely a hundred feet above the surface of the terraced lawns.

'This way, quickly!' he whispered.

He turned to Lucy, but she had stopped in the center of the complex and was staring at the towering mountain opposite Machu Picchu.

'Huayna Picchu,' she murmured as though recalling something.

'We need to get out of sight,' Ethan snapped harshly. 'We're sitting ducks out here.'

Lucy appeared lost in thought, staring up at the jagged peak that was now a dark and foreboding presence against the faint dawn sky, rising far higher than Machu Picchu. 'It means *young pyramid* in Quechua,' she said.

'So what?' Ethan asked impatiently.

'Machu Picchu is well documented and excavated,' Lucy explained. 'It holds no further secrets, but Huayna Picchu is less well known and contains remains of the Inca's city, too. If I were a royal Incan priest hoping to conceal the remains of what they believed were the children of the gods, then I'd hide their remains up there.'

Ethan stared up at the peak of the mountain. It soared over a thousand feet above Machu Picchu, and was some eight thousand feet above the depths of the gorges surrounding it.

'Can you get up there?' he asked.

'The Incas built a trail, *Sendero a Huayna Picchu*, but it's very exposed and dangerous,' Lucy said. 'I can make it, but it's at least half an hour even if I run at it.'

'Go, now,' Ethan said. 'We'll hold them all off for as long as we can.'

Lucy set off across the plaza toward Huayana Picchu as Ethan glanced up one last time at the descending parachutists. he knew that they would be wearing night vision goggles, or at the very least infrared heat sensors that would pick out the hot bodies of Ethan and his companions, as well as the Russians. But those sensors would be unable to differentiate between friend and foe, and he could only hope that the Russians voices were as audible to the descending Americans as they were to him.

Ethan ran toward a building opposite the Temple of the Three Windows and the Central Plaza, and clambered up the steps, the stone cold to the touch as he ascended toward a dark and cavernous archway leading to the interior. He recalled from Lucy's description that this was where Hiram Bingham had allegedly found the remarkable remains that had affected the rest of his entire excavation of this incredible site, not to mention his life.

He turned and waved Lopez and Jarvis inside along with the two escorts, and then he saw the shadowy figures of the parachutists landing on the palace lawns. A Russian voice yelled at him and a light pointed directly at the palace, and then suddenly the American parachutists opened fire. A deafening clatter of machine-gun fire rattled out across the lawns and the Russians split and began dashing for cover, two of them crying out in pain as they collapsed. A chaotic flare of AK-47 fire was returned across the lawns, and Ethan ducked out of sight into the temple entrance as the Americans laid down a controlled and lethal hail of fire against the Russians, before they began retreating towards the Palace.

'They're shooting at Vladimir's men,' Jarvis observed with delight. 'They're covering us!'

Lopez shook her head. 'They're doing their job. If we get in their way, they'll kill us just as soon as they will the Russians. Get inside and undercover.'

Lopez unceremoniously shoved Jarvis further into the shadows, and then took shelter on the side of the temple entrance across from Ethan, and watched as the Americans fired controlled bursts against the Russians. Pinned against the Artisan's Wall alongside the Main Plaza, the Russians began retreating toward the temple steps.

'Clever,' Ethan uttered grimly as he watched the battle unfold. 'They're directing the Russians toward us.'

'Two birds, one stone,' Lopez replied and then ducked back out of sight as a salvo of shots smashed into the temple's stone masonry around her.

Ethan watched as two of the Russians fired several shots out across the lawns of the Plaza against the Americans, and then they panicked and fled up the steps for the safety of the temple and higher ground, their rifles pointed out into the darkness.

Ethan looked at Lopez, who nodded from her hiding place in the shadows.

The first two Russians backed into the temple entrance, each of them turning into the same area of shelter as Lopez and Ethan, no doubt preparing to cover their colleagues as they retreated toward them.

Ethan wasted no time. He lifted his left boot and then hopped down onto it as he pulled his right knee up into the Russian's side while dropping both of his elbows down in the opposite direction in order to place the maximum amount of weight and power behind his knee. The solid bone of his knee impacted at the base of the Russian's ribcage and Ethan felt the bones snap like dried twigs as the Russian let out a garbled cry of agony and crumpled sideways into the wall as he tried to turn and bring his AK-47 to bear.

Ethan grabbed the stock of the rifle with his right hand as he brought the knuckles of his left crashing down across the Russian's temple with every ounce of force he could muster. The gunman's head snapped to one side and smacked into the stone wall of the temple. He slumped, unconscious, as Ethan yanked the rifle from his grasp and looked up to see Lopez in the process of driving her right knee into the other Russian's groin and head-butting him as he folded over the blow. The soldier crumpled at the knees as a breathless wheeze of pain escaped from his lips, and Lopez swung a rock she held in one fist across his face to send him sprawling unconscious onto the cold stone floor.

Ethan checked the AK-47 in his grasp and was both surprised and pleased to see it well cleaned and maintained. A spare clip was found in the gunman's jacket pocket. As he reached down, his hand caught on something, and he realized that the Russian was wearing a parachute.

Lopez frowned down at it. 'What the hell are they doing wearing those?'

Ethan pulled at the unconscious man's arm and beneath it he saw a large, webbed fabric as though the man were wearing a bat costume. A quick check of the other arm revealed a similar web of rubber-like fabric.

'It's not a parachute,' Ethan said as he realized what the man was wearing.

'We can't hold out here for long,' Lopez pointed out as another round of gunfire smashed across the walls, two stray rounds entering the temple and causing Jarvis to duck down. 'Two guns against many,' she added as she rifled through the fallen Russian's pockets.

'We have to hold out for as long as we can. The more time we can give Lucy, the better.'

Lopez looked about her, realizing that Lucy was no longer with them.

'Where the hell has she gone?'

Ethan kept a watch on the gunfight raging outside, the noise of the shots deafening, amplified by the temple's narrow confines.

'She's going to retrieve the remains that she's looking for,' Ethan explained. 'They're not here in this temple.'

'Then what the hell are we doing here?'

'Hold the line!' Ethan shouted as the sound of gunfire intensified. 'On my mark, we take out the Russian's, okay?'

Lopez nodded as they huddled near the temple entrance, gunfire raking the stones and steps outside as Ethan waited until the Russians were almost upon them.

He stepped out and aimed down the steps at the men running up toward them just as Lopez poked her head out alongside him and they fired together. The twin muzzle flashes of the two rifles flared brilliantly in the darkness, and illuminated the surprised and horrified faces of six Russians charging up toward them.

Ethan heard a brutal and rapid *thump-thump-thump* as the bullets impacted into the Russian's bodies, and they were hurled backwards to tumble down the steps and topple over the edge, and plunged down onto the plaza below.

The remaining Russians fled the steps and hurled themselves down behind the Artisan's Wall as they sought an escape from the lethal crossfire.

'The STS men are moving in!' Lopez yelled.

Ethan saw the elite American troops now advancing by sections across the plaza, four men moving forward at a run while being covered by their comrades from behind. The four running men sprinted ten yards and then dropped into prone positions and opened fire as the four behind leaped up and ran forward under the fresh covering fire.

'We've got to flank them and get out of here!' he yelled to Lopez.

'And go where?!' she yelled back. 'There's nowhere to go but down and we won't be able to sneak past the STS men! They'll pick us off easily!'

Ethan flinched as a few wild rounds smashed into the stone wall behind which he hid, and in the distance he saw the vehicles the

Russian's had used to climb the mountain, their headlights still illuminating the visitor's center through the trees beyond the plaza and the cultivation terraces on the mountain's southern flank.

'You need to get to those vehicles and make sure nobody else can follow you!'

Lopez nodded as she looked at the visitor's center and then fired off two rounds at the cornered Russians nearby.

'What about you?'

'They'll have to finish off the Russians first,' Ethan shouted back above the gunfire as he ducked back into cover. 'Get Jarvis and his guys off the hill. If you can make it to the Temple of the Condor, you can get around behind the Russians and the Americans, and reach the main tourist trail. I'll go after Lucy.'

'If the Americans catch us, we'll be slaughtered!' Lopez protested as she fired off another couple of rounds down at the Russians.

Ethan shook his head as he looked at the steadily brightening sky. 'Neither the Russians or the Americans should legally be here. They'll have to pull out before the tourists and armed guards arrive. This will all be over by sunrise.'

'Fine!' Lopez yelled back. 'I'll just fetch my magic goddamned carpet!'

Ethan looked at the gardens and the plunging cliffs behind the Temple of the Condor. 'Don't take the normal path across.' He looked over his shoulder at Jarvis and his men. 'I hope you three are all okay with heights!'

Ethan saw the American troops advancing on the Russians' position, knowing that they were also cutting Ethan and his companions off from their escape by doing so.

The STS troops had crossed the plaza but were pinned down by the weight of the Russians' firepower. Even though they were highly trained and disciplined, they were outnumbered three to one: they either would be forced to charge the Russians to end the fire fight, or retreat to fight another day.

Suddenly, the STS troops broke ranks and charged across the plaza, firing indiscriminately as they rushed to overwhelm the Russian position. Fully occupied with hunting down their armed adversaries, Ethan knew that this was their only chance to slip away.

Ethan turned back to Lopez. 'This is it! Get to the main road and get down off the mountain. I'll meet you in Cusco! Go now, I'll cover you!'

Lopez, Jarvis, and the two escorts got to their feet and Lopez led them to the entrance of the temple. The stone steps were now devoid of Russians, who had pulled back and were crouched in groups in alleys all around the Artisan's Wall, almost a hundred yards away, as they fired desperately on the charging Americans.

Ethan turned and fired off a full clip at both the Russians and the STS as Lopez, Jarvis, and his escort hurried out of the temple and turned right, away from the steps toward the warren of alleys that descended the eastern slopes of the city and the mountain.

The AK-47 shuddered into silence in his grip as its clip emptied, and Ethan hurled the weapon to one side and made sure that Lopez and the others were away and clear. He glanced back into the temple as an idea crossed his mind, and he worked hurriedly before he fled the temple toward Huayna Picchu.

*

The sound of distant gunfire echoed off the hills as Lucy labored ever upward, virtually crawling up the stone steps and forcing herself to keep looking straight ahead and not to her right, where the faint light of dawn was illuminating ethereal veils of wispy cloud drifting over the Urabamba River eight thousand feet below the sheer face of the mountain.

Lucy had taken the lower slopes at a run, climbing the winding track between the forests, sprinting as though pursued by the gunfire that she could hear raging in the distance across the ancient citadel. She knew that it would not be long before Ethan and Lopez were overpowered by one faction or the other, and her pursuers would know that there was only one place she could have fled.

Against the dark sky rose the towering peak of Huayna Picchu, overlooking the vast citadel below it. Still clad in jungle growth and vines protruding from the rocky crags of the mountain's peak, it stood more than a thousand feet higher than its more famous companion, closer to the sky. *Closer to the Gods.*

Lucy climbed ever upwards, through tiny fissures in the rock face and across narrow ledges that overlooked the dizzying depths below, and were so precarious that she was forced to crawl across them on her hands and knees just as Hiram Bingham had once done a century before her. Her breath sawed in her throat and her pace slowed as she labored upward, driven forward only by the knowledge that somewhere, half a world away, a little girl might live if Lucy could overcome her exhaustion and fear and reach the summit.

The mountainside fell away to one side of the track, a sheer face that descended deep into the gorges far below. Wreaths of cloud hung like phantoms on the cold air around her as she climbed, her balance wavering with dizziness in the thin air as she labored up the narrow track until finally she emerged, crawling once more, onto a narrow summit marked by a battered old wooden sign.

Lucy got to her feet and sucked in great breaths of air in an attempt to recover herself as she leaned against the sign and looked at the mountain peak before her. Enshrouded in dense foliage, the far side of the peak dropped away to reveal steep terraces and a series of crumbling stone temples clinging to the precipitous side of the mountain.

Lucy staggered across to the stone steps that led down toward the buildings, and then suddenly her courage failed her as she reached the edge. The track was barely two feet wide, built from loose stone that descended alongside a stone wall to her left. To her right was literally nothing but an eight thousand foot fall down the sheer wall of the mountain toward the river far, far below. An updraft of wind billowed toward her from the plunging chasm and threatened to drag her off into oblivion.

Lucy gasped and gripped the edge of the wall as she looked away from the endless depths and tried to control her thundering heartbeat.

'Just a little further,' she urged herself.

Lucy set one foot down on the steps as she kept her face to the wall and slowly descended the treacherous path toward the temples below. Perched on craggy outcrops that seemed specifically designed to scare the hell out of anybody attempting to reach them, she could see the largest of them, a building that had once possessed a roof that had long since been destroyed by the elements.

Lucy reached the bottom of the stone steps, the view ahead consisting of a rocky outcrop and then another plunging drop into oblivion. She turned, still clinging to the wall as she stepped gingerly toward the temple, once again exposed to the sheer drop to her right. Lucy tried not to think about the fact that the only way off the mountain was to actually ascend those same steps all over again. She reached the entrance to the temple and walked inside with a deep breath of relief.

The temple was open to the elements and somewhat resembled a small church, built from stone with three openings looking out of one wall toward the mountains and gorges outside, and higher walls front and back that would have supported the roof structure. The floor was of cobbled stones that fit tightly together, and ahead was what looked like a small altar set against the far wall beneath a single opening. Above it, the sun would shine through the opening at sunrise and illuminate the temple's interior. Lucy looked to her side at the three openings in the temple wall, just like those of Egypt's religious temples, and the trapezoidal entrance, again exactly the same as comparable Egyptian buildings.

Lucy looked down at the front of the ancient stone altar, and there she saw engraved into the rock a single icon: a sun, with beams of light emanating from beneath it, or a quipu with its informative pendents. But this time the lines were all of the same length, save one.

Lucy moved forward and knelt before the altar as she examined the icon. The central line extending down from the sun was longer than the rest, as so often was the case, but this time the line extended all the way down and vanished into the ground at her feet.

'This is it,' she gasped, her voice sounding odd within the hollow building's walls and in the sepulchral silence that enshrouded the temple. 'This is where they placed you, a royal tomb, the highest in the entire empire and facing the sun.'

Lucy looked down at the stones beneath her feet. The Inca were expert stonemasons who built vast cities without mortar, shaped each and every stone to fit perfectly alongside its neighbors. Using the method, identical to that of the ancient Egyptians, they had constructed massive citadels that had stood for centuries despite the earthquakes that rocked the Andes mountain chain.

The stone floor of the temple was as neatly fitted together as any other part of the entire construction, except for one tiny detail: whereas all the other stones were fitted together so tightly that one could not pass even a slip of paper between them, a small number of the stones beneath her feet had moss growing in the gaps between them. Lucy stood up and backed away slightly from the altar to see that the moss formed a perfect rectangle among the stones beneath her feet, directly in front of the altar.

As she moved alongside the rectangle, Lucy reached into her backpack and produced a folding shovel, and placed the tip of the blade over one of the gaps in the stones. She drove her foot down onto the shovel, and the metal scraped as it dug down into the gap, ever so slightly wider than those of the stones around it so that moisture and eventually moss had been able to grow and fill the gap.

The tip of the shovel sank only two or three inches down, but it was enough for Lucy to get leverage on the handle. She leaned her boot down upon it, bouncing her weight up and down, and with a scraping sound the stone lifted out of the ground as the shovel got beneath it and pried it from the earth.

Lucy levered the stone aside and began working on the next, prying one after another out of the ancient soil until she could see bare earth in a rectangle before the altar. She got down onto her knees and began scraping the earth away with the trowel, gouging chunks of it away until her hands brushed against fabric.

Lucy gasped as she worked, pulled out more soil and scattered it all around her as she frantically excavated the tight bundle buried at the altar and stared down at it in awe.

In the shallow grave, lay a burial shroud every bit as old as the ones that had been discovered decades before in Paracus, the body within completely concealed. Around the neck of the shroud was a quipu.

'I found you,' she whispered. 'I finally found you.'

Lucy reached down and carefully pocketed the quipu, then unwrapped the head of the shroud, placing layer after layer of fabric on the soil next to her until she finally revealed the skeletal remains within. The skull appeared first, and Lucy felt a supernatural awe creep through her as she saw it.

For the most part, the remains resembled those of an ordinary child but for the fused breastplate and elongated digits with what looked like extra bones that made them longer than those of a human. But the skull was bulbous, swelling from a narrow, delicate jaw to a broad teardrop-shape somewhat resembling a giant light bulb. Two enormous cavities denoted the position of what had once been very large eyes, and even at a glance Lucy could tell that the cranial capacity was far greater than that of even an adult human.

But in that same glance her heart plummeted in her chest in disappointment.

The soil of the high Andes Mountains was damp and cold, and the flesh of the being she saw laying before her had long ago rotted away. A dense pall of grief pulled down so hard on her she felt as though it would drag her heart from her chest as she recognised the level of degradation that the remains had suffered. The bones were brittle and stained with mud, which she had no doubt infiltrated deep into the marrow. Any genetic remains, any DNA that might have been present within the bones, would by now have become so degraded as to be useless.

Lucy rested her forehead on her hands for a moment as she took a deep breath. She pulled the quipu from her pocket and sadly began sorting through the knots and strings, and then slowly she began to feel her heart beat quicken once more.

'You weren't alone,' she whispered to herself.

The quipu spoke its ancient dialect to her, and she realized that once again directions were encoded into the message, directions that must point to further tombs.

Lucy wrapped the skull once more, and then tied the shroud back in place before she lifted the remains out of the tomb and turned for the temple exit. A single click alerted her to the presence of an intruder just as Vladimir Polkov stepped into the temple entrance, a pistol in his grip and a grim smile on his face.

XXXIII

Ethan dragged himself up through a narrow fissure in the rocks, carved footholds in the stones beneath his feet that he somehow managed to get his boots into as he squeezed through the gap and out onto the flank of the mountain.

The sky above was brightening, and as he emerged onto a dizzyingly narrow stepped path that led further up the mountainside, he realized that he could no longer hear the sound of gunfire coming from behind him down on Machu Picchu. He grabbed the rocky ledge and turned to look back down toward the city, and in the growing light he could see tourist vehicles far below winding their way up the Hiram Bingham trail.

Ethan's stomach lurched as he saw the gorge wide open right alongside him, the Urabamba River's winding green course just visible through the wreaths of morning cloud crowning the immense heights. He squeezed his eyes shut and forced himself to breathe slowly before he opened his eyes once more and looked at the citadel's visitor's center far below.

The Russian vehicles were gone, several of them making their way down the mountainside. Ethan knew that there was little that he could do to help: either Lopez and Jarvis had secreted themselves somewhere and would now mingle with the tourists when they arrived and make good their escape, or they had been captured by the STS team or the Russians.

He squinted and saw several black-clad figures making their way to the city's western side and the sheer face of the mountain there, and realized that the STS troops were making to escape via rappel lines and climbing gear, avoiding the oncoming tourists and guards. As he watched, he saw them dragging the bodies of dead Russians and tossing them over the edge into the plunging gorge.

Ethan turned away and clambered up the endless steps toward the peak of the mountain, his breath laboring in his chest and his heart racing. The sky was becoming brighter with every moment, and against it the broken clouds were glowing orange as they were hit by the first rays of the rising sun.

Ethan pulled himself up onto the plateau of Huayna Picchu and squinted as a bright flare of sunlight blazed into his eyes. He barely saw the figure moving on top of the plateau toward him, but in an instant he recognised the shape of a man carrying a rifle and he threw himself to one side as the rifle clattered noisily as it opened fire.

The gunfire smashed into the ground at Ethan's feet as he rolled behind a crumbling stone wall. The gunfire ceased and Ethan remained in cover as a voice called out to him, the Russian accent filled with delight.

'Come out, Mr Warner. I have something that you'll want to see.'

Ethan remained where he was. 'The American military is here. There's no way off this mountain, Vladimir. You're finished, no matter what happens.'

'On the contrary, it is you and your friends who are finished,' Vladimir replied. 'Why don't you ask your friend Lucy, here?'

Ethan cursed and peeked around the edge of the stone wall to see Vladimir holding an AK-47 in one hand while with the other he gripped Lucy firmly around the neck, his forearm around her throat and lifting her chin so that her feet were barely touching the ground.

Under Vladimir's arm was a tightly wrapped bundle of fabric, and Ethan realized that Lucy had been able to find the remains they were searching for. Vladimir jabbed the rifle up under Lucy's throat and his delighted smile dissolved into a look of pure hatred.

'Come out now, or I swear I'll blow her head clean off her shoulders.'

Ethan searched desperately for something to use as a weapon but there was nothing but dust and soil at his feet. He grabbed a handful of dust in one hand and then he raised them either side of his head as he got to his feet and stepped out from behind the wall.

Vladimir sneered at him as he switched the rifle to point at Ethan while still keeping a firm grip on Lucy's throat.

'Excellent,' he said finally. 'I've waited quite some time for this moment, Mr Warner. You've proven yourself to be an extremely annoying distraction from my work, and one I'll be glad to erase from history.'

'Your men are defeated,' Ethan repeated. 'You won't be able to leave this place without being arrested or shot on sight. Let her go.'

'Foolish American,' Vladimir snapped. 'The Americans are now as impotent as my own men on this mountain, do you think that I don't know that? You think that you have all the answers, but so often you are so wrapped up in your own ingenuity that you miss the obvious.'

Ethan squinted, the bright sunlight flaring in his eyes between Vladimir's and Lucy's head. He thought he saw Lucy vaguely shake her head, her eyes wide as she tried to dissuade Ethan from whatever he was about to attempt. Ethan knew that she would do anything she could to defend the remains bundled beneath Vladimir's arm, that she was more concerned about finding the cure for Bethany than anything else, no matter how startling the archaeological revelations might be.

Vladimir gestured with the rifle to one side of the plateau. 'Move over there, stand on the edge.'

Ethan glanced in the gestured direction and saw a raised platform of stone, perhaps once used to worship the rising sun or maybe even perform sacrifices to the ancient Inca gods. He kept his hands in the air beside his head as he moved across to the platform and clambered up onto it. Vladimir turned with his grip still firmly around Lucy's neck, a fresh smile plastered across his face as he watched Ethan mount the platform and turn to face him.

Ethan glanced down off the edge of the platform and felt his guts turn over and his legs weaken as he saw the tremendous sheer face of the mountain falling away behind him and plunging thousands of feet into the gorge. The river below was a silvery thread beneath thick banks of mist and early morning cloud that rolled between the mountain peaks. He turned back to face Vladimir, who raised a questioning eyebrow.

'What do you think the odds are of anybody finding you down there?'

Ethan did not reply as he looked again at Lucy, this time the sun not blinding him but instead shining toward Vladimir and Lucy, Ethan's own shadow blocking the sunlight from their faces. Lucy again vaguely shook her head as she tried to discourage him from whatever he might intend to do.

'This doesn't change anything,' Ethan said to Vladimir. 'You'll never get those remains out of Peru now. Every single law enforcement officer will be watching every single airport, seaport, and road searching for you and your accomplices. You'll be arrested at the first checkpoint you reach.'

'Maybe, maybe not,' Vladimir replied. 'Either way, you'll be nothing but a damp spot in the center of that gorge.'

Vladimir raised the rifle to point at Ethan's chest, and Ethan sidestepped one pace and let the full force of the sunrise blaze into Vladimir's face. The Russian squinted and jerked his head to one side as he tried to maintain his aim, and at that moment Lucy reached up to grab Vladimir's forearm. With a single jerk of her head she opened her mouth wide and bit deeply into his flesh.

Vladimir screamed as he yanked his arm free from Lucy, and Ethan rushed down off the platform and crashed past the AK-47 as he opened his right hand and pressed the mud and dust directly into Vladimir's eyes. The Russian toppled backwards and groaned in pain as the sharp dust and sand scraped across his eyeballs. Ethan purposely let himself fall on top of Vladimir, and shoved the Russian's head back where it impacted with the ground.

Vladimir growled and his eyes rolled up in their sockets, the whites smeared with mud and grime, but he kept a firm grip on the AK-47, and to Ethan's surprise maintained his consciousness. It was only then that Ethan saw that the Russian was also wearing what looked like a parachute on his back, and Ethan realized that Vladimir intended to abandon his own men and leap from the enormous mountain in an attempt to escape into one of the deep gorges surrounding the site.

Vladimir drove his boots up towards Ethan's groin and sought to bite Ethan's face. Ethan jerked back just in time for Vladimir to ram the AK-47's stock across his jaw. Ethan rolled off the Russian, who delivered a frenzied cloud of blows to his face as he struggled to get to his feet, but holding the bundled remains under one arm slowed Vladimir and made him vulnerable.

Ethan grabbed the stock of the AK-47 and pressed it to one side to prevent the Russian from taking a shot, and then drove upward with his right boot as he swung his right fist hard across Vladimir's jaw. The impact cracked out loudly in the cold morning air and echoed off the surrounding cliffs as Vladimir staggered to one side against the stone altar.

Ethan swung a boot at his right wrist and it connected with a dull crack that sent the AK-47 spinning from Vladimir's grasp. The Russian cried out as the tendons and bones in his wrist cracked. He tried to reach out for the weapon, but the rifle had already gone over the edge. Ethan heard it clatter away down the sheer cliffs into oblivion as he stepped in to finish the Russian off, fists clenched and held before him.

Vladimir reached behind him into his waistband, and in the bright sunlight a wicked-looking blade flashed and whipped towards Ethan's face. Ethan ducked in surprise and backed off.

'Time to leave,' Vladimir sneered at Ethan.

Lucy Morgan reached out from where she lay on the ground. 'No, don't do it!'

Vladimir ignored her and leaped up onto the platform. Ethan knew that he was going to jump, and in a last-ditch attempt to snatch the remains from his grasp, Ethan propelled himself forward and leaped up onto the platform.

Vladimir crouched down slightly, and then whirled and launched himself off the edge of the platform and out into open air. Ethan's foot hit the edge of the platform and he felt it beneath the sole of his boot, the perfectly cut right-angled stone his last connection with solid ground, and he knew that he would not be able to stop himself from going further. With a cry of desperation, he pushed off as hard as he could and flew out into midair directly above Vladimir and barely a yard away.

Time seemed to stand still as he saw the Russian beneath him clutching the bundle of fabric under one arm and the knife in his other hand. Ethan felt his stomach plunge as he began to accelerate into the abyss after Vladimir. The cold wind rushed past his face and through his clothes, and his shirt rippled, moisture sprinkled his hair and skin as he plummeted towards the clouds below.

Vladimir rolled over in midair with the knife in one hand and the bundle in the other as he spread his arms and legs. Thick webbing spread out like bat's wings between his upper thighs and between his elbows and waist, and the Russian soared away from Ethan.

Ethan hurled his jacket off and mimicked Vladimir's movements as the flying suit he had stolen from the Russian gunman in the temple on Machu Picchu opened and he felt his plunge arrested as the webbed suit generated lift and he soared in pursuit of Vladimir.

He saw panic on Vladimir's face as the Russian realized that he was being pursued. For the first time in the fight, Ethan's experience as a Marine parachutist came in, and he tucked his arms and legs in and accelerated as Vladimir reached for a parachute release cord on his chest.

Ethan slammed down onto the Russian's back and his body pinned the chute in its pack as they plummeted together down the gorge, rocketing along at what felt like a hundred miles per hour as their suits let them fly like birds. Wreaths of cloud hurtled by as Vladimir turned the blade in his hand and attempted to stab Ethan in the face.

The blade flashed in the air and Ethan grabbed it, catching not the handle but the blade. He held onto it even though he felt the keen, sharp edge bite into the flesh of his fingers, and then he reached around Vladimir's chest and grabbed the handle with his good hand as the Russian turned over in midair. The lift vanished from their webbed suits, and they rocketed down through the gorge in a lethal dive as the dense clouds swallowed them whole, nothing visible around them but grey mist that streamed moisture across Ethan's face. He heard the Russian cry out in panic as he tried to pull his parachute cord again, but nothing happened. Ethan grabbed him under the jaw with one hand, and with the other he forced the knife up and under the Russians arm and plunged the blade point first toward his chest.

Vladimir cried out and tried to push the blade away. Ethan looked over his shoulder and he knew that they had only seconds before they would plunge from the cloud and down into the rocky depths of the Urabamba River. Vladimir pushed hard against the knife and this time Ethan pulled with him. Vladimir's arms were yanked away from him and the bundle beneath them tumbled away into mid air.

Vladimir reached for it and his grip on the blade failed him. Ethan tore the knife from him with one brutal yank, and then he pushed away from the Russian and slashed the parachute on his back.

Ethan plunged out of the cloud alongside Vladimir, who was grasping for the bundle falling beside him. He grabbed it with one hand and directed a savage grin of victory at Ethan before he pulled his chute cord again. The drogue chute billowed open above them with an audible boom as Ethan saw the Russian shoot away under the immense deceleration, but almost immediately the chute tore apart with a thunderous crack.

Vladimir screamed as he fell alongside the burial shroud and plummeted towards the rocks of the river below. Ethan rolled over and extended his arms and legs as his suit once again generated lift and he soared away. He found his gaze fixed upon the Russian as he plunged the last few hundred feet toward the floor of the gorge and then his body smashed into the rocks with an audible crunch and disintegrated upon impact in a dark flare of crimson blood.

Alongside Vladimir, the burial shroud plummeted into the deep water with a crash and vanished beneath the waves. Ethan looked ahead and saw the sparkling surface of the river's torrent flowing beneath him, could hear now its roar as it thundered through the narrow gorge barely two hundred feet beneath him.

Ethan reached to his chest and yanked his own parachute cord, heard the chute billow out behind him as he raced down the valley. The chute yanked him to a near-halt and his legs swung up beneath him as he fought for control. He looked up desperately for the control handles of the chute above him, grabbing them and searching for a place to land. In the turbulent airflow within the valley, he had little control over the chute as it swirled this way and that, caught on the gusts blustering through the gorge as the water rushed up toward him.

Ethan took a chance and yanked down hard on one handle, and the chute swept in a hard right turn above the waves toward a steep bank densely clogged with a thicket of trees and bushes. The branches rushed by beneath his boots and Ethan took his chance as he released both of the control handles, pinched the release buckle on the suit and pointed his hands straight up in the air above him.

Ethan dropped from the chute harness and plunged into the freezing water. He shielded his face with one arm as he tumbled end over end in the torrent until he finally broke the surface. With a scrambling, desperate frenzy of strokes he reached the shore of a narrow spit of beach hugging one side of the gorge and dragged himself up onto it.

Ethan lay there for a moment and then turned his head to see Vladimir's shattered corpse float down the nearby river, and further downstream the bobbing form of the burial shroud vanishing into the distance, never to be seen again.

XXXIV

Alejandro Velasco Astete International Airport
Cusco, Peru

Yuri Polkov sat in silence as he stared out of the Learjet's windows at the glorious sunset that swept across the western horizon. The sky was filled with vibrant colors as though a celebration was taking place in the heavens. If ever Yuri needed confirmation that there was no god, no caring omnipotent figure watching over humanity, then the spectacular festival of light and color on such a tragic day was it. Yuri barely heard the words of one of his son's most trusted aides, Allayn, as he spoke, his voice thick and his eyes focused somewhere above and behind Yuri's head.

'We were engaged by a force of American paramilitary soldiers as we entered the city of Machu Picchu. They pinned us down near the center of the ruins. I lost count of how many there were, dozens, maybe hundreds. We were forced to retreat and lost about half of our number.'

Yuri rested his chin on his gnarled old hands. 'Why was Vladimir up there with you?'

Allayn swallowed, his thick bull-neck trembling as he replied.

'Vladimir wanted to personally oversee the operation and ensure that he obtained the remains you sought. He made a break for it early on during the firefight and pursued Lucy Morgan to an adjacent peak. My men and I attempted to follow them but were cut off by the other American, Ethan Warner, who opened fire on us from close range and forced us back into the soldier's ambush.'

Yuri clenched his fingers more tightly together. 'What happened to my son?'

Allayn hesitated and then sighed as though finally surrendering to his fate, whatever that might be.

'During our retreat, we saw two people leap from the top of the adjacent mountain and fight in freefall down into a gorge. Peruvian authorities recovered a body from the Urabamba River wearing clothes that we recognised as Vladimir's. He had died after freefalling directly into the river and was killed on impact.'

Yuri stared vacantly into the middle distance and his knuckles cracked as he compressed them in silent fury.

'What of the American, Warner?'

Allayn lifted his chin. 'Warner was seen boarding an aircraft at Maria Reich Airstrip later that morning, along with Lucy Morgan and the other members of their team.'

Yuri nodded slowly, as though he had been expecting that reply all along.

'Was Vladimir successful in recovering the remains we sought from Machu Picchu?'

Allayn appeared to wince.

'No remains that I know of were recovered from the site, either by Vladimir, us, Morgan, or the American troops. My men did not observe any materials or objects being carried by Lucy Morgan when they boarded the aircraft at the airstrip, so it would appear that none of us succeeded at all.'

Yuri ground his teeth in his weary jaw. 'So it would appear.'

Allayn swallowed thickly. 'I'm very sorry for your loss, Mr Polkov. Is there anything that I can do for you?'

For the first time, Yuri looked up into the thug's eyes. 'Yes. Yes, there is.'

'Name it.'

Yuri reached into his jacket pocket and with one hand and produced a small, ornate silver pistol. 'Hang onto this for me.'

Allayn reached out for the pistol, and Yuri aimed it at his chest and fired. The shot was deafeningly loud in the jet's interior, and Allayn stared in shock at Yuri and then down at his own chest where a rapidly spreading bloodstain bloomed from within his fractured heart. Allayn gasped as his legs crumpled from beneath him and he slumped onto the walkway, his eyes staring lifelessly at Yuri's shoes.

Yuri stared down without interest at the corpse as the Learjet's pilots hurried aft from the cockpit and came to an abrupt halt as they saw the dead man lying amid a pool of blood. Yuri looked up at them.

'We have some extra trash to dispose of, gentlemen. See to it.'

The pilots looked at one another and then hurried away as Yuri leaned back in his seat and marvelled at the wondrous sky blossoming outside. His only son and heir was dead, murdered at the hands of Ethan Warner or one of his cronies. There was nobody now to inherit the vast fortune that he had built over the years, nobody to continue the family name, nobody with whom to share all he had achieved over his lifetime.

Nobody.

One of Vladimir's other thugs, the man named Sergei, strode into the jet and hesitated as he saw the dead body. Yuri watched as the two pilots returned with a large canvass sack and began hauling the dead body into it, Sergei also watching in furtive silence. Yuri realized that one day he, too, would be dead and buried with nobody to remember him, nobody to raise a glass to his memory. No doubt, there would be many who would raise a glass to his death, but Yuri cared not for their future joy, only his present revenge.

He waited until the pilots had dragged the corpse away and then he waved Sergei forward.

'Sergei,' he greeted him. 'Vladimir is lost. There is no time for remorse or condolences. There is nothing that can be done. We must honor his memory the best way we know, by avenging his death. The Americans boarded their Catalina and disappeared. They could not yet have gone far.'

'I have tracked their movements as you requested, Yuri,' Sergei replied. 'Their aircraft flew south, toward the Atacama Desert.'

Yuri fell silent for a long moment. The Atacama Desert, the driest region on Earth, was a desiccated wasteland of barren plains, soaring mountains, and extinct volcanoes. But those unenviable qualities were not what interested Yuri the most.

In 1999, three Inca mummies had been discovered on Mount Llullaillaco in Argentina, high above the Atacama plains. One, a fifteen year-old girl, was one of the best preserved ancient mummies ever discovered. Yuri had travelled to Argentina's High Mountain Archaeological Museum himself to personally inspect her remains. The girl has been so perfectly preserved that she had appeared to Yuri to be merely asleep, downy hairs still visible on her arms, lice still lodged in her thick, black hair.

The tomb had also contained a collection of gold, silver, shells, textiles, and pots for food, and elaborate headdresses made from the feathers of exotic birds. CT scans had shown that her internal organs were in perfect condition: there was still blood in her heart, her brain was undamaged, and when the blood vessels were thawed the blood that poured out of them was crimson. DNA samples had been taken and later matched to a man from a small village some one thousand miles away at the foot of Mount Ampato, making him a *"living Inca"* with a direct bloodline to the young girl sacrificed five centuries before.

If Lucy Morgan had found the location of an Incan sacrificial site that contained remains similar to those found at Paracus…

'That's it,' he said to Sergei with clairvoyant conviction. 'Track every possible known trajectory to the Atacama Range, search every database, find them and report to me as soon as you do. I want them alive when I find them, so that I can kill them myself.'

*

Jorge Chavez International Airport,
Peru

'The Russians are on the run.'

Aaron Devlin nodded as Lieutenant Veer pointed to a map of Peru that was spread on a table before them. Aaron frowned as he scanned the map. They had occupied an office in a municipal building on the airport's north-west corner.

'How many of them were there?'

'We counted thirty, of whom we killed at least twelve. All of them were Russian or Eastern European, judging by their accents. Local authorities recently pulled the body of Vladimir Polkov out of the water down-river from Machu Picchu – two of my team witnessed the recovery operation.' Veer hesitated, and Aaron saw his jaw clench as he spoke. 'I lost two men myself, sir. I want these bastards hung out to dry.'

'Patience, lieutenant,' Aaron cautioned. 'Vengeance will cloud your judgement, and we've already let Morgan and Warner slip through our fingers enough times, agreed?'

'Warner didn't make it out, or at least he wasn't with the rest of his team when we caught up with them,' Veer said with grim satisfaction.

'And the remains that Lucy Morgan sought?'

'Nobody left the site with anything,' the commander replied. 'Morgan's team made their way down the mountain among other tourists two hours after the attack. We were able to gain access to the ruins atop Huayana Picchu, and it appears that a small tomb was excavated there, but if there was anything inside it was too large to carry concealed down the mountain.'

Aaron thought for a long moment.

'Morgan's path has been guided by Inca quipu, which can fit inside a pocket with ease,' he pointed out. 'She may have found another one in the tomb.'

'That's entirely possible, sir,' Veer acknowledged.

'Where are they now?'

'They boarded a privately owned aircraft, a Catalina, which operated under an IFR flight plan filed for transit to Cerro Moreno International Airport, Argentina.'

'Do we have units on the ground there?'

'I was able to get two operatives into the city of Antofagasta at about the same time as their aircraft arrived. They picked up the trail but are having difficulty maintaining contact with Morgan's team.'

'How so?' Aaron asked, straightening a little.

'The team have hired two vehicles and a large supply of mountaineering equipment such as oxygen bottles, crampons, and ice axes. They departed the city this morning to the south-east. There's not much out there, and my men were not able to get close enough to the team to place GPS markers on their vehicles without being spotted. They're essentially tracking them blind, and contact is getting sketchy even with their satellite phones. Wherever they're headed, it's pretty much the most remote location anywhere in the region.'

'We'll deploy immediately,' Aaron ordered. 'Morgan must have at least one play left to be travelling into such a hostile region. Have you been able to plot any potential destination?'

'There's nothing out there, sir, except high mountains, volcanoes, and barren plains. Their presumed destination is the mountains of the Atacama Desert, but it will take them at least a day or two to travel that far.'

Aaron thought for a moment. 'What of Yuri Polkov?'

'His private jet is making for the same location, sir.'

Aaron nodded.

'Prepare the men,' he ordered. 'We will follow Polkov, and in time he will lead us to Lucy Morgan and her team.'

XXXV

Mount Llullaillaco, Puna de Atacama, Argentina

A brutal gale swept into Ethan's face as he climbed the steeply inclined slope, the bitter cold biting into his skin as it swept up from the arid Atacama desert far below and was chilled by the high atmosphere.

He stopped for breath and gazed around at the spectacular scenery, wide mountain ranges against a hard blue sky that, literally, took his breath away, the air at this altitude immensely thin and barely breathable. The barren wastes of the Atacama Desert stretched away into the distance far below and vanished into an asthmatic haze, a wilderness that they had been traversing for two days.

'Does anybody else have a problem with us climbing an active volcano?' Lopez rasped as she joined Ethan.

Surrounded by debris fields from previous eruptions that littered its slopes, Mount Llullaillaco was the second highest volcano in the world and the seventh highest in the Andes mountain range. Perpetually capped with snow patches, the ridge upon which they stood was thousands of meters above sea level.

'The mountain's name is from the Aymara dialect, and means *treacherous water*,' Lucy informed them as she reached the ridge, 'probably because of the snow run-off in spring that would have been laced with volcanic debris.'

'Fascinating,' Lopez murmured without interest. 'Got any decent explanations for why we're up here in the middle of nowhere?'

Behind them, a small baggage train of native *huaqueros* followed, one of them helping Jarvis and two of his men along the ascent. The climbing route selected needed no specialised techniques, but the sheer altitude was in itself a danger and oxygen was being carried as part of their equipment. Ethan and most of the team carried crampons and ice axes to cross major ice patches that they had encountered above the snow line. Nearby, Ethan could see warning signs erected to warn of land mines left since the conflict between Argentina and nearby Chile in the late 70s and early 80s.

'There have been numerous archaeological expeditions to this mountain in the past,' Lucy explained as they waited for Jarvis. 'American archaeologist Dr. Johan Reinhard directed three surveys of archaeological sites on the summit, and in 1999 on Llullaillaco's summit an Argentine-Peruvian expedition, co-directed by Reinhard and Constanza Ceruti ,found the preserved bodies of three Incan children, sacrificed half a millennia earlier. It was the highest Incan burial so far discovered in Tawantinsuyu and is now the world's highest archaeological site.'

'Sacrificed?' Lopez echoed. 'Children?'

'It was a common practice among the ancient Inca,' Lucy confirmed. 'They were conducted as part of the *capacocha*, a sacrificial rite that celebrated key events in the life of an Incan emperor. The best examples we have are of a six-year-old girl nicknamed La nina del rayo, or *Lightning Girl*, due to her remains having been partially burned by a lightning strike, a young boy, and a teenage girl nicknamed La doncella, or *The Maiden*. Their remains were perfectly preserved due to the extreme aridity and cold temperatures of this area, perhaps why it was chosen by the Inca despite its extremely difficult location.'

'Can't we just go and look at the remains in a museum?' Jarvis asked as he finally reached them, his features drained and his breath coming in short, fast gasps.

'We'll be looking at *your* remains in a museum, if you go much higher,' Lopez observed with what might have been a hint of anticipation in her tones. 'You should wait here.'

Jarvis straightened his back and sucked in a lung full of the thin air, which took a lot longer than it should have. 'I won't be quitting any time soon.'

'More's the pity.'

Ethan turned and looked up at the volcano's distant peak. 'You think that there are more of these mummies up here, something that you can use to help Bethany?'

Lucy nodded as she reached into her pocket with her gloved hand and produced both a map and the quipu she had recovered from the remains at Huyuana Picchu.

'I do,' she said, 'and this quipu is guiding us. The direction of the quipu's longest pendent pointed us to this location, but it is the knots within it that are directing us to a particular spot on the mountain side. If we find that, we should find what we're looking for.'

'Which is?' Lopez enquired demurely.

'Fresh remains preserved from decay by the extreme cold and aridity of this region, and likely the most highly protected of all Incan burials,' Lucy replied as she set off again. 'That's what we need here, and if I'm right, the remains won't be entirely human.'

Lucy marched off up the hillside, leaving Lopez, Ethan, and Jarvis looking at each other. Lopez flashed a bright smile at Doug Jarvis.

'Not entirely human. Seems likely you won't be on your own then, Doug.'

Lopez trudged off in pursuit of Lucy before Doug could reply. 'Why are you still hanging out with her?' he asked Ethan as they began climbing again.

'I'm not,' Ethan replied. 'She showed up in Cambodia, had probably been following us for some time.'

'How did she know what you were doing?'

'Lucy came looking for me in Chicago, and when she couldn't find me her first port of call afterward was Lopez.'

Jarvis peered up the hillside, squinting against the fine spray of ice crystals being whipped off the surface of the snow through which they crunched. 'But she didn't accompany Lucy.'

'Lucy said that Lopez wasn't interested in finding me, which I can imagine is probably true. I pretty much left her in the lurch when I quit Warner and Lopez Inc.'

Jarvis nodded absentmindedly. 'Makes me wonder what happened to change her mind.'

'I'm guessing that she had an attack of conscience,' Ethan replied. 'She knows what's at stake here because Lucy told her.'

'Why did you quit?' Jarvis asked, changing the subject abruptly.

Ethan did not reply for a moment as he gathered his thoughts. 'I needed a change from Chicago, from everything. After we did that final job for you in New York City, after Joanna showed up alive and well and went on her way, it just seemed like the end of a chapter and I needed to get out. I stayed working with Lopez for over a year but my heart wasn't in it.'

'And so you went to live in a damp cottage in Scotland?'

Ethan looked sharply at Jarvis. 'You've been watching me?'

Jarvis shook his head. 'Not watching, but I made it my business to find out where you'd gone after you quit. I never know when I might need to call on somebody for difficult work.'

'I don't do that kind of work, anymore.'

'And yet here you are.'

'This is different.'

'This is exactly the same,' Jarvis insisted. 'You may be working for a different cause but you're working nonetheless, looking for things that nobody else can find, travelling to the ends of the earth for somebody you've never even met.'

Ethan said nothing, shoved his hands in his pockets as they trudged ever upward. Jarvis sighed as he took another pull on his oxygen mask and gestured to the barren wilderness around them.

'I'm retired, too,' he pointed out. 'And yet here I am marching up a damned volcano because the powers that be in Washington suggested that it might be helpful to them. You and I are much the same, Ethan. We have an unquenchable thirst to discover, to solve problems, to find solutions to things that others would not have even started a quest to find, yet alone achieved their goal. You're here because you want to be here.'

'I'm here because a three-year-old girl will die if we don't find what Lucy is looking for,' Ethan snapped back. 'I consider that a good enough reason to take a trip halfway round the globe. If you're trying to suggest that you can get me working for the DIA again because you think that I somehow need to, you're pulling the wrong chain.'

'Who said anything about working for the DIA?'

'You're a government man, Doug, and you have been ever since you transferred from the Marine Corps. Even if I were working for you directly, I have absolutely no doubt that you would be on the paycheck of one government agency or another.'

Jarvis shrugged and chuckled. 'You're probably right, but we all have to pay the bills, Ethan. What would you rather be doing? Marching up a volcano in pursuit of alien remains while being chased by Russians, or shivering in a damp foxhole in the Scottish Highlands hoping you won't be found by a bunch of British infantry recruits?'

Ethan did not reply. Instead, he quickened his pace and left Jarvis behind him as the old man struggled with the steep incline and the buffeting winds. He caught up with Lucy and fell into step alongside her as they traversed a wide patch of snow that had been frozen solid, possibly for decades.

'Why on earth would the Inca bring children out here so far from their empire just to sacrifice them, and to whom?'

'Nobody knows for sure,' Lucy replied. 'Like so many ancient cultures, the Inca worshipped the heavens above them, and so the sun was a major factor in their lives along with the seasons and such. Poor harvests or perhaps conflict with other civilizations might have compelled them to sacrifice their young in order to gain support from their gods. Almost all ancient cultures have some evidence of blood sacrifice in their history, despite being separated by many thousands of miles.'

'More evidence of you believing them to be linked,' Ethan surmised. 'Isn't it possible that they simply developed the same habits as each other despite having no contact at all? I heard that the reason that pyramids that are so similar in cultures around the world is simply due to the fact that the pyramid is a stable structure and easy to build, so would be a natural choice for early civilizations.'

'Entirely true,' Lucy replied. 'But then, would they have the same legends, the same references to unusual events in the sky and visitations by unusual gods with bizarre properties that taught them how to live, how to manipulate the world around them in more complex ways? How on Earth could it be that such widely separated cultures could all simultaneously develop the ability to smelt copper seven thousand years ago, or start erecting superstructures on differing continents in the same centuries?'

'But blood sacrifice of children?' Ethan persisted.

'Children were considered pure,' Lucy explained, 'unstained by the foibles of adults. Most were prepared for sacrifice for years. Biological analysis of the mummies found on this mountain during Reinhard's surveys found significant lifestyle and dietary evidence, which included increased coca and alcohol consumption in the year prior to their sacrifice. We see these children as victims but they were feted by their people, worshipped in some ways like the gods themselves, perhaps as a direct link to the deities in whom these people placed so much faith. If those supposed deities had instead been a species not of this earth, then perhaps the sacrifices meant more to the Incas than just ceremonial or traditional events. Maybe they really believed that their powerful benefactors would return to save them, perhaps from disease or from the wars waged against them by the *conquistadores*.'

'But why would an alien species start tinkering with our DNA, anyway? What's to gain?'

'Survival,' Lucy explained. 'That's all life really is, when you think about it. All species procreate in order to pass on their genes, their DNA, to keep their family line alive. A suitably advanced species may have found a way to keep their DNA alive by means other than procreation, perhaps using human beings as a living storage facility. Viruses inject their DNA into cells in order to hijack those cells and proliferate through a victim, so a viable process already exists in nature.'

'You think that we were being used as victims in some way, that this is some kind of infection?'

'No,' Lucy replied. 'If an alien species had wanted to infect us with a disease, they could have done so easily. It's my hypothesis that they were in fact using cross-breeding in order to preserve elements of their DNA in our own bloodline for reasons that we don't really know anything about. The unfortunate consequence of this is that those strands of DNA may be the cause of many of the more bizarre genetic illnesses that afflict a small number of our population. Put simply, there are people suffering from illnesses today that have no apparent explanation other than to be described as random genetic mutation. While random mutation is one of the means through which evolution operates, and can sometimes produce bizarre deformities that are quickly removed from the gene pool through the death of the carrier, some afflictions seem to continue on from generation to generation. The genes responsible often seem out of place, much in the same way as we find out of place artifacts in the archaeological record that suggest levels of intelligence far beyond the means of the civilizations who supposedly placed them there.'

Ethan peered ahead at the ridgeline of the volcano's flank and saw a large flat area appearing, a plateau close to the mountain summit.

'We're almost at the peak,' he observed.

In one gloved hand Lucy again produced the quipu that she had carried up the mountainside, and she nodded as she rubbed a gloved thumb over one of the knots in the quipu.

'Remarkable, that even after all these hundreds of years such a simple device can prove so accurate. If I'm right, the plateau ahead is where the quipu says the remains should be buried.'

Ethan forged on at Lucy's side across the treacherous ice, and together they worked their way to the summit and clambered onto the plateau to see a remarkable vista appear before them. The mountainside dropped away on the far side of the volcano to reveal rolling rocky valleys plunging to immense depths beneath a layer of broken cloud that tumbled and rolled in the sunlight like an ethereal veil. Before them on the plateau was nothing more than a few scattered rocks, dark material as black as coal that stood out against a layer of snow frosting the surface.

'From the eruptions in the nineteenth century,' Lucy observed as she knelt down to pick up one of the thick chunks of old magma.

'I thought that there would be some kind of altar or place of worship during the sacrifices,' Ethan said as he looked around the empty plateau.

'Too far from their homeland, perhaps, or they just wanted to keep this location secret from grave robbers and the *conquistadores*,' Lucy replied as she glanced back down to where the rest of their party were following them up to the plateau. She looked back down at the snow. 'This snowfall beneath our feet may be hundreds of years old. We need to clear it to see if there's anything below – it could be what's concealed these tombs for so long.'

Ethan shrugged off the rucksack he had carried up the mountain and pulled from within it a folding shovel. Lucy mirrored his actions, and together they began breaking the frozen snow into chunks and shovelling it away from the plateau. Several inches thick, the work was hard in the thin air, and Ethan found himself repeatedly going for more oxygen from his supply as he worked.

Jarvis and his men joined them on the plateau along with the *huaqueros*, and while Jarvis watched Lopez, the two escorts and the *huaqueros* all unpacked their shovels and began helping clear the snow and ice from the plateau. Lucy directed them as they dug down, and the shovels hit the raw earth and rock of the mountainside, gradually exposing more of the surface of the plateau.

'Hold there,' Lucy said as she made her way to the center of the dig.

Ethan stood upright and sucked in deep breaths of the meager air as he let his shovel drop by his side, exhausted. He could see that Lopez, Jarvis's agents, and even the *huaqueros* were equally tired by the hard labor at such high altitude. Lucy moved to the center of the plateau and knelt down as she examined the earth. Frosted with ice, Ethan realized that the surface was probably unchanged since the first snows had fallen on the burial site hundreds of years before, frozen solid for all eternity.

'Here,' Lucy pointed at what to Ethan looked like a perfectly normal piece of earth.

He moved alongside Lucy and knelt down to see that the rocks and soil were rutted and pitted unlike the smooth, free-flowing slopes of the volcano further down where countless eruptions had produced aged lava flows of basalt rock.

'We must dig carefully,' Lucy said. 'If they're in here, they won't be far down. All the remains found previously were within a couple of yards of the surface.'

'Just a couple of yards from the surface of permafrost entombed rock,' Lopez uttered. 'And there I was thinking this was going to be hard work.'

Getting onto their knees, Ethan and the remaining members of the team formed a circle around the spot Lucy had indicated and began digging down, using their shovels as trowels in order to scrape the unyielding soil away. The first few inches were unbearably hard, frozen solid, but then they began to reach slightly softer material beneath. They dug deeper and faster until Lucy's voice rang out above the buffeting gale.

'Hold there.'

Lucy pointed to a small piece of fabric that was poking out of the ancient soil, fluttering in the wind. The group seemed to close in around her for a better look as Lucy used her trowel to pull away soil from around the fragment. Longer than it had at first seemed, Ethan watched in fascination as she worked carefully and began exposing a tightly wrapped bundle of fabric that seemed to get larger before his eyes. Lucy finally threw her trowel aside and used her hands to scrape chunks of soil away from the remains.

Driven by her enthusiasm, the rest of the team began likewise lifting chunks of soil out of the grave and tossing it across the pure white snow around them until Ethan could see the outline of a small body beneath the thick fabric. Despite the covering, he could see the shape of narrow legs pulled up under a chin and arms wrapped around them, the entire body concealed beneath swathes of patterned fabric and surrounded by a small ring of pottery, everything frozen absolutely solid as it had been for centuries.

'Is this it?' Lopez asked. 'Is this what you're looking for?'

Lucy looked down at the remains, and in the bright sunlight that was beaming down into the ancient tomb, Ethan spotted at the same time she did a quipu hanging around the neck of the ancient mummy along with a necklace of solid gold.

'This is it,' Lucy said without a shadow of doubt. 'This is the one.'

It was a Russian voice that replied to her.

'And we will take it from here.'

Ethan looked up in surprise to see a dozen armed men emerge from just below the plateau, and a crackle of rifle fire snapped out on the cold wind. The native *huaqueros* collapsed as they were cut down by the gunfire, and the gunmen rushed upon Ethan's position. Behind them was a determined looking old man, his cold grey eyes blazing with hatred.

'Yuri Polkov,' Lucy snapped as she recognised him.

The old man's features fractured like a glacier into a broad grin.

'We meet at last,' he uttered, his voice as brittle as thin ice. 'I've been looking forward to this moment.'

XXXVI

Ethan walked alongside Lopez with his hands behind his head as they were marched down the mountainside. Behind them, a Eurocopter AS350 hired by Yuri Polkov's team hovered above the mountain slopes, its rotors kicking up whirling clouds of snow as Yuri's men loaded the mummy aboard. Specially designed for high-altitude operations, the helicopter was one of only a handful of rotary craft able to reach the summit of the volcano.

Ethan watched from the corner of his eye as the helicopter lifted off with its valuable cargo and swung past them through the bright blue sky as it began descending away toward the east. Ethan saw the western horizon brooding with dark grey clouds marching their way east, the towering cumulus flaring bright white at their peaks just like the mountains around them.

The Russians had deployed twenty men to the mountaintop after they had captured Ethan and the team, and they had wasted no time in completing the excavation of the tomb that Lucy had found. Yuri had taken great delight in thanking Lucy for finding the mummy for him, regaling her with tales of his own ingenuity.

'The wonders of modern technology,' he explained as they trudged down the hillside. 'Thermal imaging cameras. They're mostly used at night, but here against these frozen mountains it was so easy to watch you and your team ascend to the plateau. And my little drones, flown by Sergei, kept watch as we followed far behind.'

Ethan had seen the disgust on Lucy's face.

'You think you're clever, but you have no idea what you're doing.'

'I am very well aware of what I'm doing,' Yuri replied with a wave of one gloved hand, in which he held a Glock pistol. 'I am preserving these remains that you found for the benefit of generations to come, for the right price of course, and for the exposure of all the world's religions for what they truly are – the darkness, the lies.'

'You're selling something that doesn't belong to you and you're taking lives while you do it.'

Yuri pulled a face as though he were genuinely insulted by the accusation. 'Come now, Lucy. My son gave you every opportunity to help me back in Chicago, but you chose to brush him off. He warned that you would regret it, and now clearly you do. There is nobody to blame here but yourself.'

Ethan looked down the mountain to where in the distance the flashing blades of the Eurocopter had swung around and it was gently lowering its cargo down onto another windswept plateau far below the snow line. Ridges of long-cold magma hid whatever was down there, but he assumed that the Russians had established a base camp before embarking on their intercept mission. This far out into the wilderness, he could expect no help from any other quarter unless Jarvis was able to call in support somehow. The Russians had no idea who he was, probably assuming him to be a scientist or similar, and Jarvis had remained silent since the Russians had arrived.

'The remains are far more valuable than you could possibly realize,' Ethan said to Yuri, speaking for the first time.

Yuri Polkov peered at him with a cold glare.

'Ethan Warner,' he said as though he were speaking of something repulsive. 'Of all people, it is you I am looking forward to getting to know the most. Tell me, what happened to my son, Vladimir?'

Ethan grinned. 'He got what he deserved. You shouldn't have let a stroppy little child play out with the big boys, Yuri.'

'You murdered him,' Yuri replied. 'Hurled him from a mountain top, so I understand?'

'He jumped,' Ethan corrected Yuri. 'I followed. Turns out he had a problem with his parachute. You reap what you sow, I suppose.'

A flash of anger twisted Yuri's features, his aged voice croaking with restraint. 'I understand that you decided to disappear once, already, and that it took Lucy Morgan here quite a while to find you. Trust me, you're about to disappear again and this time nobody is going to work out where you are, except maybe archaeologists in a few hundred years digging around in the dirt for old bones. I wonder what they would make of your remains?'

'I'm not sure,' Lopez replied for Ethan, 'but I'm fairly certain they'd figure out he was twice the man you are, whether he had a gun in his hand or not.'

Yuri grinned cruelly as he tapped the butt of his pistol against Lopez's head. 'More clever American words, but you and I shall know each other far more closely, too, before your time is done here.'

'Over my dead body,' Lopez snarled back.

'As you wish,' Yuri shrugged, the nasty grin still plastered across his face, 'as long as you're still warm.'

Yuri's men chuckled among themselves and cast their eyes across Lopez and Lucy as the entire group descended towards the Russian base camp. As they crossed the old magma flows blocking their view, Ethan got his first glimpse of the helicopter's landing site and a dense cluster of tents. Two all-terrain vehicles were parked nearby, alongside the pair that Ethan and the team had brought with them, and perhaps a dozen more men milled about in the camp and turned to watch as Ethan, Lucy, Lopez, and Jarvis were led at gunpoint into the camp, Jarvis's escort likewise marched in behind them.

In the center of the camp was the Eurocopter, which several men were now opening to reveal the tightly bundled mummy within.

'Secure the perimeter of the camp,' Yuri snapped angrily at his men. 'Have the remains moved to the main tent and then stand guard!'

Yuri gestured for Ethan and the others to follow him as he turned and began hobbling towards the main tent, six of his men flanking Ethan's team, their AK-47s pointed unwaveringly at them.

'Come,' he insisted. 'There is much that we will discuss.'

Yuri crossed the compound and entered a large tent. The interior was warmed by heaters powered by a generator that rattled and hummed outside in the cold air. Ethan let out a soft breath of relief as he felt the warmth touch his skin, and he pulled back the hood of his jacket and slid his hands from his gloves as Yuri struggled his way across to a folding chair and lowered himself into it.

Lucy Morgan wasted no time as she yanked off her hood. 'This is abduction, kidnapping!'

Yuri rested both of his gnarled old hands on top of his cane and looked up at her, his eyes cold and rheumy with age.

'Yes, it is, and it is also the theft of valuable artifacts belonging to the people of Argentina and Chile,' he pointed out as he gestured to Lucy and her team. 'I take it that you did not contact the relevant authorities before marching up this mountain and excavating?'

'Like you did?' Lucy challenged. 'We're not here to debate the semantics of ownership of these mummies. We're on a mission of our own, and it's important that we get these remains back to Chicago as soon as possible.'

Yuri humphed as a bitter little smile crossed his face. 'Then you're stealing them, which makes you no better than myself. I, too, was once a fossil smuggler, dealing on the black market for dinosaur bones from Mongolia and China to sell in the United States. I made my fortune by trading on the bones of long dead species.'

'People like you are the scourge of my profession,' Lucy spat. 'I've never sought to make money from the finds that I've made, even those that would have changed the world had my own government not confiscated them from me.'

'Your work in Israel,' Yuri acknowledged. 'So you admit that you found something extraordinary out there, although you would not share your knowledge with my son Vladimir.'

'Your son was as corrupt as you are,' Lucy replied. 'It cost him his life.'

Ethan saw a brief flicker of regret shadow the old man's face and he took the opportunity to stand forward. 'Why are we here?'

Yuri's gaze switched to Ethan, the smile returning. 'I want you to see what you have achieved, on my behalf, before I have your corpses returned to the mountaintop and buried there for all eternity.'

Yuri turned to Lucy. 'You have chased this mystery halfway around the planet more than once. I take it that you wish to see what is inside the mummy's swathes?'

Before Lucy could respond the tent flaps opened and four of Yuri's men walked inside, each bearing one corner of a stretcher upon which was mounted the mummy.

Yuri leaned forward as he looked at Lucy.

'I've waited a long time for this moment, but this is *your* discovery. Despite what you think of me, I do not wish to deny you this moment.'

Lucy turned and looked at the mummy longingly, but she held her ground. 'Let the others go.'

'No,' Yuri replied. 'Open the mummy, or I will simply shoot every one of you and then open it myself.'

'You could be a part of this,' Lucy suggested. 'Imagine the fame, the recognition, the fortune that would come from being a part of this worldwide revelation, the impact it would have on religious terrorism and the corruption of blind faith. It could make you a…'

'My son's death has ended any interest I might have had in furthering either my fortune or my reputation,' Yuri growled back. He reached into his pocket and produced a small silver pistol that he lifted to aim at Lucy. 'My part in this discovery will remain anonymous. You can thank your friend Ethan Warner for my change of priorities.'

Lucy shot an angry glance at Ethan, who remained silent as he tried to figure out a way of escaping Yuri's men.

'You'll never get the remains out of Argentina,' Lucy insisted.

'I'll have no problems in smuggling these remains out of the country to study them in private,' Yuri countered. 'I've been doing it all my life. I will make public the find and have the remains sent to a secure location before approaching my associates and arranging a bid, held most likely on a privately owned island, with the winner taking all. I do not doubt that such a find will raise many tens and perhaps hundreds of millions of dollars in revenue.'

'It won't work,' Ethan replied. 'Your vision of a world scoured of religious faith ignores the fact that, despite the success and advances made by Newton, Einstein and others, the eradication of God to a place in fantasy, people still *believe*. They'll never stop believing,Yuri, no matter what discoveries are uncovered or myths revealed.'

'That,' Yuri replied, 'I will leave in the hands of the people themselves. I suggest we hesitate no longer. Please, if you will.'

Yuri cocked the pistol hammer. Lucy stared at the old man and then took a pace back from the remains.

'Do it yourself,' she snapped.

Yuri smiled as though somehow impressed by Lucy's defiance, and the pistol shifted position. The shot was deafeningly loud in the confines of the tent as Yuri fired, and Ethan flinched as he turned and saw one of Jarvis's escorts stagger backwards, the bullet slammed into his chest, and then toppled onto the cold ground. His head thumped down onto the rocks, his eyes staring wide and lifeless up at the tent roof.

Jarvis stared down at the fallen agent and then glared at Yuri. 'Once a coward,' he uttered.

Yuri pointed the pistol at Jarvis, but Lucy leaped forward.

'No!'

Lucy stepped towards the mummy, and she quickly retrieved a pair of forensic gloves and tweezers for the pocket of her jacket, and set to work un-wrapping the dense shroud.

Ethan looked at Jarvis, who was standing with his hands in his pockets. With a start, Ethan realized that the old man still had the satellite phone tucked into his jacket pocket, and he was manipulating it as they watched Lucy begin to work.

XXXVII

Ethan watched as Lucy patiently peeled away the dense layers of frozen fabric wrapped around the mummy. The material had been woven with great care by skilled artisans hundreds of years before, the colors in the fabric still visible despite it being as hard as wood and difficult for Lucy to remove without damaging it.

As she slowly removed each layer, the figure trapped within gradually began to emerge, and it was rapidly evident that the remains within the burial shroud were anything but normal. It was subtle at first, what to Ethan seemed to be a slight imbalance between the size of the body in the shroud and the size of the head. But as more layers were revealed so it became clear that the individual inside the shroud had a skull shaped nothing like a human being.

Lucy labelled each layer as it was removed, sealing each of the ancient fragments inside plastic bags for later analysis. With forensic perfection, she began to reveal the figure huddled inside the shroud, until a vivid length of jet black hair still bound in place, was exposed, two hanks of it woven between links of brightly colored fabric in dense plaits.

Ethan moved closer, fascinated, as Lucy began to reach up to remove the final layer of fabric that covered the face of the figure within. Both Lopez and Jarvis also drew closer, Yuri moving in from the other side as slowly Lucy took hold of the last layer of fabric and gently removed it to reveal the mummy's face.

There was an audible gasp from Yuri Polkov and his hand flew to his mouth as the final piece of fabric was folded aside by Lucy's delicate touch, and they stared into the eyes of a young girl who had died several hundred years before.

It was clear that the girl had been immensely beautiful, her features elegant and symmetrical. Ethan was stunned to see that her skin still maintained a natural tan color, her eyebrows delicately arched and her lips full and sculptured. The once dark orbits of her eyes had dried out long ago but her eyelids were closed as though she were merely asleep, her face serene and peaceful.

But above her face extended a skull that was far larger than normal, her hairline at least three times higher than that of an ordinary human being and her cranium shaped like a teardrop that ended in a narrow cone hidden beneath a thick blanket of glossy black hair.

'My God, she's beautiful,' Yuri whispered as he struggled out of his chair once more for a closer look. 'I could never have imagined…'

Draped across the girl shoulders and her chest was an immensely valuable solid gold necklace, forged in complex coils that looped in and out of each other. Her clothes were woven of the finest fabrics of her time, and would have held enormous value to the Inca people, perhaps even more so than the gold. That she had been treated with the utmost respect in death was undeniable despite her obvious youth, and the fact that her life been snatched away from her by the blow of a blunt instrument that had left a dent in the back of her skull.

'Ritual sacrifice,' Yuri observed as he hobbled around to one side of the mummy. 'She was killed before her prime, struck from behind while watching the rising sun as a sacrifice to the gods that gave the Incas their knowledge and understanding of the universe.'

Lucy nodded, their predicament momentarily forgotten in the face of discovery.

'Her throat is marked by ligatures,' she observed, pointing to a line of dark bruising circling her neck. 'She was garrotted after losing consciousness.'

Ethan saw that the girl's tiny hands were gently folded before her, likely placed there by her killers after they had struck her down. She seemed at peace, and Ethan remembered what Lucy had said about sacrificial victims being plied with alcohol before their deaths to induce a state of stupefied semi-consciousness, the mediaeval equivalent of humane execution.

'What happened to her skull?' Lopez asked. 'How did it end up like that?'

'It's the result of ritualistic deformation,' Lucy said as she examined the skullcap closely without touching anything.

Ethan stepped forward as he looked at the remains. 'Does this mummy contain the DNA that you're looking for?'

Lucy shook her head instantly. 'No, she is an example of cranial deformation and not a victim of something genetically inherited.' She looked up at Yuri and smiled. 'These remains are worthless.'

Yuri scowled at her. 'How can you tell?'

'The shape of the skull, can't you see it?' Lucy asked as though it were obvious. 'Lots of people think that these skulls found all over Peru, but mostly in the Paracus region, are somehow the remains of alien children, but this has been disproven repeatedly because although you can alter the shape of a skull you cannot alter the brain volume. That's what differentiates between skulls that were deliberately deformed by boards simply changing the skull's shape, and the remains of skulls that have a brain volume far larger than an ordinary human child or adult.'

'You're lying,' Yuri growled.

Lucy shrugged. 'You know that I'm not. Go ahead, check the remains for yourself. I've seen enough of these skulls to know at a glance that this is the result of ritualistic deformation and not a genetic distortion. You lost your son for nothing, Mr Polkov. You wasted your time. The only people who will be interested in this mummy are museums, exactly where these remains belong.'

Ethan's gaze drifted to Yuri and the old man suddenly screamed at the top of his lungs. 'Take them to the mountain and kill them! Kill all of them!'

Ethan, Lucy, Lopez, and Jarvis were marched out of the tent at gunpoint as the stretcher bearers followed them out into the cold wind, their weapons pointed at their backs. The sky above, once hard blue, was now filled with tumbling clouds coming in from the distant ocean. Ethan knew that the weather could change in the blink of an eye, here on the mountains, much as it did in the Highlands of Scotland where he had made his new home. He noted the lowering cloud base and the banks of fog drifting over the high peaks and obscuring the snow line as they climbed back up the mountain.

'Over there!'

Yuri Polkov pointed to a dense drift of snow that had built up along the edge of a deep magma flow that had long since frozen solid, the black rock vivid against the white snow alongside it. Ethan judged the snow to be at least three feet deep, sufficient that it would probably never melt even in height of summer.

He looked over his shoulder and saw the camp below them as they climbed, gradually receding until it was once more no longer visible behind the lower magma flows, only the tips of the helicopter's rotors peaking from the ridgeline. The visibility was dropping quickly, thick moisture in the air and the threat of further snowfall increasing by the moment.

'Forget it,' Lopez whispered to him as she noted the direction of his gaze. 'We can't make a run for it and there's nowhere to go, anyway.'

Ethan peered sideways at their Russian escorts as they reached the dense snowbank. 'We need a distraction.'

'We're not going to find one up here.'

Jarvis and his remaining escort reached the snowbank and set Jarvis's dead guard's body down. Ethan joined them, and then the Russians pulled collapsible shovels from their rucksacks and tossed them to Ethan and his companions. Yuri Polkov pointed at the deep snowdrifts.

'Start digging,' the Russian sneered. 'You didn't think we were going to do it for you, did you?'

Ethan picked up one of the shovels and turned to Jarvis, whispering from the side of his mouth as he began digging.

'I was hoping that you called the cavalry?'

Jarvis offered him an apologetic glance. 'I'm afraid that my resources this time are limited. I did manage to send a message, but I don't know if it will reach the intended recipients.'

'Who did you contact?'

'Stop talking!' a Russian yelled as he rushed up and jabbed his AK-47 into Ethan's back.

Ethan winced beneath the blow and fell silent as they gradually excavated down to the rock below, a thin grave of ice and bitterly cold rock. Ethan's shovel hit the stones as alongside him Lucy and Lopez dug out a few more chunks of snow, and then found themselves standing on the bedrock.

'Perfect,' Yuri snarled as he cocked the pistol in his grasp and looked at his companions. 'Now, let's shoot the men first and enjoy the women to ourselves before we put them in afterward.'

The mercenaries sniggered in delight as they took aim at Ethan and his companions. Ethan was about to suggest paying them double in order to let them live when he heard a strange sound drift across the mountain tops, a droning that rose above the blustering gale. Ethan looked up from the rifles aimed at him and peered into the gray sky as he sought the origin of the sound, but the winds were in the wrong direction and were snatching the noise away.

The Russians turned and looked over their shoulders up into the slate gray sky at the tumbling clouds. Ethan judged the distance to them, but he knew that he wouldn't make it before a bullet found its mark even from the wildly inaccurate AK-47s.

Suddenly, from the gray clouds appeared a pair of bright white lights that swept like headlight beams to point directly at the Russians. The two lights seemed to hover in the clouds, pointing accusingly at the Russian gunmen.

'What the hell is that?' Lopez yelled above the wind and the rising drone of noise emanating from the lights.

Ethan felt a supernatural awe creep beneath his skin, and then suddenly the droning noise leaped in intensity as the lights brightened as something rushed toward them. From the low scudding clouds burst the shape of an aircraft, twin engines turning above broad, straight wings and a pair of bright landing lights blazing like white suns as the Catalina thundered down. Ethan's eyes widened as he realized that the aircraft was on a direct collision course, and then it suddenly pulled up, its engines roaring as the belly of its fuselage suddenly gaped open.

'Cover!'

Ethan ducked down and pulled his hood over his head as from the belly of the Catalina an immense cloud of water crashed down, the intense cold turning half of the water volume to ice in an instant that showered the mountainside with a dense hail of rain ice that pelted the Russians like bullets as the Catalina roared overhead and left a blizzard of hail and snow behind it.

His head down and protected by his hood, Ethan rushed forward even though he could not see where he was going. The hail hammered down around him and he heard the Russians crying out in panic and disarray, one of them loomed before him where he crouched on the mountain slope, his hands over his head to protect him from the onslaught of ice. Ethan wasted no time as he swung one boot on the run and it slammed into the Russian's head with a dull thump that snapped his skull to one side and sent him sprawling across the rocks.

Ethan saw the AK-47 spin from the man's grasp as he lost consciousness, and jumped for it. He landed on top of the weapon and rolled his shoulders across the snow as he stuck his legs out to lay prone on the ice. He aimed the AK-47 at the other three Russians as they struggled to find their feet in the aftermath of the Catalina's attack.

Ethan squeezed the trigger as he found the first target. Two shots cracked from the rifle's barrel and struck the man in the back, severing his spine, as the AK-47's barrel jerked upwards. The Russian collapsed onto the snow as the second man turned and tried to swing his rifle to bear on Ethan's position.

Two more shots rang out and struck the Russian in his belly and shoulder. The man twisted violently as he screamed in agony and collapsed onto the snow.

The third and farthest Russian whirled and fired at Ethan from the hip, the bullets spraying wildly, churning up the snow around Ethan as he held his own rifle tight into his shoulder and fired a single shot. The bullet struck the Russian in his chest and spun him around in mid-air to land on his back on the snow, his heart shredded.

Yuri Polkov aimed the silver pistol at Ethan, but the old man was forestalled as Lopez's voice called out.

'Freeze, Yuri!'

Ethan glanced across and saw Lopez gripping the AK-47 she had salvaged from one of the fallen Russian mercenaries. Ethan got up and strode across to Yuri, the AK-47 trained on the old man as Ethan reached out and snatched the pistol from him.

Yuri Polkov flinched, his once cruel eyes now wide with fear.

'What do we do with him?' Ethan asked over his shoulder.

'You can have the remains,' Yuri pleaded. 'You can take them!'

Ethan heard the sound of the Eurocopter's engines starting up further down the mountainside, and realized that if they didn't move fast none of them would get off the mountain alive.

'Looks like your own people are clearing out without you,' Lucy observed with a grin.

'We need those vehicles, and preferably that helicopter!' Ethan said.

'Yuri should be arrested and handed over to the authorities,' Lucy insisted.

Ethan looked at Jarvis, who shook his head. 'He'll slow us down too much, and the weather's closing in fast. He wanted to prove there's no god – how about we grant him his wish?'

Ethan nodded as he turned and set off toward the plateau below, his team following him, Yuri left standing beside the snow drifts .

'Wait!' Yuri yelled as he hobbled after Ethan and his companions.

Ethan did not reply and neither did any of the others. Together they dashed down the mountainside as the Eurocopter's blades began turning faster. Ethan ran hard down the steep slope and hit the magma flow just as the helicopter was vanishing inside a swirling maelstrom of snow dislodged by its powerful rotors.

'They're getting away!' Lopez yelled.

Ethan dropped down once more into the prone position, this time atop the lava flow and looking down toward the plateau, and he aimed the AK-47 at the Eurocopter as it began lifting off. He opened fire and saw the shots impact the side of the helicopter, and then Lopez was alongside him and their rifles clattered deafeningly loud as the bullets hammered the cockpit and engine bays.

The Eurocopter's engines howled and then screeched with the sound of rending metal as something gave within them. The transmission assembly burst through the upper fuselage, and the helicopter spun through three hundred and sixty degrees as it tilted wildly to starboard and plunged back down onto the ice.

'Down!'

Ethan ducked his head as he rolled off the rocky magma flow, and a cloud of fragments of shattered blades and engine parts raced by overhead, smashing into the snow as the helicopter tore itself apart and came to rest on its side further down the mountain.

Ethan leaped to his feet and scrambled over the magma flow to see three of the four ATVs belching diesel fumes as their engines started and they began pulling away from the encampment, the billowing tents left where they were as Yuri Polkov's men made good their escape.

'They've got the mummy,' Ethan yelled as he spotted the mummy's remains stuffed into a metal cage in the rear of one of the trucks. 'Go for the rearmost vehicle's tires!'

They were within thirty yards of the vehicle as it began to pull away, and Ethan threw himself down onto the hard rocks and pulled the AK-47 into his shoulder once more as he took careful aim and fired single shots one after the other at the spinning tire. Lopez firing with deadly aim alongside him.

The ATVs tires were designed not to be punctured, but nonetheless they could be shredded as a hail of fire ripped into it. The shape of the tire broke down in front of Ethan's eyes, and the rear of the all-terrain vehicle slumped as the rim was exposed and bit deep into the rocks. He heard the engine screech as the two occupants struggled to escape, and Ethan shifted his aim to the windows of the cab as it passed by, and fired two shots.

The window shattered and one of the men slumped forward after the bullet struck him in the forehead and sprayed blood across the glass and windscreen. The vehicle swerved violently to the right, its bumper collided with a rocky outcrop, and pulled the vehicle to a halt as the engine failed.

Ethan got to his feet and rushed to the cab, Lopez hurried to the opposite side and jabbed her weapon into the window. Ethan yanked the passenger door open, and the dead occupant tumbled out of the vehicle and thumped down onto the cold rocks at his feet. Inside the cab, the driver was slumped over the wheel, one half of his face missing where he had been struck by a lucky ricochet.

Ethan hurried to the back and checked the rear to see a spare tire firmly affixed to the rear access door. Inside, strapped to the rear seat, was the mummy. Satisfied, he turned to see Jarvis making his way down the hillside toward them. He looked up into the cloudy sky and saw the Catalina circling overhead just below the cloud base, its navigation and anti-collision beacons flickering as it turned away and began descending.

'Arnie?' Ethan asked Jarvis as the old man reached them, clearly out of breath. 'You called *Arnie*?'

Jarvis gathered his breath and gestured to the Catalina with a jab of his thumb. 'He's been a busy boy, working for us, and handsomely paid I might add.'

Ethan watched as the Catalina disappeared into the clouds while Lopez hauled the dead bodies of the drivers out of the vehicle.

'Where's the mummy?' Lucy asked, distraught as she saw the carnage around them.

'We've got it,' Ethan replied. 'We need to work fast. Let's get that tire changed!'

Lopez turned from her grisly work, her features quizzical. 'What's the rush? Lucy said that those remains were worthless, that she's just a victim of ritualistic Incan head distortion, right?'

Lucy shook her head. 'That's true, the mummy itself has no use to us as its skull was deformed by her own people when she was born. But the women and girls chosen for sacrifice were considered special, and I think that I know why. The gold that she wore, and the expensive clothes, they were not for her.'

'Well, who were they for, then?' Ethan challenged as he yanked a jack from the rear of the vehicle.

Lucy smiled. 'I'll have to let you know about that.'

Ethan turned to Jarvis. 'Where will Arnie go?'

'Presumably back to the lake,' Jarvis said. 'But right now it's not him I'm worried about.'

'What do you mean?'

Jarvis lifted the satellite phone out of his pocket. 'I didn't just send a message to Arnie. I thought we were going to die, so I sent a signal out as widely as I could on an agency distress channel.'

Lopez's features sagged. 'Oh no.'

'I'm afraid it's not just the cavalry coming, but everybody else, too.'

Ethan wasted no more time as he helped Lucy and Lopez switch the tire out, and then climbed aboard the truck. He started the engine as thick snow began falling all around them, the skies darkening as the storm closed in.

Ethan turned on the headlights, and in the beams he saw a shadowy figure struggling against the wind down the mountain, leaning on a thin cane and waving desperately at them. Yuri Polkov's heavily lined features, grey with cold, stared out at them from beneath his hood as he cried out, his mouth agape but his voice snatched away by the winds.

Ethan crunched the truck into gear and drove away from the plateau, and the old man's phantom-like form vanished into the bitter, windswept darkness.

XXXVIII

The truck bounced and rattled down the rugged mountain tracks as Ethan guided it through the tumbling veils of snow falling thickly around them. Lopez sat next to him in the cab, with Jarvis and Lucy behind them in the rear seats and jabbering excitedly as she looked over her shoulder at the mummy.

'We've got it! We've actually *got* it!'

'Who is *everybody else*, exactly?' Ethan demanded again of Jarvis.

'Anybody who was listening in on our frequency,' Jarvis replied. 'If Majestic Twelve are on our case, they'll have been monitoring all frequencies used by government agencies out here, hoping to catch us on the move. I reckoned they represented the better end of a bad deal, seeing as we were going to be shot and left on that mountain.'

'If Arnie's out of reach, we're not going to get off this mountain fast enough to evade detection,' Ethan said. 'They'll send in their STS team and finish this for good, and nobody's going to find us out here.' He turned to Lopez. 'How much ammunition do we have?'

'No more than thirty rounds between us,' Lopez replied after she examined the rifles she had tossed into the vehicle. 'Yuri had at least thirty men with him, and they're out in front of us.'

'Maybe we'll get lucky and they'll get lost,' Jarvis offered.

Ethan looked ahead and began to slow the truck.

'Lucky doesn't much apply to Lopez and me,' he said.

Ahead, a wall of flames burned fiercely across the plains as the truck descended the side of the mountain. Thick black smoke boiled up into the sky, battling the snow falling from the turbulent clouds. Ethan slowed the truck to a crawl and saw three vehicles, each identical to the one in which they sat, all engulfed in an inferno of raging flames. One of them was on its side in a ditch, blown clear off the road.

'Polkov's other men and their trucks,' Lucy identified them.

Ethan slowed the truck to a halt; before the three wrecked vehicles that blocked the track, he saw the figures of at least a dozen armed men. All were dressed in black fatigues, weighed down with webbing and weapons, hands gloved and faces concealed behind black balaclavas.

'STS,' Jarvis confirmed with a single glance.

Ethan barely heard him. His gaze was instead affixed upon a lone man who stood at the center of the STS troops. Dressed in a long, black coat that billowed in the wind, his hands shoved into the pockets, and his collar turned up high about his neck, the man was tall and his skin as dark as the magma flows on the volcano behind them. He did not move, but simply stared ahead at Ethan and his companions.

'I think that they want to talk,' Ethan said cautiously.

Lopez shot him an incredulous look. 'About *what*? How many ways they can ventilate us all and leave no trace of their ever being here? Fun chat.'

'They'd have opened fire by now,' Ethan said as he watched the STS troops. 'They're waiting for us.'

Ethan reached for his door handle and then felt Lopez's hand on his forearm. 'You go out there, you could become a hostage.'

Ethan saw a look of genuine concern on her face and it warmed him even in the cold air, the memory of the closeness of their comradery in Chicago returning to him once more. 'We're all out of plays here, Nicola. All we have is negotiation. They don't need us dead, they need what's in the back of this truck.'

'No way,' Lucy shot back. 'We can't hand this over. If we give up now, Beth won't survive.'

'And we can't help her, either, if we're dead,' Ethan pointed out.

Lucy did not respond, and abruptly turned her back on Ethan and clambered over the rear seats of the vehicle and into the back alongside the mummy. Ethan opened the door of the vehicle and climbed out. The bitter wind whipped snow around him like a tornado, and he could hear the crackling of the flames that snapped around the burning vehicles nearby. He slammed the door of the vehicle shut and began walking slowly toward the tall man and his soldiers, Lopez joining him.

'Couldn't help yourself?' Ethan asked as they walked.

'I've got Yuri's pistol,' Lopez replied. 'If they start shooting, I'll be damned if I won't take at least one of them with me. Preferably Devlin.'

Ethan glanced down at Lopez but said nothing further as they walked. Closer to the vehicles, Ethan could see the bodies of the occupants burning, blackened by flames in their seats, others scattered across the road. One of the STS soldiers was cradling a rocket-propelled grenade launcher on his shoulder, aimed directly at the vehicle Ethan had arrived in. *One false move*, he thought as he approached the tall man in their center, *and Lucy and Jarvis will be fried in an instant.*

'Ethan Warner,' the tall man greeted him.

His voice was deep and resonant, carrying even above the bitter wind rumbling across the plains. He watched Ethan without emotion, awaiting a response.

'Who are you?' Ethan asked.

'I'm your salvation,' the man replied. 'Or your doom. It all depends on what you do next.'

'Vladimir Polkov is dead,' Ethan said, 'and so is his son. The people with me don't represent any threat to you.'

'No,' the man agreed. 'But what they now possess does. We picked up the distress message from your associate, Jarvis. I suspect that the Intelligence Director will by now have been informed of the existence of the same message and will be amassing an exfil' operation as we speak. I and my men will be long gone by the time they arrive. What happens to you depends on how much you all enjoy being alive.'

Ethan glanced at the soldiers behind this enigmatic, threatening man, and recognised the features of the troops who had ambushed them days before in Cambodia.

'How have you tracked us all this way out here?' he asked conversationally.

'Good luck and charm,' the man replied.

'What do you want?'

'The remains that your team excavated from the mountain.'

'The life of a young girl depends on Lucy Morgan's extraction of genetic material from those remains,' Ethan replied.

'I am aware of that.'

Ethan squinted in the gusting snow. Although the man's expression had not faltered, Ethan felt sure that he could detect the slightest tremor of regret in his tone.

'Then let the remains go,' Ethan said. 'They mean nothing to you personally. They're just bones.'

'They're bones that could cause untold distress to billions of people,' the man replied. 'They could unseat governments, cause widespread civil unrest and religious conflict, shift the very nature of what it means to us to be human.'

'You don't know that,' Ethan said. 'The reverse could be true.

Nobody knows what will happen, only that it's going to happen one day, that people will learn the truth. The longer people like you hide them from it, the harder it will be to adjust to the new world it will create, both for them and for Majestic Twelve.'

The man's eyes widened at the mention of the name. 'Such things are not for us to decide. Your lives, Mr Warner, in return for those remains. There will be no further debate.'

Above the whistling gale, Ethan heard the STS troops shift position, preparing to fire should he refuse. Ethan sighed and looked behind him, then looked at Lopez and nodded.

He stood and waited as Lopez returned to the truck and moved to its rear to unload the mummified remains. He saw Lucy Morgan clamber out of the truck with the mummy bundled in her arms, as though it were a new born swathed against the bitter chill.

'You're taking a life,' Ethan reminded the man, hopeful that he might yet reveal some meager shred of humanity.

'Or saving many more,' the man replied without emotion. 'This has been the way of things for many, many years, and will be for many more to come.'

Ethan said nothing more as Lopez accompanied Lucy Morgan to his side. Lucy set the mummy down on the ground, the frozen remains sitting on the snow without support, and then she walked past Ethan and straight up to the towering man before them.

'You're the man behind all of this?' she demanded.

'The latest in a long line,' the man replied, his dark eyes searching Lucy's. 'Believe me, it's nothing personal.'

'If I could, if I were cold-hearted enough,' Lucy hissed, 'I swear I would kill you right here and now.'

The man smiled with his eyes only, and from his pocket retrieved a small photograph. Ethan spotted a woman he recognised in the image, Rachel Morgan, Lucy's mother.

'If I were cold-hearted enough,' the man replied, 'I would already have abducted your mother and brought her here at gunpoint. I give you the chance now to avoid any further bloodshed, and hand over the remains.'

Lucy stood for a long moment after she looked away from her mother's image and up into the man's eyes, and then she handed him a small photograph. The man looked down, and from his vantage point Ethan could just make out the photograph of Bethany that Lucy had shown him so long ago in his cottage in Scotland. Lucy's words to the man reached Ethan as a faint whisper on the wind.

'Yuri Polkov didn't believe in God,' she said. 'Neither do I, and yet, we're a world apart in our humanity. Congratulations, you're the third *non-human* being I've found on this planet in my career.'

Lucy turned her back to the man and stalked back toward the vehicle. Lopez cast him a last glance and joined her, leaving Ethan standing before him.

'You're only delaying the inevitable,' Ethan repeated.

The man nodded as he turned away. 'For as long as it takes.'

Ethan stood before the flaming wreckage as the STS team stayed in position, and watched the tall man walk away between the twisted, burning metal, and then waving a single gesture at the team's commanding officer.

The soldiers withdrew, and behind the wreckage Ethan glimpsed a pair of large Black Hawk helicopters, clad in modern, black radar-absorbent panels. Their engines were already turning as the man climbed aboard one of them, his soldiers following, two of them carrying the mummy.

Ethan watched as from behind the wrecked vehicles the two helicopters lifted off, then turned toward the north and accelerated away, hugging the ground at low-level until he could neither see or hear them any longer.

XXXIX

Washington DC
USA

Aaron Devlin strode through the corridors of the Defense Intelligence Analysis Center and boarded the elevator that would take him up to the Fifth Floor. He passed through the security protocol stations and made his way to the anechoic chamber, stepped inside, and sealed the doors behind him before he moved to the center of the room.

There, alongside the remains of the being found in Israel, the mummy of the Incan girl sat in a temperature-controlled Perspex case, her features as serene as ever.

'Report, please.'

The voices remained as anonymous as usual. Aaron spoke in a clear voice and used as few words as possible.

'Lucy Morgan failed in her attempts to recover the remains that she sought,' he said. 'No materials recovered from the expedition have made it back to the United States except in my custody, and thus no security protocols have been breached.'

There was a long silence as Aaron stood in the darkness and awaited a response.

'You're absolutely sure this time?' the voice of Number Four asked. *'The governments of well over one hundred nations have their eyes on us and are expecting absolute security surrounding this issue. They can be in no doubt that there will be no information leak, no compromise.'*

'I am absolutely sure,' Aaron replied. 'We recovered all of the remains. In addition, all evidence of human presence on the mountain peaks at the site in question have been destroyed, either in the attempt to recover them or afterwards, by my own men. I oversaw this process personally.'

'And what of Ethan Warner, Nicola Lopez, and Lucy Morgan?' asked Number Seven.

Aaron maintained a steady voice as he replied.

'We lost track of Ethan Warner in Peru. Nicola Lopez and Lucy Morgan have both returned to Illinois, Lopez to her work and Morgan to her studies. We are maintaining a track on both of them.'

'You lost Ethan Warner?' Number Nine demanded.

Aaron grinned tightly to maintain his patience with a question that sounded like an accusation of incompetence. 'Ethan Warner broke from the main group somewhere in Peru and disappeared. Due to the limited nature of support offered me on this mission, my men were not equipped to pursue him. We will maintain a watch on his family and home in expectation of his return, but given his recent life off the grid, he may not be easy to find.'

A long silence followed Aaron's reply before Number Six spoke.

'What are the chances of Yuri Polkov having survived the incident?'

Aaron shrugged, although he knew that none of the men could see him. 'Yuri Polkov's body was located during our search of the mountain. He was interred in an unmarked grave in the Atacama Desert. It'll take any of his associates ten thousand years to locate his remains. In the meantime, we have taken control of his assets to further fund our own investigations.'

Another long silence, and this time Number One spoke.

'The Director of Intelligence has been attempting to gain access to our operations, and is believed to have dispatched a former DIA analyst in order to expose us. Do you have any knowledge of this individual or what stage their work has reached?'

'Ethan Warner was in the company of Lucy Morgan, Nicola Lopez, and an unknown individual who could possibly have been working for another government agency. However, I was not able to identify them. Due to the legality of our presence in both Peru and Argentina and the need to remain covert, all individuals had to be allowed to leave to avoid an international incident. Had we continued operations, or indeed attempted to arrest anybody in plain sight of local guides and tourists, it is certain that the governments in question would have made moves to prevent us from leaving the country at all. A large number of Russian mercenaries were intercepted by my team and were killed when they attempted to resist arrest. The Argentinian government recognises that they were part of an international crime syndicate, and have repatriated their remains to Russia. Vladimir Polkov was found dead several days before in Peru. The official story is that both were killed during high-risk and illegal tomb-robbing exercises in the respective countries. Given that they were Russians and not Americans, we have nothing to fear from any further investigations into the deaths.'

Another long silence, before a final reply.

'Congress must remain unaware of our activities,' Number One said. *'Make no mistake, we cannot allow the American people to become aware that their government, their Congress, is merely a cipher for our operations. Continue your work, Agent Devlin, and ensure the security of our futures. All of our futures.'*

Aaron turned, and without another word he left the chamber.

Office of the Director of National Intelligence
Tyson's Corner,
Virginia

'I don't know where to begin.'

The Intelligence Director closed the file before him, which contained Doug Jarvis's report on the entirety of events since he had begun his pursuit of Lucy Morgan.

'This is something that we have been wrestling with for decades,' Jarvis replied, the director's office windows fogged for privacy. 'Majestic Twelve is, in effect, a shadow government, capable of pulling strings globally to advance its agenda. Ever since President Eisenhower warned of the growing power of military-industrial corporations' influence over politics, units of the intelligence community have been trying to pin down exactly who is really running our country. Suffice to say, sir, that right now it's neither Congress nor the White House. They're just the public face of something far more sinister.'

The director nodded, one hand resting on the file for a moment.

'What of the operatives you employed during this operation?'

'Nicola Lopez and Ethan Warner were not employed by me,' Jarvis admitted. 'They were called in by Lucy Morgan. Neither of them has any real love for the intelligence community any longer after their previous investigations – too many close calls fighting against our own damned people.'

The director looked at the file beneath his hand for a moment longer.

'Call them in, Doug. I want to make them an offer.'

'Of what?'

'Something that they cannot refuse. Where are they? Right now, I mean?'

Jarvis managed to slap an awkward smile on his face. 'I'm not entirely sure, sir.'

The director raised an eyebrow. 'You're *not sure*?'

'It's complicated.'

*

Pitlochrie,
Scotland

The community hospital was a small building in the town of Pitlochrie, nestled deep beneath the soaring peaks of the Cairngorns. Ethan climbed out of the car he had hired, feeling odd having to drive in the right-hand seat once again.

'This place is freezing.'

Lopez got out of the passenger side and slammed the door shut, then pulled her collar up about her neck. Her deeply tanned skin was at odds with the grey skies and cold wind.

'This is pretty mild for the time of year,' Ethan pointed out as he led the way inside the hospital.

'Good to hear,' Lopez replied. 'Remind me what the hell we're doing here?'

Ethan didn't reply as he stepped inside the hospital. The interior was hushed, the building home to only a small number of wards and rooms for elderly patients and a general practice. Ethan asked at the reception desk and was directed to one of the private rooms down the hall.

Ethan had decided not to take Jarvis's offer of a ride back to Chicago when they had finally landed in Argentina aboard Arnie's Catalina, an aircraft which had flown a considerable number of miles since they had first encountered its grumpy captain in the Philippines. Instead, wary of any repercussions from the intelligence community, he had bought various tickets to different destinations before heading for the United Kingdom.

Lucy Morgan had met him three weeks later in London, and they had then travelled quietly up to Scotland with Lopez in tow.

The private hospital room was small, a tinted observation window affording a glimpse inside. There was a single bed within the room and sitting on it was Bethany O'Learey, who was smiling and talking to a man and a woman whom Ethan assumed were her parents. Beside them sat Lucy Morgan. Bethany's head was no longer encased in its scaffolding, and her features were already looking more even than they had, her skull cap having receded in size.

Lopez stared at Bethany for a long moment. 'I don't get it.'

'It worked,' Ethan replied simply.

'I can see that!' Lopez uttered in amazement. 'What I can't see is how it can have worked? They took the mummy away from us!'

Inside the room, Lucy Morgan spotted them and smiled. She got up from her seat beside Bethany's bed and joined them in the corridor outside, closing the door behind her.

'You should come in,' she urged Ethan and Lopez after hugging them both. 'Bethany's doing great.'

'The less she knows about us the better,' Ethan replied. 'You know how trouble follows us around.'

'Don't I just?'

'Where are the remains?' Ethan asked.

'In my jacket,' Lucy replied. 'It's so much easier to just carry them around with me now that we're in the clear.'

'What remains?' Lopez asked in exasperation.

Ethan watched as Lucy reached beneath her jacket and revealed a clear cylinder some nine inches long, concealed in a custom-made pocket in the lining of her jacket. Vacuum-sealed, it was filled with a faint grey mist from the chill generated by the ice packed around the contents.

'Oh my God,' Lopez gasped as a hand flew to her lips and she stared at the cylinder's contents.

Ethan could see within the shocking form of a fetal creature, humanoid but with a tall, conical skull and elongated black eyes like giant tear-drops. In the last moments before Lopez had returned to the truck in Argentina to retrieve the mummy and hand it over to Majestic Twelve's soldiers and their mysterious leader, Lucy had performed an impromptu caesarean section on the mummy and extracted the unborn fetus she had believed resided within.

'I was telling the truth to Yuri Polkov when I said that the mummy was worthless,' Lucy explained to Lopez. 'It was the foetus that held the true value. It was why a young girl with ritualistic skull deformation was treated with such respect – she carried in her womb a true *hybrid* child.'

Working alone, Lucy had sequenced the DNA from the remains and then extracted stem-cells. That she had deceived an entire department of the United States Government, covert or not, amazed and impressed Ethan, but the work she had done since completely bowled him over.

'It's not the first time something like this has happened,' Lucy explained. 'In 1930, the skeletal remains of a fetus were found in a mine tunnel a hundred miles southwest of Chihuahua in Mexico. Dubbed the *Star Child* because of its alien appearance, modern scientists believe it to have been suffering from congenital Hydrocephalus, a condition in which excess fluid in the brain causes the skull to enlarge. It's not dissimilar to Bethany's illness, in many ways. The big deal was that the skull's volume was larger than the average adult human brain, the orbits were shallow, there were no frontal sinuses, and the optic nerve canal was situated much closer to the bottom of the orbit than the back, a highly unusual series of adaptions not common to human beings.'

'Why did they kill her, if she was pregnant?' Ethan asked. 'Surely they would have wanted to keep her alive until the baby was delivered?'

Lucy closed her jacket around the cylinder. 'I carbon-dated the remains and they were almost exactly five hundred years old, give or take a decade. The Incan Empire had been overrun by the Spanish *conquistadores* and their people slaughtered wholesale in conflict or by diseases for which they had no natural defense. Their civilization was doomed, and they likely had no option but to flee and to sacrifice their most revered people in the hope that their gods would intervene. They didn't, of course. I suppose in that respect Yuri Polkov was right – great sacrifice in the name of nothing but faith is a fool's errand.'

'What are you going to do with it?' Lopez asked. 'Blow the whole thing wide open?'

Lucy sighed and shook her head. 'I don't know, but what I do know is that this thing is staying under lock and key. I'm not letting the government of any of our countries take this away from me until it's been properly studied.'

Lucy took one last look at Bethany on her bed.

as Lopez climbed into the car and shut her door. He started the engine and put the car into gear, and then looked at her.

'I kind of like taking orders from a woman.'

'Get used to it,' Lopez shot back.

Ethan drove out of the hospital and onto the main road heading north, and pretended not to notice the faint smile touching Lopez's sculptured lips.

ABOUT THE AUTHOR

Dean Crawford is the author of the internationally published series of thrillers featuring *Ethan Warner*, a former United States Marine now employed by a government agency tasked with investigating unusual scientific phenomena. The novels have been *Sunday Times* paperback best-sellers and have gained the interest of major Hollywood production studios. He is also the enthusiastic author of many independently published Science Fiction novels.

www.deancrawfordbooks.com

22407001R00181

Printed in Great Britain
by Amazon